THE
WARRIOR QUEEN

KATHRYN KNOWLES

MAD
ENDEAVOUR

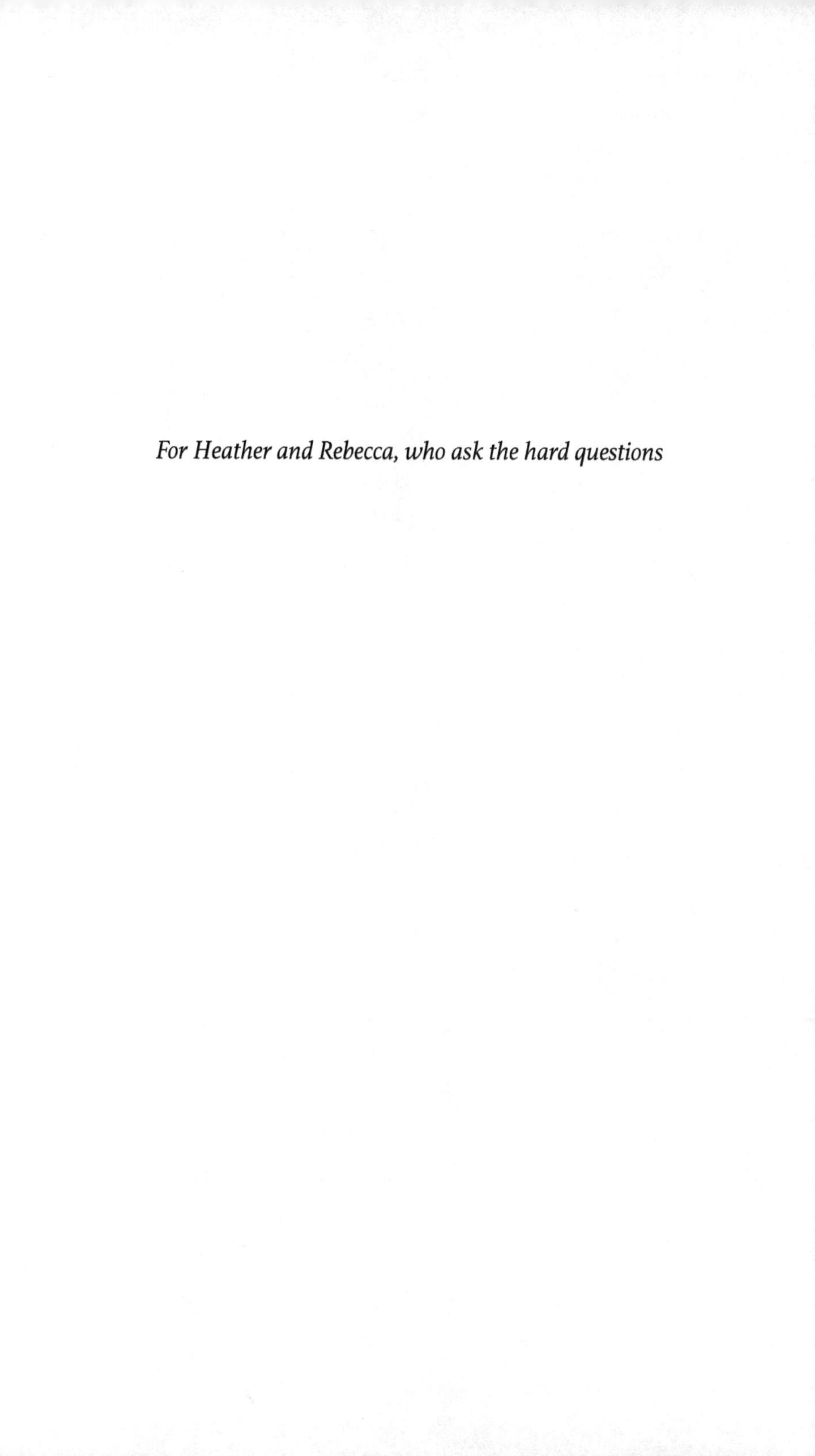

For Heather and Rebecca, who ask the hard questions

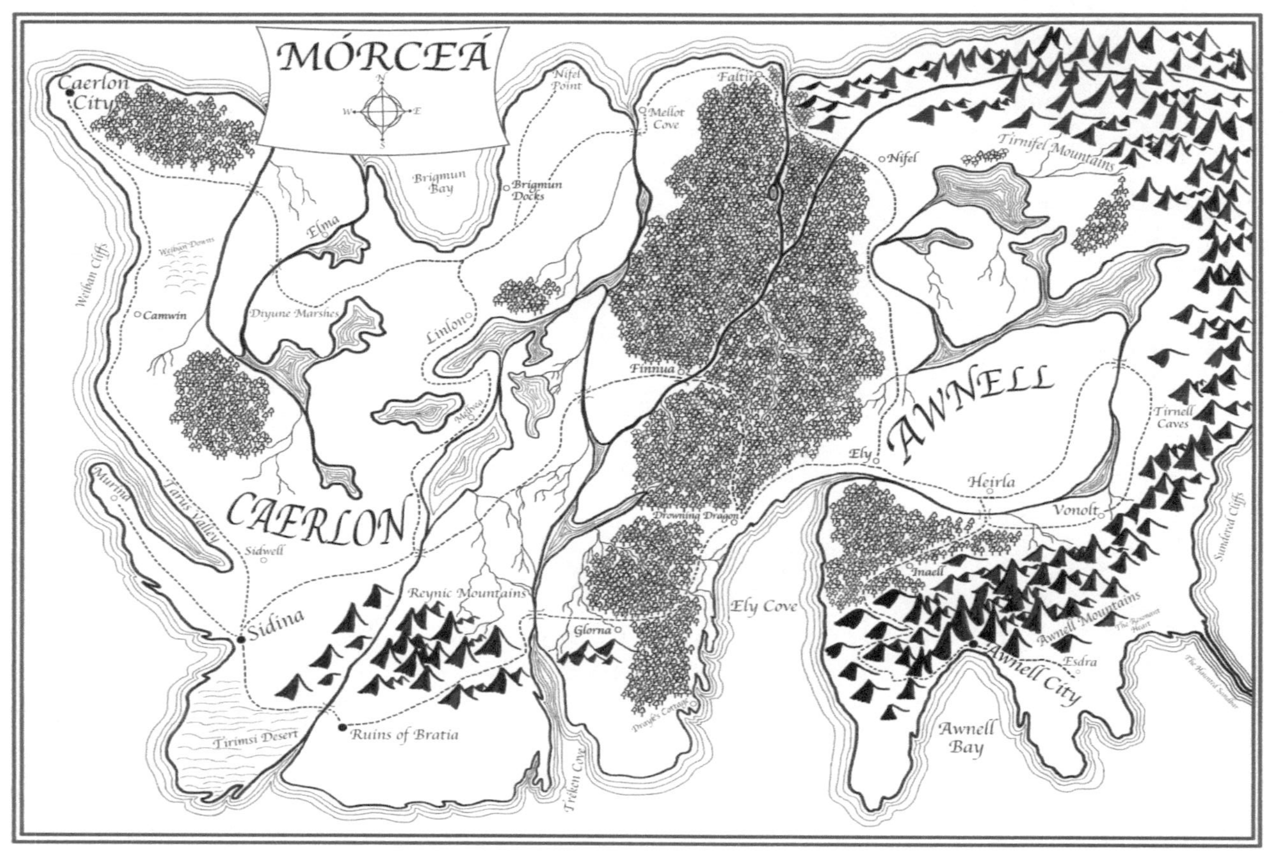

MÓRCEÁ
N
W   E
S
Caerlon City
Welfan Cliffs
Welfan Downs
Murina
Tarus Valley
Camwin
Diyune Marshes
Efma
Nifel Point
Brigmun Bay
Brigmun Docks
Linlon
Melleg
Mellot Cove
Faltii
Nifel
Tirnifel Mountains
Finnua
Drowning Dragon
CAERLON
Sidwell
Sidina
Reynic Mountains
Ruins of Bratia
Tirimsi Desert
Glorna
Drayet's Corridor
Treken Cove
Ely Cove
Ely
AWNELL
Heirla
Vonolt
Tirnell Caves
Inaell
Awnell Mountains
The Serpent's Heart
Esdra
Awnell City
Awnell Bay
Sundered Cliffs
The Haunted Sandbar

PROLOGUE

MAÍLERIER ANA

THE QUIESCENCE

Ana had never admitted it to anyone, but the thrill of combat was intoxicating to her. There was nowhere she'd rather be than the middle of battle, wielding a sword in her hand.

Not because she enjoyed taking lives. No, it was the sport of competition that she really loved. The planning and strategy of warfare, followed by the execution—the physicality of it suited her well. Her mind and her muscles were conditioned for agility, for endurance. Whenever she sat idle too long, anxiety crept in, infecting her and making her reckless. She longed to be in the thick of things, putting her life on the line. Earning every heartbeat.

But this battle was different. It was so much bigger and more important than any battle she'd fought before.

This was the last one.

The evening was clear. With no clouds obscuring it, the sky was exquisite. A black canvas, splashed with glittering stars that huddled in dense patterns, bleeding their shivering light through the blackness in smears of violet and indigo.

The moon was nearly full, and it weighed heavily upon the

world, bearing down with an intense awareness, like it knew what was about to happen.

Ana stared at it, transfixed. The familiar queasy sensation that always greeted her on the eve of battle was starting anew. Some people might consider it a sign of fear, but she knew better. No, it wasn't fear. It was excitement.

"Maílerier Ana?" One of her captains was standing nearby, watching her with a curious expression. "We are ready." He spoke with a thick, melodic accent and struggled to pronounce his consonants. Most people still spoke Awnle by preference, and this new language was difficult for them. Even Ana had to admit she didn't care for it, although she could speak it fluently. But watching everyone else struggle was tedious. She missed the simplicity of her old language, the ease of communication.

But people would learn to adjust. They had to.

Caer was right. Awnle was far too intertwined with the ancient religion—the old ways. It was time for something new.

"Very well," she said, adopting a slow, clear tone so her captain would understand. "Show me."

The captain led the way down the hill. Ana made to follow him, but paused briefly to gaze at the enormous city below her. Nearly a decade had passed since she'd last seen it, and somehow it appeared even bigger and more impressive than it had all those years ago.

She was a young child when she'd first laid eyes on the great city of Bratia, but it was one of her clearest memories. The first city she'd ever seen, she could still remember how Bratia had overwhelmed her, how it had inspired her.

Large dry-stone walls snaked around the mosaic of buildings. The Reynic Mountains loomed in the distance like fierce spectators, passing judgement on the city and its inhabitants. Foothills rolled down to the city centre, tapering off and lending a natural rise and fall to the landscape. One lone hill, Túir-Bratia, stood at the city centre. Terraced fields rose along its slope like steps towards the sacred sector, where the enormous Sun Temple sat, watching over the people below.

The temple was a massive structure, showcasing three vaulted domes with patterns of windows carved in the roof to fill the sanctuary with light at sacred hours. A dozen flaming pillars, known as the Fire Obelisks, encircled the temple, each paired with a smaller fountain that drew water from an unknown source.

The land was an unusual contradiction of dryness and bloom. Farther away from the city, the land was sparse and parched, but a magical lushness covered the city itself, as though the Natures had blessed it with life.

But every so often, when the Earth and Wind were imbalanced, a deadly sandstorm would rage through the area with enough force to tear everything apart. So, the people of Bratia had erected a Wind Tower on the plateau directly opposite the temple. It was a large, square tower built of clay and stone, with rows of ornamental chimes and bells that jingled as the tower swayed in the gentle breeze. When the winds grew wild, the heaviest and most protected bells pealed, and the people knew to board their windows and seek shelter from the violent storm approaching.

It was a thrilling sound, simultaneously terrifying and glorious. Ana could still remember the last time she'd heard it. The pounding of her heart and the warmth of blood rushing through her veins. Even then, she'd longed to brave the storm, to fight the Natures themselves, and prove she had the strength to withstand them.

But that was a long time ago, and the air was conspicuously silent tonight.

Ana followed her captain down the hill to where her battalion lay waiting. The army had been camped here for weeks already, surrounding Bratia and isolating it from the rest of Mórceá. Negotiations with city leaders had ceased two days ago. Bratia refused to surrender.

Ana couldn't help but admire their bravery, however misguided it was. Their army was outmatched and their citizens were losing steam.

Ana's cavalry patrolled the river and the streets in and out of the city, intercepting reinforcements and killing anyone who tried to flee. Ten divisions of infantry held the north with archers bombarding the barracks and religious sectors through the night. Artillery and siege engines were in place, ready to attack. The musicians, who had blasted a relentless death siren for days, preventing rest and instilling fear, had been ordered to stop.

It was almost time.

"This way," said her captain. He gestured for Ana to follow him towards the base of the incline.

They arrived at a narrow plateau. Here, her soldiers had erected a makeshift pavilion sheltering the entrance to a series of tunnels carved into the earth. The soldiers snapped to attention as Ana passed through their ranks, and she nodded curtly. She didn't have time for formalities.

"How deep does it go?" she asked, resting her hand on one of the timber supports and peering into the closest tunnel. The tunnel curved sharply. A faint light glowed halfway down where one of her men had hung a lantern, but beyond that, there was only darkness.

"All the way," he replied. "We found graves, as you say. Then we stop."

Ana felt suddenly queasy. It pained her to think of the sacrilege she was about to commit. Disrupting a sacred resting site was supposed to bring eternal shame and damnation. The Spirits would be displeased.

Nonsense. Nothing but superstition and religious naïveté. She'd long since relinquished those beliefs, even if certain instincts lingered.

Ana took a deep breath and pulled her mind back to the present. "Well done," she said, clapping her captain on the shoulder. But even without superstitious fear and shame, the gravity of what she was about to do weighed on her. She turned to gaze back at the magnificent city behind her. "It is a pity, though," she said, sighing. "I hate to destroy something so stunning, but they've given us no choice."

The longer Ana stared at the city, the more mystical she realized it was. This was definitely a city built on Resonance, and once its power was gone, Bratia would cease to exist. The land would likely die and the remnants of this glorious pinnacle of human achievement would crumble back into dust.

"We need more cities like this one," she mused, taking in the rest of its massive shape. She allowed herself to feel nostalgic for a moment as her eyes travelled over the city landmarks. There was the glorious amphitheatre where she'd seen the live retellings of the Spirit Creation, complete with elaborate costumes and sets; there was the lyceum where the maílehrs spoke on matters of scholarship and art; and in the west, set against the moonlight, stood rows of sculptures and statues, each carved by one of the eminent artists who'd lived and died in Bratia.

"Yes. When this is finished, that's what I'll do." She turned back to face her captain. "I shall return to my home in the eastern mountains and build a new city—a modern city—to mark the coming of a new age, and stand as testament to our people's strength. And it will be even more glorious than this."

She smiled to herself, content with the promise she'd made. It didn't matter if Bratia was destroyed, because she would build something even greater.

After all, soon she'd be one of the most powerful people in existence. There was nothing she wouldn't be able to do then.

Ana glanced up at the moon, wondering how much longer they'd have to wait. "Have we had any word from him?" she asked, not turning her gaze from the sky.

"Yes, Maílater Caer sends news. He will be here tonight."

Ana nodded and said nothing. Instead, she left the pavilion and walked towards the plateau's far edge, where she could see the city clearly—the city where she'd spent so much of her youth.

As children, she and Caer had come here to study with Maílehr Illayan. It had always been Caer's dream to become one of the great practitioners, but Ana was more interested in practical matters. She'd preferred her lessons with the other maílehrs much more, lessons on strategy and the sciences—tangible things. Resonance had always eluded her. She had never mastered it the way Caer had done.

She could channel the Natures in small ways, but it frustrated her that she didn't understand the Spirits as well as Caer. Resonating was like breathing to him. It was natural, and it worked. But for Ana, connecting with the Spirits required a great deal of focus and strength, and even then, she could rarely match Caer's ability.

But soon they would be true equals. Soon they would be the only remaining practitioners in the world, sharing all the power they'd siphoned.

A commotion at the camp drew Ana's attention away from the city. Half a dozen men on horseback were wending through the rows of soldiers, moving towards her.

Although it had been a while, she recognized Caer instantly. He rode in front, looking more self-important than ever. Since the last time she'd seen him, he seemed to have done away with his rustic attire, in favour of something gaudier and more elaborate.

"Really?" she asked, indicating the golden embroidered surcoat he was wearing over an unnaturally gleaming hauberk.

Caer had always possessed a flair for the ostentatious, but this was pushing it a bit far.

"What?" he asked, swinging down from his horse to stand beside her. "You don't like our new uniforms?" He gestured back to the group behind him, and Ana realized they were each wearing a surcoat with matching golden and violet undertones to complement his.

"You look ridiculous," she said, shaking her head. "This is war, not pageantry. You should dress for agility and combat."

Ana had always favoured minimal outfits designed to give her and her fighters the most flexibility. Her soldiers all wore combinations of leather and rawhide with bone inlay, and scaled metal cuirasses over the chest and stomach where they needed the most protection.

But given the speed and skill of her soldiers, it was all a bit unnecessary. Injuries were rare in her army, and casualties were even rarer.

"Well, I like it," said Caer a little sullenly. "I think it makes a statement and shows our strength."

Ana suppressed a snort as she watched the other men descend from their horses next to their leader. She recognized every one of them, and she smiled when one came striding out to meet her.

"Eón," she said, grasping arms with him in greeting, according to the customs of her people. "It has been too long."

"Indeed, Maílerier Ana." He grinned broadly as he released her arm and surveyed the camp. "It's a thrill to be on the battle-field again. I'll be honest, I have missed fighting next to you... Not that I don't appreciate the promotion," he added, casting a sidelong glance at Caer.

Ana pursed her lips sourly. A few years ago, Caer had asked her to assign a group of her most highly trained men as his personal soldiers. At the time, she'd agreed, thinking Caer planned to do some actual fighting with them. But a long time had passed since Caer last stood on a battlefield, which meant that ten of her best soldiers had spent the last two years idle. No longer warriors, they were more like a ceremonial guard.

It frustrated Ana to no end, but she knew better than to argue with Caer. It wouldn't get them anywhere.

"Well, this is it," she said, turning to address him. "The last one."

Caer nodded and glowered at the city. "I loathe this place. I look forward to watching it crumble. Finally."

Ana frowned, but said nothing. She couldn't claim she was excited to watch Bratia fall.

"Where is Illayan?" Caer asked after a pause.

"The maílehrs have stationed in the citadel, trying to repel our attacks. Illayan should be with them. Unless you believe the rumours about the community gathering in the mountains..." She cast him a dubious glance.

"Do *you* believe them?"

Ana shrugged. "I wouldn't put it past Illayan... but it doesn't matter. Over thirty practitioners are in this city. Whether Illayan is among them... it doesn't change what we're here to do."

"And what about the relics?" Caer asked.

Ana frowned again. "The last anyone saw them, Illayan had brought them to the temple for worship. They should still be there." Then, seeing the expression on Caer's face, she continued, "Tell me, what is so important about a collection of old religious trinkets? I thought we agreed icon worship was meaningless."

Caer shook his head. "They're important to me. That's all you need to know."

Ana scowled at him. "Fine," she said through gritted teeth. "You may keep your secrets for now, but when this is over, you *will* tell me what they are and why they're so important to you."

Caer gave her a simpering smile. "Of course I will," he said.

Then he clapped his hands together in excitement. "Well, shall we get started?"

Ana watched him with narrowed eyes for a moment.

When had he become so adept at hiding things? As children, he'd never been able to keep secrets from her, but now it seemed every word he spoke was a lie.

Ana took a deep breath. Her issues with Caer would have to wait. They had more important things to focus on now.

"This way," she said, turning and leading them back to the pavilion. "We've been mining since we arrived. These tunnels reach all the way into the crypts beneath the city. One good shock and they should all crumble, levelling the sacred district. Then we can take advantage of the disarray to breach. I have a dozen siege towers positioned along the strongest walls, two teams with fifty trebuchets; and over six thousand good soldiers ready to fight."

"Excellent," said Caer, grinning from ear to ear. "The city should be reduced to ruins by morning and every last maílehr will be dead."

Ana felt the excitement again. She longed to start the battle, to fight.

"Soldiers! Make ready!" she called across the hordes of warriors forming neat rows along the city walls, with swords and spears in the front and archers in the rear. They stretched beyond where her eyes could see, moving in unison like a great serpent uncoiling its writhing body across the hills. She could just make out the enormous siege towers being rolled towards the eastern wall, and she heard the creaking sound of bowstrings and catapults being drawn.

A blast of horns rent the air to signal her orders across the army. Ana felt a burst of pride as she gazed out at her soldiers. Every one of them had served her with honour and skill, and they would share in this victory with her.

"Whenever you're ready," she said, nodding to Caer. She

gave one last reflective look at the city before she drew her sword and readied herself for battle.

A second, higher horn blew, and then a low rumbling sound began. The sand vibrated around Ana's feet. She glanced over at Caer. He closed his eyes as he resonated with the Earth, sending tremors through the mines that led to the crypts beneath the city.

Bells pealed in the distance and she knew the Wind Tower was shaking. Ana whipped her head towards the city just in time to see a cloud of dust burst into the air somewhere near the western wall.

The air filled with screams as dust billows the size of rain clouds exploded from the city centre and wafted outwards. The sound of stones crashing to the ground and cracking against one another was deafening. Before long, the air was so full of dust and debris that Ana couldn't see anything.

Then suddenly her eyes were burning. An enormous inferno raged in the sacred district where the fire obelisks had collapsed, bleeding their flames onto the nearby rooftops and reducing their wood to tinder.

It was a horrifying sight, but Ana tried not to let her emotions overpower her. This needed to be done. It was a necessary sacrifice for the greater good.

The practitioners needed to be stopped. There were far too many of them, and their power had remained unchecked too long. Resonance was a powerful force, one that should not be left uncontrolled. It needed to be limited to those strong enough to cope with its burden.

It was the only way to keep everyone safe.

That's what these last ten years had been about. Ana and Caer had been fighting to liberate the people, to protect them from tyranny. The tyranny of those too weak and too flawed to use Resonance the way it was meant to be used. Those who had succumbed to their basest desires of greed and power.

It had taken years and countless battles to get here, but they were finally ending the exploitation of Resonance forever. Ana had led her army across the land, conquering settlements and suppressing the old religion, whose teachings had encouraged the practice of Resonance and led people down the path of destruction and violence.

It was important work. There was a nobility in it that nothing could taint. She was a warrior, fighting in the open air for a better future, and it didn't matter what Caer was doing in secret. It didn't matter that his experiments had grown more gruesome with each passing year, or that he relied on her to draw attention away from his actions.

He had his role, and she had hers.

And now, at the end, she knew it had all been worth it. Caer had discovered a means to extract Resonance, to remove it permanently and contain it somewhere unworthy hands couldn't reach it.

Ana didn't know how he'd done it—she wasn't sure she wanted to know—but none of that mattered. Right now, all that mattered was that she and Caer were going to save Mórceá together. They were going to usher in an era of peace and order.

The fall of Bratia was the final stage—the final community in need of cleansing. It had long been a pinnacle of the ancient religion, a home for master practitioners and their apprentices. The maílehrs encouraged communion with the Natures. They encouraged average people to explore Resonance and use it freely.

But not anymore.

The dust began to settle and Ana gazed at the heap of burning rubble where the great city of Bratia clung to life.

Coughing slightly on the dust that still lingered in the air, she turned towards Caer. "You've grown stronger," she said with a mixture of admiration and disapproval. She hated that she envied his power.

"It is a means to an end," he said, though Ana noticed a strange glint in his eye as he gazed at the devastation he'd caused. "Now... I believe you have an army to lead." He inclined his head towards her and gestured to the fragments of Bratia where the city's remaining forces scrambled to regroup.

Ana nodded and took a deep breath before giving the call for her soldiers to advance. She raised her sword high in the air, and ran forward, towards the smouldering wreckage of the finest city ever built.

Its ruins would form the foundation of a greater, stronger society.

PART I

1

AT THE FAIRWEATHER

Catanya's arms ached and burned. Exhausted, she dropped her oars and struggled to climb out of the rocking boat and into the icy water. It was early evening. Cloud cover veiled the stars above the oppressive wall of mountains before them. She and Drayk pulled their boat ashore and stared back at the vast ocean.

After an entire day at sea and the constant exposure to freezing wind and mist, the cold had seeped into Catanya's bones. Her entire body was numb, and she was shivering uncontrollably. Her breaths clung to the wintery air. She fumbled with the straps on her bag, trying to pull it out of the boat.

"I don't think we should try to go any farther tonight," said Drayk. It was too dark to see his features, but she felt his gaze on her and she heard the concern in his voice. "There's an inn at the port where we can rest and plan our next steps. If we're careful, we can make it there unnoticed."

Catanya nodded mechanically. They had arrived at the southwest side of the Kingdom of Awnell, just beyond the boundaries of its capital city. They had initially agreed to make their way through the city under cover of darkness so they could reach the mountains before dawn, but Catanya was grateful for the change of plans. She knew it wasn't safe to linger in the city, but the last two days had depleted her. The fight with Jémys and the confrontation with Cadyan...

Her weariness was more than physical. She desperately needed to rest.

They walked along the shoreline at the base of the escarpment, moving slowly to avoid attracting the sentries' notice. Catanya followed Drayk's lead as he navigated the uneven terrain, using it to keep out of sight. They walked until they reached the edge of the cape, where it angled inward towards the bay. Catanya's jaw dropped as she turned the corner and saw what lay ahead.

An enormous structure overlooked the bay like a ferocious predator bearing down on its quarry. The fortress was partly built, partly carved from the glistening black stone of the tallest mountain. The stones flickered and gleamed, giving the illusion of an ink waterfall pouring into the ocean.

"Welcome to Awnell," said Drayk.

The fortress rose in levels up from the port city, and at its peak, reaching up into the sky, stood three enormous towers with stacks of turrets, spires, and bartizans. The northernmost tower was the largest and most embellished. Hewn from the mountain's peak, it was still connected in areas along its northern edge.

At the base of the fortress, the city burst forth from the bay in a labyrinth of buildings. The port teemed with people passing between ships, wharves, and warehouses, and transporting cargo through the wide gates in the massive black walls that surrounded the inner city. Vast, savage waves hurled themselves against the docks, drenching everything and everyone and threatening to drag it all away. But the city stood unmoved and unflinching, its black-stone walls smeared with great, billowing clouds of sea foam that slid and dripped down to be reclaimed by the bay.

Catanya stared in awe, thinking the Awnadh must have built this fortress to withstand anything. It loomed over the inlet with a formidable presence that spoke of its resilience and strength.

"It's incredible," she whispered. Despite everything that had happened and everything she was feeling, she couldn't help but smile. "I've heard stories of the great city of Awnell, but this..." She shook her head, lost for words. "I never could have imagined something so... It's so glorious and terrifying at the same time."

"I suppose it is," said Drayk, following her gaze. "It's been a long time since I actually stopped to think about it."

"How is that possible?" Catanya couldn't imagine taking something like this for granted. "It's exquisite. I want to remember every detail. The facets and windows. How the lines and arches interconnect. The perfect symmetry... I need to draw it. I wish I could..."

Drayk arched an eyebrow. "Perhaps another time, yes?"

Catanya shook her head. "I know. It's just I've never seen anything so... so..." She cast around, struggling to find the words. "It's a work of art," she whispered.

"Mmm. Deadly artwork," said Drayk in a low voice. He indicated the squads of archers and spearmen lining the walls and filling the towers. "Come on, we can't stay in the open for long."

Catanya took one last longing look at the glorious fortress before she followed Drayk.

They continued along the shoreline until they reached the port, where they blended in with the workers and travellers, who were moving around and chatting animatedly.

Catanya had never seen such a teeming, vibrant place. The city was bursting with activity. A group of children ran past, apparently unchaperoned; bands of laughing people pushed through the crowd towards the taverns; and countless shops and vendors were still open, calling out deals and trying to lure in customers.

Catanya and Drayk passed a row of carts, each selling different exotic foods. The delicious smells made Catanya's stomach ache. She hadn't eaten since they'd left Caerlon, and she longed to try the different cuisines. One vendor was selling what resembled roasted pork on skewers, but it smelled of such complex spices it made her mouth water. Another vendor had small dough bowls filled with sugary-looking confetti and drizzled with a glistening syrup. It looked surprisingly decadent for street food.

As Catanya and Drayk pushed past the row of vendors and emerged at the end of the street, the crowd intensified. Drums and flutes played nearby, punctuated by people whooping and cheering. A performance was happening on the opposite side of the street.

"Stay close," Drayk muttered. He led them down a narrow alley, away from the commotion.

They finally arrived outside a large inn. A crooked sign creaked as it swung in the wind, bearing the words, *The Fairweather*. The building was old and weather-beaten, with barnacles and algae growing along its outer walls. Catanya could hear music and voices chatting happily within, and she wished she could join in the jollity.

She raised her hands to lower the hood of her cloak, but Drayk grabbed her arm and said, "Leave it. We don't want any unwanted attention." Then he raised his own hood, and, taking her hand, led the way inside.

A blast of warmth and light hit Catanya, along with a pungent bouquet of spicy food, alcohol, and sweat. The front room was packed with people of all ages and walks of life, chatting and hooting noisily. In the corner near the fire, several people were singing a sea shanty very loudly and slightly off key, while another corner housed a party of old men playing a slow but evidently heated game of dice.

"Ah, you stinkin' cheat!" shouted one gambler. He upturned the table and shook his fist at the man across from him.

Catanya jumped back as a brawl broke out. Drayk continued towards the bar, evidently unfazed. The inn was so crowded they had to push and squeeze past tables of drunken sailors and clumps of entwined couples. A portly barman stood at the bar, watching the festivities and wearing a smile.

"What can I do you for?" he asked, turning towards them. Then his mouth fell open, first in surprise, then delight. "Drayk? Is that you? My boy—"

"Shh!" said Drayk, waving his hand. "Listen, Reg, we need a room for tonight and nobody can know we're here, all right?" He gave Reg a meaningful look.

"Ah, all right, I hear you." Reg looked from Drayk to Catanya and smiled. "What have you gotten yourself into this time, eh, boy?" He shook his head in amused disbelief.

"It's nothing to worry about," said Drayk with a nonchalant shrug.

"You know," Reg leaned in and lowered his voice, "Lia's been searching for you. There are rumours going around…"

"Rumours?" Drayk cast an uncertain glance in Catanya's direction.

"Aye. Rumours. They say you've jumped ship. Gone off on your own, they say." He eyed Drayk shrewdly.

"Oh, come on, Reg. You know better than to believe the stories these old fools tell you." He jerked his head towards the drunken men nearby.

"Then how come you don't want Lia knowing you're here?"

"All in good time, Reg. All in good time." Drayk flashed a coy grin. "Now, a room, if you please?"

The barman looked like he couldn't decide if he was

worried or intrigued. But he nodded and grabbed a key off the rack behind him, handing it to Drayk. "Here you go, then, my boy. And I'll bring food up for you."

"Thank you," said Drayk.

Catanya's stomach growled her thanks.

"Oh, and Drayk," said Reg in an even quieter whisper. "I almost forgot. Someone left this for you." He slid a small envelope across the bar.

Drayk looked mildly surprised. "When did this arrive?" he asked, opening it to read the note. Catanya thought she noticed his jaw tighten, but he gave no other reaction as he slipped the parchment into his pocket.

"Couple days ago."

"What is it?" asked Catanya.

Drayk gave her a smile. "Just a message from an old lover, pining for me." He winked at her. "Nothing to worry about."

Catanya didn't believe him, but she was too exhausted to argue.

As they crossed behind the bar and started climbing the stairs, a strange prickling sensation crept up the back of Catanya's neck. She glanced behind her and watched the inn door swing closed as though someone had just left.

She felt tense as they arrived outside their room.

"Drayk, this place makes me nervous. Are you sure we're safe staying here?" She stepped through the door after him.

Inside was a modest guest room with one bed, a table and chairs, a mirror, and a wardrobe. Several candles had been lit and a warm fire roared inside a narrow hearth. On the wall beside the mantle hung a row of small rusted bells. Catanya guessed they were servant's bells, but she wasn't sure why they were necessary in a travellers' inn.

"I wouldn't exactly say safe," he said, shrugging and latching the door shut. "But Reg looks out for me. He won't tell anyone." Drayk strode across the room to check the bolt on the window shutters, then he took off his cloak and tossed it on a chair. "Besides, we're better off here than anywhere else. Ayr knows everything that happens in this city. If we want to pass through undetected, we need a plan... Assuming that's still what you want. The confrontation with Cadyan was unexpected. I think we need to discuss our options..."

"What options?" groaned Catanya, dismal and dejected. She sighed and slumped onto the bed in the centre of the room, burying her face in her hands. Her excitement at seeing the city was wearing off, and she realized she was still shivering, and her stomach burned with hunger. She heard Drayk rummaging through the wardrobe and then felt a heavy blanket drape around her shoulders. She glanced up to see him standing in front of her, frowning. Suddenly, he reached out and lowered her hood.

"What are you doing?" she asked, withdrawing from him. This close, she could see every detail of his face. A shadow of stubble outlined his jaw, and his bright eyes were especially striking inside his dark, sunken orbits.

"Looking at you," he said, unabashed. "Your hair"—he brushed it off her face—"we need to hide this colour."

Catanya pushed his hand away, uncomfortable with the presumptuous gesture. "I was concealing it fine before just by tying it up."

"Well, there's a lot more colour now, and it's spread out in multiple spots."

"How can there be more?" asked Catanya. She stood up and crossed the room to use the mirror. Drayk was right. Her face was now framed with strands of iridescent colour, which stood out dramatically against her natural black. The sight of it made her uneasy. She ran her hands through it and thought about her brother. His hair had given him such a distorted and other-worldly appearance. Catanya didn't want to look like that.

"Cadyan seemed to think the more you use your powers,

the faster your hair will turn, right?" asked Drayk, unfastening his sword and holding it in his lap as he lounged on the bed to watch her.

"Yes, he did," said Catanya as she began yanking strands apart and weaving the black over the colour into a series of tight braids. "But I've barely used my powers. I wouldn't have thought it would be this obvious." She thought back over the last few days, wondering if she could have used magic without realizing it.

Cadyan's powers had overwhelmed her on that beach. She'd tried to fight him, but nothing had happened. Cadyan had beaten her back. He'd almost killed her.

Last chance, sister. Come with me to Caerlon. His words echoed in her head.

Catanya couldn't believe she'd almost gone with him. She'd almost agreed. Had Cadyan used his powers on her mind somehow? She'd felt so calm and complacent, almost peaceful. But then that blast of golden light had erupted between them, and her strength had returned...

So, maybe Catanya's powers *had* protected her.

"Well, it's not too obvious yet," said Drayk, "but sooner or later it will be."

"I know that."

Catanya continued working on her hair in silence. Then she caught sight of Drayk's expression in the mirror.

"What is it?" she asked.

Drayk was frowning at her, his bright blue eyes pinched together. "Catya, you can't hide forever, you know that, right?"

Catanya exhaled heavily. "I know, but... I... I'm scared," she finished, turning to face him. It felt good to finally say it out loud.

Drayk sat up. "Scared of what?"

"All of it," she said, shrugging. "I'm scared of these powers and what they're doing to me. I'm scared of my brother and what will happen the next time we meet, and I'm scared for everyone around me. Everyone who keeps getting hurt because of me..." She broke off, pulling the blanket tighter around her shoulders and staring at her feet. "I just don't know what to do anymore. I never expected my life would be this... well, *this.*" She gestured around the room.

Drayk chuckled and leaned back against the headboard. "You're focusing on all the wrong things, love."

"What do you mean?"

"You think your life is frightening? Well, I think it's exhilarating. I mean, don't get me wrong, I understand. It's all new to you, which is probably overwhelming. But in my experience, new is always better. You just have to let go of whatever you're holding on to. Let go of whatever's holding you back and start looking forward."

Catanya's weary brain struggled to make sense of his words. "So, you never wanted more for yourself?" she asked.

"More? More than what?"

"More than this." She threw her hand in the air. "This life of dishonesty, drifting from one place to another with nothing and no one. Constantly running and fighting, and losing everything." She slumped down in a chair by the mirror, utterly drained.

Drayk just shrugged.

"How can that be?" she asked in disbelief.

"It's easy. I just live the life I've got, not the one I think I should have. You could make yourself sick thinking about all the opportunities you've missed. What about all the opportunities you've taken? I learned a long time ago that expectations just lead to disappointment. You can't really control anything, so you may as well learn to enjoy the journey and make the most of it."

A knock sounded on the door, and Drayk jumped to his feet, drawing his sword. "Who is it?"

"It's only Reg. I've got two hot bowls of sourwood stew for you here."

Drayk relaxed and re-sheathed his sword. "This life, it's full of shocks and surprises, but I wouldn't want it any other way," he said before letting Reg in.

After she'd finished eating, Catanya lay down on the bed to rest, still wrapped in the thick wool blanket, trying to keep warm. She closed her eyes, remembering her last conversation with Jémys and thinking over everything Drayk had just said about learning to let go. By now, she thought she'd be used to losing the people she loved, but she was wrong. Hot tears pooled under her eyelids, and she allowed herself to disappear into her emotions until she fell asleep.

It was late when Catanya opened her eyes again. It took her a while before she realized where she was. The fire had burned low, casting a dim glow over the room. She rolled over, looking for Drayk, and realized he had fallen asleep, sitting beside her on the bed.

She watched him sleep for a few minutes, thinking how strange it was to find herself here with him. It was hard to believe the man sitting beside her had once kidnapped her and tortured Jémys in the woods. She never would have guessed he'd become her ally, or that she'd come to rely on him.

Catanya untangled herself from her blanket and threw it out to cover both her and Drayk. He muttered something incoherent but didn't wake up. Catanya rolled over and fell back asleep.

Moments later, it seemed, she was being shaken awake.

"We need to go," Drayk whispered.

"What's happening?" Catanya scrambled to her feet and realized one of the bells by the mantle was jangling.

"That's Reg's signal, it means—"

The door burst open with a grinding crack and slammed against the wall. The splintered and useless lock clattered to the ground.

A cool voice spoke from the shadows of the hall, "There you are, Drayk."

Drayk exhaled and closed his eyes briefly. Then he stood up to face the woman striding into the dim firelight, flanked on either side by two burly soldiers.

"Lia, what a pleasant surprise," he said, flashing a winning smile and spreading his arms out in a welcoming gesture.

"Is it?" she asked, tilting her head and glaring at him.

"Of course. Why wouldn't it be?" Drayk maintained his calm, collected demeanour with enviable ease.

The woman named Lia marched into the room, her shrewd eyes taking in the travel bags beside the wardrobe and the empty stew bowls on the table. "I've been hearing things, Drayk. I'd hate to believe half of them." She turned her gaze back towards him and Catanya.

"Really?" He twisted his face to show benign concern. "What kinds of things?"

Lia narrowed her eyes. "Where is the rest of your crew?" she asked, ignoring his question.

Drayk cleared his throat. "Gone. It seems they wanted out." He shrugged in a way that suggested his indifference.

"Is that so?" Lia's voice dripped with disdain. "Imagine that. Every single one of them deciding to leave at the same time. And you, allowing it... I wonder why... What could have been more important than keeping your crew together?" Lia glared at him. When Drayk didn't respond, her eyes snapped towards Catanya. Lia crossed the room to stand in front of her. "So, what have you brought our queen this time, Drayk?" she asked.

Now that she was standing closer, Catanya could see Lia more clearly. She appeared to be in her mid-forties. Her greying black hair was short and choppy, like she had sliced it off herself with a dull blade, and her skin looked weathered. Numerous old scars were visible even in the dim light.

Lia studied Catanya's face. "She's a pretty young thing, isn't she? I suppose Ayr will like that."

"Nah, I didn't bring her for Ayr," said Drayk, nonchalantly refastening his sword to his belt. "I brought her to be a recruit. She has a lot of potential." He grabbed his cloak off the chair and flashed his eyes in Catanya's direction.

"Really?" said Lia, looking from Catanya to Drayk with newfound interest. "Well, that's not your decision, now, is it?" Then she rounded on Catanya. "What's your name, girl?"

"Cat-Catya," said Catanya. "My name is Catya." She glanced quickly at Drayk, who nodded almost imperceptibly.

Lia's eyes narrowed. "Well, Catya, what brings a girl like you to a place like this?"

"A girl like me?" repeated Catanya, trying to keep her voice even.

Lia smirked at her. "Pretty young thing like you ought to be married with a handful of children by now. Unless..." She looked at Drayk and let out a bark of derisive laughter. "Don't tell me that's why you've followed Drayk here." She laughed again, even louder. "Well, you wouldn't be the first person to fall under his charm. Stupid fools never can resist him."

Catanya was affronted, and her body stiffened. "I assure you, you are mistaken," she said coolly, her dislike for the woman growing.

"She probably thinks you're in love with her," continued Lia, ignoring Catanya and patting Drayk on the shoulder. The other soldiers snickered and joined in the mirth. "Oh, Drayk, you do like to cause trouble, don't you?"

"No, Lia, really—" Drayk tried to interject, but Lia cut him off.

"Well, you've had your fun with her, but it's time to go." She turned to face Catanya again. "I hate to break it to you—*Catya,* was it? But he doesn't love you. Drayk, here, knows better than that, don't you, Drayk?" Her voice was simpering and condescending.

Catanya's annoyance gave way to anger. She stared at Drayk, who seemed maddeningly unfazed by the whole thing.

"I can promise you," she said in a raised voice, "I'm not the predictable lovesick girl you think I am." Everyone in the room turned to stare at her. "I didn't *follow* Drayk here like some pathetic waif. We met during our travels, and he mentioned you might have an opening in your crew... That is all. If he was mistaken, I will gladly continue on my way. I have no intention of standing here and listening to you spout your ignorant assumptions and snide insults."

There was a long silence as Lia turned to glare at her.

"You ought to learn some respect, girl," she said in a deadly quiet voice.

Catanya sniffed and jutted her chin out. "Interesting," she said, "I was going to tell you the same thing."

A tense hush settled in the room. Catanya's heart hammered in her chest. Out of the corner of her eye, she saw Drayk grinning, but she didn't dare remove her gaze from the woman in front of her.

"Well, *Catya,*" said Lia after a pause, "you've got some nerve, talking to me that way. I can certainly see why he brought you here. But it takes more to become a Verratrí than arrogance and a brazen attitude." She stared at Catanya, sizing her up, then she turned towards Drayk and said, "Come. Ayr wants to see you. You've got a lot of explaining to do."

2

THE WARRIOR QUEEN

Catanya and Drayk left the inn, walking in silence back through the streets of the port with Lia and her guards. As they made their way deeper into the maze of buildings and warehouses, the night's darkness seemed to deepen. Catanya looked up and realized the fortress's shadow had eclipsed the sky. Thick black walls loomed overhead as she and the others arrived at the enormous gate leading into the inner city.

The gate doors seemed to be an extension of the walls themselves. The heavy stone was carved with ornate lettering and designs. Catanya barely had time to appreciate them as she passed through the gate. She chanced a glance back and saw the complex set of hinges, gears, and reinforcements that allowed a team of muscular wardens to open and close the colossal doors.

Awnell's streets were built from the same black stone as the walls. They twisted and wound tightly around the buildings, the stones glittering in the torchlight like droplets of water. They were slippery and uneven beneath Catanya's feet, and she had to work very hard not to stumble. Lia, Drayk, and the other two unknown men moved with ease. Clearly, they had all walked these streets many times.

Catanya tried to catch Drayk's eye. She wanted to know what they were heading into, but Drayk was staring resolutely forward as though he was just eager to arrive. Catanya tried to take it as a good sign that Drayk didn't seem nervous, but it did nothing to reassure her. Drayk had a knack for enjoying even the most dangerous situations.

They walked for what seemed like ages, climbing higher and higher, Catanya's legs burning from the exertion, until finally they arrived at the base of an enormous structure.

Catanya craned her neck up, but all she saw was the sheer face of black stone obscuring the stars and stretching beyond her view in every direction.

They had arrived at the central stronghold. The fortress of Awnell.

Lia led the way up the steep stone steps, past the guards, and straight through a set of heavy wooden doors into the entrance hall. The entrance hall alone was larger than any building Catanya had ever seen. Sconces lined the walls, bathing the area with an incongruously warm glow. Every few feet stood a guard, laden with weapons and wearing the crimson and black colours of Awnell. And directly ahead, there was a single set of doors.

"Wait here," said Lia in a commanding voice. She marched through the doors into what Catanya assumed must be the throne room. Catanya's heart raced and her breathing quickened as she looked around, trying to get her bearings.

She glanced at the rows of imposing guards, trying not to focus on their countless glistening weapons. Instead, she studied their faces and noticed they each bore scars at various stages of healing. Frowning, she turned to examine the two men who'd accompanied Lia. They were also sporting bruises and cuts on their faces, like they had recently been in a fight.

Why did everyone in this kingdom bear fresh wounds, as if they'd just stepped off a battlefield?

"Come." Lia reappeared and beckoned for them to follow her.

A wave of panic washed over Catanya anew, and for a second, she worried she might not be able to move. But, closing her eyes, she took a deep breath and followed Drayk through the doors into the throne room.

Catanya was momentarily speechless as she stood in the entrance, gaping at the room in front of her. She had expected something dark and oppressive, but she received a blast of colour and warmth instead. The walls and ceiling were covered by the most exquisite mural Catanya had ever seen. It depicted celebrations and scenes of the city's foundation, interspersed with all manner of flowers and animals. The designs swirled around one central image: a sprawling tree with splashes of water, ribbons of flame, and gusts of wind blooming from its branches.

The artistry of it was breathtaking—the vibrant colours combined with the intricate detail—it shone proudly, reflecting the light of the candles and torches, making the room unnaturally bright. She thought she could stare at it for hours.

"Drayk!" called a voice, breaking through Catanya's trance. Distracted by the painting, she hadn't noticed the woman sitting on the throne at the end of the room.

As she looked at Queen Ayr, Catanya's first thought was that this woman did not fit the image of a queen as Catanya had always imagined it. Ayr was clad in all black with leather boots and breeches, and she lounged in her throne with one foot on the seat in front of her and her hands resting casually on the arms. She wore her greying auburn hair in a loose braid, and her features were surprisingly soft.

Ayr leapt from her seat and strode forward to greet them with a wide smile.

Catanya's surprise became open shock as Ayr, instead of stopping in front of them, walked straight up to Drayk, put one hand on his face and kissed him passionately on the lips. Catanya gaped and looked around the room. Everyone else wore expressions of perfect indifference. Apparently, no one was surprised to see such an open display of intimacy.

Finally, Ayr let go of Drayk and stepped back, smiling as she said, "Ah, it's been too long."

"Your Majesty." Drayk inclined his head at her, his mouth twitching like he was fighting off a grin.

"I always look forward to your return," she said, patting him on the cheek. "I'm surprised you didn't come straight here, though. Lia tells me you stopped at The Fairweather."

Drayk shrugged. "Old habits," he said. "It was a long journey and I had a craving for Reg's spicy sourwood stew."

"Of course," said Ayr, though her tone communicated disbelief. "But now, I'm sure you're dying to tell me everything... Were you successful?"

Drayk cleared his throat and scratched his neck in uncharacteristic unease.

"Ah, well..." said Ayr, deflating. "We'll discuss that later. So, what *have* you brought me, then?" Her gaze roved over to rest on Catanya. "Oh, I see," she said, brightening again. "And who are you?"

Catanya wasn't sure what to say or what to do. She curtseyed awkwardly and felt her face flush as Drayk snickered beside her. "Your Majesty, my name is Catya," she said, trying to ignore her embarrassment.

"There's no need for that here," said Ayr with a kind smile. "As you may have noticed, we don't stand on ceremony in Awnell. I can't be bothered with all those silly formalities, like bowing and curtseying. Such a waste of time. So, tell me, Catya, what brings you to my city?"

"Well…" Catanya gave Drayk a furtive glance. "Drayk told me you might be looking for new recruits, and I-I'd like to be a Verratrí, Ma'am," she lied.

"Really?" Ayr looked from Catanya to Drayk. "That's interesting. It's not like Drayk to bring recruits. He's usually itching to go it alone. Incidentally…" She looked around the room again. "I see you've finally abandoned your crew. Took you long enough." She smirked as she turned to walk back towards her throne.

"Well, as I've known for a while now, they were hardly cut out for this type of work. They became disgruntled—suggested a change in leadership and a change in direction. I disagreed. Complications ensued… I tried to tell you they were weak and disloyal. Turns out I was right," said Drayk, shrugging.

"Mmm…" She looked over her shoulder at him. "Even Len?"

Drayk's face fell, but he recovered quickly. "Each and every one of them," he said without a hint of emotion.

"I see. Well, that is certainly disappointing." She settled down on her throne, her mouth quirked up in amusement. "I wonder what could have prompted such a change in attitude."

"You would have to ask them," replied Drayk.

"Believe me, I would. But as you can see"—she gestured around the room—"they're not here. So, I'm asking you, Drayk. How is it that your entire crew can stage a mutiny and yet somehow you've survived?"

"Just natural talent, I'd say," said Drayk, grinning.

"Of course." Ayr returned his coy smile. "But why now? Why, after years of loyal service, did they decide to rebel? What could have sparked such an event?"

"I'm afraid I don't have the answer to that. I'll never understand what drives a coward to forsake their duty."

The bitterness in Drayk's voice surprised Catanya. He always seemed so causal about his crew's betrayal, but his tone suggested it upset him more than he cared to admit.

"So, you haven't heard the rumours?" asked Ayr, lowering her voice to a conspiratorial whisper. She leaned forward with an obvious gleam in her eyes.

"Rumours?" asked Drayk, trying to sound innocent.

"Oh, yes." Ayr reclined again, contemplating her fingernails. "The most fascinating rumours. They speak of a young woman on the run from Caerlon. Supposedly Cadyan is offering a substantial amount of gold for her capture. Such a large amount would be tempting to anyone... You really haven't heard?" She sounded amused as she turned her attention back to Drayk.

"No, I haven't heard, but it is certainly interesting," said Drayk, lying as easily as if it were second nature to him.

"They're saying this girl has powers, you know? Powers that could rival Cadyan's and bring an end to his reign. Now isn't that *fascinating*? Imagine if we found this girl. Imagine if we brought her here to Awnell. Such a girl would be a powerful asset to my kingdom. She would be destined for more than the life of a Verratrí, wouldn't you agree?" Ayr turned her gaze to rest on Catanya.

Catanya felt hot around her neck. She wanted to avert her eyes, but the queen's stare was too intense, too discerning. It paralyzed her.

"I would," responded Drayk, and Catanya thought she heard a note of honesty in his voice.

There was a long pause, as Ayr seemed to be sizing them up.

"Very well," she said with a sigh. "You can have your secrets for now, Drayk, but I expect a full report of your crew's latest mission in the morning." She snapped her fingers and one of the guards standing behind the throne approached. "Take them to the guest chambers in the east wing. See to it they have enough food and wine." Then she stood up and inclined towards Drayk, speaking in a low voice, "I'll see you in my chambers in an hour." Then, after surveying the nearest guard, she added, "You too, gorgeous." She stroked the man's arm before winking and striding out the door.

Stunned, Catanya watched her leave without saying a word. Her mind had gone suddenly blank. She didn't know what to think as she followed Drayk and the guard through the halls towards the east wing. Ayr was nothing like what she'd expected. The queen was all charm and levity. Nothing like the cold, self-important ruler Catanya had imagined. Ayr radiated authority while barely lifting a finger. She didn't demand respect, she compelled it. Catanya had never been so intimidated or so out of her depth.

And what was going on with Drayk? Before they'd escaped Caerlon, Drayk had implied that Ayr was not to be trusted. He'd sounded nervous when he spoke about her. Yet here he was, greeting her like an old friend or lover. Catanya couldn't make sense of it. She was completely off-kilter in this world of manipulations and half-truths.

"You'll be in here, miss," said the guard, coming to a halt.

"What? Oh, thank you." Catanya peered through the door to the warm, inviting chamber within.

"And Drayk, I'm assuming you'll be wanting your usual room?" asked the guard.

"Usual room?" Catanya shot Drayk an enquiring look.

"Yeah, it's just down the hall." Drayk gestured a few doors down from her.

"So, you stay here often?"

Drayk gave her a thin smile before turning towards the guard. "Thank you, Dom, I'll join you in a minute."

The guard nodded and walked back down the corridor, leaving Drayk and Catanya alone.

"Come on," muttered Drayk, brushing past her into her room.

Catanya followed him and closed the door. Then she rounded on him. "What is going on here?"

"Calm down," said Drayk, moving to stand next to the fire. "Everything is fine." He eyed her with a touch of amusement on his face. Then he lifted the iron out of its set and began casually stoking the logs.

"Everything is not fine!" said Catanya in a furious whisper. She was straining to keep her voice down. "What was all that back there? Are you and Ayr—"

Drayk snorted loudly and shook his head. "No, that's just how it is here," he said, returning the iron to its hook and closing the grate.

"What does that mean?" asked Catanya, eyes narrowed in suspicion.

Drayk just grinned mischievously at her.

Catanya made a sound of disgust. "Why should I believe anything you say? How do I know this wasn't your plan from the start?" Her heart started pounding again. She made a move to rake her hands through her hair, but stopped, remembering the braids she'd tied to hide the colour. "I can't believe I trusted you," she said, tossing her hands in the air.

"Oh, come on," said Drayk with an edge of impatience. "I risked my life for you, I protected you from my crew, and now" —he strode over to stand in front of her, eyes searching her face —"now I've lied to my queen and my commander for you. What more do you want?"

Catanya's anger dissipated. Unsure how to respond, she turned to examine her surroundings.

The room was larger than any room she'd ever had. A wide, comfortable-looking bed sat in the centre, directly across from three large windows that overlooked the ocean. A set of sturdy armchairs framed the fire, and a tall wardrobe and mirror were tucked neatly in the corner beside a delicate dressing table.

Despite her current state of unease, Catanya had to admit that Ayr had certainly been welcoming. Catanya felt like royalty standing in this chamber. But then again...

"She knows who I am," said Catanya, in a calmer voice as she turned back towards Drayk.

"Nah, she only suspects. Besides, you heard her. She doesn't want to hurt you. She wants you to be her ally. Just like I told you at the cottage."

"Well, maybe I don't want to be her ally," said Catanya. She walked past Drayk and slumped down in one of the chairs by the fire.

Drayk pressed on his temples with his fingers, looking frustrated. "You need allies, Catya. And like it or not, we're stuck here for the time being," he said, rounding on her. "I told you it would be nearly impossible to make it through the city undetected. Well..." He gestured around at the room to prove his point. "I thought we'd be safe for a night at the inn, but Ayr knows everything that goes on in this kingdom—and Caerlon, for that matter. She probably had spies waiting for me. And I hate to break it to you, Catya, but all of Mórceá is looking for you. How do you expect to keep surviving on the run?"

Catanya didn't want to admit that he was right. "I don't trust her," she said.

Drayk laughed out loud. "You don't have a choice right now."

Catanya glared at him and then looked away, nodding resignedly.

"Right. Now, if you'll excuse me, Ayr and Dom are expecting me." Drayk clapped his hands together playfully.

It took a moment for his words to register. "Wait, what? You're really going to go to her chamber?"

"Of course," he said, giving her an incredulous look.

"Drayk, you can't!" she protested, jumping to her feet. She knew Drayk was more relaxed with his behaviour than anyone she'd met before, but this...

"Oh, I assure you, I can," he said with a smirk.

Catanya gaped at him for a moment. Then she made a sound of disgust and moved to turn away.

"What? Why not?" he asked, arching his eyebrow. "Why does it matter?"

Catanya shrugged. "No, it doesn't. I just—" She broke off and retreated a few steps. She was too embarrassed to admit the truth—that she was slightly nervous to be alone in this fortress. Drayk's company, as vexing as it could be sometimes, was still reassuring. She had grown accustomed to his presence, and she felt slightly abandoned. "I just—I," she stammered, avoiding his intense gaze. "I just think it's pathetic," she said a little more harshly than she'd intended. "It's so hollow and empty. I expected better from you, that's all."

Drayk rolled his eyes and walked away from her towards the door. "Hollow and empty. Right," he said with a scathing tone. "Nothing like the *perfect, meaningful* connection you had with Jémys. And tell me, love, how's that working out for you?" He was watching her closely for a reaction.

His words stung, and she glared at him as he opened the door.

"You know, I think it's actually a good thing that we're here," he said, glancing back at her. "You could learn a lot from watching the Awnadh. Your life might be more satisfying if you learn to relax and live in the moment a little more. You don't need to take everything so seriously. You ought to try enjoying yourself once in a while."

He flashed her a playful grin and walked out the door.

Catanya stood still, staring at the fire for what felt like ages, and fighting back alternating waves of frustration, anger, and sadness. She couldn't afford to fall to pieces. Not right now.

Eventually she roused herself enough to move. She dragged the heaviest armchair over to the entrance and used it to barricade the door. She didn't care what Drayk said. Catanya didn't trust these people. She might be stuck here for now, but she wasn't about to leave herself vulnerable. She'd learned not to take her safety for granted.

Though it was still the middle of the night, Catanya wasn't tired anymore. She strode around the room, opening the wardrobe and the dressing table, searching for anything interesting or out of the ordinary. But there was nothing. Then she sat on the bed, staring out the windows at the enormous city. Though most buildings were dark, thousands of lamps and torches still flickered through the streets, giving the impression of terrestrial stars gleaming in the dark.

She sat awake the rest of the night, watching the darkness fade and retreat, as all manner of terrifying thoughts flooded her mind.

Thoughts about Jémys. Where had he gone? Would she ever see him again? Would he even *want* to see her again?

Thoughts about Cadyan. Where was he now? How long would it take him to find her again? What would happen when he did?

Come with me to Caerlon. Let me show you what it means to be part of this family.

Cadyan's voice echoed in her head. A phantom ache burned in her shoulder where he'd seized her on that beach.

We're brother and sister.

It was getting harder to deny it—her supposed *destiny*. She'd spent so much time running from it, but with every passing day, she saw it coming closer... becoming more inevitable.

Shortly before dawn, Catanya couldn't take it anymore. She stood up and strode over to the wardrobe in search of something to wear. Half a dozen simple dresses hung inside, as well as a collection of what she'd first assumed were men's clothes. But on closer inspection, she realized they resembled the outfit Ayr had been wearing. Tempted, Catanya held out the leather breeches and jacket. She remembered how freeing it had been to wear Jémys's clothes, but she ultimately decided on one of the dresses. It was a simple blue-grey dress, made of cambric with a square neckline and laces along the front and sleeves. It was stiff and rigid, but at least it was clean.

She stopped by the mirror to check that her hair was holding in its braids before heading out to explore the fortress.

Other than the guards stationed at intervals along the corridors, the fortress seemed deserted. The sun was rising as Catanya reached the end of the east wing and stopped. She stared out the window at a courtyard terrace a few levels below her floor. Three people were setting up what looked like racks of swords, targets, and training gear. She leaned farther into the window alcove to get a better view and recognized Lia and the two soldiers from the inn.

Catanya watched them curiously for a few minutes. Lia strode back and forth with purpose, directing the others and assessing the weapons. Catanya couldn't quite place it, but there was something familiar about Lia. It was something about how she moved, how she held herself. It reminded Catanya of someone, but she didn't know who.

Just when Catanya was about to turn away, Lia looked up and caught her watching them. The two women stared at each other through the window, and Catanya thought she noticed a sinister darkness spread across Lia's face.

"Here you are," came a voice from behind, making Catanya jump.

Queen Ayr was striding down the corridor towards her. Catanya's first instinct was to brace for an attack, but the queen gave her a benevolent smile that disarmed her.

"I sent servants to attend you this morning, but was told

you'd left," said Ayr, coming to a leisurely halt. "I thought you might appreciate some food and a hot bath."

Catanya's cheeks prickled with embarrassment. "Oh," she said, suddenly self-conscious about her appearance. She clasped her hands behind her back to hide the dirt under her nails. "Honestly, that... er... didn't occur to me." It had been ages since she'd had a proper bath.

"No matter," said Ayr, waving away her discomfort. "The servants will be happy to assist you whenever you're ready. But right now, I'm hoping you might join me for a stroll."

"What?" Catanya stared at her. "Oh, I mean, y-yes, of course. I'd be honoured." She felt her face flush.

"Excellent. I'd like to show you my private garden," said Ayr, giving Catanya a reassuring nod. She led the way down the corridor and up a narrow set of stairs. "It is one of the few places where I feel truly peaceful," she added quietly.

Catanya didn't know how to respond. She watched the various servants racing around, preparing the fortress for the day ahead, and she cleared her throat awkwardly. "Running this kingdom must be very demanding," she said just to break the silence.

"It is," said Ayr. "And I confess, sometimes I would rather not have so much responsibility."

"I know what you mean," said Catanya before she could stop herself.

"Mmm. I thought you might." Ayr eyed her perceptively as she led the way up a second flight of stairs and along another corridor towards a worn, wooden door at the end. She unlocked the door and led Catanya outside into a small, bright enclosure, which was nearly overrun with exotic-looking plants and flowers.

Catanya stepped forward, gazing at the explosion of colour and taking in the wondrous smell of assorted flowers. Despite the encroaching winter, this space was warm and bursting with life. Cedar trusses bearing panels of glass were strategically placed to encourage the retention of sunlight. Songbirds chirped happily from nests in the beams.

The sound of trickling water drew Catanya into the centre of the square, where a life-sized statue stood in the middle of a small pool. Large pillars wreathed in purplish green vines surrounded the area, giving it a wonderful sense of sanctuary.

"It's beautiful," said Catanya. The smell of flowers transported her back to the meadow in Finnua... with Jémys... She tried to focus on her surroundings, to keep from losing herself in the memory.

"Yes, I've always loved this garden," said Ayr. "Ever since I was a young child. I used to come here with my sister before she died." She stood beside Catanya in front of the pool.

The statue at its centre depicted a woman holding a chalice in one hand and a long sword in the other. Two matching crowns hung from the sword's blade.

"Do you recognize her?" asked Ayr.

The question surprised Catanya. "No, I've never seen this woman before, but... there's something about her face..." Catanya tilted her head, staring at the fountain. Why did so much about this kingdom seem familiar to her. She'd never been here before. She'd never met these people. But still... It was like she could remember another time, another life spent inside these walls.

"Yes, I'm afraid few people outside of Awnell know the story anymore. Or if they do, they choose to ignore it."

"What story?" asked Catanya.

Ayr paused before responding. "She is known by many names... The Warrior Queen, The Forsaken Sister, and, my personal favourite, The Conqueror Betrayed."

Catanya frowned. "I've never heard any of those names."

"No, I didn't expect that you would have," said Ayr as she

circled the statue, admiring it from every angle. "She is said to have been the first Queen of Awnell."

"Really?" Catanya looked at the figure again with increased interest.

"Yes." Ayr stopped again next to Catanya, eyeing her with the same interest she'd shown the statue. "Tell me, Catya, what do you know about the origin of the kingdoms? The Quiescence Wars?"

"You mean the stories about Maílater Caer?"

"That," said Ayr, looking irritable, "is the abridged and revisionist version of the story. It seems Caerlon has conveniently forgotten the truth."

Catanya had never given much thought to the history of the kingdoms beyond what she'd learned as a child. But now that she thought about it, she was curious.

"So, what is the truth?" she asked.

Ayr strolled over to a bench on the side of the courtyard and gestured for Catanya to join her.

"Centuries ago, before the kingdoms were created, before there was order or structure, there was a power that flowed through Mórceá and all of its people."

"Resonance," said Catanya, nodding.

"Precisely. Now, certain people were gifted enough to harness Resonance for their own gain or to wield it against their enemies. But there were two particular practitioners whose power was unrivalled by all the others. A brother and a sister, as it so happened."

"What?" Catanya gaped at her. She'd never heard a version of the story where Maílater Caer had a sister.

"Oh, yes. A brother and a sister who were inseparable. They were the truest of friends and would have died a thousand times over before betraying each other. And for a long time, they lived simple lives, using their substantial gifts to help their community and to improve the lives of everyone around them.

But they began to realize it wasn't enough. They were struggling to keep up with the demand, and, despite all their power, they weren't strong enough to save everyone.

"Over time, more people learned to harness Resonance for themselves—immoral people who sought to wield their magic against others. Reports of feuding and crime increased. The brother and sister tried to fight back, but it was difficult. Unrest and mistrust spread through the land, and they realized they needed to do more. They needed to be stronger, to concentrate their powers somehow."

"The elixir of Caerlon," said Catanya.

"The elixir, exactly. Now, not much is known about the elixir's origin. Some accounts claim it was created from focused thought and need. Others say it was a treasure discovered by Maílater Caer during the war. Personally, I believe the stories that claim Caer and his sister created the elixir together, through experimentation and invention. I do not believe a power as great as the elixir could come into existence on its own or by mere accident.

"Whatever the truth, it has been lost to history. What we do know is that the sister, who was a skilled combatant and warrior, devised a strategy to unite Mórceá under one rule. Caer drank from the elixir first and used his powers to give the people hope while his sister marched through the land, quieting any rebels or magical practitioners who threatened the peace they were creating.

"And for a time, their plan seemed to work. But when the sister returned, triumphant, to her brother, she found him changed. Guarded and mistrustful. He refused to relinquish her share of the elixir, inviting her to serve under him instead of at his side as it should have been. When the sister refused, the brother became violent. He banished her from the land and vowed to kill her if she ever tried to take his elixir again."

Ayr finished her story and sat, gazing reverently at the

statue in front of them.

"So, the sister... she is your ancestor?" asked Catanya. Her head was spinning at this new version of the story.

Ayr nodded. "She is. And the brother is the one known as Maílater Caer—Caerlon's *great founder*, famed for uniting the people and creating the elixir that bestows unlimited power on any king who rules Caerlon."

"Hmm." Catanya frowned. "I wonder what would have become of Mórceá if the two kingdoms had shared the elixir... Maybe if Caer hadn't betrayed her, things would be different..."

"Maybe," said Ayr, standing up. She took a few steps away and then spun around to face Catanya. "Every day I receive reports of people seeking refuge in my land, people escaping Caerlon across the border in the hopes of a better life. I hear stories of Caerlon's brutality and I take pity on these refugees. No one should have to live in fear of their king."

Ayr's sudden intensity surprised Catanya. "You're right," she said, nodding.

"But even here we live in fear," continued Ayr. "In Awnell, we must live in constant fear of invasion, knowing that we cannot survive an attack from Caerlon if and when it comes."

Catanya's heart sank. *Of course.* She'd never considered that before. All this time on the run, she'd believed she might find safety in Awnell, but, of course, even the Awnadh lived in fear of Caerlon.

"So, what can you do?" she asked sympathetically. "What *do* you do?"

Ayr smiled to herself. "We drink, we eat, we make merry, we embrace our carnal needs." She winked at Catanya. "Because we know our time here is precious, and I will not allow my people to live half-alive or half-fulfilled. No, unlike Casréyan and Cadyan, who have chosen to rule with cruelty and privation, I offer repletion. I offer freedom." She held her arms out in a welcoming gesture. "As long as you are here, Catya, you are free."

Unsure how to respond, Catanya simply nodded.

As she left the courtyard later that morning, she still wasn't entirely sure she trusted Ayr, but at least she was beginning to understand. There was no one and nowhere that truly existed beyond the reach of Caerlon, but at least in Awnell, they were free to pretend.

3

A STRONG MAN

It was late, and the halls of the castle were unusually still. A cold front had crept through Caerlon, blanketing the ground and the trees with a light layer of frost. Icicles glistened in rows along the turrets, and an icy wind whistled through the windows, extinguishing candles and testing the strength of the fires.

The shift in weather had sent a bout of dry cough through the city. Diyah had just finished another busy day preparing countless coughing draughts and sleeping tonics to treat it. The work was tedious and repetitive, but Diyah didn't care. It kept her mind free to focus on other matters.

Lately, Fehla had been joining her at work. She'd become Diyah's unofficial assistant, and Diyah was slowly teaching her some of the healing arts. Diyah enjoyed Fehla's company, and she liked knowing they were helping people, despite their own hopeless situations.

As they moved around the physician's chambers, tidying after another long day's work, Fehla asked Diyah about her youth in Faltir. She seemed eager to hear stories about Diyah's childhood with Catanya.

"And then what did you do?" asked Fehla, laughing as she dried empty bottles with a cloth.

"We returned the horses, and snuck in the back door. We were sure we'd gotten away with it… but there was Lady Genna, sitting in the kitchen, waiting for us!"

"No!"

Diyah giggled. "Oh, she was furious! She made us clean every inch of the stables the next day as punishment. And we weren't allowed to leave the lodge for a week." Diyah grinned at the memory. "But it was worth it. The troupe was wonderful. I've never seen such acrobatics or heard such beautiful music in my life. And Trisyán and Garret were right. They had outstanding sparklers that lit up the sky with so many colours. It was truly spectacular."

Diyah welcomed the rush of nostalgia.

"It reminds me of a time when I was young," said Fehla. "Growing up in Awnell, every winter there was the Midwinter Carnival. It was always my favourite time of the year. My older sister, Falia, and I were very close, and we had a friend similar to you and Catanya… well… not quite, but—"

The sound of heavy footsteps and angry voices outside the door drowned the rest of her sentence.

"Get out of my way!"

"Master Julyán, my apologies, I didn't recognize you."

The door burst open and Julyán stalked into the room, looking dishevelled. His hair was matted and windswept and he looked exhausted, as though he had been travelling nonstop for days. His clothes were covered in what appeared to be a mixture of blood, sweat, and dirt.

"What has happened?" asked Fehla with a sudden return to her authoritative demeanour.

Julyán looked surprised to see her. "What are you doing here?"

Fehla stiffened. "I am the queen. I can go wherever I like.

Now, tell me what has happened." She cast a quick, nervous glance at Diyah. "Where is my son?"

"You're needed in the dungeons," said Julyán, ignoring Fehla and speaking to Diyah. "At once."

Diyah's breath caught in her throat. "Why? Who's in the dungeons?"

"Come." Julyán tried to grab her arm, but she yanked it out of his grip.

"Don't touch me," she said.

Julyán made a sound of impatience. "Your services are required in the dungeons. As a matter of urgency."

"Fine," said Diyah through clenched teeth. She turned to collect some supplies.

"I'm coming with you." Fehla joined Diyah on the other side of the worktable.

"No." Julyán's voice was flat and direct.

Fehla raised her eyebrows. "You, *Fírkon*, do not tell me what to do."

Julyán jerked his head irritably, but didn't protest. He waited impatiently while Diyah gathered her supplies, then she and Fehla followed him out the door. They hastened through the corridors towards the west wing and the dungeons. Diyah was fighting hard to stay calm as she pictured Catanya lying bloodied in a cell.

But it couldn't be Catanya... Cadyan wanted her dead. He wouldn't want to heal her.

Relief shot through Diyah like an arrow, only to be replaced by shame and disgust.

If not Catanya, then who?

They reached the dungeons and descended the stairs to the dark corridor at the bottom. The familiar stench met her nostrils, and it made her stomach turn. The sound of dripping water and scuttling rats sent chills running down her spine.

She hated this place. It was hard not to remember what happened the last time she was down here.

Memories of pain spread across her back, and echoes of depraved laughter rang in her ears. She struggled to breathe through the fear constricting her lungs. It took every ounce of strength she had to continue following Julyán into the dark, desolate place.

"In here." Julyán pointed to a cell on his left.

The guards had lit a torch near the door. Diyah squinted through the bars and saw a man lying unconscious on the floor. His body was battered and broken, covered in filth and blood.

Anger coursed through Diyah's veins, burning away her fear. "What happened to him?" she asked, crossing through the open door to kneel beside him. She brushed his wavy, dark hair out of his face and rolled him carefully onto his back. He muttered something and groaned. "What did you do to him?" Diyah glared at Julyán.

Julyán just stared indifferently back at her and said nothing.

"Can you help him?" asked Fehla, joining Diyah in the cell.

"I don't know." Diyah looked at the man's face. He was shivering, and there were beads of sweat on his forehead. "I can't help him here. I need to move him."

"No," said Julyán.

Diyah clenched her fists, struggling to keep her fury in check. "He needs to be in a clean, safe environment where I can tend to him properly. He'll die in here!"

"Then he dies," replied Julyán.

Incensed, Diyah shot to her feet and rounded on him. "Why bring me here, then?" she demanded. "If you truly don't care about this man's fate, then why bother bringing me here at all? You—"

"Diyah?" called Fehla, interrupting her angry tirade. "I think he's waking up."

The man's eyes fluttered, and he struggled to speak. "Jay..."

Diyah crouched back down beside him. "What are you trying to say?" she asked, laying her hand on his forehead to check his temperature. He was burning up. His eyes slid out of focus again as he fell back into unconsciousness.

"All right," said Julyán abruptly. "Move him. But he doesn't leave my sight."

"He can hardly move. You really think he can cause trouble in this state?" Fehla shook her head in disbelief.

Julyán ignored her and gestured for two guards to come transport the prisoner. "Take him to the physician's quarters," he commanded.

"Be careful!" said Diyah indignantly as the guards hauled him off the ground. They carried him past her, out of the dungeons. "Who is he?" she asked, rounding on Julyán again.

"It's none of your concern," he said, and he turned to follow the guards.

When they arrived back in the physician's quarters, Diyah laid out the cot near the fire in the workroom and instructed the guards to lower the injured man onto it. The exertion of being moved had drained him, and he was mumbling incoherently again.

"Jay... JJ..."

"What is that he keeps saying?" asked Fehla, looking at Diyah with concern in her eyes.

Diyah could tell from Fehla's expression that she feared for his sanity, but Diyah had seen this before. "He's delirious. The fever may have reached his brain," she explained. "I need water and blankets. There are some extras in my sleeping room." She heard Fehla rush off to fetch them for her. Diyah felt his chest for injuries and realized his clothes were soaking wet. "We need to get him out of these clothes," she mumbled, grabbing a dagger off her worktable and slicing through the ties on his shirt.

When she saw his chest, she gasped. It was badly swollen

and covered in bruises and cuts, as though he'd been beaten to within an inch of his life.

"What is the matter with you?" She spoke in a dangerously quiet voice as she turned to face Julyán. "How could you do this to someone?"

"What?" Julyán seemed surprised by her question. He had been staring at them, eyes glazed as though not really seeing them.

Diyah clenched her teeth and turned away from him. She gazed at the man on the cot. Underneath the bruises and filth, she thought she detected something familiar about him, but she couldn't place it. He had a kind face, though—handsome, even.

Diyah was angry. She wanted to scream at Julyán, to hurt him the way he'd hurt this man. Pulling herself up to her full height, she turned to face Julyán. "Get out of my sight," she said in an icy, commanding voice.

Julyán stared at her, stunned.

"You heard me. I told you to get out of here," she repeated even louder. "Go wait outside where the sight of you can't make me sick."

They glared at each other in tense silence. Diyah could sense Fehla's unease, but Diyah was too angry to be scared. She just held Julyán's gaze, daring him to react.

To her surprise, Julyán nodded. "As you wish," he said. Then he turned and swept out of the room without another word.

Diyah watched him go, filled with deep loathing. When the door closed behind him, she returned to the injured man.

Fehla hurried over to join her by the cot. She placed the blankets and the jug of water down on a nearby table. "Who do you think he is?" she asked.

"I don't know," said Diyah. She finished pulling off his

sopping wet clothes and tossed them aside. "Has Cadyan returned?"

Fehla shook her head as she unfolded a blanket and tossed it over the injured man. "I don't know, but I doubt it. I think we'd know if he were in the city." She gave Diyah a dark look.

Diyah exhaled heavily. "Does that mean he hasn't found her yet?" she whispered.

"I hope so."

Nausea twisted in Diyah's stomach. "Catanya is strong." Her voice shook, and she had to grip the edge of the bed to stabilize herself. "I'm sure she's fine."

Just then, the injured man began frantically tossing and turning. "Catanya. No, don't. Not... no... JJ!" he cried.

Diyah and Fehla exchanged worried looks. Diyah picked up a wet cloth and began wiping his forehead. "Do you think he knows Catanya?" she asked, her hand shaking as she ran the cloth along his hairline.

He was muttering even more incoherently, but she caught Catanya's name mixed in with the babble.

"It certainly seems like it," said Fehla.

Diyah nodded. "Come on, we need to clean these wounds before we can treat them. We need hot water, rags, and my purifying salve. It's over there on the shelf. Some of his wounds have started to fester so we'll probably need to use the whole vial."

Diyah and Fehla worked through the night, binding his wounds and resetting broken bones. He had a big, sturdy frame, so Diyah was grateful to have Fehla's help. The damage was extensive. Any one of these wounds was dangerous on its own, but all together... It was a wonder this man had survived. He was obviously strong. That gave her hope he might recover.

When they'd finished, they wrapped him in a thicker wool blanket. Then they sat down to monitor him as he slept, periodically checking his bandages and temperature throughout the night.

By the time morning arrived, he seemed to be sleeping more evenly, so Diyah decided it was safe for her and Fehla to rest. She told Fehla to go sleep, and she was intending to do the same when Julyán returned to the room.

"Any change?" he asked, staring down at the prisoner.

Diyah glowered and crossed her arms. "He's sleeping more soundly now, but he has a long way to go," she said, stifling a yawn.

"You're tired," said Julyán.

Diyah snorted and looked up at him. His face was sallow and drawn and he had dark circles under his eyes. "Look who's talking," she grumbled.

"You should rest," he said, ignoring her comment.

Diyah exhaled stiffly. His imperious tone irritated her. "I don't need rest," she snapped, suddenly abandoning her plan. "You rest. I have work to do. I was just about to check his bandages." She strode away from Julyán towards the bedside, fully aware that she'd just checked her patient's bandages a moment before.

She sensed Julyán's eyes on her, and she thought she heard a faint sigh before he walked out of the chamber and shut the door.

The next few days passed in a similar fashion. Julyán stopped by frequently to check on the prisoner, and after a while, Diyah suspected his interest extended beyond his duty to Caerlon.

On the third day, it relieved Diyah to discover that her patient's fever had finally broken, and he was breathing normally again. She was checking his bandages to see how the bruises were healing when she realized he was waking up.

"Lie still," she said gently. "You're badly injured."

He opened his eyes and winced as he tried to adjust his position. "Where am I?" he asked, his throat rasping.

"It's okay," she reassured him while helping him take a drink of water. "You're in Caerlon City. You've been here for three days."

The man spluttered and choked, dribbling water down his chin. "What? No, no, no, no, no..." He tried to sit up and gasped in pain, clutching at his broken ribs. "No, what happened?" He cast around wildly, taking in his surroundings. "Who are you?" he asked, suddenly suspicious and trying to lift himself up on his elbows.

"You should take it easy. It's okay. I'm a healer," said Diyah, pushing him back down into the cot. "I've been tending to your wounds. Do you remember what happened to you?"

"What happened to me..." He frowned as he tried to think, but then his face fell. "Oh no. Where is she? Tell me they didn't catch her." His eyes bulged out of their darkened orbits, and he looked mad with fear.

Diyah worried he might try to jump out of bed if she didn't manage to calm him down. He looked poised for a fight. "If you're talking about Catanya," she ventured in what she hoped was a soothing voice, "she's not here. She wasn't with you when they brought you into the city."

He closed his eyes in gratitude. "Thank the Natures," he breathed, leaning back in the bed. But then his eyes snapped open again. "Who are you?"

Diyah found his frantic energy unnerving, but she kept her tone even and calm. "My name is Diyah, and—"

"Diyah?" Comprehension flickered in his eyes as he looked around the physician's chambers. "*You're* Diyah?"

"You know who I am?" she asked, surprised.

"Yes, Catanya told me about you."

Relief flooded through Diyah. Her heart swelled knowing

what Catanya must have said about her. "Then Catanya's alive? She's okay?"

"Yes. I mean, she was the last time I saw her. We were in the cottage, preparing to leave when—" He broke off, eyes darting around the room in agitation again. "Where is he? Where is JJ? I know I saw him. Where is he?"

"Who?" asked Diyah, taken aback by his sudden return of frantic energy. "I don't know who—"

"JJ is dead," said a voice behind her. She twisted around to see Julyán striding towards them, wearing an expression of deep antipathy. "He's been dead for a long time now."

The man on the cot stared at him, eyes wide in shock. "It *is* you," he gasped, trying to sit up. "I can't believe it."

"JJ?" asked Diyah, frowning at Julyán. "What—"

"I told you. He's gone," repeated Julyán.

"But you're here!" cried the man in a pained voice. "Of course, Nelle told me... but I never wanted to believe it. I told myself you'd just..." He trailed off, looking hurt. "But I don't understand. How can you be here?"

Julyán just stared blankly at him and said nothing.

"Tell me, brother, why are you still here?" he repeated. "How could you stay here all this time?"

Diyah's head reeled as she tried to make sense of the conversation. "Brother?" she repeated, turning to look at Julyán. Their eyes met briefly and Diyah realized why the prisoner seemed so familiar. That verdant green colour was distinctive. And both men had the same broad build, the same dark hair and skin. The resemblance was striking.

Julyán stared down at his brother unfeelingly.

"How can you work for him?" asked the injured man. "After everything that happened? What did they do to you to make you stay?"

Julyán smirked. "You were always so naïve, Jémys. They didn't do anything to me. I chose this."

"I don't believe that." Jémys shook his head desperately and winced at the pain. "No, this can't be you. This isn't how our father raised us."

"Father has been gone for a long time," said Julyán. "And he died every bit the naïve fool you are now. You believe society is divided into right and wrong, honour and dishonour. But none of that matters. The only thing that matters is strength. The strong will always triumph, and the weak will always suffer. And you, brother, are as weak as they come."

Jémys's face flushed, and he stared at his brother in disgust. When he spoke next, his voice shook with anger. "If you think it takes strength to be one of them, to be a tyrant, then you truly are gone. It takes no strength to do what you do. It only takes cowardice and cruelty. You used to know that. Don't you remember what Father always taught us? A truly strong man doesn't need to make others feel weak in order to feel strong."

At these words, Diyah remembered another reason she recognized Jémys.

Julyán laughed derisively. "Well, it doesn't matter what you think anymore. These precious values of yours can't protect you from reality. And you're in enemy territory now, little brother. And I will do what I've always done. I will do what I must in order to survive." Then he turned to Diyah and said, "Make sure he's strong enough to withstand interrogation," before sweeping out of the room, slamming the door in his wake.

There was a lengthy pause as Diyah surveyed Jémys and saw angry tears pooling in his eyes.

"Jémys?" She spoke his name uncertainly and laid her hand on his arm.

He looked at her and tried to smile, but it came out more like a grimace. "Sorry," he mumbled, as he wiped his eyes and looked away from her.

Diyah felt uncomfortable, like she was intruding on something private. "You must be starving," she said, not sure what else to say. She stood up to fetch food from the cupboards and give him some privacy.

A little later, as she was helping him eat, the door opened again, and this time Fehla entered.

"You're awake," she said, crossing the room to stand next to the bed.

Jémys took in her appearance and gaped at Diyah.

"It's okay," she said. "This is Fehla, Catanya's mother. She's not like everyone else here. You can trust her."

"Thank you, dear." Fehla smiled as she sat in a chair next to Diyah. "I'm very glad to see that you are faring a bit better," she added, looking at Jémys.

"Fehla has been helping me tend to your wounds," explained Diyah, standing up to take away the plate of food. "Fehla, this is Jémys, he's... well, I don't really know who he is..." She frowned, glancing back at him.

"I'm nobody," he mumbled, shaking his head. "A simple villager caught up in something much bigger than I ever could have imagined."

"I know the feeling," said Diyah darkly.

"But... you know Catanya? You know my daughter?" asked Fehla, inching forward in her seat.

Jémys surveyed her for a moment and then nodded.

Relief spread across Fehla's face, and she turned to Diyah. "He must be the one they said was travelling with her."

"Who said that?" asked Jémys.

"The maífírkon. He told Cadyan that Catanya was travelling with a man. A skilled fighter, I think he called you. And he said you and Catanya were—" Diyah broke off and glanced at Fehla.

"We were what?" asked Jémys.

"Um, well... He implied that perhaps you two were more than travel companions," said Fehla, eyeing Jémys carefully.

Jémys averted his gaze, which Diyah took to be a confirmation of the rumour.

"But you were there?" asked Fehla, ignoring the awkward atmosphere. "You saw what happened? None of the other fírkon have returned. Neither has Cadyan. What happened to Catanya?"

"I don't know," said Jémys. He shut his eyes and leaned his head back, looking utterly miserable. "I saw Cadyan destroying the cottage, and I completely lost my head. I thought she was inside so I ran back to help her, and the whole place caved in on me... She must have escaped. They both must have... unless..." He shook his head, frowning. "She trusted him, so I'm sure it's fine. I'm sure she's fine. She has to be..." His voice shook, and he stared at them imploringly.

Diyah was struggling to follow his disjointed train of thought. "Trusted who?" she asked.

Before Jémys could answer, the door opened and Julyán strode into the room. "What's going on?" he asked, looking from Fehla to Diyah, eyes narrowed in accusation.

"Nothing," said Diyah. "We're doing what you told us to do. *Tending to the patient.*" She gestured to the cot theatrically.

"I'm fine," said Jémys, trying to sound valiant.

"No, you're not," snapped Diyah. "He is absolutely not fine. He needs calm and rest, and I'll thank you to stop barging in here and disrupting the peace *every five minutes.*" She clenched her jaw and scowled at Julyán.

Julyán made an odd sound somewhere between a snort and a sigh and turned to leave.

When he had closed the door, Fehla exhaled heavily. "I should go too. Now that Julyán is back, I don't think it's safe for me to visit as often. If Cadyan thinks I'm showing an interest in either of you, he'll be suspicious. He'll want to know why, and I'm sure he won't ask nicely."

"But Fehla—" Diyah didn't want to lose the friendship they were building. It was all she had.

"It's all right, dear, we'll find another way." She put her hand on Diyah's shoulder before turning and leaving the room.

Diyah stared sourly at the door, silently loathing the man on the other side.

———

Jémys slept on and off for the next two days and Diyah busied herself with the work she'd been neglecting in order to tend to him. She was finishing corking the last of the vials of valerian root sleep tonic and cleaning off her worktable when she noticed Jémys was awake and watching her.

"How did you get here?" he asked. "How is it possible they let you live and work here?"

Diyah shrugged. "Honestly, I just think they need me right now. There are no healers here anymore... But one day, when they decide they don't need me anymore, that'll be it." She looked at Jémys darkly.

"How did they know you were a healer?"

Diyah thought for a moment. "It was Julyán. He recognized my Heiltúir satchel." Diyah pulled her satchel off her shoulders and handed it to Jémys. "I keep this with me at all times. It holds a small collection of essential remedies and ingredients."

Jémys ran his finger along the embossed symbol on the front—the symbol of the Heiltúir. It depicted a small cauldron with an ornamental design of Awnle script encircling a decorative letter H.

"Hmm... I think I've seen something like this before." He frowned as though trying to remember, but he couldn't. Jémys shrugged and handed it back to her, wincing as he extended his arm.

Diyah was watching him closely. Now that his colour had returned, she was sure she recognized him.

"You don't remember me, do you?" she asked.

His eyes widened in surprise. "Remember you? Why? Have we met before?"

"Yes, I believe we have." She gave him a warm smile. "It was about ten or eleven years ago in the woods near Faltir. You protected me. Don't you remember?"

Jémys frowned and shook his head apologetically.

"You were staying in Mellot Cove, I think," insisted Diyah. "I was in the woods collecting herbs, and Cadyan was there. They were on the royal tour. He started harassing me and you stopped him. Surely you remember that?" She smiled at the fond memory, eager to share it with him and finally be able to thank him for his help.

But Jémys was shaking his head again. "I've never met Cadyan before in my life," he said with certainty.

Diyah frowned. "But it had to be you," she said. "I'm sure of it because you told me—you said 'a truly powerful man wouldn't need to make others feel weak so he can feel strong.' I remember it clearly. Just like you said before to Julyán."

Jémys looked genuinely curious now. "My father used to say that to us when we were boys. Maybe it was my father you met?"

Diyah shook her head. "No, it was a boy—a young man, actually. Several years older than me."

"Hmm... Ten years ago?" asked Jémys. "I was just a young boy then, maybe nine years old."

Diyah felt the sting of disappointment. "Oh... right. Then it couldn't have been you..." She trailed off, looking at the door.

Almost as though on cue, the door opened and Julyán came in. He opened his mouth to speak, but before he could say one word, Diyah cut him off.

"It was you!" she exclaimed, realization dawning on her.

Julyán looked at her, perplexed.

Diyah let out an incredulous laugh and jumped to her feet. "You were the boy that saved me in the woods all those years ago." She stepped in front of him and stared up into his eyes. Underneath the layers of malice and hate, she could see him clearly now.

Julyán looked surprised, but he quickly recollected himself. "What are you talking about?" he said, trying to be dismissive.

"Oh, this is unbelievable! All this time I've been here... *loathing* you!" she spat the word at him. "Yet you were the one who stood up to Cadyan all those years ago. You were the one who defended that little girl in the woods! You can't tell me you don't remember."

Julyán stared at her. "I remember." His voice was deadly quiet.

"You were the one," she repeated, staring at him in disbelief. How had she not seen it before?

"And you are the reason I am who I am today," said Julyán coldly.

Diyah was taken aback. "What is that supposed to mean?"

They stood mere inches from each other. Julyán was towering over her, looking intimidating, but Diyah held her ground and refused to back away.

Finally, Julyán shook his head and stalked out of the room.

"I can't believe this," said Diyah, turning to look at Jémys, whose expression was confused and shocked. She paced up and down, and then, throwing caution to the wind, she stormed out the door after Julyán. He was halfway down the corridor when she caught up with him.

"Don't walk away from me," she shouted, hardly believing her own nerve. She grabbed his arm to stop him and he jerked it away.

"You forget your place," he said, turning to glare at her.

"I don't care," she retorted, matching his venom. "I want to know what happened to that boy in the woods?"

Julyán raised himself up, bearing down on her. "Nothing *happened* to him. He grew up. He grew wise."

"Really?" scoffed Diyah. "Wise? You think that's the word for it?" She rolled her eyes.

"Careful," warned Julyán as he took a step forward, his hand on his sword. "I won't tolerate much more of your insolence."

"Fine," spat Diyah. "But tell me one thing, oh, *wise sir*."

Julyán's nostrils flared. For the first time, Diyah thought he might lose control of his emotions. She knew it was dangerous, but she pressed on.

"If that boy is gone, then tell me—why do you keep coming to check on your brother? Why do I see concern in your eyes underneath that angry façade?"

Julyán shook his head and tried to turn away.

"You care about him! Admit it!" shouted Diyah, and she grabbed Julyán by the arm again.

Julyán reacted instinctively. He yanked his arm out of her grasp and wrapped his fingers around her throat, slamming her against the wall so the wind was knocked out of her.

She had gotten what she wanted. Julyán had finally lost control. She gasped for air as he stared down at her murderously.

"Watch yourself," he said in a deadly whisper.

He held her pressed against the wall for a moment as the anger in his face abated. Bright spots formed in the corners of Diyah's eyes. Her vision blurred. Then he leisurely unwrapped his fingers from her neck and backed down. His face returned to its usual impassive state, except for a tension in his jaw that hadn't been there before.

Diyah slumped against the wall, gasping and choking on the sudden intake of air. Then, rubbing her neck, she made herself stand up tall and look him straight in the eye.

"I'm not afraid of you," she said. "I know who you really are now." She smirked triumphantly. "Having your brother here changes things. You feel vulnerable so you're lashing out. But you can't hide anymore. The boy I met—the boy your brother remembers—he's buried somewhere deep within you."

"Don't count on it," retorted Julyán, a vein in his forehead pulsing.

"Why not?" she asked with a laugh. "I have nothing left to lose. But you do." She held his gaze. Then she smiled serenely and turned on her heel, striding back down the corridor to her chambers, working hard to keep her steps measured despite her sudden discomposure.

4

QUEENS AND PAWNS

A week had passed since Drayk and Catanya had arrived in Awnell. Cold weather poured in from the mountains, and a chilly fog lingered permanently in the air. It was a damp winter, damper than Catanya was used to, with storming grey skies and icy rains that misted the city streets and walls.

Catanya was grateful not to be trekking through the wilderness anymore. She was still quite uneasy in the fortress, but she wasn't looking forward to leaving again.

Drayk seemed perfectly content to stay in the city indefinitely.

"Leave?" he said impatiently when Catanya brought up her concerns one morning. She'd cornered him outside his chambers to talk.

"I can't stay here, Drayk," she whispered, glancing over her shoulder to make sure the passing guards hadn't heard. "It's not safe."

"And tell me, love, where is it you think you will be safe?"

Catanya bit her lip and didn't respond.

"That's what I thought," said Drayk, patting her arm and walking away.

Catanya returned to her room and locked the door. She'd spent most of her week alone in her chambers, avoiding contact with the Awnadh. She was on edge, waiting for something to happen or for someone to discover the truth about her. But sitting alone in her chambers was only making her more miserable. With no distractions, her mind whirled with unwanted thoughts. Echoes of Cadyan's voice spoke to her in the dark, taunting her and laughing at her. Her nightmares about Finnua and Faltir continued, blending together in scenes of terror and pain that always ended as soldiers chased her into a clearing full of faceless people.

In her waking hours, she wallowed in regret and sadness about everything she'd lost. She replayed her final argument with Jémys over and over, wishing she could go back and do things differently. There were so many things she wished she could change. So much sorrow she longed to undo. But she seemed destined to inherit her family's legacy of grief.

Ever since her talk with Ayr, she was consumed with questions about her ancestors. The more she thought about Maílater Caer and how he'd betrayed his sister, the more uneasy she became about the similarities to her own situation.

Could it just be a coincidence?

Catanya felt as if the walls were tightening around her. There was too much she still didn't understand about her family and her magic—her role in all this.

Catanya didn't want to stay in Awnell, but her options were dwindling. And maybe this place could give her some answers. Maybe Ayr *could* help her...

Late one afternoon, Catanya decided to return to Ayr's garden. She couldn't think of anything else to do, and she wanted to see the statue again. Hopefully it could show her something—some way to make sense of her life.

She left her chambers and walked through the halls, trying to remember the route back to the garden. The fortress of Awnell was a rabbit warren of interconnected corridors and staircases. It was easy to get lost.

Catanya retraced her steps from her first morning, but somehow still found herself in a new part of the building. It was a wide, windowless corridor deep in the bowels of the fortress. Dozens of paintings and tapestries hung on display along the walls, and several sculptures stood on plinths beneath torches.

It was a gallery.

Mesmerized, Catanya slowed her pace and paused to examine each work. The paintings were incredible, with colours and brushstrokes in patterns she'd never seen before. Catanya didn't know the words to describe the styles—she'd never had any formal art training—but her artistic instincts still understood. She appreciated how the painters mastered perspective with carefully measured lines and shapes, how they blended colours to create nuance and depth.

The portraits came alive as the torchlight flickered against the texture of the paint.

She didn't know how long she strolled that corridor. It could have been hours. When she'd had her fill of the paintings, she turned to examine the sculptures.

Marble, bronze, wood, clay. The detail and variety abounded. Then she reached a set of busts depicting the former Queens and Kings of Awnell. Catanya read the plaques beneath each one, pausing when she reached the end.

King Ayln. Ayr's father.

The marble bust was astonishingly lifelike. His bristly beard was short and neat, offsetting his naturally soft features. But the sharpness in his eyes spoke of intelligence. He looked like a strong leader. Just like his daughter.

Lost in thought about statues and rulers, it took Catanya

several minutes to realize she could hear Ayr's voice drifting down an adjoining corridor.

"You are, of course, always welcome here. Even if your visit is rather... ah... unexpected."

Catanya spotted a door standing slightly ajar. She approached and caught a glimpse of the throne room on the other side.

"I am glad to hear it," came a second, male voice—a voice that sent a chill down Catanya's spine.

She froze where she stood.

"What brings you to Awnell?" asked Ayr in a conversational tone that still conveyed how unwelcome the visit was.

"I am looking for someone," came Cadyan's cold drawl. "A dangerous criminal, in fact. She should have passed through these parts a few days ago. Likely travelling with a man."

In a panic, Catanya ducked behind a large pillar. Hidden from the door, she listened to the conversation.

"Curious that you should pursue such a criminal yourself. This woman must be very special," said Ayr. Her tone was light, but Catanya thought she detected a note of heightened interest.

"She poses a great threat to our two kingdoms," said Cadyan. "Several outlying villages in Caerlon have already been decimated. My men have been tracking her for some time now. And when I heard she'd crossed into Awnell, I immediately set out to offer my services. We must apprehend her before she wreaks havoc on these lands too."

An intense anger bubbled inside Catanya. She couldn't believe it. He was blaming her for what happened to Finnua. He was blaming her for all those deaths and portraying himself as the benevolent saviour.

"That is most gracious of you," replied Ayr.

Catanya heard footsteps coming down the gallery. Flooded with panic, she realized the pillar wouldn't conceal her from anyone coming from that direction. She cast around for an escape, but there was nowhere to go. She stood rooted to the spot, waiting to be discovered.

"Oh, there you are, Caty—"

Catanya reacted instinctively. She grabbed Drayk, covering his mouth with her hand, and pulled him into the shadows.

"Shh," she hissed, and then she gestured towards the door.

"So, has anyone suspicious crossed your borders of late?" asked Cadyan.

Drayk's eyes popped as he recognized Cadyan's voice. He brushed Catanya's hand off his face and looked at her enquiringly. But she just shook her head.

"We have many travellers passing through the city. Can you be more specific? Describe her to me." Catanya sensed amusement in Ayr's voice now.

"She is tall," came a new voice—a gruffer man's voice. "A few inches taller than you, I'd say. Long dark hair, sharp features."

"And grey eyes," finished Cadyan, sounding irked.

"Fascinating," mused Ayr. "That description... it sounds awfully similar to your father, and you—or at least, your old appearance. However, I must say... I believe I prefer this new hair colour. Or is it colours? It's so hard to tell."

"Yes, well," said Cadyan irritably. "Be that as it may, I assure you this woman has nothing to do with me. She is a fugitive and she must be apprehended. Now tell me, have you seen her?"

There was a long pause, and Catanya held her breath, waiting, her heart thumping in her throat. Drayk's hand tightened on her arm.

"I have not," responded Ayr at last. "I have no knowledge of a woman matching that description in Awnell."

Catanya stared at Drayk, shocked.

"Mmm. Is that so?" said Cadyan. Catanya could tell he didn't believe her. "And what about the man in this sketch?"

A rustle of turning pages sounded inside the room. Catanya wondered what Cadyan was showing Ayr. Then she suddenly remembered her sketchbook. She had lost it the night she, Drayk, and Jémys escaped the outlaws together. Had Drayk's crew found it and given it to Cadyan?

Her stomach twisted at the idea. That book was full of pictures she'd drawn. Pictures of Jémys and Olly and their happy times in Finnua. Pictures of Diyah, and even Drayk. Was that the picture Cadyan was showing Ayr now?

"I've never seen him," replied Ayr smoothly.

"And you wouldn't lie to me," said Cadyan. It wasn't exactly a question, but the threat was clear.

"We may not see eye to eye on everything, Cadyan, but I have no desire to interfere with your reign," said Ayr with an edge. "Live and let live. That is how your father and I operated."

"My father is dead," said Cadyan bluntly. "And I never much cared for his lazy tactics. I told you when I took the throne, I have much grander ambitions than he ever did."

"Regardless, I can assure you Awnell wants no part in those plans."

Cadyan gave a light laugh. "Come, Ayr. Let's not be enemies. Think of everything we could accomplish if we combined our resources."

Catanya suppressed a shiver as she remembered the similar offer he'd made her on the beach.

Imagine if we worked together. There's never been two of us before... Imagine if we combined our powers. We could be unstoppable.

Catanya shook her head and wrenched her focus back to the present.

"Your father said something very similar to my father once," replied Ayr coolly. "I believe you are the result of those... *combined resources*. Would you call that a successful venture, or have there been any... I don't know... complications?"

Catanya and Drayk exchanged looks. Was Ayr toying with Cadyan now?

When Cadyan spoke again, his tone was discordantly bright and carefree. "Very well. I see old grievances require more than a few months to mend. But come, let us grasp arms in Awnell fashion. As a mark of respect for you and your people."

Ayr seemed to hesitate before responding. "As you wish."

"There we have it," said Cadyan, sounding glib and child-like. "And I have your word you'll search Awnell for this woman? You'll bring her to me?"

Ayr didn't reply immediately, and when she did, her voice sounded unusually strained. "I will search Awnell for your fugitive. If I find her, I will march her into Caerlon myself. You have my word."

"Very well," said Cadyan. "Then I shall take my leave." There was a sound of shuffling feet and a rustling of cloaks. "A pleasure as always, Queen Ayr."

Catanya and Drayk stood still, listening to the footsteps fade towards the exit until, finally, they were gone. Catanya let out a sigh of relief. Just as they were preparing to leave their hiding spot, the door swung open to reveal Ayr staring at them.

Catanya and Drayk froze in place.

"You can come in now," Ayr said. "He's gone." She led them back into the throne room and closed the door behind her. "So" —she rounded on Catanya—"it's true."

"S-sorry, what's true?" asked Catanya, trying to sound innocent.

"You're her," said Ayr, surveying her with a sharp eye, like an appraiser authenticating a piece of art.

Catanya felt a twinge of irritation. She was tired of hearing that.

"You are Cadyan's sister. I suspected it the moment I met you, but of course, here's the proof." She gestured towards the opposite end of the room where Cadyan had just exited.

"What are you going to do?" asked Drayk uneasily.

The three of them stared at each other, not daring to breathe. Ayr gave Drayk a hard look. The corners of her mouth twitched and her face broke into a wide grin. "I should have known you'd be the one to find her." She clapped him on the back and chuckled to herself.

"I don't understand," said Catanya.

"I've been looking for you for quite some time," said Ayr, her face alight with excitement. "Ever since I first heard the rumours. I didn't completely believe it at first, but then reports started reaching me about the firkon searching the kingdom for someone—a young woman. I knew then it was true. And now Cadyan." She let out a long whistle and laughed. "You've got them all running scared!"

"I—" Catanya tried to interject, but Ayr was too agitated.

"Finally!" she cried, pacing back and forth in front of them. "Finally, we have a real chance."

"What do you mean?" Catanya looked from Ayr to Drayk, who was wearing an expression of amused comprehension.

"I told you," he said as he leaned against the wall behind the throne.

Ayr frowned at him. "Don't you see?" She turned to stare at Catanya, her eyes gleaming. "Now we can take the fight to Caerlon! March through the city. We can defeat him."

"You want me to fight for you?" said Catanya, a lump forming in her throat.

"No, I want you to fight *with* me," said Ayr passionately. "Fight at my side. Together we can bring Caerlon to its knees."

The two women stared at each other. Fear and self-doubt consumed Catanya, but Ayr's face was all determined ferocity.

"Your powers," she said, "tell me about them."

Catanya took a step back, her heart racing. "What? Who says I have—"

"There's no point lying to me. You're not very good at it. I can see the truth written on your face. So... What can you do with your powers?"

Catanya sighed and rubbed her forehead. "I don't know. I've been trying not to use them."

"What?" Ayr looked appalled. "Why?"

Catanya dropped her hand and stared at Ayr. "*Why?*" she asked tensely. Did Ayr think it was that easy?

Why not use the gift you've been given? Cadyan's voice rang in Catanya's ears, taunting her.

But she couldn't be like him. She *wouldn't*...

"Just consider the possibilities!" said Ayr. "Think about everything you could do with powers like Cadyan's!" She was pacing again, and she seemed oblivious to Catanya's mood.

"Well, that's the problem," snapped Catanya. Her irritation had evolved into anger. "Think about what Cadyan has done! Think about all the people he has hurt."

"Yes, but that's why we need to fight!" said Ayr, taking an urgent step closer.

Catanya shook her head. "These powers are dangerous! And I don't even know how to control them."

"You'll never learn to control them if you don't try," said Drayk from the wall. He gave Catanya an apologetic look. "I'm sorry, Catya, but it's true. You have to learn to control them. You got lucky on that beach, but Cadyan won't let his guard down again."

Catanya wanted to retort but her anger dissipated in response to Drayk's calm reproof. "I know," she admitted in a quiet voice. "But it's so unpredictable. I don't know what triggers it." She looked down at her hands again.

"It happens whenever you lose control of your emotions," said Drayk, walking to stand next to her. "Whenever you're angry or scared."

Catanya looked up at him, surprised.

"It's especially strong when you're trying to protect someone you love," he added, scratching his chin.

Ayr looked at Drayk with interest. "How do you know this?" she asked.

"I've seen it," he said, shrugging.

Catanya thought back to all the times she'd used her magic. Drayk was right. It had almost always happened when her emotions were heightened: when she was escaping Faltir, or saving Jémys in the woods, or Olly in the barn.

And when she had watched Olly die...

As she remembered that night—all the pain and suffering —her hands began to prickle. A stinging sensation spread from her fingertips towards her palms, as though itching to unleash their power.

She closed her eyes and took a deep breath, trying to wrestle her emotions back into balance. Her hands burned and her heart raced even faster. After a few forced breaths, her body relaxed slightly. She opened her eyes again and said, "All right. Suppose I wanted to learn how to control them. How do you suggest we do it?" She looked from Ayr to Drayk, wringing her hands and trying to rub away the burning sensation.

Drayk looked sidelong at Catanya. "Well, I know where I'd start. But without Jémys..." He trailed off, shaking his head.

"Jémys?" Ayr looked at Drayk curiously.

Catanya vaguely heard Drayk explaining who Jémys was, but she wasn't listening. She was lost in her memory of that night in the woods, the night when Drayk had tortured Jémys, forcing her to use her powers. Even then, Drayk had known how to incite her magic, and he was willing to do anything to achieve it. She could still hear Jémys screaming in pain. She could remember the vindictive triumph on Drayk's face.

Catanya's palms burned anew, and she had the sudden urge to hit Drayk, to strike him down and cause him pain.

"What?" asked Drayk, frowning at Catanya.

Catanya had been glaring at him, rage bubbling inside her again.

"So that's how you knew who she was?" asked Ayr, ignoring the look on Catanya's face. "And as soon as you started hurting him?"

"She stopped me, yes," said Drayk, looking reluctantly away from Catanya.

"Astonishing," whispered Ayr.

"Excuse me?" spat Catanya.

Ayr stared at her for a moment, confused. "Oh, no," she said, backtracking as she realized the problem. "I mean to say, it's astonishing that your powers seem to be triggered by your desire to save the ones you care about."

"Well then, we have a problem," said Catanya, glaring at Drayk. "Like you said, Jémys isn't here. Everyone I love is gone. There's no one left I care about."

Drayk gave her a sardonic grin and turned away.

"Hmm…" Ayr was watching Drayk closely. Catanya thought she saw something gleaming in the back of her eyes. "We should bring Lia and Rey in on this," said Ayr.

"What? Why?" Drayk sounded vexed.

"Who is Rey?" asked Catanya. She didn't like the idea of letting more people know her identity.

"He's Lia's first lieutenant," said Drayk with a slight grimace.

"They will work with you. Train you," said Ayr. "They are the best warriors in Awnell. I'll have them meet you and Drayk tomorrow morning in the armoury."

"Wait," interjected Catanya. "I don't think this is a good idea. I'm not a fighter. Jémys tried to teach me, but I wasn't very good at it. I don't think I have it in me." She looked to Drayk for support.

Drayk tilted his head to the side, wearing a slight frown. "That's not true. I've seen you fight."

Catanya gaped at him. She had expected him to agree

with her.

"It doesn't matter," said Ayr. "Every person in this kingdom is trained to fight. If you wish to stay here, you must also learn. There are no exceptions. And especially not in your case. To live in Awnell is to be a warrior."

Catanya let out a faint huff. "What if I don't want to stay?" she asked, chafing against the command.

Drayk groaned. "Catya," he said reproachfully. "Where else is there to go? Ayr is offering you her protection and a safe place to learn. What more do you want?"

Catanya bit her lip. She couldn't help remembering what happened the last time she'd allowed herself to stay in one place. Catanya felt cornered. She didn't want to learn how to use her magic, but she was running out of excuses not to. Bit by bit, she was losing her argument with herself and with Drayk. She knew she needed to learn, but why couldn't anyone understand how much that scared her?

"Okay, fine," she said. "I'll stay for now and work with Lia and this Rey person. If you think they can teach me, I will give it a try." She didn't relish the idea of revealing her magic to more people, but it seemed like it was her only option. "But I don't want anyone else involved. No one else can know who I am. It's too dangerous."

Ayr gave her an appraising look. "I agree," she said. "Only Lia and Rey."

Catanya and Ayr stood surveying each other until Ayr broke the silence. "You can trust me, Catya. I want to help you."

Catanya nodded, but she didn't feel any more relaxed.

"Very well." Ayr clapped her hands together. "I suggest you get some rest while you can. You're going to need it."

Catanya's mouth went suddenly dry at the thought of what the morning would bring. As she turned to leave, Drayk made a move to join her, but Ayr blocked his path.

"Oh, Drayk," she said, "stay a moment, would you?"

Catanya glanced at him, but he just shrugged and stayed back to talk to Ayr.

When she reached the hallway, Catanya hesitated. But then curiosity got the better of her, and she stepped behind the pillar to listen.

"Drayk, I'm surprised at your willingness to support my plan. Usually you're itching to leave the city as soon as you've returned."

"What can I say? Years of trekking through Caerlon have finally taken a toll. I'm ready for a little rest and relaxation."

"No..." Ayr's voice was low and calculating. "There's something you're not telling me. You railed against your training with Lia for years, despising every minute of it. You'd never agree with me about Catya unless you had a reason to want to stay here. What is it?"

"Maybe I'm here for you," said Drayk, his voice full of mischief.

"Hmm... Or perhaps you're doing it for her?"

Drayk scoffed and said nothing.

"No, of course it's not that simple..." said Ayr, sounding equal parts amused and irritated. "I know you like keeping secrets from me. Normally, I rather enjoy our little games, but my patience won't last forever. Consider that your last warning..."

"I haven't got the faintest idea what you mean."

"Mmm... We'll see about that. Now," she switched to an abrupt, matter-of-fact tone, "if you wish to be a part of Catya's training, I want your honest opinion. Do you think she has it in her to bring down Cadyan?"

Catanya expected Drayk to continue being flippant, but his response took her by surprise.

"I have no doubt," he said without hesitation. He paused for a moment and then continued with a sudden fervour, "Can't you see it? Can't you sense it in her?"

It stunned Catanya to hear such admiration in his voice.

"Just wait," he continued. "You'll see it. She has this strength within her. I don't think even she understands it yet. But I can see it. I know."

"I'm amazed at you, Drayk," said Ayr in a quiet voice. "It's not like you to get so... *attached*. You care for her, don't you?"

Drayk laughed out loud. "Oh, come on. Do you know who you're talking to?" he said with a stab at his usual cheek.

"You do," insisted Ayr with a hint of amusement. "You really care for this woman."

"What does it matter if I do or don't? It's not about me, is it?" asked Drayk, sounding frustrated.

There was a long pause.

Catanya was beginning to think the conversation had ended, but then Ayr's low voice drifted out the door. "Well, not to worry. I have the perfect plan to solve both of our problems."

The smile in her voice made Catanya uneasy.

As she walked back to her chambers that evening, Catanya was thinking over everything she'd just overheard. She couldn't understand Drayk. She wanted to hate him—she knew she should hate him. But then there was this kindness in him, a kindness he rarely showed anyone. And she had to admit that his words had affected her. The amount of faith he had in her was overwhelming.

But Catanya knew there was something Drayk wasn't telling her. He was lying to her, and to Ayr. He seemed to enjoy keeping secrets and fostering doubt.

Trust is overrated, she'd heard him say once, and she'd naïvely thought he was joking.

But now that Catanya had lost everyone she'd ever loved, everyone she'd ever trusted, she supposed Drayk was right. She needed to make do with what she had, and Drayk was the closest thing to a friend she had left.

5

———

A MATTER OF MOTIVATION

Catanya had been awake for hours. In fact, she wasn't sure she'd ever fallen asleep. She spent the night tossing and turning and dreading what the morning would bring.

In ten minutes, she needed to meet Lia and Rey in the armoury to begin her training, and she was nervous. Everything had happened too quickly. Suddenly all these people knew about her, and they expected her to learn how to control her powers and use them to fight Cadyan.

Catanya paced anxiously up and down the room. What if she couldn't control her powers? What if she let everyone down? And worse yet, what if someone got hurt?

There was a sharp knock on the door.

"Come in," she called, and Drayk entered.

"Ready?" he asked, surveying her attire. Catanya had donned the leather breeches and vest from her wardrobe. The bone inlay and concealed metal plates made the vest surprisingly heavy. She understood these clothes were part of the Awnadh combat uniform, but she felt uncomfortable, like a child playing dress-up.

"Not really." Catanya tugged on the vest and gave a nervous laugh. "But it seems I have no choice."

Drayk was unusually quiet as they walked down to the armoury together. Catanya recalled the conversation she'd overheard the previous day and wondered if he was self-conscious. Ayr thought Drayk had feelings for Catanya... but if that were true, why hadn't he acted on them? Catanya had never known Drayk to let fear inhibit him. On the contrary, fear seemed to bring him to life. He thrived on it. He also wasn't the type of man to deny what he wanted or pretend. His desires were clear. It was obvious he felt a physical attraction to Catanya, but there was nothing special about that. Drayk seemed to have a physical attraction to most people.

No. Whatever was going on between them—whatever he wanted from her, it wasn't that straightforward.

They descended several flights of stairs until they arrived at a wide atrium at the back of the fortress. Columns the size of oak trees separated a series of archways that opened onto small, sheltered courtyards. Groups of Awnadh were visible outside, already warming up for their day's training. One group was practicing sparring in pairs, while another group performed a series of slow, focused movements in synchronization like some kind of meditation.

Catanya and Drayk continued towards the narrow door at the far side of the atrium. It opened into the armoury—a long room, lined from floor to ceiling with weapons. Swords, maces, poleaxes, bows and arrows, spears, quarterstaves... Catanya had never seen so many weapons before.

Lia and Ayr were standing in the middle of the room with a man Catanya knew must be Rey. He was tall and broad with a heavy brow, close-set eyes, and neatly shorn hair. It was difficult to tell his age, but Catanya thought he might be about ten years older than her.

"Ah, perfect, you're here." Ayr clapped her hands together.

She seemed delighted, unlike Lia and Rey. They exchanged apprehensive looks as Catanya and Drayk approached.

"Rey," said Drayk warily, inclining his head. "It's been a while."

Rey gave a stiff nod and extended his hand in reluctant greeting.

Catanya was curious. She'd never seen Drayk look so awkward before. There was evident tension between him and Rey, but neither of them seemed keen to address it now. She made a mental note to ask Drayk about it later.

"So, you are Fehla's daughter," said Lia, examining Catanya, her lip curled in disapproval. "I should have seen it earlier. You look just like your brother... and your father."

Catanya was slightly insulted. "You knew Casréyan?" she asked, trying to keep the tetchiness out of her voice.

Lia rolled her eyes and turned away. "Everyone knew Casréyan," she said. "But only Fehla was stupid enough to marry him."

Catanya looked at Ayr for an explanation.

"Didn't you know Fehla was raised here with us in Awnell?" asked Ayr. "She and Lia were my father's wards. We grew up together."

Catanya wracked her brain, trying to remember the stories she'd heard about the royal family. Somewhere in her memory, she recalled the stories about Fehla and her sister. "So, you're Falia, then?" she asked. "You're my aunt?"

Lia twitched at the word. "Hardly," she said with a sneer. "I have nothing to do with Fehla or her family anymore. Your mother turned her back on us, and I haven't spoken to her since. She chose that man over Ayr. She chose Caerlon over Awnell." Lia turned slowly to stare at Catanya, her face set with contempt. "How do we know you won't do the same?"

Catanya was stunned. She raised her eyebrows at Ayr,

seeking an explanation, but Ayr just rubbed her forehead and sighed.

"Come now, Lia, it's been nearly twenty-five years. I've moved past it. Why can't you? In Awnell, we do not punish the child for the offenses of the parent."

Lia exhaled stiffly.

"Look," snapped Ayr, suddenly losing her cool. "It doesn't matter how you feel. I just need you to train her. Catya is one of us now."

Lia showed no reaction to her queen's harsh tone. "Well, we'll just have to see about that, won't we?"

She glared at Catanya in silence until Rey cleared his throat. "Shall we begin, then?" he asked.

"Yes," said Ayr before Lia could speak again. She motioned for Rey to approach.

"Very well," he said. "Now, every warrior must be able to defend themselves, with or without magic."

"Meaning?"

"Meaning... grab a sword," said Lia, gesturing to the rack behind her.

Catanya took a deep breath and approached the rack. There were half a dozen swords with different shapes and designs. There were curved blades and straight blades, single-sided ones and double-sided ones. Some were longer than others, and some were broader at the point. She had no idea which one to choose.

"Here," said Rey, pulling one down. It had a long, thin blade, and a complex hilt with rings and plates to protect the hand. "Start with the basic rapier." He flipped it in the air and grabbed the blade with ease, holding the hilt out for her.

Catanya swallowed hard and curled her fingers around the leather-wrapped handle.

"Wouldn't it be better to start with a wooden blade?" she asked under her breath. She remembered the way Jémys had worked with Olly in the orchard, using sticks. His method seemed much safer.

Rey smiled at her and shook his head. "Real battles are fought with sharpened steel. Training without the threat of injury limits us. We fight harder when we fear the consequences of failure. Now, come with me."

He beckoned for her to follow him through a door at the back of the armoury, into one of the enclosed courtyards. It was still early, the sun had not yet risen above the mountain, so the area was cold and bleak. An icy layer of dew blanketed the walls and floor.

Rey led Catanya into the centre of the square where the hard stone floor was coated in a compact layer of frostbitten sand. He began doling out instructions about how to hold the blade and how to stand.

Ayr and Drayk sat on a nearby bench to watch. Lia stood stiff with her arms crossed, presiding over the affair with impatience.

"Good," said Rey, watching Catanya practice her lunges. "But keep your blade higher and step with your front foot first. Good, that's better. Now let's practice defensive manoeuvres."

They spent the entire morning drilling positions and postures. As the sun crested the sky, Catanya was already exhausted. Her muscles were shaking and her hands were clammy. Sweat drenched her hair and poured down her back. She longed to take a break, but she suspected that wasn't an option.

"That's enough," said Lia after another hour of drills.

For a brief moment Catanya felt relief, until Lia beckoned for Rey to step aside. "That's enough theory," she said, pulling her own sword out of its scabbard and pointing it towards Catanya. "Now, defend yourself."

Catanya had no time to prepare before Lia lunged. A sharp pain grazed her arm and she stumbled, losing her footing. She grasped the wound and felt hot blood leak through her fingers.

"Pitiful," said Lia with venom. She motioned for Catanya to stand up. "Try again."

Catanya ground her teeth, biting back her retort as she returned to her defensive position.

This time she was ready. When Lia lunged, she managed to block the attack, but her triumph was short-lived. Lia twisted her blade. The sharp steel sliced Catanya's knuckles and she cried out, dropping her weapon.

"How do you expect to fight the firkon, when you can't even keep your sword in your hand!" shouted Lia. "Again!"

Catanya recovered her blade and took up her position.

This time, Lia didn't even lunge. She merely used her blade to swat the sword out of Catanya's grasp. The force of the hit reverberated painfully along Catanya's arm. She cringed, shaking out her hand.

"I've trained children with better hand-eye coordination! Retrieve your weapon."

"Lia, maybe we should—" Drayk tried to interject, but Lia cut him off.

"No. The girl is undisciplined and weak. She needs to learn. Again!" she called to Catanya.

Time and time again, Lia lunged, beating Catanya back, breaking her down. She was merciless, thrashing and slicing until Catanya's body was raw. Patterns of wounds cut through her clothes. Blood trickled down her face and her hands, blurring her vision and slicking her palms.

"Enough!" said Ayr, finally stepping in. "That's enough for today."

Catanya was doubled over, panting and dripping bloody sweat onto the cobblestones as she struggled to reclaim her weapon once again.

"Fine," said Lia, sheathing her sword.

Drayk came forward to help Catanya. "It'll get easier," he whispered. "Lia's just showing off. She's always hard on new trainees."

Catanya appreciated his effort to reassure her, but she knew better. There was more to it than that. She saw it in Lia's eyes, felt it in her attacks. It was hatred. Pure hatred.

Lia saw nothing but Cadyan's sister. Casréyan's daughter.

To her, Catanya was the enemy.

They spent the next few days in the arena, running through different sword-fighting techniques, forms, and stances. It was a far cry from the friendly stick fights with Jémys and Olly beneath the trees. This was brutal. After two days, Catanya was just as bruised and battered as every warrior in Awnell. Her joints ached, and her muscles had seized with exhaustion.

Soon after swords came the bow and arrow, and then the staff. There was no end in sight. The days stretched into weeks, and the longer Catanya spent with Lia, the more she grew to despise her. Catanya did her best to be polite, but it was difficult. In all her life, she'd never met anyone so callous or so impatient. She had imagined Lia as some sort of motherly figure who'd rescued Drayk as a child, but nothing could be farther from the truth. Although Lia seemed to care for Drayk, she did so with the same harsh exigency she showed everyone else.

Rey was a much more patient teacher. He had the same high expectations, but he managed to be demanding without showing irritation or frustration. He could explain concepts in a way that was easier for Catanya to understand. She wouldn't say she liked Rey, but she definitely preferred him to Lia.

Ayr was too busy to attend all the training sessions, but Drayk had been with Catanya throughout every one, often stepping in as her opponent or helping demonstrate manoeuvres. He seemed to be enjoying himself, and Catanya noted how adept he was at fighting. From what she could tell, he was equally as capable as Rey, if a little less disciplined. She hadn't given it much thought before, but she supposed he must have trained in Awnell with Lia as a boy. Only now did she realize how lucky she'd been to escape him in the woods all those months ago. If not for her magic, she never could have bested him that night. Even Jémys wouldn't have had a chance.

"So how does it work?" she asked one afternoon when they were taking a break.

"How does what work?" said Drayk absentmindedly.

"The hierarchy here. Lia's the commander, she runs the army. And Rey is her first lieutenant. What does that mean?"

"Rey is Lia's second in command. He stands in for her as necessary, overseeing the other lieutenants and their units and coordinating training. Most trainees work their way up to Lia, training with second and third lieutenants before progressing. But you're special." He winked at her.

"Lucky me," said Catanya sardonically. "But what about the Verratrí? Is that a rank like lieutenant?"

Drayk chuckled as he took a swig from his canteen. "No, Verratrí aren't officially part of the army here. Or at least, not on paper."

"What do you mean?"

"Well..." He took another drink before continuing. "Verratrí are an ancient order of emissaries, devoted to knowledge and freedom. The order was founded in the early years after the Quiescence Wars to try to learn Caerlon's secrets. Most of them were caught—tortured and killed. So, over the centuries, the order died out. But Ayr reinstated them about ten years ago. Now, Lia and Ayr handpick the Verratrí to work in secret. Only one or two crews exist at a time, and we're typically the ones who don't conform very well. Don't like rules," he added, flashing Catanya a grin. "They choose people who are most likely to pass unnoticed in Caerlon, people who can handle living a double life—living on the run."

"That sounds... difficult," said Catanya, thinking about her own situation.

"Nah, it's great... Or at least, it was until my crew turned on me. But I suppose living a dishonest life warps you a little after a while. You need to work even harder to stay who you are."

"Do you think that's what happened? They just lost sight of who they were?"

Drayk tilted his head. "Well, after years living like outlaws, it's pretty difficult to give that up. The freedom, the independence..." He seemed to lose himself momentarily in the memory.

"Drayk?"

"Mmm..." He pulled himself back to reality. "Yes. It's hard to give it up."

"I guess now that Cadyan knows your face, you won't be able to continue as a Verratrí," said Catanya, eyeing him.

"No, I suppose not." He sighed, meeting her gaze. "Oh well, I was pretty much done with that life, anyway. I'm ready for something new."

"War?" suggested Catanya darkly.

Drayk chuckled. "Maybe."

Their conversation ended when Lia and Rey strode back into the courtyard, accompanied by Ayr.

"Ah, Catya, Drayk. How is it going?" asked Ayr.

"Fine," said Catanya with a shrug. She had certainly made improvements, but she wasn't very confident yet.

Lia cleared her throat impatiently. "The queen believes it is time for us to move on," she announced with a definite note of resentment. Clearly, the commander didn't appreciate being overruled. "She would like you to begin harnessing your magic for combat."

Catanya's breathing tightened, and she looked uncertainly from Lia to Ayr. She hated to agree with Lia, but she didn't envy the idea of trying her magic.

"First things first," said Ayr. "We need to know everything. In order to train you, Catya, we need to know everything that has happened since you got your powers."

"Why?" asked Catanya.

"Because," said Lia, her tone expressionless. "I need to know what I'm up against. I need to know how far you've got to go."

"And we need to know everything Cadyan knows," added Ayr. "So, start from the beginning."

Catanya reluctantly launched into her story. It was difficult to talk about everything that had happened, and Lia was ruthless. She wanted every single detail, no matter how painful the memory might be. When Catanya reached the part at the cottage, she found it difficult to continue, so Drayk took over for her.

"And that's when you found us at The Fairweather," he finished, giving Catanya a small sympathetic smile.

Catanya managed a half-smile in response.

Lia and Ayr started exchanging theories on how best to proceed, but Rey just watched Catanya and Drayk with a shrewd expression that made Catanya nervous.

"Ayr tells us your magic seems to be connected to your emotions," said Lia. "Whenever you experience a particularly strong emotion, your powers manifest. Is that true?"

"Well... no, not exactly."

"No?" asked Ayr, surprised.

"No. It's not as if my powers manifest every single time I get emotional. It's just that when they *have* manifested, it seems to coincide with times when I'm experiencing strong emotions... usually."

"Hmm..." said Rey, as he started pacing back and forth.

"Now, Catya, you told us the strongest you ever experienced your magic was on the night Finnua was destroyed. Is that correct?"

"Yes," said Catanya warily. "I nearly tore the entire village apart."

Rey stopped pacing and turned to face her. "Okay, I want you to try to remember how it felt that night when you unleashed your magic. Try to remember every little detail and imagine it happening again."

Catanya got slowly to her feet. "You want me to remember what it felt like to watch a village burn? To watch a little boy being murdered as he screamed for me to protect him?" she asked, raising her eyebrows.

Rey and Ayr exchanged apprehensive looks.

But Lia just clicked her tongue impatiently. "Yes," she said, her voice as condescending as ever. "We need to understand how your powers work. To do that, we must return to when they were strongest."

"Couldn't we start with something—I don't know— simpler?" asked Drayk, looking at Catanya.

"No," said Lia. "So far, the girl has been incapable of controlling the powers. She allows them to control her, instead. So, the burden falls to us. We must find a way to stimulate them for her."

In that moment, Catanya would have loved nothing more than to hit Lia. "Fine," she said. "But I'll warn you now. If this works, I can't guarantee your safety."

Lia sneered at her. "We'll take our chances," she said.

Catanya bit back her angry retort. Instead, she closed her eyes, thinking back to her last night in Finnua and trying to remember how she'd felt. She tried to picture the men on horses stampeding through the village, burning everything in their path. As much as it hurt, she tried to picture Olly running towards her and calling her name. She saw the pain on his face as he fell to the ground, the sword cutting through him. She tried to conjure the unbridled rage she'd felt, but all she found was a hollow pit. A hole inside her that only widened with each passing day, with each friend she lost.

Tears pooled beneath her eyelids, and her face burned with embarrassment. She didn't want these people to see her cry. She took a deep breath and swallowed before opening her eyes to look at them.

"I can't do it," she said. "I can't remember how it happened that night, and I can't just force myself to feel how I did then. It's not possible."

"Why not?" asked Lia.

"Because feelings don't work like that," Catanya snapped. "If you could fabricate them, they wouldn't be real."

"Hmm..." Rey was walking back and forth in front of her. "What about the other times you've used your powers? That time in the lake. What was going through your mind then?"

Catanya frowned as she tried to remember. "I think that day I was... peaceful," she said. "Yes, it was the first time I'd felt safe in days. I was exhausted beyond my limits but the water was comforting. It felt like home."

"Peaceful?" repeated Rey.

"Yes, but it was more than that." Catanya cast around, trying to find the right words to describe it. "It was the place. I remember thinking the place itself was magical. The water and the trees... I can't explain it."

"But there was nothing magical about Finnua," said Lia. "So, what's the common thread here?" She sounded irritable.

"Well, there isn't one, that's the problem," said Rey, but instead of sounding annoyed, he sounded invigorated, as if the challenge of solving such a complicated puzzle intrigued him. "We just need to find one spark. One way to trigger your magic and then we can study it from there."

"Drayk, do you have any thoughts you'd care to share? Any

valuable information you've been holding back about this or... anything else?" asked Ayr, looking at him with a hard gleam in her eye. "Now is the time to speak up. What do you think would be an effective way to incite her powers?" She tilted her head, staring at him expectantly.

"Well, I did find one way..." Drayk glanced from Ayr to Catanya, wearing an almost apologetic expression. "But it won't work this time," he said, trying to brush the idea away. "We need to find something else." He stared back at Ayr with a mulish look.

A tense, silent exchange seemed to pass between them.

Ayr narrowed her eyes. "I see..." she said, sounding disappointed.

"Why won't it work?" asked Rey. "What was it?"

"Oh, it was love," said Ayr before Drayk could respond. "Drayk, here, forced her to use her powers to protect the man she loved. Isn't that right, Drayk?"

Catanya was uncomfortable. Her personal life was being traded like secrets in a war room.

"Of course," drawled Lia, looking at Catanya with intense disapproval. "Of course, you loved the farm boy."

Anger surged through Catanya again. "What is that supposed to mean?"

"It means you have behaved predictably and foolishly," said Lia. "You wear your heart on your sleeve like so much armour. You will be an easy target for Cadyan."

Without thinking, Catanya stepped towards Lia, itching for a fight. "How dare y—"

"In this instance"—Ayr raised her voice to be heard over the building squabble—"I believe this can work to our advantage."

"How?" spat Catanya.

"Well, Catya... as Lia puts it, you wear your heart on your sleeve. So..." She made an apologetic gesture and then gave Lia a meaningful look.

"Oh, I see." Lia nodded and then rolled her eyes. "Very well. Rey?" She beckoned for him to approach. "You've been wanting to do this for a while, haven't you?"

And before Catanya knew what was happening, Rey pulled his arm back and smashed it against Drayk's face.

Drayk swore and spit blood onto the cobblestones.

"What are you doing?" Catanya cried, lurching towards Rey.

But Rey ignored her and kicked Drayk's knees, causing him to crash down hard on the ground. Before Drayk could react, Rey punched him across the face again, sending blood spraying over Catanya's clothes.

"Stop it!" Catanya tried to intervene, but Lia grabbed her arm and restrained her. "Let go of me!" She struggled against Lia's iron grip.

"No," said Lia simply.

Catanya watched, powerless, as Rey lifted a staff off the ground, snapped it over his leg and began flogging Drayk on the ground where he lay.

Drayk cried out in pain and tried to shield himself.

"What is the matter with you?" shrieked Catanya.

Lia wore a mask of cold indifference. Ayr looked mildly entertained as Rey raised his leg up, preparing to stomp on Drayk's face.

Fury and loathing eclipsed Catanya's mind, and she shouted in anger. A scalding heat coursed through her, scorching against her skin. Lia gasped and released her grasp, clutching her fingers as though they'd been burned.

Time seemed to slow as everyone stared at Catanya.

A powerful wind came from nowhere, hurling Rey away from Drayk so he crashed against the fortress wall.

Catanya welcomed the gale, letting it swirl around her. She clenched her fists and felt her fingers lace around the cold steel hilt of her weapon. Without hesitating, she lifted the sword and threw it at Rey. It flew in perfect, soaring arcs. Rey ducked, and it plunged into the wall mere inches from his head. The sound of metal scraping into stone reverberated around the entire yard. Its echoes were unnaturally loud, ricocheting off the walls and refusing to subside until the wind slowed.

Gradually, the energy drained from the courtyard until a strange quiet settled around them. Catanya's energy sapped away, and her muscles trembled with exhaustion. Not taking her eyes off Rey, she held out her hand to help Drayk onto his feet.

"Magnificent," exclaimed Ayr, her voice jarring against the unnatural quiet.

"Yes. Surprisingly impressive," said Lia with a reluctant nod.

Rage bubbled inside Catanya. "Excuse me?" she hissed, her voice shaking. She had to work very hard to stay calm. "What is *wrong* with you people?"

"It's okay, Catya," Drayk tried to reassure her, but he grimaced as he wiped blood from his face. "I'm fine."

"It is *not* okay," she snapped, her voice rising now. "I'd expect this kind of behaviour in Caerlon. But if you really want me to believe you're better than Cadyan, you'd better start acting like it!" Her voice was full of acid.

"Oh, come now, Catya," said Ayr, her smile faltering. "We needed to test it. We needed to confirm what drives your magic, and we did."

"What? *Love*?" spat Catanya in the most scathing tone she could muster.

Ayr nodded. "Or more specifically, a strong desire to protect the people you care about. This is a good thing."

"How's that?" Drayk scowled at her, struggling to stand upright. Rey made a move to help him, but Drayk shoved him away.

"Well, if you want to protect people, Catya, there's no better way to do it than by defeating Cadyan. Think of all the people who need saving. Just think about that for a second. Tell me that doesn't inspire you to fight."

"Of course it does!" shouted Catanya. "Don't you think I want to stop him? To end all this suffering?"

"Then let's do it!" said Ayr, throwing her arms out in excitement.

But Catanya shook her head. They still didn't understand. "It's not that easy! I'm not a leader or a fighter. I don't have what it takes to cut people down in front of me, to wage war on my enemies and wield unfathomable power. It's not who I am. I wasn't raised in this. I was purposely removed from it, sent to live a normal, boring life. No matter what I do, or how I train, Cadyan will always be stronger than me because *this is who he is*."

Ayr put her hand on Catanya's shoulder and squeezed. "It's not a matter of strength, Catya. It is a matter of motivation," she said, her eyes gleaming in the light of the setting sun. "I believe you will rise to the occasion. You may not have been raised for this, but trust me when I say your upbringing actually gives you an edge. Just as it did for me. You'll need to earn your leadership every day, but that's good. It means you will respect it—honour it more than anyone else would."

There was a long pause when no one spoke.

"I'm tired," said Catanya finally, shrugging off Ayr's hand. "I've had enough of this for today."

On her walk back to her chambers that afternoon, Catanya considered what Ayr had said. It wasn't a matter of strength, it was a matter of motivation.

For the first time, Catanya imagined herself as the victorious warrior. She imagined herself defeating Cadyan and taking the throne in his stead. But this image did not fill her with pride, nor did it inspire a desire to fight. Instead, it filled her with a queasy chagrin and discontent that she couldn't understand.

6

CADYAN'S PROMISE

Several weeks had passed since Diyah had met Jémys. His wounds were beginning to heal, and he was slowly recovering. Although she was pleased with his improvement, she dreaded the day when Julyán would insist he return to the dungeons.

She didn't understand how Julyán could be so unfeeling towards his brother, nor how he could have changed so dramatically from the young man she'd met years ago in the forest. It was as if his time with the fírkon had scraped away all the decency inside him, replacing it with something dark and callous.

For generations, the first-born son of every noble family had been promised to the fírkon. Diyah had never seen the damage that could do to a family. Until now.

It was difficult to imagine a time when Jémys and Julyán had resembled brothers. They seemed to loathe one another with such intensity that Diyah wondered if something deeper fuelled their animosity.

It hadn't taken Diyah long to decide she liked Jémys. He was everything his brother wasn't—kind, open, and warm. It was obvious how much he cared about Catanya, and Diyah liked him even more for it.

She liked having someone to talk to about her friend, someone who could tell her what Catanya had experienced since leaving Faltir. Diyah was happy to learn her friend hadn't been alone all these months, and, although she didn't know where Catanya was now, she had a renewed sense of hope. Hope that wherever she was, Catanya was fighting back.

The weeks passed, and the weather grew steadily colder. Jémys had healed enough that he could walk for short stretches with Diyah's help. Yet Julyán made no attempt to move him. Every day Julyán came to check on his brother, and every day Diyah expected it to be the last time. But most days, Julyán stayed only briefly before leaving without saying a word. It grated on Diyah's nerves.

"Don't you have anything better to do with your time?" she spat one afternoon when he strode through the door. She was helping Jémys move from his bed and the sudden interruption made them both jump, causing unnecessary strain on his injuries.

"How is he?" asked Julyán, unfazed by Diyah's rudeness.

"What do you care?" said Jémys through gritted teeth as he struggled against the pain. He had one arm around Diyah's shoulder and was taking slow, careful steps.

Julyán frowned slightly but remained silent.

"Was there something you needed?" asked Diyah. "Or is this a social visit?" She rolled her eyes as she guided Jémys over to a chair by the fire and helped him sit.

Then she placed her hands on her hips and turned to face Julyán obstinately. Julyán's forehead creased, and he eyed her like he was trying to figure her out. Then he left the room without another word.

Diyah turned back to Jémys. "I don't understand him," she said.

"Mmm." Jémys closed his eyes, obviously still in a great deal of pain. "What is there to understand?" he asked morosely.

Jémys seemed to shut down whenever Diyah broached the subject of his brother. He was obviously reluctant to discuss what had happened between them, and Diyah couldn't really blame him. Jémys had been through enough already. He needed time to adjust, time to heal. So Diyah didn't press the matter. As much as she wanted to learn about Julyán, her priority was helping Jémys recover.

The following days passed uneventfully. Diyah's security had relaxed somewhat since her initial posting as the physician. Guards were still stationed outside the physician's quarters, observing her—and Jémys—and she still required an escort if she wanted to venture into the city. But she was now free to move throughout the castle during the day without constant supervision.

At first, Diyah had hoped she might be able to use this newfound freedom to her advantage. She could explore the castle and learn its secrets, searching for a way out. But every inch of the castle was crawling with guards and soldiers. They feigned disinterest, but she felt their eyes tracking her through the corridors.

This annoyed her almost more than the constant escort had done. She knew the guards were watching her and reporting everything she did back to Julyán. The attempt at deception was insulting.

One afternoon, lost in thought as she made her way to visit patients, Diyah found herself in a part of the castle she'd never seen before. The wide expanse of ocean visible through the window told her she was somewhere in the northwest wing. But she didn't know where.

Cold winter air blew through cracks in the windows, making her shiver. She pulled her shawl tighter around her shoulders, and continued along the corridor to see where it led. The farther she walked, the darker and more isolated the passage became. She supposed that, at some point, the corridor had angled in towards the central castle. Steadily fewer windows lined the walls, replaced by rows of torches. And suddenly she realized there were no guards in sight.

Diyah's curiosity intensified, and she started walking faster. What could be so important that it was contained in the strongest part of the castle, but also so unimportant that the area wasn't swarming with guards?

The corridor ahead curved sharply to the right. Diyah turned the corner and found herself in a dead-end. Four heavily armed guards stood vigil outside an enormous locked door.

"Hey, what are you doing here?" shouted one guard as he grabbed Diyah to restrain her.

"Ow!" Diyah struggled against his vice-like grip. "Let me go. I'm not doing anything. I just got lost."

One of the other guards snorted. Evidentially they didn't believe her. They pinned her up against the wall and began searching her with rough hands. They emptied her pockets and tossed everything aside. Diyah heard the distinct sound of glass breaking.

"Hey!" she shouted. "Those are medicines. Do you have any idea how long it takes to brew that tonic? OW! Get off me!" They slammed her against the wall so hard that she felt it in her bones.

"That's enough," came a voice from behind. She craned her neck to see Julyán standing in the corridor, looking aggravated.

"Master Julyán," said the guard holding Diyah. "This girl is trespassing. Only the king and the chaplain are allowed down here. We have orders to protect—"

"Yes, I'm well aware of your orders," snapped Julyán. "Now, return to your posts. I'll deal with her." He held out his hand expectantly.

The guards exchanged dubious looks. The one holding Diyah hesitated before shoving her aside, so she lurched backwards, stumbling on the hem of her dress. Diyah steadied herself, then stooped to collect the items scattered across the floor. She left the glass shards of her broken vial and walked over to Julyán. He grabbed her arm and steered her away.

They walked quickly and quietly until they'd put several corridors between them and the guards. Then Julyán tossed Diyah's arm out of his grip and rounded on her.

"What do you think you're doing?" he snarled. "You gain a modicum of independence, and the first thing you do is go nosing around the strong room?"

Diyah scowled at him. "I wasn't *nosing around*," she said. "This castle is enormous. You can't expect me never to get lost. Besides, what independence do I really have if you always know exactly where I am?"

"You should be grateful that I do," he snapped. "If I hadn't arrived, you'd be back in the dungeons now, or dead. And if the king ever heard..." He broke off, shaking his head darkly.

Diyah was stunned. She couldn't imagine what was so bad about stumbling down the wrong corridor. But then it hit her.

"The elixir," she whispered, turning to look back down the hall. "That's what's behind the door?"

Julyán didn't respond, but Diyah knew she was right. A shiver ran down her spine as she thought about the potion that had bestowed powers on every King of Caerlon since Maílater Caer—the potion that had somehow affected her friend too.

"Come on," said Julyán, grabbing her arm again. "I'm taking you back to your quarters."

They walked in silence for a while until Diyah began to recognize her surroundings.

"Wait," she said, stopping in front of a familiar door. "That spilled tonic was meant for the chaplain. I need to tell him I have to make it again."

Julyán nodded grudgingly and let go of her arm.

Diyah knocked on the chaplain's door and waited for a response. Scuffles and bangs of hurried movement echoed within, and Julyán frowned almost suspiciously.

The door opened and the chaplain appeared, looking flustered.

"Ah hello, dear," he said, sounding relieved. "What can I do for you?" His smile faltered when he noticed Julyán standing behind her.

Diyah explained about the tonic and apologized for not being able to deliver it on time. As she spoke, she noticed a maidservant clearing away dishes and wiping off a table in the room.

"Oh, not to worry," said the chaplain. "I'm in no hurry. Whenever it's ready." He held the door for the maidservant who exited, carrying his lunch, which—Diyah noticed—he had barely touched.

As she and Julyán walked away, it surprised Diyah to see a slight frown set on his face. He was as taciturn as ever, and she wondered what he was thinking.

It was so hard to believe he was the same person she'd met in the forest years ago. She couldn't help remembering how full of life he had seemed back then. She remembered the way he'd smiled at her. The way he had swaggered around, brimming with confidence and cheek. It was difficult to imagine this Julyán ever behaving like that.

A sudden heaviness settled in Diyah's chest. It took her a while to recognize the weight for what it was—sorrow. She'd never dreamed of a day when she'd feel anything other than hatred for Julyán. And now that she did, it made her uneasy.

They continued walking in silence until a sudden commotion roused Diyah.

They had arrived in the entrance hall. Half a dozen fírkon were milling around, covered in mud and slush, and looking frostbitten and exhausted.

"What's going on?" Diyah wondered aloud.

Her answer came as Cadyan strode through the open doors, shaking snow off his cloak.

"Your Majesty," Julyán said, inclining his head. "You've returned."

Diyah's breath caught in her throat. She cast around, anxiously searching for a sign of Catanya, but all she saw were fírkon.

"Yes." Cadyan jerked his head stiffly. "I've returned for the Offering tomorrow."

Julyán nodded and glanced around the room. "And the maífírkon?" he asked.

Diyah followed his gaze and realized with a jolt that Slaedir wasn't there.

"He remained behind," said Cadyan. "Wars are fought by soldiers and spies, and make no mistake, we are at war. Ayr will pay dearly for ever believing she could hide things from me. Send word to Zadílar. We need our shipments early. And recall every single fírkon who isn't in the city already. Ready the army for war."

With that, Cadyan swept past them, down the corridor and out of sight.

Later that night, as Diyah sat talking with Jémys, she struggled to control her nervous energy. Jémys had told her about Catanya and Drayk's plan to escape through Awnell. At the time, she'd thought it was a good idea, but not anymore. It seemed Cadyan was determined to reignite the conflict between kingdoms. Nowhere was safe anymore—especially not Awnell.

Mórceá was on the brink of war, and Catanya was at the centre of it. Diyah had always believed her friend had the power and strength to challenge Caerlon, but this didn't feel right. It was too soon.

"What if she's not ready?" whispered Diyah for the hundredth time. "What if she still can't control her powers?"

Jémys shook his head, looking bleak. "I don't know, but she has made it this far, hasn't she?"

Diyah sighed and nodded. Jémys was right. They just had to have faith that Catanya could handle whatever came next.

Now that Cadyan had returned, the Royal Offering was set to take place the following sundown. Diyah wasn't looking forward to the subsequent surge in her workload. Every month, Cadyan made all manner of empty promises to his sick and dying subjects. Diyah tried her best to help the ones she could, but often there was nothing she could do.

Cadyan seemed to delight in getting their hopes up. He was all too quick to take credit for Diyah's work when it was successful, but equally quick to blame her when it wasn't.

Diyah found it infuriating the way he boasted about having a *devoted Heiltúir* under his employ. It made her skin crawl. She hated to think what her father would say if he could see her now.

She could still remember his serious tone when he'd taught her what it meant to be a Heiltúir. It was the earliest memory she had of her father.

A Heiltúir is first and foremost honest. We do not mete out death, nor do we fear it. Our sacred knowledge is our gift and our privilege, and we use it, not for glory or for fame, but for peace.

She tried to tell herself that as long as she was helping people, nothing else mattered. But it was difficult to watch her people's legacy become associated with such a twisted, self-serving ruler. There was no peace or honour in what Cadyan was doing.

On the morning of the Offering, Cadyan came to see Diyah in her chambers.

"Well, physician," he said as the door swung closed behind him. He wore an embellished silk tunic and a bright gold surcoat bearing the Caerlon coat of arms. His long, fur-lined cloak was draped across his shoulders and it trained along the floor behind him. "I trust you'll do everything in your power to uphold our promises today."

Diyah's body stiffened. "Of course," she said through clenched teeth. She glanced at Julyán—who had followed Cadyan into the room—and noticed that he looked especially rigid.

Cadyan strolled leisurely past her, sneering at his surroundings. Then he halted in front of Jémys, who was sitting up in his cot, as though bracing for a fight.

"Well, well, well," Cadyan drawled. "If it isn't the boy from the sketchbook, alive and in person." He reached into his pocket and pulled out a small leatherbound book, waving it through the air.

Jémys's eyes darkened, and Diyah was sure he knew what it was.

"Let's have a look, shall we?" said Cadyan, then he swung a chair around and sat facing Jémys. "Here's one of you lounging in the grass—very expertly drawn, I must say—don't you agree, Julyán?" He flipped the page before Julyán could even pretend to respond. "And here's one of you smiling. How sweet!" He taunted Jémys, clearly relishing each pained expression that crossed his face. "And another one, oh! And another one! Well, now, she seems to really enjoy drawing you, doesn't she? I wonder why?" He pulled a face of mock wonder. "But here now, this one... this one is my favourite." He stopped on a page halfway through the book, his eyes gleaming with a malicious light. "Tell me, who is this little boy with you?"

Jémys's entire body tensed. He looked like he wanted to strangle the king.

"Is that your son?" sneered Cadyan.

Diyah was startled, and she actually noticed Julyán shift uncomfortably at the question.

Cadyan grinned from ear to ear. "Is that your boy? He's very sweet looking, isn't he? What do you think?" He turned the book to face Diyah.

Diyah was standing far away, but she could still make out the image. It depicted Jémys holding a boy of about four or five over his shoulder. The pure joy on both their faces made her insides twist.

"I'd say she likes him," said Cadyan triumphantly, turning his attention back to Jémys. "You must be so *proud*." Cadyan waited, watching Jémys with an air of utmost glee.

"He's not my son," said Jémys finally, lifting his chin. His tone was hard and dignified, like he refused to show emotion. "And he's dead now. Your men killed him."

Diyah watched Jémys's forced stoicism, sorrow twisting in her chest.

"Oh, dear. What a shame," said Cadyan in false sympathy. "I suppose he would have become one of my fírkon one day. Oh, the things he might have seen and done if only he'd lived... Such a pity he'll never get that honour."

Diyah closed her eyes for a beat, and gripped the countertop so hard it hurt.

"It's not an honour," said Jémys through clenched teeth. "Being forced to join your fírkon would be a fate worse than death."

Cadyan raised his eyebrows. "Worse than death, really? That's interesting..." He scratched his chin thoughtfully, then shrugged and returned to the sketchbook. He stood up, still flipping pages absentmindedly, and strolled back to where Julyán and Diyah stood. "Oh, you're in here too, look." He suddenly slammed the book down on the worktable in front of Diyah. "But you know, I don't think she captured your likeness very well. You see, there's no sneer of sanctimonious hostility on this girl's face." Cadyan's playful tone was gone now, as he glared at Diyah across the table. "You know, *healer*, you're one of the few people in this book who isn't dead yet. I suggest you do whatever it takes to keep it that way. Do I make myself clear?"

Diyah longed to strike him, to tell him how much she hated him. But she knew that wouldn't end well for her.

"Yes, Your Majesty," she mumbled.

Cadyan narrowed his eyes before snatching the book back off the table. "Good. Now let me make something else perfectly clear." He stood in the entrance and turned to face them both. "There are any number of ways I could hurt you—punish you for your misguided allegiance to my sister. Executions are good for public displays. But they're over so fast... Physical pain is always satisfying, of course." A quick flash of gold shot across Cadyan's eyes.

Diyah and Jémys both gasped in pain.

White-hot pain stabbed through Diyah. It felt like her blood was boiling, steaming and scalding as it pumped through her veins. Eyes blurry, she grabbed the table and bit back her cries of pain. She watched Jémys double over his bed, coughing blood onto the floor.

"Ugh. On second thought..." Cadyan stared at Jémys with disgust. "It's not really satisfying to beat an already broken body."

Cadyan released his hold, and Diyah slumped onto the worktable, panting and sweating. Jémys retched again and spasmed from the pain in his broken ribs. He wiped blood off his mouth and leaned back on the cot. The colour had drained from his face.

"I suppose mental torture is always an option," mused Cadyan, twisting the ring on his hand. "I could make you do things. Make you hurt each other until you learn to enjoy it."

Diyah noticed Julyán make an odd gesture, like he was suppressing a shudder. She stared at him, but he returned to his air of practiced indifference.

"So many options for punishments, I simply don't know which one to choose," continued Cadyan, taking no notice of anything unusual. "But I promise you that before this is over, you will come to regret ever having met my sister. Your loyalty and affection for her has brought you here, and it will bring you both unimaginable pain and sorrow before the end. Your survival now depends upon how quickly and how completely you can prove your devotion to me. The longer you resist, the more elaborate your punishment will be."

Then, apparently satisfied with the reaction he'd caused, he strode out of the room.

7

———

DELIRIUM

Catanya's training had completely taken over her life. Day in and day out, Lia and Rey expected her in the courtyard. Although she had not forgiven them for their stunt with Drayk, she was soon too preoccupied and too exhausted to give her anger much thought.

Lia had relaunched Catanya's training with increased intensity. It seemed Catanya's outburst of magic had temporarily satisfied everyone's curiosity. They wanted to ensure she had a strong foundation of combat skills—a strong sense of control—before trying to integrate magic.

This suited her well, since she was still reluctant to push forward with her powers. A pit formed in her stomach any time she even thought about using them. She couldn't shake the sense there was something important—something dangerous she still didn't understand about how they worked.

So, for now, she was content to train like any other Awnadh soldier, to learn how everything worked in this kingdom.

Catanya had been in Awnell City for over a month, and it still felt surreal to her. Her entire life, she'd dreamed about visiting this city, never really believing she'd get the chance. And now she was actually living there.

Of course, spending every day trapped on the training yard and every night alone in her chambers wasn't really *seeing* the city. She desperately wanted a day to herself, a day when she could venture outside the fortress to explore.

Finally, one morning, her opportunity arrived.

Lia and Rey had been called away to manage a dispute in a far corner of the city, and Ayr was trapped in meetings with her steward, detailing arrangements for the upcoming Midwinter Carnival. Catanya was free to explore the city at her leisure.

After wolfing down some porridge and grabbing a thick, fur-lined cloak from her wardrobe, she set off in search of Drayk. Surely, he could show her the best places and sights in the city. He'd know all the hidden secrets that only the locals knew. That was the Awnell she wanted to see.

She arrived outside his chambers and knocked excitedly.

No response came.

It was quite early. He was probably still asleep.

She knocked a little louder. "Drayk," she called, pressing her ear against the door and listening for movement, but nothing happened. After waiting and knocking a few more times, she finally gave up.

I wonder what he's doing, she thought, embarrassed that she felt a little disappointed. She hadn't seen Drayk much since the incident with her magic the week before. After the beating he'd taken, she couldn't blame him for not wanting to join her training anymore. But she had to admit, she missed his company.

With a slightly dampened mood, Catanya left the fortress and emerged onto the streets of Awnell. The blast of cold, wet air on her face reinvigorated her spirits as she breathed in the smell of salt water and seaweed.

Despite the early hour, the streets were already bustling. Everywhere she looked, she saw people busy with morning routines and activities. Groups of fishermen trudged back from the port after their early morning catch; launderers hauled baskets of fresh-washed linens; labourers re-mortared the corners of crumbling buildings; and all manner of transient traffic moved around in a lively but unhurried fashion.

In a small common near the fortress, a group of young soldiers had gathered together. They were dressed in the same black leather outfits that Lia and Rey always wore, and they were practicing spear techniques under the tutelage of one of Rey's second lieutenants.

Catanya stood on the slick cobblestones, watching them for a while. From what she could tell, they were already quite advanced, despite their young age. They handled their spears with surprising dexterity and precision, flowing through different positions and stances without the slightest hesitation or interruption.

She made a mental note to ask Rey to show her the move that involved swinging the spear over the head in rapid circles. *That,* at least, looked like it might be enjoyable.

Smiling to herself, Catanya set off down the street, watching the people jostle by her. The city was waking up. Shutters withdrew from windows as the various shops opened their doors for business. A sign above a nearby display read *'new sealant for wading boots, half price'* and a group of older tradesmen had already formed a line outside the door, waiting for it to open.

"Watch out!" squealed a voice from behind. Catanya whipped around just in time to watch a group of children run past, laughing as they chased a large metal hoop, which tumbled down the steep streets into the crowd below.

Catanya chuckled and continued on her exploration.

She dodged aside as a door opened in front of her. A group

of dishevelled young people poured out, squinting in the daylight.

"I don't know what you're talking about, Syln, I'm obviously the better dancer," said one young man to his friend.

The one named Syln snorted. "Yeah, in a competition for lumbering mules." The girl on his arm snickered and giggled, and the boys continued arguing as the group disappeared around the corner, out of sight.

Around midday, a delicious smell met Catanya's nostrils. She had arrived at the same food carts she'd noticed on her first night in the city.

Catanya made her way over, eager to try everything. She didn't have a lot of money, but Ayr had given her a small stipend as a member of the army, which Catanya was eager to spend.

She stared at the cart serving skewers of grilled meat. There were several options, but she chose the one the vender told her was a local delicacy: peppered boar. The meat was tender and delicious, but it was very spicy. Her mouth burned and her eyes watered as she spluttered her thanks to the vendor.

When she finished the skewer, she moved down the line of carts, trying samples of everything, including five different local cheeses, grilled prawns, and something called ogderblu, which looked like roasted chestnuts but tasted more like salted radish. Finally, she reached the vendor she was most excited to try— the one serving the dough bowls filled with sugary confetti. Apparently, it was called shredcake.

As she finished the dessert, licking the syrup off her fingers, she commended herself for saving the best for last.

Gradually, the afternoon sun warmed the winter air, prompting her to remove her cloak and drape it over her arm. The breeze was still cold, but she'd worked up a sweat hiking the steep streets all morning.

She passed an alcove packed with rows of horse-drawn

carts, each big enough to fit one or two people. The coachmen were milling about idly, chatting and waiting for someone to rent their curricles. She briefly considered renting one so she could take a break and rest her feet, but ultimately, she decided that walking the streets was the best way to experience the city.

A short time later, she turned down a narrow laneway lined with assorted shops and displays. She peered through the grimy windows as she passed. A pastry shop, a wine emporium, a chandler, a tannery, a—

She paused and turned to look through the window more closely. Behind the glass, stretched a precarious labyrinth of furniture carved from all different woods. Unique designs and intricate engravings decorated every single piece in painstaking detail. They were truly unique.

Catanya had never seen furniture like this. Everything at the lodge had been plain and serviceable. It needed to be durable enough to withstand wear and tear from countless children over the years.

Even the furniture in her current chambers wasn't as complex as the craftsmanship displayed in this shop.

"Can I help ye, miss?" came a voice beside her.

Catanya started. A lanky man stood in the street, staring at her with wide, droopy eyes. He was carrying a steaming pot of something that smelled strongly of fish and wearing a damp, stained apron tied around his waist.

She gestured back at the shop. "They're beautiful, aren't they?" she asked.

The man grinned. "Aye, tha' they are. Come on in, then." He jerked his head, motioning for her to follow him as he shoved the shop door open with his shoulder and marched through like he owned the place. "Hey, Bir, someone to see ye," he called into the bowels of the store as he deposited his steaming pot on the counter and turned around to face Catanya.

"Name's Niq," he said, wiping his hand on his apron before

holding it out for her to grasp in the Awnadh greeting. "This is me husband's shop."

"Catya," she said, doing her best to hide her surprise. She knew the Awnadh were free to love whomever they chose, but she hadn't really thought about it in terms of marriage. Drayk's relationship with Len hadn't exactly been romantic. And Ayr seemed to be equally unrestrained in her behaviour.

Catanya smiled and watched a broad-faced man emerge from the backroom. "Niq, did you remember to bring the lacquer I asked—oh, hello." The man stopped when he saw Catanya standing there. He had a heavy brow and a long, braided beard adorned with wooden beads. The beads were intricately carved in the same style as the furniture.

"Told ye, someone to see ye," said Niq, shaking his head. "And lunch. 'Cause I know ye forget to eat when yer workin' on a commission."

"Thank you," said Bir, bending down to smell the soup. Catanya noticed him grimace slightly and wrinkle his nose. Luckily, Niq didn't see.

"Your work is exquisite," said Catanya, gesturing around the room. "I was admiring it through the window. Have you been doing this long?"

"All my life." Bir beamed, fiddling with his beard as he surveyed his shop. "Even while I was active in the army, I always used my leisure time to work on pieces."

"We're both recessed now," explained Niq, pulling three bowls out of a nearby cabinet and ladling a generous portion of fishy stew into each. "Bir was a righ' accomplished fighter too. They offered him a promotion and everythin'. But he wasn't interested. Were ye?"

Bir shook his head and clasped his hands behind his back. "Nah. Being good at something isn't the same as *wanting* to do it."

"That's right'." Niq smiled at his husband. "So, we decided

to pursue our passions instead. Bir has his woodworkin' and I'm fixin' to be a chef. Goin' to open me own pub one day."

Catanya caught Bir's eye briefly and read the dubious expression there. Once again, Niq didn't seem to notice. He pulled a spoon out of his pocket and dunked it into the nearest bowl. He blew on the spoon before tasting it, then he smacked his lips and shrugged.

"So..." Catanya cleared her throat, exchanging another awkward glance with Bir. "Recessed. Does that mean you don't have to fight?"

"Yeah. We on'y fight if we go to war," said Niq. "But tha's not likely to happen in our lifetime, now is it, Bir?"

Bir just shrugged.

But Catanya's insides twisted.

War.

Wasn't that exactly what Ayr wanted? Wasn't that what all this was about—her training with Lia and Rey? To wage war on Caerlon?

Catanya's enthusiasm for her day of whimsical exploration evaporated instantly, replaced by the harsh reality of her situation. If she succeeded in doing what Ayr wanted, Catanya would lead Awnell into war, and people like Niq and Bir would pay the price.

No longer able to look them in the eye, Catanya lowered her gaze. It was stupid of her to think she could explore the city like any normal person.

"I should go," she muttered, overcome with guilt and shame as she moved towards the door.

"Wait, don't ye want to try some soup? It's a new—"

Catanya was out the door and halfway up the street before Niq could finish his sentence. She felt miserable. Everywhere she went, she brought pain and suffering with her. No one was safe.

What was she thinking? That she could just gallivant

around the city, enjoying the sights and local cuisines like nothing was wrong?

Whatever choice she made, people were going to suffer. If she ignored her role in all this, people in Caerlon would suffer most, and if she tried to fight, it would be the Awnadh.

There was nothing she could do to protect anyone.

"Is this my choice?" she asked to the empty air. "Pick between *this* suffering or *that* pain, and never mind the damage I'll cause?" She kicked a pebble in frustration and watched it skip down the black cobblestones and ricochet off a door that was opening onto the street.

Loud voices boomed out of the building.

"No offense, mate, but I'd sooner believe you sprouted wings than believe you could stick that bet. You're not exactly—"

She received a sudden jolt, realizing she recognized that voice.

Catanya rushed forward just as the door swung shut, wafting a familiar noxious stench into the open air.

She coughed and read the sign above the door. *Delirior Ece.*

Delirior. Did that mean what she thought it meant? She craned her neck to see a series of enormous smokestacks on the roof, each spewing streams of thick grey fog into the sky above the city, away from the streets.

Catanya reached into her pocket and pulled out a handkerchief. Then she took a deep breath, held the cloth to her face, and pushed open the door.

A wave of hot, dense air hit her with suffocating force. The den was dark and crowded. A thick haze filled the space between people, clouding the windows and clinging to every surface. The smell was so strong it made Catanya's skin crawl as she pushed her way through the crowd, searching for Drayk.

Instead of tables, every few feet stood a small stove enclosed by padded benches and thick cushions. The stoves fed into pipes in the ceiling, but a series of thin hoses dangled from their bases, pouring concentrated bursts of smoke into the room.

"Amber, willow, or ruddy?" said a sultry voice at Catanya's side.

"Huh?" She turned to see a petite woman holding out a tray of different-coloured pouches. "N-no, thank you," she stammered. "I'm just looking for—"

"Knock it off, Von, we know you're lying," came Drayk's voice from a seat near the corner.

Catanya gestured to indicate she'd found what she was looking for. The petite woman smiled placidly and walked away with her tray.

As Catanya wove through the stove compartments, she noticed the wide range of occupants. They appeared to be all different ages, comprising everyone from servants and trade workers to soldiers and city officials. They mingled together with ease. Most of them sprawled across benches in stupors, wearing glazed looks, but many were giggling and socializing. She passed several groups that appeared to be in various degrees of mind-altered debauchery, oblivious to any onlookers.

The scene made Catanya incredibly uneasy.

A burst of raucous laughter greeted her as she stopped in front of the farthest compartment. Drayk lounged inside with a group of scantily clad men and women. His hair was unusually dishevelled and his tunic was unlaced, exposing his chest. His sleeves were rolled up past his elbows, and his cloak and vest lay forgotten on the seat behind him.

"Catya," he cried jubilantly as he caught sight of her. "Come meet everyone. This is Von, Pai, Mri, and Kae, no wait Kie?" He frowned at the girl on his left. "Oh, I can't remember. Anyway, sit! Sit with us." He indicated the open seat across from him and grinned lazily.

Catanya made no move to join them. "How long have you been here?" she asked, choking on the rancid air.

"Well, that depends... What day is it?" He chuckled and stretched out on the bench, resting his head on Von's lap. Von had one arm wrapped around Mri and the other was holding one of the pipes. He took a big puff and handed the pipe to Mri before resting his hand on Drayk's chest.

"Who cares what day it is?" he asked in a hoarse voice as he slowly released the smoke from his lungs.

Catanya pursed her lips underneath her handkerchief. "Drayk, are you all right? The thing with Rey and Ayr—"

"Ah, forget Rey, Drayk. He's an ass." Von laughed and patted Drayk on the cheek. "And Ayr... well... Ayr is Ayr."

The others snorted.

"It's forgotten," said Drayk. But even in the dark, Catanya could still see the faint outlines of bruises on his face and arms.

"Drayk, why are you spending your time in a place like this?" she asked. "Delirium is so dangerous."

"Nah, s'not," said Drayk, brushing away her concern. "It's only dangerous if it's made wrong, but Ece is the best blender in the city." He gestured to the petite woman who had offered Catanya the delirium pouches at the door. She was circling through the den, chatting with her patrons and refilling stoves.

"Nnea is pretty good too," said Mri as she puffed on her pipe, blowing out the smoke in perfect rings.

"Nnea only makes the one variety though," said Von. "Here, Ece gives you choices. I like this new ruddy batch." He took the pipe back from Mri, closing his eyes as he inhaled. "It doesn't have any of the burnt aftertaste, you know?"

The others intoned their agreement and Catanya just watched them, bewildered.

"Oh, come on, Catya. Relax, will you?" said Drayk, gesturing around the room. "It's not dangerous, it's not illegal, so what's the problem?"

Catanya frowned. She didn't have an answer for that. Growing up in Caerlon, she'd learned to fear delirium, believing it was wrong to use it, immoral even. She'd been taught that anyone who used it was either stupid or reckless... But maybe Drayk was right, maybe in an environment like this one delirium was perfectly fine. Nobody here appeared to be in any danger. They weren't behaving erratically or violently like the stories she'd heard growing up. In fact, everyone here seemed relaxed and happy.

"There, see, we're convincing her," said Von, holding out his pipe for Catanya to try.

Catanya took the pipe, holding it gingerly in her hand. Part of her wanted to try it, but she couldn't help wondering what Diyah would say if she could see her friend now.

"Hang on," said Drayk, pulling the pipe out of her hands. "She can't try the ruddy stuff on her first go. Way too potent. We'd have to switch to willow."

The others groaned.

"No. It's okay, don't bother," said Catanya. "I'm not interested." She was relieved to have the excuse not to try it. Even if it wasn't dangerous, she didn't think she wanted to risk it.

"You've been breathing it the whole time you've been in here, love," said the girl whose name was either Kae or Kie. "Even without using the pipes... That cloth on your face might have filtered most of it, but you'll still get some of the effects, I imagine."

"O-oh right," stammered Catanya, embarrassed that she didn't already know that. She looked at Drayk, who just shrugged and nodded. Catanya's pulse quickened. The already sweltering heat of the room increased, causing sweat to trickle down her back. "I have to go," she said, desperate to escape the lounge before she inhaled any more.

She made eye contact with Drayk, silently urging him to come with her.

Drayk sighed and nodded. "Well, friends, I believe I should be heading out now too."

"Oh, no, Drayk don't go." The group groaned and pleaded with him, apparently sincerely sorry to see him leave.

"No rest for the wicked," said the one named Pai as he lifted a pipe off the stove and pressed it to his mouth, inhaling deeply.

"Rest is for dullards and elder citizens," declared Drayk, punching his fist in the air. "One I have never been and the other I surely never shall!"

The group laughed.

"Drayk..." Catanya pressed him to hurry. Her heart pounded faster and faster in her chest. She didn't want to be exposed to the delirium any longer.

Drayk groaned and swung his legs on to the ground, righting himself. "All right, I'm coming. Von, Mri, thanks for the info. I owe you one."

Von nodded and puffed on his pipe. "Aye, let us know what you find out there."

Drayk nodded.

Catanya was too preoccupied to care what they were talking about. Drayk made a move to join her, but Mri stopped him.

"Wait," she said in a demanding voice. Drayk cocked an eyebrow and looked back at her. Mri just grinned and pointed at her lips. The others guffawed as Drayk bowed in mock submission and then leaned in for a very sloppy goodbye kiss.

When they pulled apart, Mri turned her gaze to watch Catanya, obviously enjoying her reaction as Drayk moved down the line, exchanging equally passionate kisses with Von, and Pai in turn. But when he reached Kae/Kie, she held up her hand to block him.

"It's Kiua," she said in reproof. "And you'd know that if you'd bothered to ask before leaving the other morning."

Drayk laughed. "My mistake," he said, grinning as he snatched his clothes off the bench and stumbled over to join Catanya. "Shall we?" He gestured towards the door and waved a lazy goodbye to Ece as they passed.

Drayk pulled on his coat as they made their way back onto the street. He eyed Catanya with mild exasperation. "Calm down, Catya, you're barely going to feel it at all."

"I just want to get out of here," she said. Her day had started so well, but between the delirium lounge and her conversation with Bir and Niq, she was utterly drained and miserable now.

"Suit yourself," said Drayk, nodding for her to lead the way.

Catanya had only taken a few steps when suddenly everything went black. The light of the setting sun extinguished, submerging the world in suffocating shadow.

"What's happening?" she asked, spinning around in the dark, looking for Drayk. He wasn't there anymore. The streets and buildings were gone, and all sense of direction was lost. There was nothing but dense, blinding blackness.

"Hello?" She tried to move, but her feet were stuck to the ground. She buckled and fell over, landing on her hands and knees.

Footsteps sounded nearby. Softly at first, and then louder. They were coming closer and closer, picking up speed. Catanya tried to stand up, to unstick herself from the ground, but she couldn't. There was no escape from whoever was walking towards her. Her heart thumped in her chest and her breathing constricted. The footsteps stopped mere inches away, and Catanya looked up hesitantly. A pale light surrounded the person before her, and Catanya's jaw dropped.

"Diyah?" she gasped, gazing at the smiling woman.

"There you are," said Diyah, but her voice sounded distant. "I've been looking for you for ages." She held out her hand to help Catanya to her feet, and the blackness evaporated. Warm midsummer sunlight illuminated the scene. They were standing on the beach in Faltir.

Catanya glanced at her familiar surroundings. It was just as she remembered it—the waves drenching the sand, the sound of birds, and the soft breeze in the air.

"Who's he?" asked Diyah, indicating someone behind them. Catanya turned to see a faceless man standing just inside the tree line. His features were blurry and he had no eyes, but somehow, she knew he was watching them.

"I-I don't know," she said. She'd seen people like that in her nightmares, but never one standing so still, lurking in the shadows.

Diyah snorted. "Well, that's not true," she said as if by rote, turning her gaze out towards the water. "But we can pretend it is, if that's what you want."

"What?" asked Catanya, frowning. Diyah had said those words before, hadn't she? But not like this. "Do you know who it is?" Catanya glanced back at the strange blank person behind them. She felt a tight sensation in her chest, like something was tugging her towards the unknown figure. It was unnerving.

"I know you're scared, Catanya, but you have to carry on, you have to fight. I'm sorry."

Catanya's heart sank, and she looked back at her friend—the person she loved most in this world. "No, Diyah." She shook her head, aching with guilt and regret. "I can't watch any more people die. I can't keep causing all this death and destruction." Diyah had sacrificed everything to save Catanya, but it was all for nothing. Catanya wasn't strong enough to be who Diyah believed she was. To be the person Diyah deserved.

"Everyone dies, Catanya. It is just one part of the journey."

Catanya wanted to find comfort in her friend's familiar words, but she couldn't. "What if I can't do it?" she asked.

Diyah gave her a sad smile. "You are the only one who can."

As quickly as it had started, the vision disappeared into smoke. Once again, she was standing on the streets of Awnell, the black cobblestones especially dark after the brightness of the beach.

"You all right?" asked Drayk, reaching out to stabilize her.

Catanya was queasy, and a sharp ache pounded in her head. "What happened?" she asked, spinning around and looking for a sign of Diyah.

"Just a little delirium dream," he replied with a shrug. "You were only gone for a second. I'm surprised you had one at all, actually, you usually have to inhale a lot to get one..."

"It seemed so real," whispered Catanya, glancing behind her to check that no faceless men lurked in the shadows. The street was empty, but the tight tugging sensation in her chest remained. Fainter, but still there.

Drayk nodded. "Yeah, they always do."

"It felt like..." She trailed off, remembering the strange vision she'd had of Jémys's childhood in Finnua and the one of Drayk at the sea cottage. But this new vision hadn't been like those. It had been too dreamlike. Too vague. She was convinced that her previous visions had been glimpses of the past—real events. And in those, she'd always been an observer, unable to interact.

But this strange dream-Diyah had seen her and talked to her. And the faceless man...

Catanya suppressed a shudder.

"I don't like delirium," she said firmly, deciding she never wanted to try it again.

Drayk shrugged. "I used to like the visions," he said. "I used to like the escape of it. But I don't get visions anymore." He sighed and rubbed his forehead. "Ece once told me that delirium gives you only what you ask of it. So, I guess somewhere along the line, I stopped asking to live in a dream." He paused, eyeing her pointedly. "Maybe you should too."

Catanya stared at him, lost for words.

"We should walk for a while," he said. "The fresh air will clear your head faster." He gave her a sympathetic pat on the shoulder and led the way forward.

They walked the rest of the afternoon together, returning to the fortress only after the sun had set.

8

ARMOUR

The wind bit at Diyah's face as she trudged up the frozen streets through the gently falling snow. Her muscles were heavy and her mind was exhausted. She'd spent the entire night and early morning cramped in a one-room house on the border between the commercial district and the poor quarter, tending to her patient. She was covered in blood and sweat, and her hair had matted uncomfortably against her neck. All she wanted was to regain the privacy of her quarters to sleep.

She glanced over at Julyán. He was walking beside her, looking distinctly unruffled and perfectly awake.

It irritated her.

"How wonderful it must be to care so little about other people's welfare that you can simply go about your day after the night we had," she muttered under her breath.

Julyán glanced at her. "It is not my responsibility to care about every person I meet," he said.

"Oh, how *gallant*," retorted Diyah.

Julyán rounded on her. "Tell me, does the ability to sympathize with their pain affect the outcome of their treatment?" he snapped. "Or does it merely drain you, leaving you broken when you fail?" He stared at her long and hard, waiting for a response.

But Diyah had no response. Not today. His words had cut right through her defenses.

"I see," said Julyán. He turned and continued along the road towards the castle.

Diyah followed him. She was mad at herself for opening the conversation with him at all. She should have known it would only make her mood worse.

But as they continued walking in silence, she noted how unusual it was for Julyán to respond so vehemently to one of her snide remarks. He usually excelled at ignoring her. Perhaps he was more affected than he wanted to admit...

Diyah exhaled quietly and shook her head. *Or maybe he's just tired and irritable.*

As they arrived at the front courtyard outside the castle, Julyán slowed his pace. Diyah groaned when she saw the reason why. Cadyan was standing on the steps, wearing a thick fur-lined cloak, and speaking with someone who had his back turned.

This was the last thing she needed after such a miserable evening.

"Your Majesty," said Julyán, inclining his head and coming to a halt in front of the king.

"Ah, Julyán, there you are. I was wondering where you'd gone. What could possibly have been important enough to keep you out all night?"

He didn't seem to require a response. He gestured to the man standing beside him, and with a quick jolt, Diyah realized she recognized him. His boyish face gleamed with interest as he surveyed them, and his ashy hair seemed unusually metallic under the drab sky.

"Zad arrived late last night with a shipment of armour. I had hoped you would join us for drinks, but you were nowhere to be found."

"Zadílar," said Julyán, inclining his head to the man. Diyah thought she noticed a faint smile on Julyán's normally stonelike face. "I am sorry I missed the opportunity to see you." He sounded sincere, which surprised Diyah.

"Ah, nonsense, my boy," said Zadílar jovially, waving away the comment. "Who in their right mind would spend their evening sequestered away with a boring old man when they could spend it among finer company, the finest in Caerlon, I'd say. Our lovely healer here. I commend your good judgement —" He broke off, noticing the state of Diyah's smock. "Oh, perhaps I misspoke. I fear you had a rather trying evening, my dear. Is everything all right?"

Diyah grimaced as she looked down at her bloodstained hands. "Ah, no, not really," she replied. "Mother and child both lost." She was surprised at how small her voice sounded. The stinging sensation in her eyes warned of tears approaching.

"I've never understood that," said Cadyan in a cool, conversational tone. "Why people insist on marrying and having children."

Zadílar chortled and clapped Cadyan on the back. "Well, no. I can't claim I ever relished the idea myself, but still... Loss of life before it even begins. Sad business, very sad business."

Cadyan made a sound like a snort, but he covered it with a cough.

Diyah squeezed her eyes tight in frustration, trying to hold back her sudden urge to strangle the king. She could probably do it. She felt angry enough. But of course, Julyán would kill her if she did.

For a brief moment, she found she didn't care, as long as it meant Cadyan was dead.

Startled by the darkness of her thoughts, she dragged

herself back to the present. She'd lost the thread of the conversation around her.

"Excellent tensile strength. The shipment includes our new designs, lightweight for easy travel, but durable. I think you'll find them to your liking. Oh, and Julyán, I recommend you try the new flash-plated mail. Excellent stuff, that is. So light it feels like water moving with your muscles. But it'll stop even the most sharpened steel. You can depend on that."

Armour. They were discussing armour.

"And this is the final shipment?"

"Yes, Your Majesty. Everything you ordered, plus an additional few hundred spears and some new swords for your fírkon to test. If they like the designs, I can produce more in the coming year."

"Excellent." Cadyan clapped his hands together and Diyah noticed Zadílar eyeing the ring on his hand.

"That's new," he said, pointing to it. "Not exactly a handsome ring, though, is it?" He chuckled and looked at Julyán, who showed no reaction.

Cadyan held out his hand, eyeing the ring with a mad glint in his eye. "True, it is plain, but I tell you, Zad, it's the greatest thing I've ever worn. Isn't that right, Julyán?"

He grinned knowingly, but Julyán just frowned at the king. "I have no opinion on the matter," he said.

Cadyan smirked. "Come on," he said. "You don't have to pretend. You know how valuable this ring is. So, tell us what you really think." He placed his hand on Julyán's shoulder, which Diyah privately thought was a very dangerous decision, but Julyán did nothing. She thought she noticed a fog pass through his eyes, but she blinked and it was gone.

Julyán cleared his throat. "I have no opinion on the matter," he said again with surprising force.

A strange flash of light forced Diyah to blink, and Cadyan

yanked his hand away from Julyán as though he'd been burned. He looked suddenly angry as he glared at the firkon. Julyán shook his head and frowned.

"Come, come," said Zadílar, intervening before either man could say or do anything else. "If you like it, Your Majesty, that should be sufficient testament to its value. Isn't that right, Julyán, my boy?"

Julyán stared at Zadílar, his eyes slightly glazed. "Yes, of course," he replied, rapidly regaining his cool.

"Our king need not concern himself with our opinions. An old man and a soldier. Who are we to talk?"

Cadyan smirked and nodded his agreement, but Diyah thought he looked deeply unsettled. She couldn't fathom what was so important about a stupid ring, but Cadyan was vain. Maybe he desperately needed to be showered with praise every thirty seconds or he'd break down in tears.

Diyah shook her head. She was too tired to deal with this nonsense. She just wanted to sleep.

"Now, gentlemen," said Zadílar. "I believe I must be on my way, and our young healer looks quite ready to faint from exhaustion. Why don't I take her off your hands? I'll escort her to her quarters so you two can be free to inspect the new weapons and test them at your leisure." He rocked back and forth on his heels, with his hands clasped behind his back, looking perfectly serene.

"Excellent idea. Come on, Julyán." Cadyan grabbed the tall firkon by the arm and steered him towards the door, leaving Diyah and Zadílar alone on the steps.

Zadílar waited until they were out of earshot before speaking. "My dear?" he said, holding out his arm for her.

"Thank you," she mumbled, reaching out and interlocking arms with him.

They made their way through the castle halls in silence.

Any other day, Diyah would have seized the opportunity to ask Zadílar questions, but her brain was so groggy today, she couldn't remember any of her questions.

"I am sorry for the losses you witnessed last night, Diyah. I know a Heiltúir is supposed to respect the flow of life and understand death's inevitability, but I expect it does nothing to alleviate the sting of loss in the moment, does it?"

"No," replied Diyah in a small voice, "it doesn't."

"Have you been keeping well otherwise?" he asked, with a stab at casual conversation. "I hear you've had an addition to your chambers."

Diyah looked at him, perplexed. "Oh, you mean Jémys?" she asked, suddenly realizing what he meant. *What a strangely provocative way to phrase the question.* "Yes, I've been tending to him in the physician's chambers. He sleeps in the workroom," she added, in case Zadílar had other ideas.

"Jémys. Is that his name? I only know there is a young man healing in your quarters. A dangerous criminal, if the rumours are to be believed. *Treason.*" He pronounced the word with mock shock and awe.

Diyah snorted. "Apparently it's practically treason to dislike the king's choice in jewellery, so I suppose the bar for criminality has lowered as of late."

Zadílar let out a boisterous laugh. It was infectious, and before she knew it, Diyah was smiling too.

"Oh, I am sorry, Diyah. One as smart and witty as you deserves to be surrounded by smart and witty people. But all you've got are these dullards."

"Well… Jémys is nice."

"Nice is not witty," said Zadílar. "And I am convinced that wit is rarely ever nice." He winked at her and she chuckled.

They lapsed into silence again, and after a while, he started humming to himself. It was an oddly spirited tune. It reminded Diyah strongly of something, but she couldn't place it.

"You gave them weapons," she said, suddenly remembering what she'd overheard earlier.

"Mmm, that is my job," replied Zadílar.

"But... weapons. Weapons they will use to kill Catanya." Diyah pulled her arm out of Zadílar's. "What do you want from me?" she asked, some clarity breaking through her fatigue.

Zadílar sighed and glanced around to make sure the corridor was empty. "My dear, all I want is to be your friend. To help you in whatever way I can."

Diyah narrowed her eyes. "Fehla says you're untrustworthy."

Zadílar sniffed haughtily. "Fehla is a fool, incapable of seeing a bigger picture. Incapable of conceiving of a reality where rules do not apply. My dear, you should not put your faith in someone like that."

"And I should put my faith in you instead?" she asked, offended to hear him disparage Fehla so openly.

"By the Natures, no," he replied with a laugh. "You should put your faith in yourself. That is the only person you can understand completely. The only person you can truly trust."

Diyah stared at him for a moment.

"My dear, what do your instincts say?" he asked patiently.

Diyah's instincts were a little fuzzy at present, but she couldn't deny that something about Lord Zadílar seemed familiar to her. She was inclined to trust him, but she didn't know why.

Zadílar seemed to understand what she was thinking. "Over the years, I have learned to be adaptable," he said. "I told you when we first met, honesty is not your friend... Well, it hasn't been my friend either for quite some time. How do you imagine I've lived this long if not by being adaptable?"

"So, you're only interested in your own survival? You're only loyal to yourself?" she asked, still confused.

Zadílar exhaled heavily. "No, no, no. My loyalties are resolute, it is my behaviour which adapts. I play the roles they need me to play in order to blind them to the truth."

"The truth?"

"That everything I do, I do for the good of my people." He spoke in a whisper so low, his lips barely moved.

Diyah frowned, trying to make sense of his logic. "That doesn't necessarily mean what you do is moral or honourable," she said.

"No, it does not," he agreed, nodding. "Regrettably, there are many times when the greater good can only be achieved through distasteful methods. So, I adapt... into someone who can use such methods."

Diyah pursed her lips. "I can't be like that," she said firmly. He could present it however he liked, but Diyah would never be able to make the 'distasteful' choice.

"You believe that *now*, but I am not convinced." He gave her an apologetic look. "I'm sorry, my dear. I do not wish to belittle your efforts, merely to put you on your guard, to prepare you."

"Prepare me for what?"

Zadílar shrugged. "Anything and everything that may come your way."

They paused, staring at each other for a moment.

"Now come," he said, extending his arm and smiling again. "You are exhausted. Let us continue to your rooms. I would very much like to meet the dangerous criminal known as Jémys."

Diyah sighed and took his arm again, allowing him to escort her through the halls and back to the physician's quarters.

Zadílar didn't stay long once they'd arrived. He exchanged pleasantries with Jémys and asked a few questions. Then he ensured Diyah had a tall drink of haymead in her hand before he bid a fairly formal farewell, promising to visit again as soon as he was able.

Diyah didn't know how she felt about that.

"What a strange man," said Jémys after Zadílar left.

"Yes, he is," she said, eyeing Jémys suspiciously. He was reclining in his cot in an awkward position, trying not to move too much as he chatted with her. She suspected he'd over-exerted himself while she was away. He remained stubbornly convinced that he should be healing at an inhuman rate, and often required several reminders to take it easy.

Jémys adjusted his blankets, then winced and tried to brush it off as some sort of twisted grin.

"You reopened a wound, didn't you?" said Diyah. She recognized the behaviour. Catanya had always done the same thing whenever she'd tried to hide an injury.

Jémys looked at her, baffled. "How did you—"

Diyah clicked her tongue and stood up, moving over to where he was sitting. "I told you Cadyan's powers aggravated your injuries. You need to take it easy," she reprimanded him for the hundredth time. Even Diyah still had some lingering pain from Cadyan's brief torture. But her body had recovered faster than Jémys's.

"I'm not good at that," he mumbled, but his tone was apologetic.

"Yeah, I've noticed." Diyah unwound the bandages on his side and began inspecting his injuries. It was one of the shallower cuts that had reopened, but it needed to be salved and re-bound.

"If you keep reopening these, you'll never heal," she said, exasperated. "I know you're impatient. You want to be out there doing something. I do too. But if you bleed out and die, you'll be no good to anybody."

Jémys looked at her with sadness in his eyes. "I'm dead either way, Diyah," he said in a quiet voice. "Once I'm healed, Cadyan is just going to—"

"Hush," said Diyah. She couldn't bear to think about that right now. "We'll find a way out of this. You and me together."

She worked slowly, insisting on double-checking everything so she didn't make any mistakes in her exhausted state. Jémys flinched as she spread the salve over the wound. It always stung a bit, but perhaps her fatigue made her clumsier than normal.

"Serves you right," she grumbled.

After a few minutes, he was freshly bandaged and lying back in his bed.

"Thank you," he said.

Diyah grunted and tossed the soiled bandages into the fire. She watched the fire engulf the linens, charring the edges as the flames bled into the centre, reducing the fabric to ash. She'd had enough blood for one day.

As she rinsed her hands in the washbasin by the fire, her mind drifted back to the family she'd spent her night trying to help. In particular, she wondered what the father was doing now.

"Jémys, can I ask you something?" She hesitated before adding, "It's about the sketch that Cadyan showed us... the one of you and the boy."

Jémys's expression darkened. "What do you want to know?"

Diyah cleared her throat, conscious of the fact that this was likely a difficult topic for Jémys. "Well, you said the boy wasn't your son, right? But you obviously cared about him like a... like a father..." She was having trouble keeping her voice steady.

"Yes," he replied, watching her closely. "What's your question?" He seemed to sense how much she was struggling to find her words.

"I guess I'm wondering what goes through a parent's head when they lose their child? Is it just grief or is it anger?"

Jémys frowned and closed his eyes. "Both," he said in an uncharacteristically weak voice. "Pain, rage, devastation, and then... just a hollow sensation. Like you've forgotten how to feel..." He sighed heavily and opened his eyes again. "And then the questions consume you. Why is this happening? What did he do to deserve this? What did I do wrong? Why couldn't I prevent it? What if I had gotten there earlier..." He trailed off, staring at the fire. The light of the flames danced on his face.

After a few minutes, Jémys cleared his throat and turned his gaze back to her. "Why do you ask?"

Diyah shook her head, blinking away the tears that had formed as she'd listened to him. "I just... I can't stop thinking about the father from last night. He lost everything... his wife and his child. One minute he had a family, and the next he had nothing." She bit her lip, trying to hold back the tears as she looked up at the ceiling, taking several steadying breaths. "I wonder if he will come to regret it... if he'll regret ever having a family. Will he wish he'd never loved them at all?"

"He will for a time... but eventually he'll emerge out the other side. He'll remember how precious it was when he had it."

It surprised Diyah to hear such reassuring and hopeful words, given everything Jémys had said just a moment before. "So... is that how you feel?" she asked.

Jémys smiled faintly. "I'm getting there."

Diyah nodded and downed the rest of her haymead in one gulp, coughing as it burned and tickled her throat.

"I never gave much thought to the idea of family." The words tumbled out of her before she even registered what she was saying. "I lost my parents when I was so young, I forgot. But today... today was the first time in a long time that I revisited it... that pain." Her voice sounded strangely distant. "A young family... That's the picture of hope, isn't it? The picture of love and joy... and then just like that"—she snapped her fingers—"it's gone. So fragile..." She looked down at the glass in her hand, turning it around in her exhausted fingers.

"Diyah?" Jémys sounded concerned.

"I'm okay," she mumbled, pouring herself another helping of haymead. She took a deep breath and plastered a smile onto her face. "I just forgot... I forgot how beautiful it could be."

136

9

———

THE MIDWINTER CARNIVAL

Awnell City was bursting with activity as preparations for the Midwinter Carnival began. The carnival was an enormous celebration in Awnell. Catanya found it difficult to resist the excitement building within the fortress.

Caerlon had long since banned the practice and celebration of the ancient religion, so events like the Midwinter Carnival were never observed in Faltir. But growing up, Catanya had heard stories about them. She knew the ancient religion had worshipped the Natures, and each celebration marked the change in energy from one Nature to another. The Midwinter Carnival celebrated the Wind and Sea in dominance over the Earth. It was a time when communities gathered to sing and dance. This celebratory dance was said to be what woke the Earth beneath their feet and gave it energy to reclaim its place among the Natures.

In Awnell, the carnival had also taken on another meaning. It had become a mode of expression for the Awnadh, an act of fellowship and defiance against Caerlon.

In addition to the two weeks of pageantry, spectacle, and festivities, the entire carnival would culminate with a grand banquet inside the fortress. Everyone within a ten-mile radius would come to dance until the sun rose the next day. Ayr had hired the best chefs, musicians, and entertainers in Awnell to make sure the event was unforgettable.

Although Catanya's training continued, Ayr insisted Lia relax their schedule so Catanya could enjoy the festival.

"Combat training can only get you so far," Ayr said. "A soldier is only as good as their motivation for fighting. It's important for you to experience the freedom and joy that's possible. You need to understand it, to *want* it. Go explore. Live."

So Catanya spent every free hour exploring the festival. The city streets were bursting with acrobats and players performing for eager audiences. Minstrels, troubadours, and artisans came from all over Mórceá to share their work.

Catanya visited each stall, admiring the wide range of artistry and craftwork. She imagined herself setting up a cart and selling her own drawings or offering to do portraits for a penny. The thought brought a smile to her face as she remembered her innocent days in Faltir, when her greatest excitement had been selling her jewellery in the village.

One afternoon, as she watched two acrobats twisting and flipping around the square, she noticed Rey coming to join her.

"Are you enjoying the carnival?" he asked.

"Yes, very much," she responded somewhat stiffly. She didn't particularly want his company.

"It's a pity they don't celebrate in Caerlon. I find these sorts of celebrations bring our people closer together. They give us something to share. Especially in times of sadness," he said, watching the other spectators with pride. "Perhaps, when you are queen, you will reinstate it in Caerlon."

He smiled down at her before heading back to the fortress.

Catanya continued her progress through the carnival exhibits, trying not to think about Rey's comment. She still didn't like the idea of being queen. She had been doing her best to put one foot in front of the other lately, focusing on her training despite grappling with the tough decisions she'd need to make soon. But now, surrounded by so much excitement and creativity, she didn't want to worry about war or her responsibilities. She wanted to pretend, at least for a little longer, that she was someone else entirely.

Later that afternoon, she found a cart selling art supplies unlike any she'd ever seen. They had inks and paints in every colour of the rainbow next to stacks of empty canvas. There were lead pencils bound in leather to keep the fingers clean, and knives specifically designed for sharpening them evenly. Catanya looked at everything longingly. She sat for hours watching one painter as he depicted the fortress of Awnell on his canvas, all the while wishing she could do the same.

The weeks of the Midwinter Carnival ended up being some of the most relaxing weeks of her life. The hopeful joy in the air was contagious, and the beauty and artistry of it spoke to her on a deep level. She felt like these artists were her true kin. This was the life she ought to have had. This freedom and passion was everything she'd ever wanted for herself, and everything she could never have.

As she stood in her chamber on the evening of the banquet trying to get ready, she replayed some of her favourite memories from the week. She remembered a young troubadour singing his song with such a clear and piercing voice, and she started singing to herself absentmindedly as she wove her hair into her usual tight braids.

Someone knocked on the door, and Catanya opened it to find Drayk looking unusually proper in his formal attire. He still wore all black, but his clothes were custom fitted, with a high collar fastened on one side of his neck that snaked across his chest towards his belt. The pattern of alternating leather and satin was striking. He was clean-shaven, but he smelled faintly of smoke.

"I'm almost ready." Catanya turned around, leaving the door open for him, and ran back to her dressing table to finish her hair.

"It's okay, there's plenty of time. And actually..." He closed the door and crossed the room to stand with her. "I have something for you."

Catanya looked up at him, puzzled. "What is it?" she asked. For a wild second she wondered if he'd somehow known how badly she wanted art supplies. She had been resisting the urge to buy them for herself, in part because they were expensive, but mostly because she felt guilty for losing the book Jémys had bought her.

"Well, it's from Ayr actually," he said. "She wanted me to give this to you." He handed her a small velvet box.

"Oh." Catanya took the box and opened it to reveal an ornate necklace. It featured a series of black and red swirled gemstones set in a heavy festoon style.

"Flamestones," said Drayk, eyeing the necklace. "They're only found in the deepest depths of the Tirnell Caves. The Awnadh wear them to inspire passion." He stifled a cough and shook his head knowingly.

"They're beautiful," said Catanya, overwhelmed by the generosity and trying not to read into the significance of it. She lifted the necklace out of the box.

As soon as her fingers touched it, a familiar dizzy sensation greeted her. Her vision blurred just like it had done that afternoon in Finnua and that morning at the sea cottage.

"Catya? Are you all right?" Drayk's voice disappeared into the haze that was enveloping her.

When her vision cleared, she was still standing in her

chamber, but Drayk was gone. Several comfortable chairs were arranged around the fire, and a large tapestry hung on the wall. The room was cozier than Catanya knew it. Not simply a guest chamber, but someone's home.

Two young women stood before her.

Ayr was instantly recognizable. Her long auburn hair was tied up elegantly and the flamestone necklace hung from her neck like it had always belonged there. She was much younger than the Ayr Catanya knew, perhaps in her early twenties.

The second woman had her back turned, but she was tall and slim with dark hair that cascaded softly over her shoulders.

"I'm so excited about tonight. Do I look okay?" she asked, turning towards Ayr. Catanya's heart leapt. She recognized this woman too.

"You are beautiful, as always, Fehla," responded Ayr, beaming at her.

Fehla blushed and looked at her feet.

An abrupt knock on the door startled them. Fehla chuckled and opened it to admit a third woman, who strode into the room with an agitated energy.

"You'll never guess who's here!" she said.

It took several seconds before Catanya recognized Lia. This younger version of her aunt had a brightness about her that her future self lacked completely. "Your parents are going mad out there, Ayr," she said.

"Why? Who's here?"

"Prince—I mean *King* Casréyan," she said scathingly.

"What? Why is he here?" asked Fehla.

Ayr and Fehla exchanged baffled looks.

"Oh, probably to remind us what we're *not* missing," said Lia with a laugh.

Fehla frowned. "Have you met him before, Ayr?"

Ayr nodded and shrugged. "A few times. I've never liked him, though. The way he talks and the way he treats everyone...

Something about him makes my skin crawl. And he always seemed a bit pompous to me." Ayr made a flouncing gesture and everyone laughed. When they had stopped, Ayr sighed morosely. "Oh, well, I guess I'd better go join my parents. I suppose I have responsibilities now, don't I? I'll see you both soon." She waved and left the room.

Fehla watched her go, eyebrows pinched in concern. "This has all been so hard on Ayr," she said. "Losing her sister and becoming her father's heir. I don't think she's ready for all the responsibility."

"Nonsense!" said Lia. "Ayr is going to be a wonderful queen one day, Fehla. Just wait. I bet she's the one who finally stands up to Caerlon."

"Maybe Casréyan won't be as bad as his father," said Fehla. It struck Catanya how innocent Fehla sounded. How naïve.

Lia sniffed. "He will be. They always are... But enough of that! Today we're celebrating. And I have a gift for you." She held out a small wooden box that was oddly familiar to Catanya. "This belonged to our mother. She gave it to me before she died, and, well, you know I'm not that fond of jewellery." She grinned at Fehla and opened the box.

Inside was a second, but much more familiar, necklace. Its iridescent colours danced and sparkled as Fehla lifted it into the light.

"Oh, Falia, really? You're giving this to me?"

"It's yours," said Lia, nodding. "I think it would make Mother happy to know you're wearing it."

Fehla rushed forward and flung her arms around her sister. "Thank you!" she cried.

"Catya?" Drayk's voice came through the fog.

Catanya teetered and opened her eyes to find him staring at her, wearing a concerned look on his face. "Are you all right? You went sort of rigid and stopped responding."

"I'm fine," she said, trying to act like nothing had happened.

"I was just lost in thought." Then—more for the distraction than because she was interested—she turned her attention towards the flamestone necklace. "Flamestones inspire passion, you say?" She repeated his words without really hearing them. Her mind was still lost in the vision she'd seen of her mother's youth—in the memory of her own shattered necklace, and the weight of the one she held in her hand now.

She sensed Drayk's eyes on her and turned to see him still watching her with concern. But then he shrugged, seeming to understand that she didn't want to talk about it. "Yes, I know. Passion isn't really your area of expertise," he said, relaxing his posture. "If you don't want to wear it, I'm sure Ayr will understand." He held out his hand as a familiar twinkle played in his eyes.

He was baiting her, and Catanya had a sudden urge to wipe the smirk off his face. Without taking her eyes off him, she slid the necklace out of the box and began fastening it around her neck.

She tilted her head and examined her reflection in the mirror. The necklace draped elegantly across her chest, and the colours matched the red embroidery on her formal outfit. Another gift from Ayr, the outfit comprised a set of patterned leather and silk breaches beneath a tight, tapered jacket with exposed boning. The jacket fell to the ground at the back but pinched in at the front where it met her belt, leaving space for weapons if she chose. Even in formal attire, the Awnadh never strayed far from battle-ready.

"So, is this supposed to be Ayr's way of apologizing?" she asked, touching the necklace and remembering how it had looked on Ayr's neck in the vision.

"Apologizing?" asked Drayk. "For what?"

Catanya dropped her hand and made eye contact with him in the mirror. "For hurting you in order to force me to use my powers!"

Drayk shrugged. "Well, it worked, didn't it?" he said with a cocky grin.

"Ugh, I forgot who I was talking to. You probably enjoyed taking a beating," she said, striding away from the mirror. Then, immediately regretting her words, she turned back towards him. "I'm sorry," she mumbled. "I didn't mean..."

Drayk brushed away the comment with a casual wave. "So, I've been meaning to ask," he said after a pause. "Why *did* it work?"

"What do you mean?"

He sauntered forward, scanning her face. "Why did it work this time?" he repeated. "I know why you protected Jémys, but why me?"

Catanya stared at him in disbelief. "Well, I assume you're not sorry I did."

"No, of course not! I'm just curious." He shrugged and tilted his head, grinning cheekily.

"Don't flatter yourself," said Catanya, irritated and embarrassed at the same time. "I would have saved anyone in that situation."

"Oh, really?" Drayk grinned even wider.

Catanya rolled her eyes and ignored him. She finished pinning her hair, and, without another word, she turned and led the way out.

As they walked down the hall in silence together, Catanya felt a prickling on the back of her neck like someone was watching her. She glanced behind her, but no one was there. It wasn't the first time she'd sensed someone following her...

Her uneasiness remained as she and Drayk turned the corner and descended the stairs. She couldn't help but remember the faceless man in her delirium vision. He had made repeated appearances in her nightmares over the last two weeks, always accompanied by a tugging sensation in her chest. She was beginning to see shadows everywhere she went.

Worried that her delirium vision had made her paranoid, she did her best to cast her discomfort aside. This was a night of celebration.

The banquet was in full swing by the time Catanya and Drayk arrived. The throne hall had been lavishly decorated with garlands, bells, and ornate lanterns. Along one side of the room, an immense table overflowed with food and countless varieties of wine, haymead, barkbeer, and sourwood rum. On the other side, a small stage had been erected where a group of musicians took turns singing and playing different instruments, including harps, tabors, pipes, and several instruments Catanya didn't recognize.

In the centre of the hall, the dancing had already begun, but it was unlike any dancing Catanya had ever seen. The dancers had a freedom and fluidity in their movements. There didn't seem to be any predetermined choreography. These people danced from their souls without inhibition or hesitation. Some danced alone, some in groups, and some danced in couples.

With a pang, Catanya remembered the last time she'd danced. It had been a different type of celebration, but that night with Jémys had been one of the best nights of her life.

She shook her head, trying to push the memory away. She couldn't afford to dwell on thoughts of what might have been. Jémys was gone. Finnua was gone. This was her life now.

She continued looking around the room and found Ayr leaning against her throne, smiling as she watched her people. When she spotted Catanya and Drayk, she came over to greet them.

"Welcome, welcome!" she exclaimed, embracing them both. "What an evening." She grinned and turned to admire the splendour.

"It's incredible," said Catanya. "Everyone seems so..." She trailed off, at a loss for words.

Ayr nodded as though she understood Catanya perfectly. "There's something liberating about a dance, isn't there?" She smiled at Catanya. "Please eat, drink, dance! Enjoy yourself." Then she grabbed Drayk and pulled him towards the dance floor. Drayk laughed and wrapped his arm around her waist as they left.

Catanya felt a slight irritation at their sudden departure. As she made her way over to the banquet table, she watched them start to dance, their bodies intertwined. Catanya helped herself to a glass of spiced wine and turned to watch the musicians. Another taborer joined the group on stage, and the steady pulse of low drums resounded off the walls and reverberated through the floor.

Catanya was scanning the room for other familiar faces when her gaze landed on a droopy-eyed man and his burly dance partner.

Niq waved energetically and dragged Bir off the dance floor to talk with her.

"I was hoping I might see you tonight," said Catanya, grabbing each of their arms in greeting. "I need to apologize for running out on you the other day. Sometimes I have these... er... headaches that come over me. I hope you weren't offended." She tried to smile at them, doing her best to ignore the sadness underneath.

"Offended? Nah, I just assumed you didn't want any of that nasty stew," said Bir, snickering and stroking his beard. He had new beads braided into it today. They were carved from reddish wood with pale flames descending from their centre. "Oh, that stew was something awful, that was." He seemed to be in a gregarious mood, and Catanya noticed the slight pinkness warming his cheeks.

"Oy!" Niq smacked him on the arm. "I'll have ye know, tha' recipe is a delicacy in some parts o' the world."

"Those would be the parts of the world where food is

scarce, no doubt?" suggested Catanya, flashing a cheeky grin towards Bir, who laughed and spilled wine down his front.

"Oh, righ'. I see how it is," said Niq in a tone of mock offense. "Well, jus' for that, I'd say ye owe me a chance to prove meself." He wagged his finger at Catanya.

"Yes, we noticed you arriving with Drayk. He's an old friend of ours. You two should come for dinner one night soon." Bir sounded sincere as he jerked his thumb towards Drayk on the dance floor.

"Oh, really? How do you know him?" Catanya shouldn't have been surprised. Drayk seemed to know everyone in this city.

"Oh, he used to work for me aunt," said Niq.

"Doing what?"

"Doing what he's best at," said Bir with a snicker. This prompted another smack on the arm from Niq. "Ow! What are you hitting me for? You know it's true."

Niq laughed and shook his head. Catanya didn't understand the joke, but she decided not to ask.

They chatted happily for a while until Niq grew distracted by the food table and ran off to inspect the most popular dishes, dragging Bir along with him.

As she watched them go, Catanya noticed Rey dancing nearby with a woman she didn't recognize. Unfortunately, Rey spotted her and whispered something in the woman's ear before they both left the dance floor to head in her direction. Catanya tried to leave before he could reach her, but a large group of drunken girls blocked her path.

"Catya," called Rey.

Catanya turned resignedly back towards him. "Hello Rey," she said with an affected smile.

"I'd like you to meet my wife, Isa." He presented the woman at his side.

Catanya was slightly surprised. She had assumed that Rey, like Ayr, Lia, and Drayk, had never married.

"Nice to meet you," she said to cover up her moment of hesitation.

Isa looked to be about five years older than Catanya. She had a plain, impassive face, much like her husband, but she had one particularly noticeable scar extending from above her right eye and along the bridge of her nose. She had muscular arms and a curvy frame, but she was at least a foot shorter than Rey.

"Catya, yes it's nice to finally meet you," said Isa, extending her hand. "My husband tells me you've been training with him and the commander."

"Well, yes." Catanya gripped her arm, noting how strong and rough it felt against her own.

"You poor thing. I definitely don't miss it." She flashed her husband an affectionate smile.

"You mean you trained with them as well?" asked Catanya, surprised.

"Oh, yes. Everyone in Awnell trains under the commander and her lieutenants. That's how we met," she added, nodding at Rey.

"Yes, I was just a third lieutenant, and she was a particularly stubborn student," teased Rey.

"Wait, *everyone*?" asked Catanya, surprised. She hadn't really registered what that meant until now. In Caerlon, only first-born sons were trained as firkon, and the levy had only recently expanded to included commoners. But women had never trained as soldiers.

"Yes. We don't advertise it outside Awnell, but Ayr believes everyone in the kingdom must learn to defend themselves," said Rey, shrugging and reaching across the table to grab some food. "When she became queen, she redefined our warrior class and resurrected certain ancient traditions."

"*Tenacious and loyal, we live for now and we fight for the future,*" recited Isa as Rey smiled. "That's our old warrior's adage, passed down from the first commander. Ayr made training mandatory for at least a year, but I stayed longer. I'm one of the second lieutenants now... And we've been married for nearly three years," she added, taking her husband's hand.

"Oh! Congratulations," said Catanya clumsily. She wasn't sure what else to say, so she sipped her wine and watched the dancers. Her eyes immediately fell on Drayk and Ayr, who had retreated from the dance floor. They appeared to be in the middle of a heated discussion. Ayr gesticulated angrily and Drayk wore an obstinate scowl.

Their change in attitude perplexed Catanya. She couldn't get a handle on their relationship. "So, what is Ayr's story?" she asked, unable to contain her curiosity.

"What do you mean?" asked Rey, following her gaze.

"Well, why has she never married? Shouldn't she be, I don't know, trying to produce an heir?"

Isa frowned and looked at her queen. "Ayr has never shown much interest in anyone."

"I don't know about that," Catanya scoffed as she eyed Ayr and Drayk.

Rey snorted into his wine and then exchanged knowing smiles with Isa. "Well, let's just say the queen enjoys numerous dalliances with different men and women. Drayk just happens to be one of her favourites," he said.

"Why?" asked Catanya.

Isa smiled at Catanya meaningfully. "Well, there's just something about him, isn't there? And... well... he's sort of the same as her, isn't he?" She looked at her husband apologetically.

Rey rolled his eyes and shook his head.

"All right, what's going on?" asked Catanya finally. There

was obviously history between Rey and Drayk, and she wanted to know the story.

Rey took a deep breath. "Drayk *is* the same as Ayr. I learned that the hard way many years ago. Being with him was exhilarating—intoxicating. It was easy to convince myself that our passion was enough, or that he would change over time. But Drayk and Ayr, they don't want to be tied down, either of them. Me, on the other hand…" He gave his wife an affectionate smile and kissed her on the forehead. "I need something to fight for."

Catanya thought she understood. And she actually found herself relating to Rey in this instance. She knew what it meant to be in love. It made her sick to realize she'd likely live the rest of her life without experiencing that joy again. "Don't they want more for themselves?" she asked, gesturing to Ayr and Drayk.

"Well… rumour has it that Ayr was in love once. A long time ago." Isa looked at Rey for confirmation and he nodded.

"Really? What happened?" asked Catanya. It was difficult to imagine Ayr being vulnerable or open enough to fall in love.

Rey shrugged. "I don't know. It was before my time. I don't think it ended well though."

They continued watching the dancers in silence, but Catanya's eyes kept drifting back towards Ayr and Drayk, who seemed to have stopped arguing. Now they were talking with their heads inclined together in an almost conspiratorial whisper. Drayk appeared to be sliding a piece of parchment into his inner coat pocket.

Catanya was curious about them. One minute they were kissing in front of everyone, and the next minute Ayr was ordering Rey to torture him. Now they were intimate again? It didn't sit well with Catanya.

She was completely lost in her thoughts, and it took her a while to realize Drayk had left Ayr and was walking to join her at the refreshment table. His skin was flushed and his eyes shone spiritedly.

"Shall we?" he asked, holding out his hand. His conversation with Ayr obviously hadn't damped his spirits. If anything, he looked livelier than before.

Catanya was caught off guard. She hesitated before taking his hand and following him onto the dance floor. Drayk twirled her around and placed his hands on her hips as he began steering her in time with the music.

Catanya struggled to keep up with him. Her body was tense. She had never danced like this before and she was self-conscious.

"Are you all right?" asked Drayk.

They were pressed so closely together he had to pull back in order to see her face.

"Yes, I'm fine. It's just all so..." Catanya trailed off as she observed the other dancers around her.

"It takes some getting used to," said Drayk. "But I wouldn't have it any other way. I love the freedom of this place. Nobody judges anyone or expects them to be something they're not. We're all free to be whoever and behave however we want." He pressed his cheek against her head and took a deep breath, his grip on her waist tightening.

Catanya's heart raced and her head began to fog. She was extremely aware of Drayk's body and the warmth of it pressed against hers. She was unsteady, not sure if she wanted him to let go or squeeze her tighter in his arms. The rhythm of the drums swelled through the air, getting faster and louder. All the bodies around them reacted, smashing together in frenzied excitement. The floor shook with the weight of pounding feet, and the air was thick with the haze of hot breath and sweat.

Catanya stumbled, jostling against the impassioned dancers, clinging to Drayk for support. He responded by sliding one hand up her back and embracing her against his chest. His other hand squeezed her hips against his harder and harder.

Catanya's breathing quickened in pace with the drums. She

started almost involuntarily moving her hands up to Drayk's shoulders, towards his neck.

The spell broke abruptly as someone wrenched Drayk away, leaving Catanya dazed and confused, surrounded by unfamiliar dancers. She turned to see who had interrupted them and realized it was Lia. Her face was red with anger.

The music was so loud Catanya could only hear fragments of what they were saying. She thought she heard Lia mention Caerlon and something about being selfish and untrustworthy. Drayk seemed to disagree, at which point Lia accused him of being naïve. Catanya had heard enough. Spinning on her heel, she pushed past the other dancers and left the dance floor.

She wasn't surprised. She knew Lia didn't trust her. If Lia was determined to hate the entire Caerlon royal family, including her sister and her niece, there was nothing that she, Catanya, could do about it. Besides, Catanya didn't trust Lia either. In fact, she felt especially offended to discover that even her mother's side of the family was spiteful and cruel.

Fuming, Catanya snatched another wine glass off the table and downed it in one gulp.

"You looked good out there," said a familiar voice.

Catanya noticed Ayr standing behind the table, grinning at her.

"I mean it, you and Drayk looked good. I thought for a moment you were actually enjoying yourself," she said with a laugh.

"Mmm..." Catanya took another glass of wine. "For a moment, so did I." She glowered at Lia and Drayk, who were still locked in their argument.

Ayr followed Catanya's gaze. "Ah, don't take it personally. Lia has never been a very warm or tactful person."

"No. Nor trusting, I imagine." Catanya made no effort to hide her displeasure. "But Lia trained Drayk, right?" she asked. "She's like a mentor to him?"

Ayr frowned. "Yes, I suppose she is. In a manner of speaking." She lifted a wine glass off the table and crossed to stand beside Catanya so they wouldn't have to shout over the noise. "Theirs is an unusual relationship."

Catanya pursed her lips. Unusual relationships appeared to be the norm in Awnell.

Ayr seemed to guess what Catanya was thinking. "Awnell has long been a home for free-spirits such as myself, but also for refugees fleeing the torment of their former lives."

"You mean Drayk?" asked Catanya, remembering the vision of the young boy and his mother.

"Yes... among others," said Ayr vaguely as she took a sip from her wine.

When Ayr didn't elaborate, Catanya decided to press. "I saw the sea cottage," she ventured. "Drayk took me there."

"Ah, yes... Then you know."

Catanya thought for a moment. "Well, no actually. Not really. He didn't say much while we were there. But that was his childhood home, wasn't it?"

Ayr nodded. "It was. But by the time I met him, Drayk had been living on the streets of Awnell City for many years."

Catanya was shocked. "Living on the streets?" she asked. "What happened with his mother?"

Ayr made a sour expression that communicated her obvious distaste for the woman. "From what I understand, after several failed attempts, the woman finally drank herself to death, leaving her young son to fend for himself. But Drayk was clever, even then. He was resourceful." She grinned at some distant memory. "Oh, he caused a lot of trouble. Best pickpocket I've ever known. And wily too. I can't count the number of people he swindled or the number of other children he roped into his schemes."

A smile tugged at the corners of Catanya's mouth. She could picture it clearly. Young Drayk with his band of misfits wreaking havoc on the city. "So, how did Drayk go from a petty criminal to one of your Verratrí?" she asked. Now that she was finally getting some answers, she was eager to learn more.

"Well, he managed to evade our capture for a long time, but eventually we caught up with him. I was all set to lock him up for his crimes, but Lia talked me out of it. She saw something in Drayk. She offered him the choice. He could either join the Verratrí and use his skills to help the kingdom, or he could go to prison."

"I guess I know which option he chose," said Catanya wryly.

"Yes, but it still took many years before he was able to forget his past and learn to expect more for himself. Lia worked with him every day, and it took him a long time to trust her."

"Understandable, given his upbringing," said Catanya, thinking about the vision again, and the scars on Drayk's chest. "I'll never understand how his mother could treat him like that."

"It is inexcusable," Ayr said with a heavy sigh. "But I don't think she considered him to be her son... not really." She shook her head darkly. Then, seeing the question on Catanya's face, she continued, "Drayk's mother did not conceive by choice. From my understanding, she was enslaved at the Bratia camps before being sold to a wealthy racketeer. When she became pregnant, he simply cast her aside to die... I think, to her, Drayk was a constant reminder of her own pain and vulnerability. A reminder of the man who broke her. She hated Drayk and everything he represented... So, I suppose we mustn't judge her too harshly. She was a victim too."

Catanya felt sick. She scanned the room for Drayk, but he wasn't arguing with Lia anymore. Now he was talking and laughing with some people Catanya didn't recognize. He seemed so carefree and light, back to his usual charming self. But now she saw it, the darkness and pain underneath the bravado.

"You care for him," said Ayr, tilting her head. "I can tell that you do. Why bother hiding it? Why not just admit it?"

Catanya cleared her throat. "I'm not hiding anything," she said, nettled. "It's just... pointless. Drayk is too... I mean, *I'm* not —" She broke off, shaking her head. "It doesn't matter. I'm not interested in getting involved with him. Nothing is ever going to happen between us."

"And why not?"

Catanya gave her an incredulous look, and Ayr chuckled.

"No, really. Why not? What's holding you back?"

"Where do I start?" said Catanya with an exasperated sigh. "With everything that's going on... It just wouldn't be right."

"Right? Who said anything about right and wrong? I'm talking about feelings, emotions, *desires*." Ayr raised her eyebrows suggestively and took another sip of her wine.

"We can't always trust our feelings," muttered Catanya.

Ayr laughed outright. "Well, speak for yourself," she said. "I trust my feelings and instincts over facts any day." She raised her glass as if in salute and finished it in one gulp. Then she winked and walked off to join a group of cheery dancers.

As the night progressed and inebriation levels rose ever higher, the dancers lost all sense of inhibition and propriety. The musicians played increasingly rhythmic and boisterous music, and the noise and energy in the room reached a fever pitch. The harder the musicians played, the harder the dancers' feet hit the floor. People were sweating and losing layers of clothing as the heat became overwhelming.

Everywhere Catanya turned, she saw people entwined in passionate embraces. At various points in the evening, Ayr could be seen entangled with (at Catanya's last count) three different men and four different women. Rey and Isa were locked together in the centre of the dance floor, and a pack of eager-looking partners surrounded Drayk.

Catanya wondered what her younger self would say if she

could see herself now. Never in her wildest dreams had Catanya imagined she'd end up at a celebration quite like this one. This kind of behaviour would never have happened in Faltir—or anywhere in Caerlon. At first, she'd found it all rather unseemly, but the longer she spent in the hall, the more she realized there was something genuine about it—something instinctive and wild. It was blissful abandon. It was what a celebration ought to be.

As the sun rose the next day, people filtered out of the banquet. Some had fallen asleep in the hall and needed to be woken up. Others had run off together to continue the festivities in private. Catanya was turning the corner, heading back to her own chambers when she nearly ran headlong into Drayk.

"Oh, there you are!" He had taken off his formal jacket and was looking much more like his usual casual self.

"Here I am," said Catanya, returning his grin. She was tired, and feeling the effects of the third bottle of spiced wine she'd shared with Niq and Bir.

"So, what did you think? Your first Midwinter Carnival?"

"It was..." She contemplated her response. "It was unusual, unexpected, unruly, and... rather spectacular," she finished, chuckling.

Drayk smiled and closed his eyes as though relishing the moment. "Yes, I knew you'd love it."

Catanya frowned. "I mean, it wasn't without its flaws or its low moments, but..." She shrugged.

"Yeah, I'm sorry about Lia," he said, opening his eyes to give her an apologetic look. "She can be... well, close-minded."

Catanya met his eyes and read the genuine regret in them. "What did Lia say to you?" she asked.

Drayk made a sound of disgust and shook his head. "Nothing worth repeating."

"I mean, I think I caught the important points." Catanya adopted a tone of false levity and continued, "Now, correct me if I'm wrong, but she doesn't trust me because I'm Caerlon royalty, and she wants to make sure you don't trust me either?"

Drayk smirked. "Something like that."

"Lovely," said Catanya, leaning against the wall and closing her eyes.

Drayk took a deep breath. "She told me not to fall in love with you, actually."

"What?" asked Catanya, flabbergasted. She opened her eyes to look at him.

"Oh yes," said Drayk, with a caustic laugh. "Apparently, I've become weak and sentimental, two traits which do not sit well with her."

Catanya gave Drayk a sceptical look. "Sentimental and weak? You?"

A smirk twitched at his lips. "My thoughts exactly," he said, nodding. "I assured her she has nothing to worry about. I wouldn't know how to fall in love, even if I wanted to." He made an attempt at a jaunty grin, but Catanya noticed it didn't reach his eyes.

Suddenly overcome with pity, she sighed and stood up straighter so she was level with him. "Ayr told me, you know?"

"Told you what?" he asked unsuspectingly.

"Your story. About how you came to live in Awnell, about Lia and... your mother..."

The light-hearted expression slid off Drayk's face.

"I'm sorry, Drayk." Catanya put her hand on his arm. "I can't imagine..."

Drayk just shook his head. "Don't do this," he said, pulling his arm out of her grasp and looking irked. "Don't look at me like I'm some vulnerable child who needs protecting. I am who I am, and it's never going to change."

"What are you talking about?" asked Catanya, mildly hurt by his abrupt shift in attitude.

"You're looking for some sign of tenderness and affection,"

he said in disapproval. "You want me to be different, be a better man—like Jémys." He laughed and moved in closer to her. Then, lowering his voice, he continued, "I like who I am, Catya. I make no apologies for the things I've done."

"I'm not asking you to," she said irritably. "But—"

"Good. Because I'm just this"—he threw his arms out and smiled sardonically—"I'm a liar and an outlaw. A philanderer and a vagrant, nothing more."

"You really believe that?" she asked, giving him a steely look.

"I know it," said Drayk, stepping forward and inclining over her. His bright blue eyes danced in the light of the nearby torch. "But I have to admit," he continued, his voice softer as he searched her face. "I rather like that you want there to be more." He brushed a loose strand of hair out of her face.

"Why is that?" asked Catanya in a low voice, barely a whisper.

Her heart was thumping so loudly she thought it might be trying to break free from her chest. She gazed into his eyes, transfixed, and her body leaned forward instinctively as Drayk brought her face over to meet his. Their lips touched, and Catanya finally gave in. Before she knew it, she had arched her back and wrapped her hands around his neck.

He drew her tighter into his body, like he had done on the dance floor. His lips moved fervently as they parted hers and he ran his hand down her neck, lingering briefly as he touched the necklace on her chest. Then he gripped her waist and pressed her firmly up against the wall.

And for a brief moment, Catanya experienced the blissful abandon everyone else had experienced that evening. But too soon, reality came crashing down on her.

"Wait," she said, pushing him away. "We can't do this."

"Sure, we can." He grinned, leaning in again.

She shook her head and stopped him. "No, I mean *I* can't."

Drayk exhaled quietly and backed away.

"I'm sorry, Drayk, but despite everything, I'm still in love with Jémys. My heart, it's... I..." She trailed off, too sad to continue.

Drayk smiled wryly. "Well, Catya, it's not exactly your heart I want," he teased, brushing her cheek with his hand.

Catanya pulled back, staring at her feet. "It's too difficult," she said. "Please don't..."

Drayk chuckled under his breath. "All right," he said, nodding and backing away from her completely. "But you let me know when you change your mind." He flashed her another playful grin, and Catanya couldn't help but smile in spite of herself.

She shook her head and took a deep breath as her pulse resumed its normal pace.

A few minutes later, as they walked down the corridor together, Catanya felt the same prickling sensation on her neck that she'd experienced at the beginning of the evening. But once again, when she glanced behind her, the corridor was empty.

They continued through the halls until they arrived outside her chambers. Catanya moved to open the door, but Drayk stopped her.

"You know, Catya," he said, leaning in. "One of these days, you'll need to let go of that fear that's controlling you. You'll feel a lot lighter if you do, trust me."

10

SLAEDIR'S NEWS

"Ow!" Diyah pulled her bleeding hand back and clutched it tightly. She had been rifling through one of the upper cupboards in her physician's chambers and cut her finger on something sharp. She grabbed a cloth off the counter and wrapped the wound. Then she dragged a chair over and stood on its seat so she could see the highest shelf.

She found the culprit at once. A large sewing needle lay at the back of the cabinet. She snatched it up with her uninjured hand and jumped off the chair.

"Are you all right?" asked Jémys. He was sitting near the fire, watching her run around the room.

"I'm fine." She tossed the needle into a jar full of similar rubbish and climbed back onto the chair to finish cleaning.

"Please sit down," said Jémys. "You've been jumping around all day and you're making me nervous. You need to relax."

"I can't relax," she said. She was a mess of nerves and she hadn't been able to rest for days. She'd spent the last two hours frantically cleaning the physician's chambers just to have something to distract her.

There had been a significant lull in her work this week. She'd never realized before how much she relied on that work to keep her busy and her mind occupied. Without it, she was left to dwell on everything that was worrying her.

Cadyan had been back in Caerlon for weeks already, and he'd instructed the firkon to prepare for war. A mad rush to amass resources and make preparations had ensued. Zadílar had made a special delivery of weapons and armour... but then nothing. The firkon were ready to leave, ready to fight, but Cadyan still hadn't given the order. It seemed he was waiting for something, but nobody knew what.

Diyah was certain the answer would come with Slaedir's return. She didn't know where he was or what he was doing, but she knew his arrival would not bring good tidings.

Until that day came, she needed to keep busy.

She spent the rest of the afternoon re-organizing everything she'd removed from the cupboards and tossing away anything unusable.

All sorts of strange items were stashed away in the cupboards. She found a collection of old rusted surgical tools that made her skin crawl; several vials of liquid, which were completely congealed; a basket full of something brown and rotten that might once have resembled milk thistle; and dozens of unlabelled jars whose contents she needed to identify.

After a while, Jémys gave up trying to convince her to rest and decided to help. Overall, his wounds had healed considerably well. Although he still had severe pain, he could move around on his own and perform minor tasks without too much difficulty. He still had bandages wrapped tightly around his chest and ribs, and one of his arms was cinched across his front, but his left arm was free to work. So, he positioned himself near the worktable where he could sort through the stacks of books and replace them neatly on the shelves.

"Oh, that is gruesome," he said, coughing on the dust that

emerged when he opened one of the massive tomes. He held up a vivid depiction of a naked man contorted in pain and bleeding from the nose and mouth. "How can you look at these images?" he asked, slamming the book shut and putting it on the nearest pile.

Diyah shrugged and turned back to her collection of jars. "I don't know, I guess it just doesn't bother me."

It was getting late and Diyah had finished labelling all the jars except one. It was the same vial of bright green liquid she'd found months ago. She still didn't know what it was.

She covered her mouth and nose with a cloth and uncorked the vial slowly. It gave off a pungent, musty smell, and it had a slight filmy quality.

She swirled it and tipped a dollop of the green liquid into a shallow bowl that she'd mounted to a stand. Then she lit a candle and placed it under the bowl, waiting for the metal to warm as she probed the contents.

"What is that?" asked Jémys.

"I have no idea," said Diyah through her cloth. "I found it in the cupboard, but I've never seen anything like it."

As the liquid heated, the colour slowly turned from brilliant green to sickly brown. Before long, it had dried up completely.

"Hmm..." said Diyah, discarding her face covering. "It's not a concoction, which means whatever it is, it's a naturally occurring substance... but then why have I never seen it before?"

"Is it important?" asked Jémys.

Diyah raised her eyebrows thoughtfully. "I suppose not, but it just bothers me. I memorized the uses of every known poison and remedy before the age of five. My father was very strict about it. He said that a Heiltúir couldn't waste time searching for answers, they needed to have them already in their head."

Jémys gaped at her. "Before you were *five*? That's impossible."

Diyah shrugged. "Our people have excellent memories,"

she mumbled, too tired to elaborate. She scraped the dehydrated contents out of the bowl and re-corked the mysterious vial. "But if I don't know what this is, it means my father didn't either, and most likely none of the Heiltúir... That troubles me."

Later that night, after Jémys had fallen asleep, Diyah sat up alone, searching through all of her books for anything that might explain the mysterious green substance. She couldn't find anything. In fact, it shocked her to discover how out-dated most of these books were.

The fire had burned down, and the candles were nearly extinguished when someone knocked on her door.

Surprised that someone would call on her so late, Diyah grabbed a nearby candle and walked to open the door.

It was Fehla. Her hair hung in a loose braid and she wore a thick knitted shawl wrapped around her shoulders.

"Hello, Diyah," she said. "I'm sorry to wake you, but it's my head again. May I come in?"

"Of course," said Diyah, holding the door for her and ignoring the guards' scowls. She and Fehla had decided weeks ago that they needed a story to cover for their visits. They'd decided that whenever Fehla wanted to see Diyah, she should feign a recurring headache that required treatment.

When they'd closed the door, Fehla turned to face her. "I just wanted to check on you both. Are you all right?"

"We're all right for now," said Diyah. She led Fehla to a set of chairs near the window where they wouldn't wake Jémys. "Cadyan needs me, but I'm worried about Jémys. I don't know what Cadyan's planning to do to him."

Fehla glanced over her shoulder at him, eyebrows pinched

in sadness. "He seems like a good man," she said. "And he obviously loves Catanya a great deal. But do you think she loves him?"

Diyah frowned as she thought about it. "I don't know. I've never known Catanya to fall in love before. But then again—" She broke off, staring at Jémys. In the dim candlelight, she could see the wounds on his face had faded. Once again, she remarked how handsome he was, lying there asleep. He bore a striking resemblance to his brother, but there was a softness about him that Julyán lacked. Then she recalled the stories he'd told her about his time with Catanya in Finnua, about his aunt and the other villagers.

"I've never met anyone like him before," she said thoughtfully. "I think I could see why she might love him." She smiled, hoping Catanya might have known happiness for a while with Jémys.

"I hope not," said Fehla darkly.

Diyah was surprised. "What?" she asked reproachfully. "Why?"

Fehla sighed and looked at Jémys, her face clouded in sadness. "Because heartbreak is the worst pain of all. No one heals after losing the one they love. Not completely. I don't want that pain for her. Not on top of everything else."

"But she hasn't lost him," protested Diyah. "They might find their way back to each other."

Fehla looked sceptical but said nothing.

And deep down, Diyah knew Jémys and Catanya had very little chance of reuniting. Even if Jémys survived whatever punishment Cadyan had planned, how could he ever hope to find her? How could any of them ever hope to find her?

"Do you think Catanya is still in Awnell?" she asked. She'd been wondering it for weeks, and she didn't know what to hope for. She knew Cadyan had his sights set on Awnell, which made it dangerous. But then again, Awnell was a massive kingdom with soldiers and resources it could use to protect her.

"I expect so," said Fehla.

"But—that's a good thing, right?" asked Diyah, desperate for a confirmation.

"It is difficult to say... Queen Ayr is a very cunning and strategic leader. I'm sure she would recognize Catanya as a valuable ally for her... but I'm concerned about Falia, actually." She bit her lip. "I haven't spoken to my sister in years, not since I left Awnell. She made it quite clear to me that if I went with Casréyan, she would disavow all connection to me. She was true to her word..."

"Oh." Diyah fidgeted with the hem of her apron. "I'm sorry. Were you two close?"

"We were. Ayr, Falia, and I were inseparable as children. But when I agreed to marry Casréyan, Falia told me I was aligning myself with the enemy. I was abandoning Ayr, my rightful queen and my—" Fehla broke off and Diyah thought she noticed tears glistening on her cheek.

There was a long silence as Fehla recollected herself. "I don't know what my sister has been doing all this time, but if she's still at the fortress with Ayr, I can't imagine she'll be too happy to encounter her niece."

"Well, she can't be as bad as Cadyan, can she?" muttered Diyah half-heartedly.

This didn't seem to cheer Fehla up. If anything, it just made her feel worse. But Diyah couldn't bear to dwell on her worries anymore. She'd managed to keep herself distracted all day, but now her fears were taking root again. She cast around for a new discussion topic, but she couldn't settle on anything. So, they sat together in troubled silence until Fehla needed to leave.

The next day, Diyah was tired from her lack of sleep, but she wanted a change of scenery. She left her chambers early to call on the chaplain and ensure he had enough tonic to last throughout the week. But when she arrived, she found his room empty.

She was making her way back towards her quarters, wondering where the chaplain could be at this early hour, when she heard raised voices coming from somewhere nearby.

She looked around to get her bearings and realized she was standing in a corridor off the entrance hall. The guards outside the throne room hadn't noticed her.

"Excellent news," came Cadyan's voice. "You're sure?"

"Positive," said another voice Diyah recognized. Her heart started hammering inside her chest. Slaedir had returned to the castle. "I saw her myself," he continued. "She's been getting real friendly with Ayr. And that other fella."

"I knew it!" exclaimed Cadyan.

The loud rumble of voices told Diyah dozens of firkon were crowded in the throne room.

"Quiet," called Cadyan in a low but carrying voice. The chatter died immediately. "Well, Maífirkon," he continued. "Ready the army. We leave tomorrow. The time has come for Awnell to fall."

An excited buzz ran through the room, and Diyah realized almost too late that the buzz was moving towards the entrance hall. She hurried away and slipped out of sight just as the firkon surged into the corridor.

Diyah ran up three flights of stairs, taking them two at a time, and hurtled down the hall towards the physician's quarters. She burst through the door to find Jémys sitting near the fire.

"He found her!" she cried breathlessly, clutching a stitch in her side. "Catanya. He found her in Awnell. They're preparing the army."

"What?" Jémys looked aghast. "When do they leave?" he asked, jumping to his feet and shuddering at the pain.

"Tomorrow."

The door burst open again, slamming against the wall with a deafening crack. In came Julyán, looking irritable. "Come." He beckoned for Jémys to follow him. "We're moving you to the dungeons."

"You can't!" protested Diyah. "He's not finished healing—"

"He's healed enough," Julyán snarled, cutting across her. "I've allowed this charade to continue for too long. The army rides tomorrow, and we cannot leave a prisoner loose in the castle. When we return, he'll be transported to the work camps."

"The camps," repeated Diyah, her voice hollow. She watched the colour drain from Jémys's face.

"Now, are you going to come willingly or will I have to force you?" asked Julyán, laying his hand on the hilt of his sword.

"Well, well, well," said an unctuous voice from the doorway. It was Slaedir. "Still alive, I see." He stared at Jémys as he crossed the room to stand in front of him. "I guess it helps when your brother is your warden, eh?" He sneered at Julyán.

Diyah noticed that Julyán's demeanour had changed completely. He was still standing with his hand on his sword, but his entire body had stiffened as if waiting for an attack. He was staring at Slaedir through narrowed eyes.

"I didn't put it together at first, but now he's healed up, I can see it. You didn't think I'd remember, did you?" asked Slaedir, looking at Julyán. He let out a bark of laughter. "Did you explain the situation to our dear king? What do you think he'll say when I tell him your little brother has been bedding his sister?"

Julyán stood perfectly still, but Diyah noticed a muscle in his jaw twitch slightly.

"I mean, sure, Cadyan, he hates his sister," continued

Slaedir, obviously enjoying himself. "But I reckon he'd still want to kill anyone who'd dared to touch her, don't you?" He smirked and turned back to face Jémys. "Mind you, I *am* curious..." He leaned in and lowered his voice. "How did she taste?"

Diyah made a sound of disgust. To her surprise, Jémys hit Slaedir so hard on the face that he stumbled back.

"I recognize you from Finnua," Jémys shouted. "You killed him! Trampled him! You—" He tried to step forward, but Julyán drew his sword in a flash of steel and pressed it against his brother's neck.

"I'm warning you," he said in a low voice.

Jémys froze in place, glaring at Julyán with heightened loathing.

"Aye, what are you waiting for? Just kill him already," roared Slaedir, spitting blood, and what Diyah thought might be a tooth, on the floor.

"No," said Julyán, taking a deep breath and sheathing his sword. "The king has plans for him. He's still useful to us."

"I can't see how," said Slaedir. "She's obviously moved on from him, hasn't she? I saw her with that other fella. The pretty one from her book." He made a sound like a grunt of pleasure and closed his eyes reminiscently. "Pretty steamy those two. He didn't waste any time, now did he?" He gave Jémys a taunting smile.

Diyah looked at Jémys and saw comprehension dawning beneath his anger.

"Oh, I've hit a nerve." Slaedir laughed and raised his hands up in a mock apology. "Now don't you worry, sonny. I'll be sure and bring you back both of their heads."

Diyah was furious. She marched forward and slapped Slaedir in the face as hard as she could. "You're despicable," she spat.

Slaedir clutched at his cheek and swore loudly. He made a

move as though to hit Diyah, but Julyán grabbed his arm in the air.

"No," he said. "She is not to be harmed. We need her."

"Need her?" spat Slaedir, yanking his arm out of Julyán's hand. "You know what, I've had just about enough of your self-righteous talk. Whose side are you on, anyway?"

"I serve my king," said Julyán matter-of-factly.

"*I serve my king,*" repeated Slaedir in a mocking voice. Then he shoved Julyán away from him. "I am your maífírkon! You do not tell me what to do!" he shouted, spraying spit in Julyán's face. "You've been a thorn in my side too long. I can't wait for you to get what's coming to you. Just do us a favour and try not to get yourself killed in battle, will you? I am very much looking forward to watching you choke on your own blood when I finally gut you in the tournament next month. It'll be like killing your father all over again. And you'll be a coward in the end, just like him."

Diyah watched the scene, utterly transfixed. She had always sensed a tension between Julyán and Slaedir, but she had never seen them behave like this.

"Don't be so sure of your victory, Slaedir," said Julyán in a threateningly quiet voice. "Overconfidence has been the death of many a more talented soldier."

"We'll see," said Slaedir before he turned and stalked out of the room.

Julyán turned to face his brother again. "Come," he said. "Don't make this harder than it needs to be."

But Jémys stood stock-still, refusing to move. "What was that about Father?" he asked, giving Julyán a piercing stare. "What did he mean?"

Diyah's pulse quickened. She looked from Jémys to Julyán, sensing the tension mount between them.

"You heard him," said Julyán, meeting his brother's gaze.

The colour drained from Jémys's face. "All this time, you've known who killed our father?"

Julyán nodded.

"That man killed our father?" Jémys's voice was unsteady, and Diyah noticed he was clenching his fists. "He killed Olly too. Olly, Nelle, Finnua... and now you tell me he killed our father?" Jémys seemed to be struggling to understand. He backed away from Julyán, eyes wide like he was seeing him for the first time. "And you work with him? You work *for* him?"

"Yes," responded Julyán.

"How?" Jémys's tone was strained with betrayal and revulsion.

"It doesn't matter," said Julyán. "I serve my king and I serve my maífirkon." He gestured for Jémys to follow him. Then he turned to Diyah and said, "The guards will permit you to make periodic visits to tend his wounds, but he will not leave his cell. Is that clear?"

Diyah glanced over at Jémys and saw the shock and anger on his face. "Fine." She said through gritted teeth. "But tell me, why make this effort to save his life if you're just planning to condemn him for the rest of it?"

"The king wants him alive," said Julyán.

"Yes, you said that already. But why?" she demanded.

Julyán gave her an appraising look and then shrugged. "Enslavement is infinitely worse than death."

Diyah gaped at him, appalled.

"It's okay, Diyah," said Jémys, although his voice shook and he had tears in his eyes. "The only thing that matters now is Catanya. As long as I know she's alive and fighting, I can endure anything." He gave Diyah a reassuring smile and then turned cold, furious eyes towards Julyán. "And when she unleashes her power on Cadyan and his *fírkon*," he pronounced the word with spite, "maybe they'll have time to repent before they die. But either way, we'll have justice."

A shadow flickered in Julyán's eyes, but he showed no other reaction as he steered his brother out of the room.

Diyah watched them go, overwhelmed by the despair she could no longer keep at bay. Her only hope now lay in the strength of an unknown army and the support of a distant queen.

11

———

THE CABIN NEAR INAELL

A week had passed since the carnival banquet, and the city was resuming its normal functions. The last vestiges of the celebration were cleared, and the visiting artisans, troubadours, and entertainers had departed the city.

Catanya's training with Rey and Lia had resumed in full force, but with one modification. Now that she'd mastered the basics of most weapons, Lia and Rey expected Catanya to augment her skill with magic. However, so far, she'd been unable to incorporate magic in any way. She hadn't manifested any powers since the day she'd protected Drayk.

Catanya worried Lia and Rey might continue using Drayk to provoke her, but it seemed once was enough for them. In fact, Drayk hadn't even attended her recent training sessions. Catanya had barely seen him since the carnival.

Though she was grateful not to watch him being tortured every day, part of her worried his sudden absence might be thanks to their awkward interaction at the banquet.

Catanya wanted to be frustrated with Drayk, but she actually felt slightly abandoned and hurt. She had grown accustomed to his company and support, and she'd been counting on him to help her deal with Lia.

"You need to focus!" shouted Lia after landing a particularly forceful blow on Catanya, sending her crashing to the ground.

"I'm trying," said Catanya through gritted teeth.

"Obviously that's not true, otherwise I would never have been able to lay a finger on you. I don't understand. Do you enjoy taking a beating?"

"Of course not," spat Catanya, standing up and wincing at the pain in her ribs.

It was late in the afternoon. They were alone in the court-yard, and Lia was pacing angrily. She had taken away Catanya's weapons, trying to force her to use her magic. But so far, the only result of their day's work was a beaten and bruised Catanya.

"This is pointless," she said. In her bitterness and fatigue, Catanya was losing her patience.

"Pointless, is it?" said Lia. "Pointless for me to train you to protect yourself? You don't think you need to learn this? You think you're above it all?"

"No!" shouted Catanya. "But I think your methods are pointless. You don't know what you're doing."

"I have trained hundreds—nay thousands—of Awnell's best soldiers, and yet my methods are not good enough for *Your Highness*?" sneered Lia.

"Don't call me that."

Lia's lip curled back like a predator spotting a weakness. "What's the matter? Afraid to admit who you really are?"

"You have no idea who I am," Catanya snapped.

For a moment they just glared at each other, filled with contempt. Lia opened her mouth to retort, but the door swung open and Ayr and Rey marched into the courtyard.

"So, how are we faring?" asked Ayr. She strode over to them and clapped Catanya on the back. "Any progress?"

"None," said Catanya, jerking away from her.

"None?" Ayr sounded disappointed, and she glanced at Lia. Lia just pursed her lips and nodded. "Hmm, well, let me see what you've got." Ayr sat on one of the stone benches at the edge of the courtyard and gestured for them to continue. Rey joined Lia and Catanya.

The rest of the afternoon passed in an equally frustrating manner, except Catanya and Lia did not dare continue their bickering in front of Ayr.

Catanya tried everything she could to summon her magic. She tried concentrating her mind, flexing various muscles, focusing on breathing... But nothing worked. It was like the harder she pushed, the more elusive her magic became—as if the powers themselves didn't want to be used.

As the sun dimmed, the door opened again, and Drayk strode across the courtyard towards Ayr. His cheeks were flushed, and he was wearing a thick travelling cloak.

Ayr's face brightened, and she jumped to her feet. "Confirmation?" she asked.

"Yes," said Drayk. "Not far from here. Looks like he's staying still for now. But then there's these. They just arrived for you."

Catanya turned to see Drayk handing two sealed letters to Ayr. Her moment of distraction cost her dearly. Lia landed yet another heavy blow, splitting open Catanya's lip.

"That's enough," called Ayr before Lia could reprimand Catanya. "That's enough for today, I think." She was staring down at the letters, wearing an odd expression of resignation. "Lia, Rey, I need you to wait for me outside." She gestured to the door with her head and exchanged glances with Lia.

Lia seemed to understand some unspoken meaning. She nodded and cast Catanya a scathing look as she strode out of the courtyard. Catanya rolled her eyes and wiped her lip on her sleeve. As she began collecting her things, she strained her ears, trying to hear what Drayk and Ayr were saying.

"Sooner than I expected," muttered Ayr. "We need to get moving." She folded up the letters and put them in her pocket. "Are you ready?"

"Of course," replied Drayk.

Catanya was curious. She wanted to hear more, but Rey drew her attention away from the conversation.

"Don't get discouraged," he said, holding out her gloves for her.

"Oh, no, why would I be discouraged?" she asked acerbically, taking the gloves and shoving them in her pocket.

Rey gave her a faint smile and turned to leave. But then he paused and said, "Far be it for me to criticize my commander, but if you ask me, we've been going about this all wrong."

"What do you mean?"

"Well, we can only teach you what we know. It seems to me that you need a more qualified instructor."

Catanya snorted. "And who do you suggest? Cadyan? Oh, no, wait, he wants to kill me."

"Mmm, yes..." Rey frowned seriously, and then he left without another word.

Catanya shook her head in disbelief. She collected the rest of her belongings and walked over to Ayr and Drayk.

"Are you going somewhere?" she asked, gesturing to Drayk's travelling cloak.

"Just got back," he replied.

"Oh... really?" Catanya was a little stung to discover Drayk had left the city without telling her. "From where?" She tried to sound nonchalant.

"Long story," he said, waving his hand. "It's not important right now."

"Actually," said Ayr. "I think it is. His latest note said to come, didn't it? Then you should go first thing tomorrow. Both of you. I need Lia and Rey with me for the next few days, and, quite frankly, I don't think these training sessions are going well anymore." She paused thoughtfully. "I think a change of scenery and pace would do you good, don't you agree, Catya?"

Catanya frowned and looked at Drayk, but he just shrugged. "Where are we going?" she asked.

"Not far. It's a cabin just south of Inaell. We'll be there and back before the day is done."

Catanya nodded. She didn't really care where they went or what they did, as long as it meant she didn't have to see Lia.

"Excellent," said Ayr. She brushed her hands together, gave an odd, resigned sigh, then she turned and swept out of the courtyard.

An awkward tension filled the space she left behind. Catanya couldn't think of anything to say to Drayk. Her mind was suddenly blank.

"That looks painful," said Drayk, breaking the silence for her. He pointed to the bruises on her face. He seemed perfectly at ease, like he hadn't spent days stressing about their kiss the way she had.

"What, this? Nah, it feels good," said Catanya in a droll tone. She wiped the blood off her lip, covering up for her foolish discomfort. If Drayk wasn't embarrassed, then she wouldn't be either.

Drayk grinned. "Well, don't worry. I'm sure you'll regain your looks in time." He winked at her.

Catanya stifled a laugh. *Same old Drayk,* she thought with a touch of relief. And just like that, they regained their old rhythms. Nothing had changed.

"So... What's so important about this cabin?" she asked as she headed towards the armoury door.

"Nothing special about the cabin, really," he replied, following her into the room. "In fact, I'd say it's a rather dull, dreary sort of place. Plain architecture, boring history... not interesting or significant."

Catanya sighed and returned her weapons to their various

racks. "All right, then what's inside the cabin that's so important?" she asked, leading the way out of the armoury and into the atrium.

Drayk looked at her with a twinkle in his eye. "They say an unpredictable recluse lives there," he said, lowering his voice to a taunting whisper. "A dangerous drifter."

Catanya shook her head in exasperation. "I see. So, you've been chasing tales of an eccentric drifter. What, just curious to see what the future holds for you?" She stopped walking and turned to face him with a deadpan expression.

Drayk laughed and cuffed her on the shoulder playfully. "Well, let's just say this particular drifter has something valuable we want. But I'll tell you all about it on the journey tomorrow." He chuckled to himself as he walked off in the opposite direction. "You should get some rest," he called back. "We'll leave at first light."

Catanya watched him go, feeling a mixture of irritation and relief to see him acting like the same carefree and infuriating fool he had always been.

<hr>

Catanya's entire body hurt that night as she undressed to bathe. Her arms and legs were covered in large purple bruises and her jaw was swollen and tender. The months of training had sculpted her muscles into hard, sinewy knots, but she felt tight and sore. The servants had filled a deep cast-iron tub by the fire with hot water. As she lowered herself in, she felt the filth and stress of the day begin to wash away. With her head resting against the edge of the tub, she closed her eyes. She couldn't remember the last time her body *hadn't* ached from one injury or another.

She took a deep breath and plunged her head into the water. Opening her eyes, she watched her hair float and sway around her like gossamer seaweed. The strands of colour were luminous against her natural dark. Although her hair had hardly changed since her first night in Awnell, she still found it unsettling to see. She supposed she'd never really get used to it.

She slept unevenly that night, and it was still dark when she awoke. Her body was heavy and tender as she stumbled out of bed and dressed for her journey. She had grown accustomed to the breeches and vest uniform that the soldiers of Awnell wore, but she still felt uncomfortable when she strapped the leather baldric over her shoulder. The weight of the sword pressed uncomfortably against her back. She hoped, in time, she'd learn to like the sword too.

After a hurried breakfast in her room, she rushed off to meet Drayk. As exciting as Awnell City was, she had to admit she was strangely excited about the prospect of an excursion today. After weeks of staying still, she suddenly realized how much she was itching to be moving again. It seemed the time she'd spent running and trekking through the woods had rubbed off on her.

"Ready?" asked Drayk, as she arrived outside the fortress and found him waiting for her.

The pale light of dawn and the wet, chilly air hovering above the black-stone streets gave the impression of smoke rising from smouldering coals. It surrounded Drayk, lending him an eerie appearance.

Catanya nodded, and they set off together towards the north-western edge of the city.

As they left the inner city and moved farther from the port, the buildings became sparser. They were built lower to the ground, as if designed to withstand great forces of wind. Large conifer trees peppered the area with increasing frequency, as wilderness slowly reclaimed the space.

Finally, all the streets converged onto one large road that led directly out of the city on the western side. They passed several scouting outposts, who simply nodded and let them pass.

"Not very intimidating," said Catanya as she surveyed the feeble groups of sentinels. "This is all Ayr has watching the main road into the city? What about the mountains? What's stopping people from sneaking in that way?" She pointed to the rolling landscape, where thick trees provided dense cover.

"These are just the sentinels you see," said Drayk nonchalantly. "There are dozens of archery posts scattered through the trees, not to mention snares, trapping pits and other spring-loaded weapons."

"Oh." Catanya stumbled on the uneven earth and glanced around furtively, looking for any sign of movement or hidden traps. But there was nothing.

The sun had fully risen when they left the city behind. The soft morning rays peeked through the dense cloud cover, causing swirls of yellow and pink amongst the grey.

"Here we go," said Drayk, stopping in front of a patch of enormous trees with long, straight trunks. He stepped off the road and continued into the forest along the foothills of the Awnell Mountains. Catanya hesitated before following him.

"So... are you going to tell me?" she asked after a while. She was trudging along after him, struggling to keep pace. The muscles in her legs burned from the prolonged uphill climb, not to mention all the aches and pains from her training the previous day. "What are we looking for?"

"We're looking for a map," he replied without looking at her. Then he stopped and turned, squinting at the horizon as though trying to find his bearings.

"A map," echoed Catanya, panting slightly and massaging her stiff thigh. "A map of what?"

"You wouldn't believe me if I told you." Drayk started walking again, faster than he had before. "I'm not even sure I believe it."

"What is that supposed to mean?" Catanya jogged to catch up with him, while trying to ignore the sting in her muscles. "Drayk," she prompted when he didn't answer.

Drayk stopped and turned around to face her. "A map to Túir-Avlea," he said with a slight defensiveness.

Catanya snorted. She stared at him for a moment, waiting for the rest of the joke to come, but he held her gaze unblinkingly. "No," she said, unable to hold back her grin. "You can't be serious."

Drayk just shrugged.

"You *are* serious," she called, hurrying after him and doing her best to contain her amusement. "You know, I was just teasing you yesterday when I called you eccentric, but this... You can't really believe Túir-Avlea exists. It's a legend. A *story*."

"Well... We'll soon find out," he replied.

"Drayk, be serious." She grabbed his arm to stop him. She needed to talk some sense into him.

"I *am* being serious. I didn't always believe. But now..." He shrugged and looked at her meaningfully. "I don't know, I guess I'm open to the possibility."

"So, what changed?" Catanya couldn't imagine any argument compelling enough to make her believe in Túir-Avlea.

Drayk gave an exasperated sniff. "I met you," he replied.

Catanya opened her mouth to respond, but closed it again, frowning. She didn't know what to say to that.

"Look," said Drayk, "this isn't some whimsical fancy of mine or Ayr's. We've been searching for this map for years. It's the reason I was in Caerlon. It's the reason—well, one of the reasons—she reinstated the Verratrí after centuries of dormancy. Ayr sent me to track down old storytellers and poets, trying to find any information or proof that the map was real. For years, I roamed Mórceá with a crew, following every tenuous theory I could find. And a few years ago, I started hearing stories about a man. He was a drifter, wandering the outskirts of Caerlon, supposedly very erratic—raving about a map that was tormenting him. I knew I'd finally found what I was looking for.

"So, I started hunting him. I tracked him to the Reynic Mountains, then the Tarus valley, the Diyune marshes, the Weiban Downs... But every time I thought I was getting close, I'd arrive and find the place deserted. No sign anyone had ever been there... except for a single note."

"A note?" repeated Catanya, frowning.

Drayk sighed and reached into his coat, withdrawing a small bundle of papers. He handed them to Catanya.

Catanya took the papers and saw a series of messages scrawled in tight, jagged handwriting.

You think you can catch me, boy?

Catanya shuffled the pages, reading the other notes.

Nice try... You're getting slower... This is too easy. At least give me a challenge... Your new crew is worse than your last... No wonder your mother hated you.

At this, Catanya stopped reading and stared at Drayk. "He knew about your mother?"

Drayk nodded and took the notes back, returning them to his pocket. "Yes. He knew everything about me. It turns out, I wasn't just tracking him. He was also tracking me. Over the years, the notes became more specific, more taunting. He knows who I am and what I want, but I still don't know anything about him. It's infuriating."

Drayk turned and started walking again.

"So, this man," said Catanya, following him, "this is the dangerous recluse you told me about yesterday?"

"Yes."

"If he's so difficult to find, what makes you think he'll be in this cabin?" she asked.

"Well, a few months ago, I tracked him to Linlon, where I learned he'd left Caerlon entirely. He came back to Awnell."

Linlon. A distant memory came back to Catanya. A memory of a day spent unloading carts after the harvest in Finnua. She'd overheard the workers talking about Linlon, talking about the devastation in the small lake town.

"Wait... *you* ransacked Linlon?" She remembered how scared she'd been the day she found out about it. Everyone in Finnua had assumed the firkon were responsible. But now...

Drayk snorted. "We didn't ransack the place we just... you know... plundered a bit. We raised a little havoc and mayhem. Acted like bandits." He winked at her.

Catanya scowled at him. From what she remembered, the accounts sounded worse than a *little havoc.*

"Oh, come on," said Drayk with a laugh. "We had to play the part, you know? It's how we survived out there in Caerlon."

Catanya shook her head and stayed silent. It was so easy for her to forget who Drayk had been before they'd met.

"Anyway," he continued, ignoring her silent reproof. "Since I've been back in Awnell, I've been searching again. You remember Von and Mri?"

Catanya pursed her lips and nodded. It would be a long time before she forgot her experience at *Delirior Ece.*

"Well, they're both members of Ayr's advanced scout teams. They patrol the outskirts of Awnell and keep track of everyone who comes and goes. I gave them the description I had of the man, and they remembered seeing him. After that it only took me a couple days to track him." Drayk stopped walking and pointed to something in the distance.

Catanya followed his gaze and was surprised to see a small trail of smoke rising into the sky. It looked like it was coming from a chimney somewhere deep in the forest.

Drayk beckoned for her to follow him and they clambered up the next set of hills in silence together. Catanya didn't know what to make of his story about the supposed map. Túir-Avlea was just a legend, a myth. But whether or not this map existed, she was curious to meet the man who'd successfully evaded Drayk for so long.

"How do you know he's actually in there?" she asked, panting as she struggled to climb the hill in Drayk's wake. "You've been in Awnell for weeks now. If he's been tracking you, why would he stay so close to where you are? That doesn't make sense, unless... Wait a minute..." Catanya trailed off, watching Drayk. "You got a note at The Fairweather."

She had completely forgotten about it until now. Drayk had tried to pretend the note was from an old lover.

"Is that why you wanted to go there? That's why we went to that inn?" Catanya slowed her pace as she grappled with her mounting distrust and dread.

"No, actually. That was a surprise," he said, continuing his forward climb without concern. "But, like I said, he knows everything about me. He must have known I'd end up at the inn."

"Drayk, what was in that note?" she called after him. "Why do I get the impression there's something else you're not telling me?"

"Because there usually is," he rejoined, tossing her a playful smile.

Catanya stopped dead in her tracks, hands on her hips. "That's enough! I'm not taking another step until you tell me the truth."

Drayk sighed and slowed to a halt, facing away from Catanya.

"I mean it, Drayk," she insisted. "I'm tired of your lies and manipulations. Tell me the truth now, or I'm turning back."

Drayk stared up at the sky as if collecting himself, then

turned to face her. "Fine," he said resignedly. He pulled out three more papers from his jacket, and handed them to Catanya.

She read the words scrawled across the first page, and her mouth went suddenly dry.

Find her again. Then I'll find you.

"What is this?" she asked, her hand shaking as she lifted the paper. "Who is he talking about?"

"Who do you think?" Drayk asked with a touch of exasperation. "He left that note for me in Linlon... right after I met *you* in the woods. That's when everything changed."

Catanya nodded mechanically, still staring at the page without understanding.

"And the note I got at The Fairweather." He motioned for her to read the next page.

Well done. Now wait. I'll send word when it's time.

Catanya let out a short nervous laugh. "He's giving you instructions," she said. "And you're obeying him?"

"Without a second thought," said Drayk. He took a step forward, a manic gleam in his eyes. "I've spent ten years of my life tracking this map. Now I'm closer than ever before. I won't stop now."

Catanya didn't know how to feel about that. She lowered her eyes and shuffled the papers to read the last note.

Out of time. Come now. Bring her.

A chill settled over Catanya's body. "You're bringing me to him," she said, feeling hollow. "He wanted you to find me and bring me to him." She stared at Drayk as if it were her first time seeing him. "You used me—you and Ayr. You've been planning this together. This is the only reason you helped me."

"It's not the only reason," said Drayk, shaking his head. "No, Catya, I'm not using you. Ayr didn't even know about this until a week ago—when I got the last note. Ayr may have launched me on this journey but this is personal for me now. It's about more than my duty to the Verratrí or to Awnell. It has been for a long time... The truth is, the moment I met you in the woods, I knew I'd follow you. I didn't need him or anyone else to tell me. *I knew.*" He paused and stared at her long and hard. "I'm on your side, Catya. You and me. I want us to find this man together, find the map *together.*"

"How am I supposed to believe you?" she asked.

Drayk sighed. "You can believe whatever you want. It doesn't change anything. We're here now. Are you honestly going to claim you don't want to see this through? You don't want to meet the man who seems to know so much about us? You don't want to find the map to Túir-Avlea?"

Catanya didn't respond. As much as she hated to admit it, Drayk was right. She was burning with curiosity about this man. She wasn't going to turn back now.

Drayk seemed to understand. "Come on," he said.

As they crested the last hill, they saw a small, dilapidated cabin nestled between the trees. It looked like an old hunting cabin, but from its appearance, it hadn't been used for years, possibly decades.

The roof sloped perilously into the centre. Several wood panels had separated from the frame, and the rest of the walls bore cracks and water-damage.

As they approached the front of the building, Catanya curled up her nose at the sudden stench. The smoke rising from the chimney smelled wrong, like whoever was inside was burning rotten eggs and mouldy fish.

Catanya coughed and cast an uneasy glance in Drayk's direction.

Drayk wrinkled his nose and nodded.

Suddenly, the door swung open with a bang, loosening three more wooden planks from the wall. A flock of birds burst from the trees in protest, scattering into the sky.

Catanya's first instinct was to hide from whoever was coming out of the shack, but before she could react, a wizened man hobbled through the doorway. His hair was matted in two large clumps on either side of his head. He wore ripped breaches with a pair of overlarge boots flapping loosely around his calves and a grey tunic, stained with what looked eerily like blood. He held a large, rusted hunting dagger in one hand.

The man didn't seem to notice Catanya and Drayk. He was muttering to himself, and making erratic movements as he began rooting around in front of his house, searching for something.

"Soon, soon, soon. Can't wait around all day. What's taking so long?" He lifted a rock off the floor, held it up to the light, and cast it aside. "Always wanted to go myself, but no, no, no. Not for you." He spoke in a taunting, nasal voice.

"This is the man you've been searching for?" whispered Catanya incredulously. She couldn't believe this frail old man had managed to avoid Drayk and his gang while tramping all across Mórceá on his own.

"Trickery and tomfoolery," grumbled the man as he continued inspecting the rocks outside the cabin. "A daft fool's obsession, huh? What does she know? I proved her wrong, didn't I? Ha! And look at the damage she did. Ungrateful brat took everything then up and died without any thought for my suffering."

"Who is he?" whispered Catanya, watching the man. Something about him seemed familiar to her.

Drayk shrugged. "Nobody," he said.

But Catanya knew that wasn't true. This man was important. It was as if she'd met him before, but couldn't remember.

Drayk kept his hand firmly on the hilt of his sword as he moved closer to the cabin. "Hello," he called, "You there. Can you hear us?" When the man didn't react, Drayk took a step forward and waved, trying to catch his attention.

The man stopped and turned to look at them. His shock changed into anger then resignation in an instant. "Ah, finally. Kept me waiting, didn't you?" he called, stooping down and lifting a rock off the ground. He tossed the stone up and caught it a few times and then, without warning, hurled it at them.

Drayk dodged and Catanya gave a surprised yelp, but the stone just rebounded off a nearby tree and landed in the grass.

"Chasing me all over Mórceá like some kind of bloodhound. Ha!" He cackled and scratched a bald patch on his head. "You actually thought you could find me? Cocky little shit. I remember you, you know? Scared little boy. I watched you walk out there, and make it farther than everyone else... Bet you didn't know that, eh? Bet you didn't know how long I've known."

Drayk looked puzzled. "You watched me do *what*?"

The man gave a sharp cry, brandished his rusty dagger, and charged towards them.

Drayk stepped back automatically, but the man stopped short a few inches away, staring at him with wide eyes darting rapidly. Then he tilted his head. "What makes you so special, eh? Why you?" He glowered at Drayk before turning his gaze to rest on Catanya. His eyes bulged. "And you," he said in a dead voice. He watched her intently for a moment. "You might be the only one who can do it. But what will be left of you when you do? Will you even survive?" He lurched forward again so he was directly in front of her. "I hope not..."

Catanya didn't know whether to run or brace for a fight.

"But all things considered, I suppose I'm glad it's you and

not the other one," he said in a whisper, and Catanya recoiled at the stench of his breath. "And perhaps... I can see a bit of her in your face. But too much poison obscures it..." He heaved a great sigh and stepped away. "Well... I had hoped to get some answers before the end, but we're out of time. And I'm ready. Come along, then." He ambled back to the house, beckoning for them to follow.

Drayk and Catanya stood in stunned silence for a moment.

"What do we do?" whispered Catanya, watching him go.

Drayk shrugged. "Follow him..."

The two of them approached slowly. They pushed open the door and entered the dank, musty cabin. It was only one room, with a crooked fireplace in one corner and various piles of debris scattered across the floor. There were heaps of what looked like old clothes, rusted tools, dilapidated books, and rotten food jumbled together in a mess.

The man sat in a lone chair by the fire, sorting through the nearest mound of debris and tossing items into the flames.

"Have to dispose of a broken lifetime," he called to them without taking his eyes from the flames.

"How long have you been here?" asked Drayk, stepping over what might have been the remains of a deer pelt.

The man didn't respond. Catanya lifted a tattered sack off a nearby table. The fabric crumbled in her fingers.

"Oy," Drayk clapped his hands, trying to get the old man's attention, but he didn't react.

"Drayk!" Catanya gave him a reproachful look. "What are you doing?"

Drayk frowned and shook his head. "You know, I don't think he can hear."

Catanya turned and looked at the man. He stared at the fire, muttering incoherently. She waved at him. "Sir, can you hear us?"

"'Course I can't hear you. I'm deaf," he grumbled.

"Er..." Catanya and Drayk exchanged confused glances. "But you heard me say that?"

"'Course I didn't. Idiot girl. Your mother lay with inbreeds or what?" He snickered at his insult. "Mind you, you'd be better off if she had."

Catanya raised her eyebrows and looked at Drayk for support. "I don't understand."

The old man laughed. "That's an understatement. None of you people ever did. Taking things that weren't yours. Thieves and murderers, that's all you are."

"Well obviously he *can* hear us," said Drayk under his breath.

But Catanya was still watching the old man. "No... I don't think he can hear you... it's only me."

"What?"

Catanya couldn't explain it, but she knew it was true. Then she recognized the sensation. The connection, like a thin rope running between them, tugging at her lungs and heart. It had been there since the delirium dream, pulling her towards this man. But now it was stronger. It tightened in her chest, restricting her breathing.

"Who are you?" she asked.

The old man just sniffed and shrugged. "Map keeper, fool, prodigal castaway... meagre conduit, apparently... But I can't say I'm surprised. Always knew it wasn't meant for me. And I knew one of you would find me, eventually. Your friend there's been chasing me for years. It's been entertaining and exciting evading him, actually. He's a good tracker." He chuckled to himself. "But then there's that troll of a firkon working for her —stupid girl sullied our blood and now she thinks she's entitled to something." He screwed his face up in disgust and spit on the ground. "But I wasn't running from them. No..."

"Who were you running from?" asked Catanya, taking a step closer to him.

The man turned to stare at her, his expression blank. "The dead."

A chill ran through Catanya's body.

"What's he talking about?" asked Drayk.

"I-I don't know," she said, shaking her head.

A cruel smile twisted across the old man's face, exposing his discoloured teeth. "Ha!" he pointed and laughed at them. "You don't even know, do you? Can't you feel them inside you? Itching and scratching away... I heard them..." He gestured at his ears and shrugged. "Never heard nothing again."

The old man launched out of his chair, and for a wild moment, Catanya thought he would charge at them again, but he just yanked something out of his pocket.

"Is this what you want?" he asked, brandishing a worn piece of parchment. "Túir-Avlea? Ha!" He unfolded the parchment and held it out to show them the crudely drawn map on one side. "You think this is the answer to your problems? Resonance? The Natures? Wind, Fire, Water, Earth, and then..." He broke off, shuddering. Then he groaned and rubbed his face with his hand. "I should never have gotten involved," he said in a plaintive voice. "But I thought my family would inherit paradise. Not this dark, distorted world. And now we're so tangled up in it. My daughter... her daughters... you and that other one." He shuddered again. "I should have ended this all years ago. Should have tracked everyone down and slit their throats while they slept. End the bloodline before it was poisoned."

Drayk grabbed Catanya's elbow to get her attention. He shook his head warningly and tightened his grip on his sword. "Give us the map," he said, but the man didn't respond.

Catanya tried to approach, but Drayk tightened his hold on her arm.

"It's okay," she said, trying to reassure him.

"No, it's not," said the old man in a deadly quiet voice. "You're here to kill me."

Catanya stopped moving and stared at him. "No. That's not true. I don't want to hurt you," she said. "Neither of us do."

The old man laughed. "Well, I bet he wouldn't mind getting in a few good blows." He nodded at Drayk and cackled. "A little revenge for the years of torment? Wouldn't that be nice? Ha! I reckon you're entitled after everything I put you through. I gave you a good run there." He chuckled and eyed Drayk with an almost affectionate gleam in his eye. "But you won't get the chance. She's going to kill me. I'll make sure of it."

"No," said Catanya, her heart thumping in her throat.

"Yes," he said, staring into the fire. "You have to. I've been searching for Túir-Avlea my entire life. But now I know I'll never get there. My life never belonged to me. I'm merely a conduit, a tool." He turned the parchment in his fingers and stared at it. "I spent years trying to make it past that shoal, hearing those voices. I can still hear them. And they've grown louder of late, more persistent. They're following me, urging me to find you. You understand? My life means nothing. It never did. All this time, I made sacrifices, believing I was chosen. But I have nothing... So, what do I do now? We're out of time, I have to decide. The conflict is coming, and I can't let him find it. But can I let you?" He gazed at Catanya, like he was sizing her up.

"I could give you the map." He made a move like he wanted to hold the parchment out for her, but stopped. "Although... perhaps I should do something truly meaningful with my life," he whispered more to himself than to them. "After all, it doesn't matter if you're one of them. You're one of his descendants too. Isn't it my duty to protect Mórceá? To protect everyone? Yes. I've finally decided. This is my sacrifice for the greater good." He hung his head and sighed. Then he held the map towards the open flame.

"No!" Drayk launched forward. He grabbed the man's outstretched arm and wrenched him away from the mantle, trying to pry his fingers off the map.

Catanya was aghast. "Drayk, don't hurt him, he's just an old man! Let go!"

But the moment the map left his fingers, the man backed off, looking dazed and angry.

Catanya reached forward, wanting to help him. When she touched him, he let out a bone-chilling scream and recoiled in pain.

"Wrong," he said. "*So wrong.* Can't you feel the connection? Right here." He hammered his fist on his chest and stared at Catanya, tears in his eyes. "Please, just kill me."

"What?" Catanya looked at Drayk for help, but before Drayk could respond, the man lunged at Catanya, taking her completely by surprise and knocking her to the ground.

Catanya gasped in pain as she collided with the hard floor. The baldric on her back pressed painfully into her shoulder blade. And suddenly, the man descended on her, pinning her arms under his legs and trapping her. With a violent anger, he wrapped his bony hands around her neck and started squeezing.

"You thief! You usurper! *Murderer.* Draining it from me, just like he did to them. How can you live with yourself?"

Catanya spluttered and flailed, struggling to breathe. She saw Drayk try to wrench the man off her, but he cast Drayk aside with surprising strength.

Catanya's vision blurred. Drayk reappeared, sword in hand, and he held it to the man's throat.

The man's grip on her neck slackened slightly, but Catanya still struggled to breathe.

"You want to kill me?" he asked, turning to glare at Drayk. "Do it, please. If you kill me instead of her, I might not be trapped." Then, to Catanya's utter shock, he reached up and grabbed the blade, squeezing it until blood streamed between his fingers.

"Go on, kill me!" he cried. "The dead have been calling me my entire life. But I can hear them calling *you* too."

He cackled hysterically and let go of the blade before proceeding to swat at Catanya with his bloodied and tattered hands. "You should be used to the feel of blood on your skin. Your strength was forged in the blood of a million slaughtered souls."

Drayk looked stunned and mortified. In his moment of hesitation, the man started choking Catanya again, this time with more urgency.

"Perhaps I can kill you first," he whispered. "I could save everyone."

Catanya spluttered and flailed on the ground. She couldn't breathe. She was going to die.

The familiar prickling sensation in her fingers arrived just in time. A great surge of power coursed through her.

The man yelped and loosened his grip. Then a blast of energy burst out of her, hurling him off so he crashed against a table and crumpled to the ground in a heap.

Catanya was breathing normally all of a sudden. She felt formidable and powerful as she stood up, facing the room.

Drayk let out a strangled cry of relief. He laughed feebly and re-sheathed his sword.

Catanya relished the sudden rush of strength as she stepped forward to glance down at the man who'd attacked her. Only then did she notice what was wrong.

The man gasped and clutched frantically at his throat. "You see? I told you, you'd kill me," he spluttered. His face darkened, turning red.

"What?" Catanya stared at him, frozen in shock. But then she realized she could feel it. The air had tightened around them. She was pulling the breath out of his body and into her own, compensating for the suffocation he'd inflicted on her.

"Oh no," she muttered as she watched him writhing on the ground. She tried to release the power, but the air just tightened more. Her heart thumped wildly in her chest, and with each breath she took, the air constricted more.

"What do I do?" she gasped, rushing forward and kneeling in front of him. His face was a deep purple colour as he spluttered and gasped on the floor.

Catanya shook out her hands, trying to get the tingling to stop, but nothing happened. She was completely out of control. The prickling in her hands grew stronger, burning up her arms, towards her chest, warming her from the inside.

It felt good. It felt exhilarating.

"No, no, no..." She didn't want to feel that way. She scratched at her chest, searching for any way to stop it. There was nothing, no way to break their connection.

With one last shuddering gasp, the old man lay still.

There was a long pause as Catanya just stared down at him, perplexed and overwhelmed.

Slowly, the power drained from her body. The air loosened and her breathing returned to normal, leaving her weakened—shakier and more fragile than she'd been in a long time. Her vision blurred anew. Her head throbbed, and her throat grated like the stolen air had scorched its way into her lungs.

"Catya," came Drayk's voice. He sounded miles away, but those were his hands trying to pull her to her feet. "Come on, love, let's go."

"But I..." She gestured feebly to the old man. Her muscles shook so violently, she couldn't stand. "We can't just..." She looked down to see the streaks of blood smeared across her front.

"There's nothing we can do," said Drayk in a calm, reassuring voice. He pulled a rag off a nearby chair and began roughly wiping the blood off her. When he finished, he tossed it aside.

"I didn't mean..." Her eyes burned and tears streamed down her face.

"I know, Catya," said Drayk, trying to sound reassuring. "But let's go now. Let's get out of here." He bent down to retrieve the map he'd dropped in all the commotion. He glanced at the page briefly before folding it and slipping it into his pocket. Then he took her arm and gently steered her towards the door, back into the forest.

12

THE RIGHT PERSON

Completely numb, Catanya sat at the foot of her bed, staring at the fire. She listened to Drayk moving around, but she didn't know or care what he was doing. She couldn't even remember how they'd made it back to the fortress.

"I killed him," she said, putting her face in her hands. She didn't know why she was so devastated. This wasn't the first time she'd killed someone. There was that firkon in Finnua, wasn't there? And she'd nearly killed everyone with her powers that night.

"But that was different," she muttered to herself. "I stopped myself that time. Why couldn't I stop this time?"

"Catya." Drayk sounded close. She lowered her hands to find him kneeling in front of her, eyes searching her face.

"I killed him," she repeated, pleading for him to understand.

"It wasn't your fault," he said firmly. "The man was dangerous. He attacked you. You did what you needed to do."

Catanya frowned and stared at Drayk, struggling to understand his words. "I didn't need to kill him," she said.

Drayk shrugged. "I get the sense he wasn't going to give us a choice. You heard him. All that talk about the dead calling him. He wanted us to kill him."

Catanya shook her head and rocked back and forth. "No, you don't understand... I think... maybe..." She couldn't bring herself to say what she was thinking. *Maybe I couldn't stop because a part of me wanted to kill him. Maybe I'm more like Cadyan than I want to admit.*

"You don't need to apologize for protecting yourself, Catanya," said Drayk in an uncharacteristically delicate voice, and she noted that he'd used her full name for the first time.

She turned her eyes to meet his and read the understanding in them.

Someone rapped on the door, and they both started. Drayk sighed and stood up, walking over to see who it was.

"Ah, you've returned." It was Ayr's voice, and her obvious excitement was jarring after everything they'd been through that day. "Did you find it?"

She heard Drayk explaining everything that had happened and she saw him pull the rumpled parchment out of his pocket. But Catanya didn't care about the map anymore.

After a while, the door closed. She looked up to find herself alone with Drayk again.

"Look, Catya," he said with a sudden return of his brusque, cavalier manner. "You need to accept it. Bad things happen. If you think he's the last man you'll have to watch die, well..." He trailed off and shrugged.

Catanya felt suddenly irritable. What happened to the Drayk who understood? The Drayk who was her friend. "Go away," she moaned, putting her face in her hands again. She didn't want to deal with him right now.

"What?" Drayk seemed surprised.

"Just go, please. Leave me alone."

She waited until she heard the door open and close before

kicking off her boots and crawling up into her bed. The tears came as she buried her face into the soft sheets and waited to fall asleep.

She slept poorly that night, haunted by familiar nightmares—and several new ones involving the man in the cabin. No matter what she did, no matter how hard she tried to prevent it from happening, the dreams always ended with the man lying dead at her feet.

She stayed in bed the whole next morning, not moving even when the servants brought food in for her. She just stared at the ceiling, wishing she could sleep for a year. With the covers pulled up over her head, she disappeared into darkness.

It was late in the afternoon when someone knocked on her door.

Catanya grunted, and the door opened to reveal a short, curvy woman with a large scar across her face. Catanya recognized Rey's wife.

"Catya," said Isa, stepping into the room. Catanya grunted again and propped herself up on her elbows. Why was Isa, of all people, here talking to her? They barely knew each other.

"Ayr sent me. She would like you to join her for dinner this evening." She walked over to stand beside the bed. "Catya, you need to get up."

"Go away," groaned Catanya, slumping back down and shutting her eyes. She had no desire to speak with Ayr, or anyone.

"I heard what happened," said Isa in a hard voice. "You should know, the guilt will never go away. It will never fade and it will never leave."

Catanya opened her eyes to stare at her. "Is that supposed to make me feel better?" she asked, even more irritable than she'd been before.

"No. It's just the truth. You will carry your guilt with you every minute of every day for the rest of your life. There is nothing you can do to change that."

"Why are you telling me this?" asked Catanya. She couldn't believe Isa had come here just to make her feel worse.

"Because you need to understand. In Awnell, we are trained to accept the consequences of our actions. You cannot survive in this world if you allow your mistakes to drag you down. You must use them to your advantage. Learn from them, as we have all learned from ours... Do you think you're the only person who ever regretted taking a life? No, we all have our quiet shames, Catya."

Catanya just stared at her, unsure how to respond. Part of her wanted to ask what quiet shames Isa was hiding, but she wasn't sure she wanted to know.

"Now," said Isa, straightening her posture. "You must ask yourself one thing. Are you going to wallow in self-pity until your guilt becomes your identity, or are you going to pick yourself up like a true Awnadh and force yourself to move forward?" She cocked her eyebrow and held her arm out for Catanya. The dim light cast uneven shadows on her scarred face. "Tenacious and loyal, we live for now and we fight for the future."

Catanya considered those words for a moment. Then, with a resigned sigh, she reached out and grabbed Isa's arm.

"Good." The lieutenant smiled, and pulled Catanya to her feet. "Now, clean yourself up, you're a mess." Isa nodded stiffly before leaving to give her some privacy.

Catanya took her time bathing that afternoon. She had come to quite enjoy the hot baths that the servants prepared. They mixed some sort of oil into the warm water, which was soothing on her perennially aching muscles.

She lay in the water for a long time, working through her thoughts.

Isa was right. Catanya couldn't afford to dwell on what had happened. She needed to move forward, but she wasn't entirely sure how. The fact of the matter was she hadn't just made a mistake, she had completely lost control. Her magic had killed someone, and she still didn't know how or why. Was there something wrong with her that she couldn't control it? Or maybe whatever gave her these powers in the first place hadn't worked properly. Maybe there was a reason Cadyan could control them and she couldn't.

Or maybe she just wasn't strong enough to handle it.

And if that was the case, they were all doomed.

After she'd dried and dressed herself, she set off towards Ayr's private chambers for dinner. She was still miserable, but she thought the dinner might at least distract her.

She knocked and was admitted to a surprisingly understated chamber. It comprised a small sitting room, adjoined to a bedchamber with massive windows that overlooked the city. But despite its size, Ayr had barely filled the room with anything. Aside from the wide bed, there was a cluttered desk in the window alcove, a tall wardrobe, two squishy lounge chairs, and a small dining table. The most elaborate item in the room was the large green rug under their feet, which featured intricate yellow weaving and gave the room a warm, inviting ambiance.

"You were expecting something more lavish?" asked Ayr, who was standing by the table, waiting for her. She wore her usual leather military attire, but her hair was twisted and pinned behind her head, like she wanted it out of her way.

"Well, yes, actually," admitted Catanya.

"I have simple tastes," said Ayr. "And I can't see the point of wasting the kingdom's money on pampering myself. Not when there are so many better ways to use it."

"That's very... well, honourable," said Catanya, taking the seat across from Ayr and remembering all the reasons she admired this woman.

"I'm glad you think so."

The door opened and a servant backed in, pulling a trolley. He bustled around for a few minutes, setting the table and pouring them generous helpings of spiced wine. When he finished, Ayr thanked him and he left the room without a word.

"Well, here's to our friendship," said Ayr, raising her glass. "New though it is, I'm sure it will be one for the ages."

Not sure what to say, Catanya just mirrored the queen's gesture and inclined her head.

"Now tell me," said Ayr, lowering her glass and smacking her lips, "how did you enjoy the carnival and the banquet? I've been so busy these last few weeks, I never had time to ask you." She smiled at Catanya as she tucked into her dinner.

Catanya blinked, thrown off by the casual conversation. "Oh... I enjoyed it very much. Yes, the music and the artists, especially." The carnival seemed like a lifetime ago, and it was difficult to recall those carefree memories. Everything felt so different now.

"And after our little chat at the banquet... I'm curious. Did you take my advice about Drayk?" Ayr's eyes twinkled as she watched Catanya.

Catanya choked on her mouthful of wine and coughed. Whatever she had been expecting them to discuss, that hadn't been it. Her face burned with embarrassment. "I... don't... not..."

"Mmm. I take that as a no." Ayr chuckled and shook her head. "Oh, take it from me, Catya, don't be a martyr. I believe your life is challenging enough without taking on unnecessary guilt. I've noticed you have a habit of doing that." She gave Catanya a meaningful look.

Catanya frowned. It annoyed her to have the two situations

compared. "That's different... And I don't feel guilty about Drayk. I just... it's..." But she didn't know what it was.

Ayr took another sip of wine. "Life is too short to worry about what other people want. I've learned that the hard way many times. If you don't take what you want in life, you will lose it." Her voice sounded bitter and resolute.

Catanya didn't know what to say. She wanted to disagree, but she found there was a certain amount of truth in Ayr's words. That realization made her uneasy.

After a few moments of awkward silence, Catanya found her voice again. "Well, I doubt you invited me to dinner just to discuss Drayk."

Ayr chuckled. "No, you're right. I'm sorry. Forgive my curiosity." Ayr took a moment before she continued. She seemed to be choosing her words carefully. "Tell me, what do you know about the legend of Túir-Avlea?"

Weary, Catanya scratched her forehead. "The children's story about the lost mountain?" she asked. A part of her still thought Drayk was joking about the map, but it seemed Ayr was going to pursue the same ridiculous theory. Catanya couldn't help feeling resentful that everything they'd gone through yesterday was to retrieve something so ludicrous. A map to Túir-Avlea.

Ayr clicked her tongue impatiently. "It's hardly a children's story. It is a legend. And it's as true as any other."

"Right, but legends aren't true, are they?" said Catanya.

Ayr raised her eyebrows. "Aren't they?" she asked with a lingering pause. Then she stood up and crossed to the desk in the corner. She lifted the parchment and held it up, turning to face Catanya. "This map shows the path to Túir-Avlea," she said as calmly as if she'd said it was a map of Awnell.

Catanya stared at her in disbelief. "You can't be serious. Túir-Avlea isn't real. It's just a story, a simple story to give hope to little children."

"And what does the story tell them?" asked Ayr, unfolding the parchment in her hands and staring at it, her face full of wonder. Then she looked back at Catanya expectantly.

"Oh, come on, you know the story."

Ayr smiled. "I do, but I would like to hear you tell it."

Catanya heaved a great sigh, halfway between amusement and exasperation. "Okay," she said, standing up to join Ayr by the desk. "Well, legend has it that, before the dawn of the kingdoms, before the Quiescence Wars and the loss of Resonance, there lived a powerful practitioner named Illayan."

It wasn't her most enthusiastic telling of the story. When she'd recounted it to the girls at the lodge, she'd used a lot more description and dramatic emphasis. But Ayr wasn't a child, and Catanya was too tired to take this seriously.

"Illayan lived in the great city of Bratia where he communed with the Natures and crafted some of the most potent magical relics of all time, each with their own unique power. Students flocked from all over Mórceá, desperate to study with him, and learn the secrets of Resonance. But Illayan was very guarded with his knowledge. He shared his wisdom with only the worthiest few.

"And as they say in Caerlon: just when Illayan was about to give up his practice—when the Fire had left his soul, and the Wind had dried the Water from his skin—the Earth gave a mighty shudder. This is when a young boy arrived in Bratia. Illayan's last and greatest student. The one who would grow up to become Maílater Caer."

Ayr gave a derisive snort, but motioned for Catanya to continue her story.

"Illayan took the boy under his wing and taught him everything he knew, training him harder than any other practitioner. And it wasn't long before the student surpassed the master. Years later, when the abuse of Resonance ran rampant, and the Quiescence Wars began, the student sought his old teacher's guidance. But Illayan refused to relinquish his final secret, the secret behind his mystical relics. He opposed Caer's mission to cleanse Mórceá of Resonance, and this led to conflict.

"When the army came to quash his rebellion, Illayan hid his relics and escaped to the mountains with a group of loyal students. There, he invoked the Natures to hide his community and shield them from harm. Using the last of his Resonance, Illayan detached the entire mountain from the earth and carried it out, beyond the borders of the emerging kingdoms.

"They say the mountain, Túir-Avlea, has remained a safe haven for all those who still possess magic. The combined power of all its inhabitants keeps it hidden and its people safe and free. According to legend, they will re-emerge when magic has been returned to Mórceá."

"Mmm..." Ayr nodded, a slightly manic gleam in her eye. "Resonance," she said.

"Right. But it's just a fable—a folk tale. It can't be true."

"And why not?"

Catanya opened her mouth to retort, but a sharp knock on the door interrupted her.

Ayr exhaled heavily, folding the map and returning it to her pocket. "Excuse me, I'm afraid there are rather a lot of things happening at the moment." She walked over to the door, and opened it to reveal Rey.

"Forgive the intrusion," he said in a hurried voice. They descended into a hushed conversation about something Catanya couldn't hear.

The distraction suited Catanya. She was rankled and she wanted a minute to think. Why was everyone so willing to believe these stories about Túir-Avlea? Ayr and Drayk were both intelligent, strategic thinkers. So why were they both so willing to accept this?

She glanced around, and her eyes fell on the pile of papers scattered on Ayr's desk. Curiosity nudged her frustration aside.

Catanya moved closer under the pretext of looking out the window. Out of the corner of her eye, she scanned the papers. Assorted bills, a few rolled-up maps, and what appeared to be an official notice, sealed and stamped. She was about to turn away when two smaller papers caught her attention.

The letters Ayr had received two days ago.

Catanya glanced behind her to make sure Ayr wasn't looking, then she leaned in closer to inspect them. They jutted out of the pile at odd angles, so she could only make out snippets of writing.

... been ready for weeks, but you were right, my queen...

The handwriting on the first letter was sloppy, like it had been written in a hurry

... taking the Murbanya... slow... should give you a few days.

Catanya remembered Jémys talking about the *Murbanya*. It was supposed to be the largest ship ever built, but she thought it was chartered to Caerlon... Why did Ayr care about it?

Catanya glanced over her shoulder. Ayr was engrossed in her discussion with Rey, so Catanya chanced a closer look at the papers.

The second letter was written in a much neater, loopier handwriting.

... offense, my dear, I was merely trying to offer my guidance, but I'll do as you instruct. The first shipment will arrive within the week, and I'll wait to receive word before sending the second. I hope you know what you're doing.

"Very well," came Ayr's voice from the doorway. "Thank you, Rey, that's all for now."

Catanya turned to see the queen walking to join her as Rey left.

"Ah, forgive the mess," said Ayr, scooping up the papers from her desk and rifling through them. Then she walked over to the fire and tossed them unceremoniously into the flames. "I should know better than to keep such useless clutter." She smiled at the surprised look on Catanya's face. "Come, sit." She gestured to the dinner table. "You must be starving."

As they took their seats at the table again, Ayr pulled the map back out from her pocket. "So, where were we?" she asked, sliding the parchment along the table to Catanya.

Catanya took the map and held it up to the candlelight.

She hadn't had time to examine it in the cabin. It appeared to depict an island, perched in the middle of the vast ocean somewhere far off the coast. The island encompassed a large solitary mountain right in the centre.

Catanya's mouth went very dry.

"This looks familiar," she thought aloud. She remembered a night several months ago... A night when she'd stood on the shoreline, staring out at the hazy form of a distant mountain. A mountain only she could see.

"Really?" Ayr sounded intrigued.

"What language is this?" Catanya pointed to the cramped writing in the corner.

"It is ancient Awnle," said Ayr, taking the map back. "Few people still understand it today, other than me, of course." She grinned at Catanya as she pulled a lead pencil out of her pocket and began scratching translations on the page. Then she read the words aloud.

> *The harkened pain and sorrow,*
> *With resounding aches of defeat,*
> *Shows delusions of yearning*
> *To burn and scold at innocence*

> *Like bitter truth that bites*
> *The years of tart neglect,*
> *Whose jagged fear cracks and grinds,*
> *Paring down to soothe the dread,*
> *Where balms of closing breaths*
> *Respire their final essence.*

When she finished, she turned her eyes towards Catanya, who was staring at the page, lost for words.

"What does it mean?" asked Catanya in a hushed voice.

"I was hoping you could tell me. What do you think it means?"

Catanya frowned and took the parchment from Ayr, tracing the words with her hand. "I think... I think it's a set of instructions," she said, surprising even herself. "But it's more than that, actually... I think it's a lesson of some sort. I think whoever wrote this was trying to teach us something—to test us." She didn't know how, but she knew what she said was true. "What do these other words mean?" she asked, indicating the labels written above the map in specific areas.

"Ah, yes." Ayr nodded. "Those are names of places, steps along the journey." She gestured for Catanya to lay the map down, and then she pointed to the first label. "The Windy Shoal," she read, scratching the translated name just beneath it.

Catanya glanced at the picture, frowning. The images were quite rough, but she supposed it could be a depiction of a sandbar.

"The Burning Cove." Ayr slid her finger along the image. "The Reflecting Channel, the Shrouded Caves, and, finally"— she translated the last label and tossed her pencil aside—"the Dead Wood."

"Dead Wood," repeated Catanya, shivering as a chill swept over her body.

"Yes... Perfectly spine-tingling, isn't it?" asked Ayr with a wide grin.

Catanya let out a shaky laugh as she lifted the map back up, examining it from all angles. She could tell the age of the parchment from one touch. It was coarse and unevenly stretched, with blemishes on the edges. It was handcrafted, likely from calf skin. Nothing like the cheap, mass-produced vellum that came from Elma these days.

"So, how did you learn about this map?" she asked, hearing the awe in her voice.

"Mmm..." Ayr took a sip of her wine and leaned forward, resting her arms on the table. "It began as an idle story I heard as a young woman. The person who told me—one of my lovers at the time—she must not have expected me to listen, much less believe the story so strongly that I'd spend decades of my life and countless resources trying to locate the map." Ayr snorted and downed the rest of her wine in one gulp. "Never underestimate the power of curiosity and tenacity," she said.

Catanya laughed. If Ayr had tracked this map down based on nothing but a rumour she'd heard as a young woman, she was infinitely more determined and intelligent than anyone Catanya had ever met.

"So, what are you planning to do with it?" she asked.

"Well, I had always assumed I'd go there myself. I'd be the one to finally find the lost mountain, *Túir-Avlea*, but now I think... perhaps it is not meant for me." She spoke slowly, watching Catanya for a reaction. "Your encounter with that man in the cabin has led me to believe that this map"—she tapped the parchment in Catanya's hand—"won't take just anybody to its destination. I believe it has been waiting for the right person."

"The right person," repeated Catanya. Her hands shook, rattling the page. The man in the cabin had tried to burn the map rather than let Catanya take it. He'd seemed so determined to protect its secrets, so frightened of what Catanya would do…

She couldn't be the right person, could she?

"Oh, yes." Ayr smiled again. "I can't say I'm not a little disappointed, but I expect this will turn out for the best."

Before Catanya could say anything, the door burst open and Isa rushed inside, flushed and panting.

"Ayr! It's happening. The city is under attack!"

13

A BATTLE

Ayr sprang to her feet in an instant.

"They've taken out the sentries on the western escarpment," said Isa. "They're advancing on the city as we speak."

"Caerlon?" said Ayr, and her voice was eerily calm.

"Yes."

Ayr launched into action. "Alert the commander. Notify the outlying villages. Start moving people from the city into the stronghold. It will take a great deal more than an army to break these walls."

Almost on cue, the wind outside began to howl violently, rattling the windows and ripping at the shudders. A torrential rain burst down upon the fortress.

From somewhere deep within the fortress, they heard a deafening crash, followed by the sound of screaming.

"That's not possible." Isa sounded terrified.

Catanya's breath caught in her throat. A storm like this could only mean one thing.

"He is here, then," said Ayr, nodding. For a brief moment, Catanya thought she detected triumph on the queen's face, but then Ayr turned to address her lieutenant, her expression all steely resolve. "We have to hurry, Isa. Find Rey and send him to me, then report back to Lia."

Isa took a deep breath, nodded stiffly, and hurried out the door.

"Come with me, Catya." Ayr rushed to the trunk by her bed and thrust it opened to reveal a small cache of weapons. "Arm yourself," she said, grabbing a leather baldric from the top and fastening it around her shoulder.

Catanya didn't need telling twice. She pulled out a matching baldric and an ornate sword. It had a broad, slightly curved blade, with Awnle script etched down one side. The pommel and hilt were bound with leather, which formed perfectly to Catanya's hand. She flung the baldric over her back and tightened the strap before sliding the sword inside.

"Where are we going?" she asked, hurrying to keep up with Ayr.

"To the western tower. I need to assess the damage." Ayr snatched the map off the table where Catanya had left it, folded it hastily, and shoved it into her pocket as she ran out the door.

They hurried through the shadowy corridors together. Catanya tried to catch a glimpse out the windows, but all she saw was darkness. Another loud bang shook the floors beneath them. Catanya paused, bending her knees to keep from falling. But Ayr kept moving without so much as a waver. Catanya raced to catch up.

They turned the corner into the west wing, and a horrifying sight met their eyes.

The outer wall of the fortress had been blown apart, leaving a gaping hole and a sheer drop to the mayhem below. The entire western bank of the city was alight with bright orange flames that flickered as swarms of arrows flew through the sky. A great host of soldiers teemed through the streets. The vivid gold and violet of their uniforms shone through the night like harbingers of death. And everywhere, people were running, screaming.

There was another resounding crash, and Catanya stumbled. She grabbed hold of a torch bracket to stop from falling through the hole in the wall.

"What was that?" she asked, terrified. But her question was soon answered. Soaring through the sky with the ease of a bird was an enormous stone slab—the same glistening black stone that formed the city. It hurtled through the air and crashed down upon the western bank, crushing at least ten people.

"He just killed his own men too!" shouted Catanya, aghast. She watched as another even larger stone was ripped from the earth with a terrible shudder and sent careening towards the front gate.

The subsequent crash sent a reverberation throughout the fortress that threatened to bring down the already weakened walls.

"I don't believe he cares who lives and who dies." Ayr's voice was dripping with disgust as she watched another stone soar through the air and shatter against the western bank. "Not as long as he gets what he wants." She shook her head. "Come on." She grabbed Catanya by the hand and pulled her along the corridor towards the staircase at the end.

They climbed the stairs two at a time and burst into the cold night air, atop the tower. Dozens of Awnadh archers were already in position, sending targeted arrows at the firkon on the ground. Despite their exceptional speed and aim, they were outnumbered and outmatched. It would only take Cadyan a flick of his wrist to bring the entire tower down.

Catanya's attention was drawn towards the ocean. She turned slowly to watch three massive ships emerge through the fog and hover in the deep waters just offshore. The pale moonlight shimmered through the mist that hung in the air like phantom dust, and the ships loomed over the bay as daunting grey spectres.

"He's out there," she said in a hollow voice, nodding towards the water. "He's on one of those ships, I know it. I can feel it."

Catanya's head suddenly throbbed, and the pain made her stomach churn. She could sense the force of Cadyan's power bearing down upon the fortress, bearing down on her. Ayr shouted something at her side, but Catanya couldn't understand it. She couldn't make out the words. The weight of the surrounding air was pressing in and suffocating her. She was drowning.

Not again, she thought. *Not here, not these people too.* She fell to her knees, clutching her head in her hands. The sound of screaming poured into her until it was all she knew. The screams of these people here, the screams of everyone in Finnua, and Faltir.

"Catya! Stop, stop!" Someone grabbed her hands and pried them away from her face. Suddenly, the screaming stopped and Catanya realized it had been coming from her.

"Get up!" shouted Drayk, trying to pull her to her feet. "Get up and fight!"

"I can't," she said numbly. Tears poured down her face, and she trembled from limb to limb. "I'll only make it worse. Everything I do makes things worse. I can't..."

"You have to. Hey!" He shook her violently, trying to get her attention. When she still didn't respond, he smacked her hard on the face.

"Ow!" She clutched her cheek, glowering at him.

"Well, pull yourself together," he said. "If you don't do something, we're all going to die."

Catanya looked around, wide-eyed, and realized that in the few minutes since she'd lost focus, the battle had gotten much worse. Several soldiers were lying dead on the tower around them. Ayr called orders to her remaining fighters as another boulder flew through the sky and collided with the south tower, reducing it to rubble.

"You have to do something," said Drayk in a quieter voice. "You have to." He squeezed her hand and helped her to her feet.

Catanya's legs shook as she crept towards the parapet. She could see the entire city laid out below, and all the people still trapped in it. Her mind raced, trying to think of something she could do to help. The wind howled around them again and the tower swayed precariously beneath their feet. Chaos continued, pouring into Catanya's mind and drowning every thought but one: Cadyan had to be stopped.

The powers she loathed—the powers that had burned so out of control yesterday, draining the life from an old man— scorched through her body anew. Catanya didn't try to fight them. She breathed in the fear and the fury, relinquishing her sense of self.

Catanya stared through the storm at the ships on the bay, and her vision burned gold. She needed to do something. At least this was something she'd done before, albeit not to this degree.

Catanya lifted her hands in front of her and began pushing them back and forth, imagining the movement of the waves.

"Cover her," hollered Ayr to the remaining Awnadh on the tower. The archers turned their bows to eliminate anyone with a clear line of sight. Arrows hissed past Catanya with incredible speed. The archers' hands were mere blurs as they loosed and reloaded their weapons with unrelenting vigour.

Please let this work, she thought urgently. *And please let me have the strength to stop.*

A scream rent the air, and the archer closest to her tumbled over the parapet, a flaming arrow through his heart. Catanya watched him fall and knew in that moment that it didn't matter.

It didn't matter if she had the strength to stop. Death and destruction were in the air, whether they came at her hands or at Cadyan's.

Catanya focused her mind on the water and imagined forcing it back from the shore, leaving the ships behind. She urged the water to move, and she could feel the weight of it pushing back at her, but she didn't relent. She squared her shoulders and heaved.

It took every ounce of strength she had, but eventually the shoreline began to extend farther out to sea. The tide retreated slowly, leaving the ships behind in increasingly shallow, muddy water. The vessels teetered and threatened to fall.

Catanya closed her eyes and focused on pushing the water still farther out to sea. Her arms seized, and she cried out in pain, shaking uncontrollably. It was as if every fibre in her body, every muscle, tendon, and ligament, was being pulled from her bones. Her feet slipped on the stones as she struggled to stay upright.

She couldn't hold on any longer.

With an inarticulate shout, she gathered one final, excruciating force and hurled. When she released her hold, she collapsed against the parapet, her entire body shaking and burning with pain. She opened her eyes in time to watch an enormous tidal wave cascade over the tops of the ships, engulfing them and tearing their masts apart. Crippled and bursting at their seams, the ships were finally dragged down by the overpowering weight of the sea.

The violent winds suddenly stopped and the flames in the streets died.

But as Catanya looked out over the city, she realized it wasn't enough. The firkon were still moving, barrelling through the streets and forcing the Awnadh to retreat. The entire western bank was in ruins, and the fortress continued to hemorrhage stones, weakening its structure. Catanya tried to stand, but she collapsed from the exertion. Her grip on the parapet was the only thing keeping her from falling.

"That won't stop him," she said, feeling nauseated. She could still sense his power in the air, dimmer, but still active. "It'll only slow him down for a few minutes." Her legs slipped and Drayk grabbed her by the waist to help her stand.

Just then, Isa and Rey charged up the stairs and burst onto the tower.

"My queen." Rey strode over to join her. "The eastern city has been evacuated, and the south is nearly done. But I'm afraid the west is lost."

"We can't win this," said Isa. "Not this time. Not with him out there."

"I know," said Ayr, nodding. She closed her eyes and took a deep breath. "Very well, Isa, you know what to do." Her eyes snapped open, and they burned with a sudden, renewed clarity. "Go find the commander and tell her it's time. Lia won't be happy, but tell her to enact retreat protocols. I'm relying on you. I trust you." She grabbed Isa's arm momentarily in hers and inclined her head in salute. Then she turned to address Rey. "Hold them off as long as you can." She took Rey's arm just as she had done Isa's, nodded soberly, then released him and walked away.

Catanya watched Isa and Rey exchange grave looks. They ran forward and embraced each other only briefly before breaking apart and continuing in their respective assignments from Ayr.

Catanya wanted to ask what those assignments were, but she was still having trouble standing and she was afraid if she spoke, she'd retch.

"Drayk," said Ayr, moving to stand in front of him. "Now is the hour when you must decide. Will you do what I've asked you to do?"

Drayk looked sidelong at Catanya. Then he turned back to Ayr and nodded.

"Good. Then, Catya," Ayr turned to face her, "you must go." She reached into her pocket and withdrew the map, holding it out for her.

"What? No, I need to stay and help," protested Catanya, pushing away from Drayk and standing up. Her legs shook, but they managed to hold her weight.

"There's nothing more you can do. Awnell will fall tonight, and we cannot afford to lose you. You are our only hope of ending all this."

"But—"

"Do not argue with me," snapped Ayr, holding up her hand to stop Catanya. "You must trust me when I say that certain battles must be lost in order to win the war. This is one of those battles."

There was a loud crash somewhere below them. The sound of shouting voices grew louder.

"But I can't just walk away," said Catanya, looking at Drayk for support.

"I'm not telling you to walk away," said Ayr, shaking her head. "But you need to learn to control your powers. Tonight was a good start, but there is only one place where you will truly learn what you need to win this war. You must find Túir-Avlea."

"But it's a myth!" shouted Catanya. In her frustration, her strength faltered again. She grabbed Drayk's shoulder to steady herself.

"I don't believe that," declared Ayr, thrusting the map into Catanya's hand. "And neither, I think, do you. Trust your instincts, Catya. They are the instincts of a queen." She nodded encouragingly at her. "Until we meet again," she said. Then she turned and strode through the door, back down the stairs into the fortress.

Numb and helpless, Catanya just watched her go. Her mind and body were drained, and she couldn't understand half of what was happening around her. Ayr believed she had a queen's instincts, but in this moment, Catanya had never felt less like a leader.

"Come on." Drayk wrapped her arm around his shoulder and steered her towards the staircase.

They half-ran, half-stumbled down the stairs and through the corridor towards the eastern wing. The floors shook under the weight of thousands of feet stampeding through the halls. The battle had made its way inside and everywhere they turned, they saw soldiers fighting. Dozens of bodies were strewn across the floor, and Catanya couldn't tell whether they were friends or enemies.

She was struggling to stay conscious. With every step she took, a shock ran through her bones, aggravating her already aching body. Her eyes slid in and out of focus and she could feel Drayk struggling to support her weight.

They turned a corner and found their way suddenly barred by two massive firkon. Drayk swore loudly and let go of Catanya to fight.

Catanya fell against the wall. All of her training fled from her mind, so the sword on her back was useless. She slid onto the ground, shattered, watching as Drayk fought alone.

She wanted to help him, but couldn't. When she tried to stand, she just slid farther down the wall. Drayk twisted and turned, blocking the firkon's attacks, but his body was nothing but a blur to Catanya. There was a flash of metal and someone hit the floor. Catanya squinted through the fog, but she couldn't tell who it was.

Another thud rocked the ground.

"Catya!" Drayk's face appeared in front of her. He was sweating and breathing heavily, with blood splattered across his front, but otherwise, he seemed fine. "Come on." He wrapped his arm around her again and hoisted her back to her feet. "Can you walk?" he asked.

Catanya nodded and leaned on him as he led the way onwards.

They came to an abrupt stop outside a door and Drayk pushed it open. Catanya steadied herself on the doorframe. She was still faint and disoriented, but as she looked around the room, she realized they were inside Drayk's chambers.

She needed to focus on something concrete. "Ayr... What did you tell her you'd do?" she asked numbly, pulling her arm out of Drayk's grasp.

"I promised her I would go with you," said Drayk. He eyed her to make sure she wasn't about to fall, then he ran into the room.

"What? Why?" Her mind was still fuzzy, but she wanted answers.

"Do I need to have a reason?" he asked as he began rummaging through one of his wardrobes.

"Yes, I think you do," murmured Catanya, slurring her words. She pressed her forehead against the wall and let the cool stone soothe her aching head. She turned her gaze to survey Drayk.

Drayk shook his head as he pulled two cloaks from the wardrobe and tossed one to her. Then he yanked two travel bags off the door, stuffed them with food from his table, and ran to meet her. "We need to hurry." He pulled her arm back over his shoulder and continued down the corridor.

They pushed deeper into the fortress, struggling to avoid the chaos, and hurtled down two flights of stairs. They finally stopped at the foot of an old wooden staircase in an area Catanya didn't recognize.

"I don't understand," she said, as she pulled away from Drayk, using the railing to keep herself steady. "You knew about Túir-Avlea this whole time and you said nothing?"

"Yes. Well, no... I mean, sort of." Drayk was shaking his head as he looked around frantically. "It should be here somewhere..." He was muttering to himself and pacing back and forth, examining the wall. Then he started running his hands along the wood panelling under the stairs. "It's been so long since... Aha!"

There was a faint click, and the panel swung open to reveal a narrow tunnel leading underground. "This will take us out to the eastern shore beyond the ridge," he explained, brushing away the cobwebs that covered the entrance. He poked his head through, wrinkling his nose at the musty smell. "No one will see us. The original Verratrí created these tunnels to conceal their movements in and out of Awnell," he added. He grabbed a torch off the wall beside him and hoisted himself up into the entrance. "Are you coming?" He held out his hand for her.

Another booming crash prompted Catanya to look behind her. She knew that, somewhere above them, Cadyan had resumed his destruction of the city. Her legs wobbled, and she tightened her grip on the stairs. She felt her breathing constrict as fear and envy twisted inside her. It was all so much easier for Cadyan. His powers didn't overwhelm him. He didn't fall apart whenever he used them...

Cadyan was going to decimate this beautiful city without breaking a sweat.

"If you stay, we all die," said Drayk quietly. He was watching her closely and seemed to understand what she was thinking.

Catanya finally met his gaze, wishing she could disagree. But he was right. There was nothing she could do to stop Cadyan tonight.

"We have to go," Drayk insisted.

Catanya took a deep breath and nodded. As she took Drayk's hand and followed him into the tunnel, she made a silent promise.

Never again.

Never again would she be forced to flee, leaving people she cared about behind. Never again would she find herself too weak and incompetent to fight.

She clutched the musty bit of parchment in her pocket. The map to Túir-Avlea. If the legendary place truly existed, Catanya was determined to find it.

14

A LIE

I t was chaos everywhere as Ayr hurtled down the main stairs and back towards the entrance hall.

"Get to the keep!" she shouted as she ran past the bottleneck of terrified people scrambling to push through the front doors. Although everyone in the kingdom had been trained to fight, most people in the city were recessed—out of practice. And Ayr had enacted retreat protocols, requiring half her active warriors to withdraw and fall back amongst the civilians. It was a risky manoeuvre, but it was a strategic gamble. It had to work.

Despite the protocols, the corridors were still crammed with swirls of red and gold as the Awnadh men fought to keep the enemy at bay.

She heard someone cry out and turned to see a young boy cowering on the ground beneath his attacker. Without hesitation, Ayr drew her sword and blocked the firkon's path.

"Run!" she called to the boy. She whirled her sword through the air with speed and precision, and the soldier had no time to react. She struck him down where he stood. But before his body reached the ground, three more attackers emerged from the crowd to continue his fight.

Ayr twisted and spun with such ease and grace that her movements felt dance-like. She'd honed her body for this, training every day. She always knew where her assailants would strike before they'd even begun. Within seconds, she'd knocked one unconscious and killed another. But a brief moment's distraction allowed the third man to strike. Hot pain grazed her side as his sword slashed her arm. She stumbled backwards into the wall and cried out in rage.

Without waiting, she kicked off from the wall and leapt into the air. Torchlight reflected in the firkon's eyes as he realized, too late, what was about to happen. Ayr's sword slashed down upon him. His shock still lingered on his face as his head fell to the ground with a dull thud.

Ayr barely paused before launching through the mass of people towards the throne room.

When she arrived, the room was in ruins. She manoeuvred through the piles of bodies, looking for any survivors. Three pillars had collapsed, causing sections of the ceiling to cave in. The remnants of a once beautiful fresco littered the floor like gruesome confetti, and a torch had fallen over, igniting the tapestries along the rear wall.

Something grabbed her foot. Ayr braced for attack, but, looking down, she saw one of Cadyan's men lying half dead on the floor, gazing up at her imploringly.

"Please," he spluttered. "Help me."

She stared down at him. He was young, no older than eighteen. His body was broken and mangled beyond repair, and there was fear in his eyes—the kind of fear only experienced by someone near death. Ayr shook her head and brought her sword down in one swift flash of steel. The man lay still.

"I don't think that's the type of help he was looking for," said an oily voice behind her.

Ayr's body stiffened. She turned slowly to watch Cadyan's maífírkon saunter along the aisle towards her. His uniform was spotless, unsullied by battle. It filled her with rage.

"It was the only help I could give," she said, tightening her grip on her sword.

Slaedir stopped in front of his now dead soldier and clicked his tongue. "Such a pity. He was so young, one of the newest recruits. I think his name was Earnin, or Nirnin—something like that. But no matter. He played his part." Slaedir shrugged and stepped over the soldier's corpse to stand in front of Ayr. "Where is she?" he asked.

"Where is who?"

"Don't insult me," he said. "You know who I'm talking about. Now I'll ask again, where is she?"

Ayr smirked and said nothing.

"Come on, woman. Your kingdom is in shambles, you're hurt." He indicated her wounded arm. "You can't fight me. I'm the best warrior in Mórceá. Even on your best day, you'd be no match for me."

"Is that so?" said Ayr, amused by his ignorant presumption. She spun her wrist so her sword twirled in an arc at her side. Then she brought it to a halt, pointed directly at him. "Prove it."

Slaedir laughed in her face. "Fine," he said, drawing his own weapon. The ostentatious gold inlay gleamed in the fire-light as he pointed its tip towards her.

They stood perfectly still, locked in mirror image for what felt like ages. Ayr took slow, measured breaths to maintain her calm and clear her mind. But Slaedir looked restive and eager, like he was struggling to contain his excitement.

The burning tapestries along the walls bathed the room in hot, orange light. Out of the corner of her eye, Ayr noticed the flames spreading across the rubble and bodies on the floor.

"This is foolish," said Slaedir. "War is not a woman's trade.

Neither is ruling a kingdom. I'll teach you your place." He gave a lecherous grin and lunged.

But Ayr's reflexes were too fast. She met his blade with her own and whipped it out of her way without yielding her position. Slaedir stumbled back, his arrogance slipping.

"You were saying?" she asked with a smile, ignoring the aching pain from her wounded arm and the flames inching towards them.

Slaedir straightened up and advanced again, this time with more focus. Ayr met his blade with equal force, and they began to circle one another. Again and again, Slaedir attacked and Ayr parried, delighting in watching his frustration consume him. The angrier he became, the more viciously he fought.

The clanging of metal reverberated off the remaining stone pillars. Slaedir's blade sliced through the air so fast, at times the metal became a blur.

He swept his arm straight through the air, as if to decapitate her, but Ayr ducked, avoiding the blow.

She laughed as she righted herself. "It seems your skill has been grossly exaggerated," she taunted. "Or perhaps you've just gotten slow with age? Don't be embarrassed. After all, not everyone can expect to age with the grace of a queen." She brandished her arms to indicate her own muscular form, then winked at him and lunged.

"Shut your mouth," he growled, dodging her attack with a surprisingly graceful pivot. "You want to talk about getting slow?" he asked, dodging another swing. "Well, you're supposed to be this great leader, aren't you? But you didn't even notice a spy living in your city. I was here for weeks—*weeks*! And you never knew. Ha! You think you're so clever, but I bested you. And I told Cadyan everything he needed to know. My actions brought your kingdom to its knees."

Ayr laughed again. "Oh, Slaedir, you really are naïve, aren't you?"

"What's that supposed to mean?"

Ayr gave him a pitying smile. "Of course I knew you were here!" she exclaimed with a laugh. "But stopping you or killing you... it wouldn't have made any difference. Do you honestly think your presence here had any *real* impact on Cadyan's decision to invade?" She waited for Slaedir to catch up with her, but he didn't seem to grasp her implication. "Think about it. Why would Cadyan send his maífírkon—supposedly his most important soldier—to spy on another kingdom? Surely that's a job for some lesser fírkon... Someone the king doesn't need or want in his city with him. Someone... *disposable*."

Slaedir's face turned an angry purple colour and he lunged again. Ayr blocked his attack with a rapid parry.

"He just wanted you out of his way!" she jeered. "He *wanted* me to catch you and kill you! After all the years you tormented him as a child, he longs to watch you suffer the same slow, painful death as Casréyan. Trust me, he would have invaded Awnell with or without you. He just hoped your death would give him an excuse. And you'd do something useful for once. He doesn't trust you. Certainly not with anything important."

Slaedir snorted. "Cadyan's an ignorant little boy. He knows less about ruling than you do."

Ayr clicked her tongue in mock disapproval. "Now, now. You mustn't speak about your king with such disrespect."

Impatient, Slaedir slashed out and Ayr spun around, elbowing him in the back so he stumbled and fell to the floor. When he sprang back to his feet, he was clutching a chunk of stone debris in his hand. He hurled it at her.

Ayr reacted just in time, but the jagged rock still grazed her arm, aggravating her wound. When she turned around, Slaedir was in front of her again. He jabbed his sword out, but she dodged it. She grasped his arm with her free hand, smashing it down against her knee.

He cried out in pain. Ayr cast him aside, but as he staggered, he kicked her legs, nearly tripping her.

A sudden violent shudder rocked the floor and the walls. Bangs and shouts echoed in the hallway. Momentarily distracted, Slaedir dropped his guard.

Ayr brought her weapon through the air, deliberately slicing down inches from his cheek, nicking his ear, and stopping just before hitting his shoulder. His eyes bulged in fear, and she laughed. Then she flicked her wrist so the flat steel slapped his face and he stumbled, looking outraged and humiliated.

Ayr laughed again and lowered her sword, sliding it back into its scabbard.

"What are you doing?" snarled Slaedir, confused. "Fight me!"

"No," said Ayr. She strode over to her throne and sat down, crossing her foot over her knee and watching the curtain of flames swell along the walls. "Tell me, Slaedir, what is the point of you?" she asked, looking him up and down with abhorrence. "You may be a decent fighter, but you're a poor excuse for a military mind. Your king hates you, and your firkon don't even respect you. How can you expect anyone to take you seriously?"

Slaedir's face flushed. He opened and closed his mouth several times, evidently struggling to find a retort. "The king trusts me," he said lamely.

Ayr laughed outright. "You really believe that?"

Slaedir scowled at her. "When Cadyan learns that I've beaten you, and brought him his sister's head, I'll be rewarded."

"But you haven't beaten me," said Ayr, stroking the arms of her throne.

"Look around you, woman!" shouted Slaedir. "You have nothing left but your arrogance. Now tell me where the girl is and maybe I won't kill you. Where is she?"

Ayr leaned forward, letting the heat of the approaching fire warm her face. "Gone," she said with satisfaction.

Slaedir gaped at her. "What do you mean 'gone'?"

"It's a simple word. I should have thought even you would understand it. I mean, the woman you're looking for is *gone*." She smiled even wider at the horror on Slaedir's face.

"She can't be," he said. "We have the entire city blocked. There's no way she escaped without us finding her."

Ayr cackled and reclined in her seat, feeling nonchalant and amused. The flames spread from the tapestries behind her, creeping across the bodies on the floor towards the throne. But Ayr wasn't concerned. The flames flickered and licked at the body nearest her, and an idea formed in her head.

"I can assure you, Maífirkon," she said, "my kingdom and my fortress have more secrets than your insipid brain can even imagine. Did you really think I wouldn't have a way to evacuate her safely?" Ayr gave him a pitying look and shook her head. "Oh dear, dear, dear... How many times have you let her escape, now? Is it four or five? I can't imagine Cadyan will be too happy with you." She gave an affected sigh. "Poor Slaedir. Growing more useless every day, aren't you?"

"Shut up!" he snapped, his face flushed and his eyes bulging in panic.

"Well, at least your shame won't last long. I'm sure, in his anger, Cadyan will make it quick. Probably not painless... No. But quick. Who do you bet will be maífirkon next?" she asked, as if she were just making pleasant conversation. She savoured the moment as outrage overtook his features.

"I said, shut up!" Slaedir bellowed. He took an angry step and nearly tripped over the rubble.

Ayr fought the urge to laugh.

"Well..." She feigned a pensive expression. "You could always—no, I'm sure you wouldn't..." She trailed off, staring at her feet and waiting for Slaedir to take the bait.

"What?" he spat.

She lifted her shoulders and looked at the ceiling. "Well, I was thinking... You could always... well, *lie*."

"What do you mean?" he said.

Ayr darted her eyes towards him, and rested her elbow on the throne's arm. "Well, you could just lie to him... Tell Cadyan his sister is dead. He never needs to know she escaped. I imagine that news would go over a lot better than the news that you'd failed to capture her... *again*." Ayr shrugged and waved her hand dismissively. "But I understand, a man like you... I'm sure you'd never dream of lying to your king. No, I'm sure you'll accept your punishment with dignity." She sighed exaggeratedly and allowed her gaze to rest on the body closest to her once again.

It was a young woman with long, dark hair and a slender frame. The flames crawled out towards her and licked at her dress. Ayr knew almost everyone who lived in the city. She tried not to think about this woman's family as she watched the flames engulf her body. The temperature of the fire rose, and the woman's skin turned red. It bubbled and blackened until her distinguishing features were gone.

An anonymous dead woman.

Ayr could practically hear the slow grinding of Slaedir's mind as he struggled to piece it together.

The shouts in the hall grew louder and louder until a sudden, terrified cry rent the air. A great force sent the heavy doors flying off their hinges into the room where they crashed against the already damaged stone pillars. As the dusty air cleared, they saw Cadyan standing in the doorway flanked by soldiers, and not all of them wore Caerlon's colours.

"See, I told you she'd be here," said Rey, leading them into the room. "She always claimed she'd die before abandoning her throne." He kicked the rubble out of his path as he walked towards her.

"Rey," said Ayr uncertainly. "What is the meaning of this?"

"It seems not all of your warriors are as loyal as mine," sneered Cadyan as he came to a halt in front of Ayr.

Ayr looked from Cadyan to Rey, disbelief on her face. "No..." she breathed, shaking her head.

"Yes," said Rey. "I know a lost cause when I see one. The time for Awnell is over. I'm looking to the future."

"A wise decision," said Cadyan with a condescending nod. "Your queen sealed her kingdom's fate when she lied to me and harboured my enemy. Now, where is my *dear* sister?"

Slaedir cast Ayr one furtive glance before saying with pride, "She is dead, Your Majesty."

"Dead," repeated Cadyan, staring at Slaedir.

Slaedir moved aside to reveal the flaming body beside the throne. "She was trying to defend the queen. She put up a good fight. But her ill-performed magic was no match for the maífirkon's sword." He brandished the gilded blade in his hand.

Cadyan strode forward and knelt in front of the body. With a wave of his hand, all the flames abated, leaving behind the smoking and charred remnants of the girl's body.

Ayr watched Cadyan with bated breath. She screwed her face up into one of anguish and defeat as she waited for his gaze to reach her. Hot tears tingled in her eyes and she looked away as Cadyan stood up again and addressed his maífirkon.

"Well, I had hoped to do it myself, but I suppose under the circumstances, I should be happy..."

It surprised Ayr to see that Cadyan looked troubled, almost sad. He stared at the burnt corpse, evidently lost in thought.

"My king?" said Slaedir, taking a hesitant step towards him.

Cadyan flushed and looked around the room, apparently self-conscious. Then he cleared his throat and straightened his posture. "Well done, Slaedir," he declared, clapping him on the back. He strode over to stand in front of Ayr, and then his face contorted into a nasty grin. "Oh, this is wonderful! The girl is gone *and* I've captured Awnell. It's a glorious day, don't you think?"

"What now, my lord?" asked Slaedir.

"Kill her." He gestured casually towards Ayr.

But before Slaedir had taken even one step, Cadyan stopped him. "No, wait! On second thought, we'll bring her with us. I want her to watch her kingdom crumble. I want her to suffer, knowing she was too weak to protect her people. We'll have a public execution later. Make a display of it." He cackled and turned to face Rey. "You. How would you like to join the ranks of a proper kingdom?"

"I would be delighted." Rey inclined his head and shot a smirk in Ayr's direction.

"In fact"—Cadyan turned around, gazing at the room—"all this is mine now. Tell your men they have two choices. They can either join me, or they can die. Anyone who needs persuading can be sent to Bratia until further notice. The women and children may stay here for now. They're too weak to be much use in Bratia anyway. We don't need them distracting the workers."

Ayr fought hard to keep her face impassive as she listened.

"Yes, my lord," said Rey, smiling. Then he bowed and left.

"We leave for Caerlon tomorrow," announced Cadyan to the room at large. A dozen more fírkon had entered and were watching the scene with interest. "We leave tomorrow with my new prisoner, and however many men are left standing."

But as the soldiers bustled around, Ayr noticed one fírkon break free from the crowd and approach the charred body on the ground. He knelt down to examine it, a frown set on his otherwise handsome face.

"What about the man?" he asked, turning to address his maífírkon.

"What man?" said Slaedir.

"The man who escaped the cottage with her. Where is he?" He stood up, looking around for evidence of Drayk.

"Likely died in the battle, didn't he?" said Slaedir, shrugging and walking away.

But Ayr saw doubt written on the firkon's face as he glanced back at the body. She knew the lie would not protect them for long, but she only needed to buy Catanya and Drayk some time.

INTERLUDE

AYR

THE NEW QUEEN

Ayr took a deep breath and wiped away her tears. She twirled her new, wrought iron circlet around in her hands. She had taken it off as soon as she'd regained the privacy of her chambers. It didn't feel right yet.

Brushing her thumbs against the rough metal, she stared down at it numbly. Her father had worn this crown every day for as long as she could remember. It was his. It belonged on his head, not hers.

King Ayln had been a natural leader. He was wise and prudent, and he'd led his people with strength and dignity. Ayr would never be able to fill the hole he'd left behind. It was absurd to even try. She should just march back out there and return the crown. Surely there was someone better suited to this than her...

Ayr snorted and shook her head. Her father would scold her for being so cowardly.

When I am gone, you mustn't waver. You must seize control and own it. Never flinch. Never relent. She could still hear the fire in his voice as he'd said it, still see the proud gleam in his eye.

Ayr had always known this day would arrive, but a part of

her never truly believed her father would die. He always seemed too strong, too good. A man like that should have lived forever...

Ayr walked over to the mirror. She stared at her reflection, half expecting to see someone else standing there, but it was the same reflection she'd seen her whole life. Nothing had changed. Not really.

Ayr exhaled heavily before raising the crown back up to her head, doing her best to ignore the tremble of her hands. The crown fit well. Her long red hair pushed through the gaps in the iron weave, and it opened up into a point at the centre of her forehead where the cold metal was oddly soothing on her skin.

The setting at the front was shaped like an arrowhead, and it bore a single black stone in its centre. The stone, known as the Eye of Awnell, was so smooth and glistening that when she rotated her head, it seemed to move like liquid. Legend said it was the first stone carved from the mountain during the city's construction.

Every ruler since Awnell's beginning had worn this crown. Now it was her turn. But she felt a little ridiculous, like a child playing dress-up.

She wasn't born to be a leader. She was the second child of the king. By rights, she should be a warrior or an explorer. Those were the things she'd dreamed about in her youth. She had dreamed of fighting and running—combat and action. Not politics and governance. Ayr had always been too impatient... too restless, unlike Aane.

Ayr closed her eyes as the image of her sister's lifeless body crept unbidden into her mind again. *When will I stop seeing that?* she thought angrily. *It's been years. Why does that image still haunt me?*

Ayr sighed and rubbed her tired eyes.

Of course, the answer was obvious. That was when everything had changed for her.

"It doesn't matter what you want," she said in a low voice, addressing the girl in the mirror. "Not anymore. This is your life now. There's nothing you can do to change it." She took a deep breath and straightened out her dress. "More still, you owe it to Father and to Aane to try—you owe it to your people to serve them the best you can. You can do this. You *will* do this."

A sudden, loud knock on the door made her jump.

"Enter," she called.

The door opened to reveal Lia standing in its frame, looking sour.

"It's time," she said. Ayr could tell from her tone that Lia was dreading this party as much as she was.

Ayr nodded and followed her out of the room.

As they walked the corridors, neither of them spoke. Lia wasn't one for idle chat, and Ayr was grateful for the silence.

After a few minutes, they arrived in the gallery outside the throne room. Hundreds of voices buzzed behind the doors, and Ayr's stomach did an uncomfortable flip.

In a moment, she would be formally presented to the crowd as the new Queen of Awnell. She hated the artifice of it, but a part of her knew that, with Caerlon delegates behind those doors, she needed to maintain a certain level of formality, a level of self-importance to rival that of Caerlon.

But it didn't mean she had to like it.

The doors opened and the sound of voices ceased, evaporating into suffocating silence. Somewhere in the distance, a voice announced her, but she didn't hear what it said. She was too overwhelmed by the sea of faces staring at her, staring *through* her. It was like they knew she was an imposter... deep down they knew she wasn't meant to be their queen.

She had never felt more removed from her people than she did in that instant.

And then the deafening sound of applause engulfed her. A

rumbling beat of drums cued the laughter and conversation back to life. Suddenly, she was home again. These were the same people she'd always known, and she was still just Ayr.

She laughed in relief as she beamed out at the crowd, watching them enjoy this latest celebration. This was how the Awnadh were meant to be. Full of life and joy.

"Are you all right?" asked Lia.

"I am," said Ayr. "I really am." She stared out at her people, finally coming to terms with her new role.

So, as she turned towards the line of attendees waiting to pay their respects and saw the two individuals she'd been dreading most to see, she knew exactly how to react.

"King Casréyan," she declared, spreading her arms wide in welcome.

"Queen Ayr," he replied with a hint of derision in his voice as he inclined his head. Casréyan wasn't a large man, but he stood with an overbearing presence. He wore an ostentatious silk coat in the violet and gold colours of Caerlon. His thick crop of black hair was neatly styled, and his cold eyes scanned the room with obvious distaste. "Congratulations on your ascension, you must be very pleased."

Ayr plastered a smile onto her face. "Thank you. It is so generous of you, coming all this way to join me on this important occasion." Her voice strained against the forced civility. "Both of you," she added, turning her gaze towards Fehla, who just stared at her feet.

Nearly two years had passed since they'd last seen each other. Now they were standing so close, it struck Ayr how pale and drawn her old friend looked. Dark shadows framed her eyes, and she wore a smile that looked just as contrived as the one Ayr was using.

"Are you planning to stay in the city long?" she asked, trying not to let Fehla's dejected appearance affect her.

"No," said Casréyan. "We return tonight. The demands of

my kingdom are such that I cannot spend an entire evening engaged in meaningless frivolity. I have important matters to address."

"I understand," she said in her best condescending simper. "Well, I hope you will enjoy your time... however long it may be."

Casréyan gave her a sour expression. "I'll have one of my men draw up the new trade agreements," he said abruptly, lifting his chin. "Before your father died, we were planning some revisions. I won't bore you with the details. I'm sure one of your advisors can explain it to you." He waved his hand and turned his attention towards the festivities, clearly communicating how little respect he intended to show her.

Ayr narrowed her eyes. She had expected this. "I assure you I am quite well-informed." She motioned for her steward to approach. He had been standing off to the side holding a stack of ledgers and paper. "I think you'll find these contracts reflect the changes you were discussing. You'll note, though, that I took the liberty of recalculating the distances and the fees associated with restructuring the routes. It's all quite detailed, but I've made a copy here for you to peruse at your leisure. I think you'll find it benefits both kingdoms nicely."

Casréyan gaped at her. He obviously hadn't expected her to be so well prepared.

But King Ayln had taught her well. Even though it made her skin crawl, she knew how to play this game.

"Very well," he said through gritted teeth, as one of his firkon took the stack of papers. "I'm sure we'll find time to discuss this further once your celebrations have ceased."

"I'm sure we shall," said Ayr.

Casréyan scowled and beckoned for Fehla to join him as he turned and strode off into the crowd.

As she moved to follow him, Fehla made eye contact with Ayr briefly. Ayr was taken aback by the profound sorrow she read in those eyes—eyes she'd once known better than her own. Now they were pale replicas of what they used to be. Fehla looked nothing like the woman Ayr remembered. Who was this pitiful wretch now standing before her?

A sudden, inexplicable anger burned through Ayr.

How dare she? she thought, watching Fehla disappear into the crowd. *How dare she come back here, seeking my pity?*

Ayr had tried everything to convince Fehla not to marry Casréyan, but Fehla hadn't listened. She'd turned her back on the people who loved her. As far as Ayr was concerned, whatever had happened since then was Fehla's own fault.

Ayr refused to allow herself to feel sorry. She refused to care about Fehla anymore.

"What do you think?" asked Lia, joining Ayr. She had watched the exchange from a distance so she wouldn't have to speak to Fehla.

"I think I have an entire kingdom of people whose happiness and safety are my responsibility. Fehla is not my concern anymore."

Lia nodded stiffly.

When she had finished greeting everyone, Ayr finally joined the festivities. Realizing how famished she was, she wandered towards the food table.

"My queen," said one of the servants, bowing as he offered her a tray of meat pies. He looked about eighteen and he was gazing around the hall in apparent awe.

"What's your name?" she asked, giving him a smile.

"My name? It's Hes, Your Majesty." He seemed flattered and surprised that she would ask him.

"Well, Hes, I believe everyone can serve themselves from this point on. You and the others should enjoy the merriment." She helped herself to some spiced wine and gave him an encouraging nod. "Go on," she said, chuckling at his delighted smile as he ran off to join the dancing.

When Ayr had eaten her fair share of food and made her way through two glasses of spiced wine, she felt much happier. She strolled around, watching the festivities and chatting with different groups of people.

After a while, she noticed someone making his way over to join her. He was a lanky man, with dark skin and threaded black hair. He wore a boyish grin on his face that was impossible to resist.

"Zad," she said jovially as he stopped in front of her and took her hands in his. "It's so good to see you." Zadílar was only ten years older than Ayr, but he had already been the Lord Steward of Sidina for nearly twenty years. He'd inherited the position at the early age of twelve when his older brother had died. Because of this, Ayr felt a unique kinship with him. Neither of them had been born into leadership.

"And you, my dear." He smiled at her, his remarkably even teeth glinting in the light of the nearby torch. "It delights me to see you looking so well in your new role. Although, I was sorry to learn of your father's passing. He will be missed deeply." Zadílar patted Ayr's hand and gave her a warm smile. "But I am sure he would be grateful to know his throne is in such intelligent and capable hands."

"*Can* hands be intelligent?" asked Ayr with a grin.

Zadílar laughed boisterously. "Well done," he said, inclining his head before taking another large sip of wine. "You've always been quick with a snappy retort. I love it!" he cried to the room at large, drawing several stares and giggles. "You have all the makings of a fine queen, my dear. A very fine queen. All you must do is decide how best to apply that brain of yours." He wagged his finger at her, grinning from ear to ear.

"Thank you," said Ayr. She had always liked Zadílar. He was one of the few Caerlon delegates who'd always respected her father. He seemed to value the Awnadh and their way of life, even joining their celebrations whenever he could. Zadílar was a man who was equal parts intelligent and gregarious. He could talk business with a drink in his hand and still dance until sunrise the next morning. He fit in well in Awnell.

"And how are you enjoying the celebration this evening?" he asked, snatching two more drinks off a nearby table and handing one to her.

Ayr smiled as she took a sip from the glass. "I am actually enjoying it much more than I expected."

"That is as *I* expected," said Zadílar, winking at her. Then he chuckled to himself. "Yes, by rights, the crowning of a queen should be a dreary, tedious affair, shouldn't it? But not here. No, everything is a celebration in Awnell, isn't it? Your people are so dynamic, so much more alive. I confess, I've spent years trying to understand, trying to replicate that spirit in Sidina."

"Really?" It surprised Ayr that anyone in Caerlon would be interested in emulating Awnell.

"Oh, yes." He nodded before taking a large sip and draining most of his new glass in one gulp. Then he smacked his lips, as though relishing the taste. "But I'm afraid no matter what we do, we will never be able to reproduce what you have here. Yours is a kingdom built by warriors. It's in your blood and it's in theirs." He nodded towards the crowd of dancers. "This entire kingdom was founded on the tenets of combat. Fight hard and live hard because every moment could be your last. It is, quite simply, *magnificent*." He chortled as he watched a couple stumble past him, doubled over in hysterics as they re-filled their goblets and returned to the dance floor.

"But in Caerlon, we have something else. I'm afraid there is a pervasive apathy and hopelessness that underlies our entire society. So, despite my best efforts in Sidina, I have only ever succeeded in creating veneers and empty parodies of jollity. Oh, it can be satisfying enough if you don't look too closely, but this..." Zadílar sighed as he gazed at the lively crowd. "We will never have this. So, I have contented myself with the charade. I would take that over the darkness any day."

Ayr nodded, thinking about the implications of what Zadílar had said. She had never given much thought to the general culture of Caerlon. The actions of its king were so loud and distracting that she'd never stopped to wonder how that could seep into the society's fabric. For the first time in her life, she felt truly sorry for the people of Caerlon.

"I wish there was something I could do to help," she said out loud.

"Mmm." Zadílar rocked back and forth on his heels, observing the dancers. "Of course, there are certain areas where Awnell's interests intersect with those of Sidina," he said.

Ayr frowned. "Such as?" she asked, trying to match his quiet, casual tone so as not to attract attention.

"Well, my dear, you are warriors, and, in Sidina, we make weapons."

His directness surprised Ayr, and she didn't know how to respond.

"Perhaps the warriors of Awnell have been idle too long, mmm?" He turned his eyes on her, his expression full of meaning.

Ayr glanced around to make sure no one was listening. "Are you telling me to wage war on Caerlon?" she whispered, hardly daring to believe it.

"*Am I* telling you that?" he asked. Then he shrugged. "No, my dear. I am simply pointing out the potential for a renewed sense of purpose in your kingdom. Don't get me wrong, I had the utmost respect for your father, but I must say that I'm pleased your people have new leadership. It is an opportunity for refreshment, wouldn't you say?"

"Refreshment," repeated Ayr, her mind racing with the ideas Zadílar raised.

"Yes, you're right," he said, snapping his fingers with a

sudden carefree energy. "We *do* need more drinks. I'll go fetch us some, then." He downed the rest of his drink and winked as he swept off in search of more wine.

Ayr watched him go, as a nervous sense of excitement crept into her mind. Zadílar was right. Maybe her reign didn't need to be consumed by policy and control, maybe there was an opportunity for her to take action.

"What did old Zaddy have to say for himself?" asked Lia, coming to stand next to Ayr.

"He gave me a great deal to think about, actually." Ayr made eye contact with Lia, her mind racing with ideas. "Yes, a great deal..."

Ayr remembered the old adage the warriors used to repeat in the early days of her father's reign.

"*Tenacious and loyal, we live for now and we fight for the future,*" she spoke the words under her breath as she stared out at the crowd of people. *Her* people.

Her warriors.

PART II

15

THE RESONANT HEART

Catanya was flying. Hurling above the world in violent, unnatural arcs. Then everything twisted and contorted, and she fell. Through flames and ice, she crashed into the earth's core where the rock walls pressed in around her, suffocating her. She cried for help, thrashing against the sides of her cage, but nobody came.

The walls morphed into mahogany wood. She was a little girl again, trapped in that old, dark cabinet in the lodge basement. But she was just playing hideaway with Diyah. What happened? And why wasn't Genna coming to help her this time?

"Catya?"

She recognized that voice.

"Catya, wake up."

She heard a faint rustling nearby, but she didn't open her eyes. It took her a long time to realize she was awake. Her dreams had been a swirl of random images mixed with memories from her childhood that she thought she'd forgotten. A cool draught blew against her cheek. The floor underneath her was hard and uneven.

She didn't know where she was.

Groaning, she struggled against the stiffness and pain in her body as she rolled onto her back.

"Catya?"

She opened her eyes. Drayk was crouching beside her with his arms outstretched. It looked like he had been about to shake her. The room was dim, and it reeked of horses.

"Where are we?" She managed to speak, but her voice was raspy. "What happened?" She tried to move, but her muscles were too sore. The violent pounding in her head threatened to knock her back down.

Drayk helped her into a seated position and handed her a canteen. "Here, drink this."

Her fingers fumbled with the stopper as she tried to remove it, so he uncorked it for her, and helped her to drink. The water was soothing on her parched lips and throat. She closed her eyes and drank deeply before trying to speak again.

"So?" she asked, waving at their surroundings. Now that she was awake, she realized they were sitting in what appeared to be a rundown barn. Faint rays of light poked through the wooden slats of the wall. The floor was strewn with hay and dried manure, but she saw no horses.

"We're in Esdra," he replied, taking the canteen and handing her a chunk of bread and cheese. "Just east of Awnell City. We made it out, but then you collapsed. You've been unconscious for three days. I had to find somewhere for us to hide out."

"Three days?" repeated Catanya, choking on her mouthful of bread. "I've been asleep for *three days*? What happened to Awnell?"

Drayk's face darkened. "I don't know for sure," he said. "But this village has been evacuated, which means Ayr gave the signal for retreat."

"Evacuated where?" Catanya grabbed hold of the wall and

pulled herself up to her feet with a great deal of effort, ignoring the throbbing in her head. "We should go find them, make sure everyone is safe." The added weight of her guilt was heavy on her weary body.

"No." Drayk stood up, his jaw set in a hard line. "We can't."

"What do you mean, we can't? We need to—"

"We need to follow that map," said Drayk. He pointed at the pocket where Catanya stored the parchment. "We need to find Túir-Avlea."

"Drayk, we can look for this mythological mountain later. But right now, there are real people who need our help."

"Our *help*?" Drayk seemed agitated, and he looked at Catanya like she'd lost her mind. "How do you expect to help anyone? Catya, look at you!" His tired, sunken eyes bulged with fear and anger. "Three days! I've been here, hiding and waiting. Just watching you—hoping you would wake up! Whatever happened to you on that tower, it almost killed you. Do you understand me? You nearly died because you don't know what you're doing with those powers. You need to learn how to control them. That's the only thing that matters."

"But I—"

"No." He cut her off impatiently. "Awnell is gone now. Ayr sacrificed everything so you and I could make it out. Catya, we need to do what she said. We need to follow that map and find Túir-Avlea. You've seen what Cadyan can do. He decimated an entire city with a wave of his hands and when you tried to match him, it took everything you had. It almost killed you... I —" He broke off, shaking his head in frustration.

"I know," said Catanya in a quiet voice. Drayk's outburst had humbled her. "You're right. I let the powers overwhelm me. I don't know what I'm doing and I need to learn, but..."

"But what?"

Catanya sighed and looked him in the eye. "I feel sick

leaving them behind. I'm tired of leaving devastation in my wake."

Drayk nodded and rubbed his forehead. "I know, Catya, but it's too late to change what happened. All you can do is move forward, hopefully towards a solution. Come on, let's look at that map."

Catanya pulled the parchment out of her pocket and unfolded it. "I'm not sure how useful this will be," she said, frowning. "It shows the names of locations and the landmarks, but I don't see any sign of where it actually begins, do you? There's nothing on here that looks even remotely familiar."

She waited as Drayk read the poem on the side of the page. When he finished, he pursed his lips like he'd tasted something sour and then turned to examine the images. "The Windy Shoal," he read aloud, frowning as he tapped the first label. He seemed lost in thought for a moment. Then he gave a resigned sigh. "That old man at the cabin, he mentioned hearing voices, right? And he mentioned something about watching me make it farther than anyone else..." Drayk's tone was strained, like he was reluctant to hear the answer.

"Y-yes, I think so." Catanya thought back on their interaction with the man. So much of what he'd said had seemed jumbled and disconnected. She wasn't sure how to make sense of it.

"I think I know where this begins," Drayk muttered. "Farther east, a few miles past the boundaries of Esdra and before the Sundered Cliffs, there's this old monument of sorts... It was built towards the end of the Quiescence Wars. Nobody knows exactly when or by who. But people who follow the ancient religion travel there to pray and make offerings to the Natures. I always thought it was meaningless, but..." He exhaled and turned his eyes to her. "About a day's journey beyond the monument, there's a narrow beach and a sandbar stretching into the ocean."

"Right..." Catanya frowned, waiting for him to continue.

"Well, the locals call it the Haunted Sandbar," he said. "Because anyone who ventures onto it comes running back, raving about voices on the wind."

Catanya struggled to suppress a laugh. "And you believe those stories?" she asked.

Drayk scowled. "I don't have to believe the stories because I've experienced it myself. I've been there before."

There was a long pause as Catanya stared at him, struggling to contain her laughter. "You've been there?" she repeated dryly.

"Yes. When I first arrived in Awnell. I was young and ignorant and I was an outsider, you know? So, the older street kids thought it would be entertaining to bring me out there and scare me." He shrugged, acting like the memory didn't bother him. "See, every child growing up in Awnell knows about that sandbar. It's a sort of rite of passage for kids to run out on the shoal and set a record for the farthest point reached. But nobody ever makes it very far. They all come running back before long." Drayk's voice trailed off, and Catanya was surprised to detect a quaver in it.

"You're scared," she said, stunned. He was always so dismissive of his past experiences. This was the first time he'd spoken about them with anything close to earnestness, which actually gave her pause.

"Well, let's just say I made it farther than anyone ever has, and I have no desire to do it again, but..." He shrugged, grimacing at the idea of going back.

"Okay, so you think this Haunted Sandbar is the same one on this map? This Windy Shoal?" she asked, glancing back at the crude drawing. Catanya was reluctant to believe his story. She didn't believe in ghosts or disembodied voices, but Drayk seemed so serious... Perhaps as a child, the wind had sounded otherworldly to him. She could understand how a frightened child might confuse hissing and wailing squalls with the sound of voices tormenting them. And any place with gales that strong would surely qualify as a "windy shoal" wouldn't it?

"It fits, doesn't it?" he said. "And the old man knew about it. I'm sure of it... I'd say it's worth a try."

Catanya pursed her lips and continued staring at the parchment. Could it be true? Genna had told her the stories of Túir-Avlea as a child. But they were only ever stories, tales of hope and comfort to soothe bad dreams... could Túir-Avlea actually be real?

"All right," she said finally. "We'll go." She let go of the wall, trying to steady herself as her legs wobbled under the pressure. "How far is it?" she asked, clenching her teeth as she took a step forward. Her entire body ached with pain from her exertion on the tower.

"Not far," said Drayk, eying her nervously. "We should arrive by sundown tomorrow." He cringed as he watched her taking awkward steps. "Or perhaps a little later," he said with a playful grin.

"Shut up," she muttered, trying not to smile at the look on his face. But as she took a few more steps, her strength seemed to return to her. It wasn't long before they were able to leave.

Outside the barn, the overcast sky gave a pale gloom to the world. The air was damp, and the ground was a mixture of mud and ice.

The village of Esdra was very small. Its buildings were built of the same glistening black stone as Awnell City, but they were simpler and more rustic. They were designed for modest shelter, nothing more. The proximity to Awnell City likely meant people in Esdra didn't need to worry about much else. They farmed and lived, and if they needed anything more, they could always find it in the city.

As Catanya and Drayk crossed the abandoned streets and fields, they saw signs of the villagers' quick retreat. There were scattered supplies strewn everywhere and half-filled carts left unattended. Catanya glanced down as they stepped over a fence and saw a single child's slipper lying intrenched in the hardened mud. The sight of it filled her with a sudden and profound sadness.

She glanced back at the desolate village one last time, wondering where the villagers were now and whether they'd ever be able to return to their homes. She closed her eyes momentarily, holding back the tide of her grief. Then she turned to follow Drayk.

They walked in silence together for hours that day. Catanya wondered if Drayk was privately mourning the loss of his home or if he was so used to living like a wanderer that it didn't even faze him. Or maybe he blamed her as much as she blamed herself.

How many more homes are you going to destroy? How many more lives are you going to ruin? said a nasty voice in Catanya's head. She tried to shake it off, tried to focus on the journey, but she couldn't help but remember all the people who'd suffered because of her.

Now she could add everyone in Awnell to that ever-growing list.

It was early afternoon when they slowed their pace. By that point, Catanya had been wallowing in regret and sadness for hours. Mud caked her boots, and the intermittent drizzle of chilly rain had dampened her hair and clothes.

"We're nearly at the monument," Drayk said, and the clarity in his voice sounded jarring against the gloom of her mood. "There." He pointed forward. A small stone structure was barely visible in the distance. It stood alone in a wide open plain, the ocean behind it stretching towards the horizon. "The

Resonant Heart," he said in an oddly reverent voice. "That's what it's called."

"Really?" Catanya hadn't expected something so strangely sad, yet hopeful at the same time.

She squinted out at the monument. From a distance, it looked like a freestanding stone wall. As they approached it, Catanya realized that what she'd mistaken for a wall was actually a series of pillars, spaced evenly apart. It was a simple structure, with a broad plinth that supported five separate columns, each stretching about ten feet into the open air.

Between the pillars lay the remnants of wreaths and bouquets, likely left as tokens and offerings during the Midwinter Carnival. The flowers had wilted, and the wreaths were droopy and waterlogged. It was clear nobody had been here for several weeks.

Up close, Catanya noticed each pillar was identical and perfectly hewn from matching grey stone. The monument was remarkably plain, with no ornaments or carvings anywhere except the bottom, where a few words were etched into the plinth.

The words were ancient Awnle, and they were badly faded and weathered, not to mention covered in moss and grime.

She crouched down to get a closer look. "Do you know what it says?" she asked Drayk.

"*Into silence, but not in peace,*" he recited the words from memory and shrugged. "That's what I was told."

Catanya frowned and stared at the words. She held her hand a few inches above the plinth, where she thought she detected a strange energy emanating from the stone. When she pressed her fingers against the engraving, a sudden vibration ran through her body. "It's a cenotaph," she breathed. "A monument to the dead, but—"

A sharp burning sensation shot through her fingers and she yanked her hand back, wincing in pain. And then the air filled with screams. Not just one scream, but thousands… hundreds of thousands. The screaming grew louder and louder. It sounded like it was coming from the pillars as it barrelled towards her.

She cried out, clasping her ears and falling to the ground. The screams were part of her now. Somehow, they were inside her, torturing her and ripping her apart from the inside out. They weren't just any screams, they were the screams of the dead and dying. The gut-wrenching, desperate pleas for life, and the final, rattling howls of loss. Catanya's body threatened to explode. She couldn't contain the pain.

Nothing had ever been more excruciating.

And then, as suddenly as it had started, it stopped. The gentle rush of the nearby ocean swept the echoes away.

Catanya lay panting on the ground, clutching her burning fingers, with her eyes squeezed shut and her face drenched in tears.

"What happened?" came Drayk's panicked voice.

Catanya groaned and strained to open her eyes. All she saw was blackness. Her heart raced, and she grasped around blindly. Everything was obscured and jumbled, as though her eyes had forgotten how to make sense of images and light. Gradually, Drayk's face swam into focus, and the cenotaph's blurry edges came back into view.

"Y-you didn't hear the screams?" she asked, climbing to her feet. She held up her fingers to examine the damage. But they were fine, no burns or marks at all.

Everything was fine now.

Drayk shook his head, glancing around nervously. "I didn't hear anything."

Catanya nodded, barely listening to him. The air was thin, and she was lightheaded, like she hadn't slept in days. "I-I don't understand," she sputtered. She took several laboured breaths as she looked back at the pillar. "Unless…"

She couldn't explain it, but she knew that she'd needed to hear those screams. She knew that, somehow, they were connected to her—a part of her.

They *belonged* to her.

Catanya shuddered as a frigid chill settled into her bones. It was as if all her warmth had drained from her body. She could still feel the sorrow of those voices. It flowed through her like a poison, infecting her spirit. And it had always been inside her, hidden just underneath everything else, waiting to be acknowledged...

She was ashamed she hadn't realized it before.

"I'm sorry," she whispered, closing her eyes and bowing her head.

"Sorry about what?" Drayk's voice broke through. She turned to see him eyeing her with his face set in deep concern.

"Nothing," she said, her throat chafing.

Suddenly parched, she pulled off her bag and rummaged around for her canteen. She drank slowly, trying not to think about what she'd just experienced.

She didn't want to know what it was or why it had happened. All she wanted was to push that sorrow back into the depths of her soul and ignore it forever. She had enough of her own pain to contend with, without taking on more.

"Are you all right?" asked Drayk.

Catanya nodded as she replaced her canteen and faced him, deliberately turning her back on the cenotaph. "I'm fine," she said, forcing her voice to sound confident. "Should we continue?"

Drayk surveyed her momentarily. Then, seeming to accept her assurance that she was fine, he nodded and gestured for her to follow him.

Catanya cast one last furtive glance at the monument and felt a shudder run down her spine.

16

AWNELL HAS FALLEN

It was early in the morning. Soft light bathed Diyah's small sleeping compartment, as she lay in bed, staring at the ceiling and listening to the chilly wind whistle through the window. Almost a fortnight had passed since the king and his soldiers had left for Awnell. With each passing day, Diyah found it increasingly difficult to get out of bed in the mornings.

There had been no news from Awnell and she was beginning to fear the worst had happened. For so long, she'd been clinging to the knowledge that somewhere out there, Catanya was alive. That knowledge had given her enough hope to withstand everything else. But doubt and despair were slowly clenching around her heart. If Catanya died, any chance of overthrowing Cadyan would die with her. Diyah didn't think she could bear to live the rest of her life under his regime.

Diyah sighed heavily and sat up, swinging her legs over the side of the bed. The room was freezing cold. She shivered and dressed herself as fast as she could, her fingers fumbling with the ties on her wool bodice. As cold as her chambers were, she knew the dungeons would be worse, and she needed to check on Jémys. She might not be able to help Catanya, but she was determined not to let Jémys die.

However, it surprised Diyah to see how well Jémys could withstand the living conditions in the dungeons. Despite his circumstances, Jémys had developed a newfound optimism. He seemed convinced that Catanya would be fine—that the battle for Awnell would not end in Caerlon's victory.

Diyah didn't know if it was denial or guilt, but, for whatever reason, Jémys was adamant that Catanya would defeat Cadyan and everything would be okay. Diyah wished she could have his conviction. She hated herself for her doubt.

"Any day now," said Jémys, as she sat outside his cell that morning. "Any day now, we should hear the battle is over. I bet there will be parties and celebrations everywhere. It's going to be wonderful, Diyah. Just imagine what it will mean to defeat Cadyan, to end the royal tyranny in Caerlon."

Jémys was sitting with his back against the cell bars, staring at the wall across from him. Most of his wounds had finally healed, but Diyah insisted he keep his arm cinched for another week.

"I hope you're right," she mumbled.

"I am," he said. "Trust me, Catanya is powerful, and she has an entire kingdom to support her. I know she can win. She'll defeat him and his entire army, just wait."

"You really want that?" asked Diyah, a little surprised.

Jémys looked at her in amazement and laughed. "Of course, I do! That's what we all want, isn't it?"

Diyah frowned, picking at a loose thread on her sleeve. "What about your brother? Surely you don't want him to die."

Jémys's shoulders stiffened, and he turned to stare back at the wall. "Julyán chose his side. His fate should be the same as his king and the rest of the firkon. He doesn't deserve our mercy."

"You don't mean that," she said in a small voice.

"He's a traitor and a coward. Diyah, he tortured you! He killed Lady Genna and the girls at the lodge, and he would have killed you too if it came to it. How can you defend him?"

"I'm not defending him," said Diyah quickly. She regretted telling Jémys about the attack in Faltir and her early days in Caerlon. When he'd first asked her about it, she was grateful to have an attentive listener. But now she could see how much it fuelled his anger towards his brother. "I know what he's done," she said. "Believe me, I know all too well. But he's still your brother..."

"No," said Jémys, shaking his head. "My brother died years ago. Whoever that man is, he's not him."

Diyah found Jémys's words unsettling, and she didn't know how to respond. She could tell he was in a lot of pain, and he was just masking his pain with anger. But if Julyán died, Jémys would never get the chance to heal and move on. He would be left with his pain and his anger for the rest of his life. As a healer, it grieved Diyah to know she wouldn't be able to help him.

***

Diyah spent the rest of the day making rounds to visit her patients throughout the city. After months of living and working in Caerlon, she'd met hundreds of people. She was beginning to feel like one of them, despite the continued presence of her mandatory castle chaperone.

She often imagined what it would be like to live in Caerlon under Catanya's rule. To move about the city unaccompanied, mixing and mingling with everyone at her leisure. She missed having the freedom to come and go as she pleased, and she hated having to bring a guard with her everywhere. The people were slowly coming to trust her, but it was obvious they found the guard's presence upsetting. The castle guards did not engender trust or inspire comfort. Diyah was sure that, without their presence, her work would be a lot smoother.

The next afternoon, as Diyah made her way back up to the castle with the surly guard at her side, she found herself, for one brief moment, actually missing Julyán's company. She almost laughed out loud at the absurdity. But for all his faults, Julyán was still more interesting company than the average castle guard.

And she had to admit that something about him puzzled her. She'd always prided herself on being a good judge of character, but in Julyán's case, she still had trouble deciding. She couldn't reconcile the man who'd suggested torturing little girls with the boy who'd defended her years ago in the woods. It didn't add up, and Diyah felt an intense curiosity about the entire situation. She needed to know what had happened. What had caused Julyán to change so dramatically?

That night, she decided to visit Jémys again. She wanted to get some answers. Moreover, she remembered how important Fehla's visits had been to her when she was the one locked in the dungeon. She knew Jémys could use that same support now.

After dinner, Diyah packed up some of her poached chicken and cabbage and headed towards the west wing for the second time that day. As she reached the entrance, she prepared to argue with the guards about why she was visiting again so soon. She opened her mouth to deliver her rehearsed speech, but the guard just waved his hand.

"Of course, they're expecting you." He opened the door without another word.

Diyah tried to conceal her surprise as she crossed the threshold into the dungeons. She could hear voices below—a lot of voices. It sounded like at least a hundred men were arguing down there.

She emerged onto the first floor and her jaw dropped. Each

cell was full to capacity with men sporting injuries that ranged from minor bruises to life-threatening wounds. They all wore strange black and red leather outfits with exposed bone and metal lining.

The noise level was ear-splitting as they rattled the bars and called insults and threats across the vast, underground space. It took several seconds before Diyah realized who they were shouting at. There, in the middle of the dungeon, stood three men. Slaedir, Julyán, and someone she didn't recognize—a tall, muscular man with shaved hair and a grave face. He wore the same outfit as the men in the cells.

"Ah, there you are," Slaedir said, striding towards Diyah. "As you can see, we have some new... ah... *guests* who need a healer's attention... after you've finished tending the injured fírkon, of course."

"What happened?" said Diyah, aghast. "Who are all these people?" She'd heard a commotion during dinner, but she'd assumed it was just the guards handling some argument or altercation. She had no idea the fírkon had returned.

"This is what's left of Awnell's army," announced Slaedir.

Diyah teetered where she stood, suddenly dizzy. She cast around, searching for Jémys. She found him standing in his cell, surrounded by bloodied and grimy soldiers, looking stunned.

"*What's left?*" echoed Diyah, staring blankly at Jémys.

"Yeah, that's right," said Slaedir. "Awnell is gone, and so is your precious *princess*."

Diyah shook her head in disbelief.

Jémys banged on the cell door, defiance in his eyes. "I don't believe you."

Diyah stared imploringly at Julyán, desperate for him to deny it. But Julyán said nothing. He just turned his attention back to the prisoners.

"No!" cried Diyah, half shouting, half sobbing as she fell to her knees.

The noise in the dungeon mounted again, but Diyah couldn't understand anything they were saying. She wasn't listening.

It couldn't be true. Catanya couldn't be dead, she couldn't be. Not after everything that had happened.

"Get up," snarled a gruff voice in her ear as someone hauled her to her feet.

Her head was spinning as she turned to see Slaedir gripping her arm so tightly it hurt.

"Let go of me!" she shouted, trying to yank her arm out of his grasp, but he just tightened it even more. She dropped the food she was carrying and tried to hit him with her other hand, but he blocked it and pushed her against the nearest cell door. She hit her head on the cold iron bars and winced as he wrenched her arms behind her back.

Hot tears poured down her face as she stared into the cell at the bloodied men lying on the floor. She tried not to picture Catanya's body, broken and bleeding on a floor just like it, somewhere in Awnell.

The dungeon door opened and closed again. The atmosphere changed, and the noise died down.

"Slaedir, what are you doing?" Cadyan's cold voice rang off the walls.

"Trying to teach this girl some manners, my lord," he replied. "She refuses to obey, but she's too pretty to leave unbroken."

His hot breath clung to Diyah's neck, making her skin crawl. Anger and disgust burned away her sadness. She struggled to wrestle free.

"Let her go," said Cadyan, sounding bored. "We have more important things to discuss."

Slaedir sighed and released his grip. Diyah turned around, rubbing her hands and grimacing.

"Now, where is she? She should hear this." Cadyan craned his neck to see into the cells.

"Over here, Your Majesty," said the man Diyah didn't recognize. He was standing at the end of the corridor next to the only empty cell.

"Excellent." Cadyan walked to join him.

Diyah squinted at the shadowy cell and realized that it wasn't actually empty. There was a woman inside. She stood in the middle of the cell with her hands clasped behind her back. She looked formidable, wearing the same leather clothes as the Awnadh soldiers. But her reddish grey hair was slipping loose from its ties, framing her face with a strange delicacy.

"How do you like your accommodations this time, my lady?" asked Cadyan, his voice thick with irony.

The woman in the cell just stared at him, and said nothing.

"Not in the mood for talking? Very well, then you can listen." Cadyan turned to address the rest of the chamber. "Soldiers of Awnell, you have fought well. You have fought with honour and skill, and I applaud you. These are traits I admire and respect. It is not your fault that your queen has led you astray. I do not think you should suffer for her mistakes. Join me, and your skill and bravery shall be rewarded. Join me and you will know what it means to serve a real monarch. Your lieutenant, here," he gestured to the man beside him, "has selected you from the remaining Awnadh. He tells me you are some of the best warriors he's ever trained. I offer you the opportunity to join my ranks, no questions asked. You will not get this opportunity again. Join me now, or die. Those are your options."

A heavy silence settled in the air as the men in the cells exchanged dubious looks.

"Gentlemen!" cried the lieutenant from Awnell. "Don't be foolish. You followed me once, now follow me still. Tenacious and loyal, we live for now and we fight for the future!" he cried.

The mood in the room shifted slightly, and some of the men frowned. Diyah noticed several of them shooting apprehensive glances at their queen, who stood perfectly still, looking smug.

"Aye, Lieutenant," called one man, nodding and stepping forward. "We live for now and we fight for the future!"

"Long live the King!" shouted another man, nodding towards Cadyan.

A lot of murmuring broke out as most men in the cells seemed to decide they'd rather follow Cadyan than die.

Diyah watched in disbelief as, one by one, the soldiers of Awnell renounced their queen and their kingdom as easily as if it had been inevitable all along. She glanced at Queen Ayr in her cell and could have sworn she saw a smile flicker across her face. But Diyah blinked, and the smile was gone, replaced by a look of deepest betrayal.

Cadyan was standing, victorious, surrounded by a sea of traitors. Diyah's anger drained away, leaving hopelessness in its place. If these were the soldiers who'd fought alongside Catanya, then her friend never stood a chance.

"And you... don't think I've forgotten about you." Cadyan walked over to stand in front of Jémys, who was watching the scene with tears staining his cheeks. "You must be simply *devastated* to learn about your beloved's demise. It's tragic, really," said Cadyan with false sympathy. "Now, I am not without mercy. Despite your role in helping her escape, I will offer you the same deal I have offered them. Join me, or die." Cadyan made an odd sound like he was suppressing a laugh. "Choose which fate is *really* worse. Become the firkon your *little boy* never got to be, or die just like him."

Jémys looked absolutely revolted as he stood there, staring at Cadyan. Diyah held her breath, waiting. She knew Jémys would never join Cadyan, but she couldn't bear the thought of watching him die. Jémys shook his head, trembling from head to toe.

"Jémys—" said Diyah, taking a step forward. But she was cut off by the sound of cackling behind her. She turned to see Slaedir doubled over with laughter, pointing at Julyán.

"Oh, this is rich," he howled as he drew his sword. "First your father and now your brother. I'm going to enjoy this."

"No!" shouted Diyah, stepping in front of him and blocking his path to Jémys.

"Out of the way!" Slaedir shoved Diyah aside. She fell to the ground in front of Jémys's cell, and her wrist twisted painfully.

"All right!" shouted Jémys, and everything went silent. He was glaring at Slaedir with such loathing that he looked almost mad.

"Say again?" said Cadyan, gesturing towards his ear. "A little louder."

"I said all right, I'll join you," repeated Jémys, not taking his eyes off of Slaedir. "I'll join your fírkon, and I'll fight for you. After all, what else do I have left?" He finally turned to look at Cadyan with an air of steely resolve.

"A wise choice," said Cadyan, nodding. "You have all made a wise choice today," he said to the dungeon at large, "and you will be rewarded for it. However, do not mistake my mercy for weakness. If, at any point, I even *suspect* you are acting against me or the interests of my kingdom..." He trailed off as he surveyed the room. A flash of gold gleamed in his eye.

At first nothing happened, but then one by one, the soldiers of Awnell fell to their knees, crying out in pain. Diyah stared in horror as the men thrashed on the floor, whimpering like frightened children.

Then Jémys fell, landing hard on his still-injured arm. He let out a strangled cry, then clenched his teeth as though trying to bite it back. Diyah lurched forward instinctively, but a sudden wrenching sensation in her chest stopped her. The sensation spread out towards her legs, arms, and head. It felt like her flesh was being peeled away from her bones. The air in her lungs felt like shards of glass, slicing and scraping her as she struggled to breathe.

The pain overwhelmed her and she collapsed, writhing on the floor. Her eyes filled with tears of pain, but she could still make out the blurry outlines of Cadyan, Julyán, Slaedir, and the Awnadh lieutenant looming above her.

The torch flames flickered and dimmed, casting the room into darkness.

"A small taste of the vengeance I can unleash," called Cadyan, his golden eyes glowing like embers through the dark. "You have all seen what I did to your kingdom. Trust me when I say you don't want to learn what I do to those who betray me..."

The pain in Diyah's body mounted until she thought her bones might break from the strain and pressure. With a final excruciating wrench, it stopped.

The torches flickered back to life. Everyone was lying on the floor, shivering as their breathing slowly resumed its normal pace. Everyone except Queen Ayr.

At first Diyah assumed Ayr had been spared the pain, but then she noticed the beads of sweat on the queen's face and her shortness of breath. The whites of her knuckles were visible where she'd clenched them around the cell bars. But the queen hadn't collapsed. She hadn't even screamed. She'd endured her pain in silence.

Diyah felt a mixture of envy and awe, watching the woman hold her ground with pride and dignity. She wished she had that fortitude.

The soldiers gradually regained their composure, panting as they hauled themselves back up to their feet.

"Now," continued Cadyan in a calmer tone, "I've instructed my firkon to watch all of you and report back to me. Any, shall we say, *odd* behaviour, will not be met with mercy again. The Maífirkon Tournament begins next month. I expect every man to compete. Your rank at the end of the tournament will determine your station in the fîrkon for the next four years. Those who rank the lowest will be sent to the work camps to join the other Awnadh. Whether you join them as fellow workers or as their guards... I haven't decided. So, I trust you will use this opportunity to prove your loyalty to Caerlon. Now, let me hear you say it..." He held up his arms as though conducting a chorus.

The Awnadh exchanged confused looks, but then a voice at the back called, "For Caerlon, For Might, and For Glory!"

A satisfied smile spread across Cadyan's face.

"For Caerlon, For Might, and For Glory!" echoed the room in unison. Jémys and Diyah locked eyes as they reluctantly spoke the words.

"Excellent," said Cadyan, clapping his hands together. "Now, where is my mother? It's time she heard the good news."

Diyah took advantage of Cadyan's momentary distraction to crawl towards the bars where Jémys stood.

"Jémys," she whispered, beckoning for him to crouch down. "What are you doing? You're really going to join him?"

Jémys shook his head. Speaking in a voice that was barely audible, he whispered, "I'm going to kill him, Diyah. One way or another, I'm going to kill them all. I owe it to my family. I owe it to her." His voice broke, and he averted his eyes.

Diyah reached her uninjured hand through the bars to rest it on his.

"Whatever it takes," she agreed, nodding.

There was movement all around her. Diyah realized Cadyan was preparing to leave the dungeons.

"Wait a second," said Slaedir. "What about her?" He pointed to Diyah on the floor. "Someone's got to teach her to stay in her place."

Cadyan laughed. "Well, what do you suggest?"

Slaedir crouched down and grabbed Diyah by the chin. "It would be an awful shame to waste that pretty face," he said, leering. "And she's a Heiltúir. That's some rare blood she's got in her." He leaned in and inhaled a deep, rasping breath before his face split into a nasty grin. "What if we added another prize to the tournament this year?" he suggested, turning to face Cadyan. "Someone ought to have her, don't you think?"

"You suggest that whoever wins the maífírkon title should also win himself a wife? Is that it?" asked Cadyan. Diyah couldn't tell if his sneer was directed at her or Slaedir.

A great degree of murmuring and whistling came from the other men. Obviously, Slaedir wasn't the only one who liked this idea.

But from inside her cell, Queen Ayr made a sound of disgust.

"What was that?" hissed Cadyan, walking over to her cell.

"Just like your father," said Ayr. "I guess that's just how things are done in Caerlon. None of you can actually convince a woman to love you. No, you have to *force* them. Pathetic," she declared, staring Cadyan straight in the eye.

"Well, now that I know you hate the idea, it's settled. Slaedir," he addressed his maífírkon, "if you manage to keep your title, she's all yours!" With a hearty laugh, Cadyan strode towards the exit. "Otherwise, may the best man win!"

Diyah thought she might be sick to her stomach. She couldn't believe what had just happened. The sound of cheering and laughter threatened to engulf her.

"It's okay," said Jémys in a forced calm voice. "It's okay, we won't let that happen. There's still time... We can do this. Whatever it takes, right?" He squeezed her hand.

She turned her eyes to meet his, and, despite the horror she read in them, there was something reassuring about their warm green colour.

"Yes," she said more calmly than she felt. Jémys was right. They had to fight back. They had to avenge Catanya. "Whatever it takes."

17

THE WINDY SHOAL

It was just after dawn when Catanya and Drayk finally reached the beach at the eastern shore. The sky was overcast and gloomy, and a fine mist hung in the air. Only a few gulls dared to inspect the stranded seashells dotted across the grey sand.

The harkened pain and sorrow, with resounding aches of defeat...

Catanya had been reciting the poem nonstop in her mind, trying to make sense of the words. It also helped to drown out the memory of what happened at the monument.

"Drayk, what do you think about the poem on the map?" she asked. She had repeated the words so many times that they were making less and less sense to her.

"Search me, love. I've never been one for poetry. I always figured if you had something to say, you could just say it directly."

"That seems consistent with your personality," she said dryly. She was a little disappointed that he wouldn't be interested in discussing it with her.

They walked along the beach for another hour until they reached a point where the shoreline curved outwards. As they rounded the bend, Catanya saw it. There, stretching through the ocean like a path towards the horizon, was a half-drowned and narrow sand shoal. The wind whirled up the grey sand and mixed it into the mist, but the water framing the shoal was eerily still.

"It must stretch on for miles," said Catanya in awe. She squinted into the distance, hoping to see where it ended, but the overcast sky was too dense.

Drayk shuddered beside her and she saw the apprehension on his face.

"So, what exactly happened to you out there?" she asked.

Drayk heaved a great sigh. "It's hard to explain," he said in a low voice. "But I heard voices, whispers on the wind." He looked back towards the shoal and shuddered again.

Catanya pulled out the map from her pocket and unfolded it. As far as she could tell, the shoal would lead them to an island somewhere in the middle of the ocean. She squinted through the mist, but she couldn't see anything resembling a landmass. There was nothing but water, sand, and mist as far as the eye could see.

"Well..." She took an uneasy breath. Now that she was standing here, it was harder for her to deny that this shoal could be haunted. It really was isolated and bleak, and the otherworldly chill in the air made her skin crawl. "I suppose we have no choice, do we?" She tried to give Drayk a reassuring smile as she stepped onto the sandbar.

It relieved her to discover how solid the sand was beneath her feet. She peered into the water on either side of her, wondering how wide the shoal reached before it dropped into the depths of the ocean.

She turned back to look at Drayk expectantly. He seemed to be steeling himself to step forward. "Well, maybe it's not as bad as I remember," he said as he took a deep breath and walked out to join her.

They walked together until the fog and spray swallowed the land behind them and all they could see was water.

As Catanya stared out at the unforgiving expanse of ocean on either side of her, a tightness settled in her chest. She had always felt safe near the ocean, but for the first time in her life she understood how daunting it was. This far from land, they were so untethered and isolated. They were so insignificant compared to the enormity of the ocean surrounding them. All it would take would be one wave, one powerful gust of wind, and they'd be lost forever.

As they made their way along, the water seemed to press and tempt them as if it longed to drag them into its fathomless depths. The wind blew gently at first, but the farther out from land they trekked, the wilder the gusts became. After a few hours, Catanya had to fight hard to stay on her feet. The cold made her skin burn and her head pound. Her nostrils filled with the smell of seawater, and her clothes became drenched from the ocean spray.

A sudden and violent squall whipped at her ears, and she thought she heard someone call her name. She glanced at Drayk, but he made no sign of having spoken. She was so exhausted that she assumed she was hearing things.

But after another few minutes of walking, Catanya caught the unmistakable sound of children giggling. She stopped dead in her tracks and held out her hand to stop Drayk.

"Do you hear them?" she asked, her voice raspy and hushed.

"Hear who?"

"The girls." She was surprised to discover she knew exactly whose voices they were. "Alli! Gréys?" Excited, she whirled around, expecting to see them, but there was nothing and no one—nothing but sand and water.

"They're not here, Catya." Drayk spoke quietly, and he gave her a sympathetic look.

"What do you mean, they're not here? They have to be. I recognize the sound of their voices." Her mind was racing. Her entire body ached, and she was exhausted, but she knew what she'd heard.

"It's the wind," said Drayk. "It plays tricks on your mind."

"So... you didn't hear them?" asked Catanya, crestfallen.

Drayk shook his head, wearing a morbid expression.

Catanya nodded and tried to ignore the sense of disappointment and queasiness she now felt. For one brief, shining moment, she had deluded herself into thinking the girls were there with her—that they were all right. But that was absurd. She knew that now.

As they continued walking, she noticed Drayk grimacing beside her.

"What is it?" she asked.

"It's nothing." He tried to sound casual, but the pain on his face was too obvious.

Catanya came to a halt. "What do you hear?"

I could just stay here you know? I like it up here! called a discordantly happy, high-pitched voice through the wind.

Catanya gasped and grabbed Drayk's arm.

Eww. What are you doing? Only old married people do that.

"It can't be." Catanya looked around reflexively, though she knew it was impossible.

"Try not to listen to it," Drayk said, shaking his head violently, as though trying to ward off a bee. "We should keep moving."

Catanya nodded, trying to hold back the sudden tears burning in the corners of her eyes.

They pushed forward together, walking for several more minutes.

Are you listening to me? squeaked Olly's voice on the wind. Catanya had to close her eyes to block it out.

More giggles and squeals.

You're going to leave, aren't you? asked Diyah, and Catanya nearly tripped in her astonishment.

The wind grew more insistent, fighting against Catanya and Drayk as they struggled to walk. They stumbled onwards, slipping in the wet sand and struggling to stay upright as the powerful gusts threatened to blow them out into the ocean.

It was agonizing. Every movement was a physical struggle as they battled the forces of the wind. With every step she took, Catanya heard more voices in the air. They started out more like echoes—hints, and murmurs that blew past her in the squall, leaving a lingering impression she could almost ignore. But the more she ignored them, the clearer and more directed the voices became.

The voices were fighting them, trying to prevent them from crossing the shoal.

Oh dear, it's just dreadful, just dreadful, came Genna's voice.

I've been looking for you for quite some time, said Ayr.

"Stop it!" shouted Catanya, clutching her ears. The voices only grew louder, spurred on by her reaction. She tried to plow forward, with her hands cupped over her ears, but the wind laughed and shoved her back with a great heave.

Can't you feel them? Itching and scratching away, cackled the man in the cabin.

What's the matter? Afraid to admit who you really are? sneered Lia.

The voices snapped at her from every direction, pushing and pulling her with violent insistence.

Out of the corner of her eye, Catanya saw Drayk fall to his knees. She strained to turn against the wind, and was shocked to see tears pouring down his face.

"No, I'm not," he moaned, clutching his head with his eyes closed and his face screwed up against the pain. "No! Stay away from me!" He swatted at something she couldn't see.

It alarmed Catanya to see him like that. "Drayk," she

croaked, but the storm drowned her voice. She tried to go to him, but the wind swelled around her, drawing the air out of her lungs.

You could stand up to Caerlon, said Diyah.

I don't want to join the fírkon! Olly's voice cried.

Shh, it's only a nightmare, dear. Go back to sleep, cooed Genna.

I don't want to lose you either. I can't. Please. I love you, Catanya.

At the sound of Jémys's voice, Catanya fell to her knees. "Please, stop," she moaned.

The wind cackled even louder now, a vindictive, unforgiving sound.

My personal favourite, the Conqueror Betrayed.

"Stop!"

Maybe you were given those powers for a reason.

You're a royal—one of them. You never think about anyone but yourselves, shouted Jémys.

Catanya was sobbing uncontrollably now. The world was spinning, and she could barely breathe.

So, you're on the road to nowhere from nowhere. Sounds like a truly riveting adventure, sneered Drayk's voice, but she knew it wasn't really him. She had her eyes closed and her head pressed into her knees. She grasped around blindly, trying to find him, but all she felt was sand.

You lied to me, and now everyone I love is dead! roared Jémys.

You're the only one who can save us, so just go! cried Diyah.

Finally, we have a real chance... I want you to fight with me, said Ayr.

Catanya's entire body was shaking. She wanted nothing more than to disappear.

Pull yourself together! If you don't do something, we're all going to die.

Drayk's voice broke through, and she remembered her powers.

In a last, desperate attempt to fight, she tried to summon something, any kind of magic that might help them. Her fingers prickled, but before she could focus any of her power, the wind laughed again. And this time, it was different. It sounded familiar—a cool female voice cackling in taunting delight.

In an instant, all Catanya's power sapped away, and she collapsed into the sand, weaker than ever.

The voice cackled even louder.

It was one of the worst sounds she'd ever heard, and she needed to get away from it. She tried to stand, but her legs wobbled, unable to support her weight.

Help us, Catanya, cried the girls from the lodge, and an image burned through her memory. She saw the lodge in shambles and people screaming and running in every direction.

Catanya help me! squealed Olly.

Her legs gave out, and she collapsed again. She tried to crawl forward, but the wind pushed her down.

I told you that you'd kill me! shouted the old man in the cabin. *Murderer! You should be used to the feel of blood on your skin.*

Awnell City was burning. The screams grew louder and louder.

And the woman cackled more.

"I'm sorry," gasped Catanya, trying to block out the voices as they reached a deafening volume. The winds surrounded her, circling faster and faster until a vicious cyclone emerged. It engulfed her, blasting sand into her eyes and blinding her. It pulled and buffeted her in every direction until her body finally left the ground. The wind hurled her into the sky.

"No!" she cried out, trying to cling to the earth, but she couldn't reach it. She had become weightless as she revolved in sickening circles, rising higher and higher until she lost all sense of direction.

She couldn't see anything anymore. For all she knew, the

wind was launching her away from safety, out towards the far reaches of the sea.

It's all your fault, hissed Jémys.

She cried as the voices jeered at her, taunting her with the sounds and echoes of the pain she'd seen and caused.

More screams of people dying, and still the woman laughed.

"No, they don't deserve this. Let me help them." Catanya reached out blindly, trying to find her way forward. "I can help them. I can fix it, just let me go to them!" She desperately wanted to undo everything. It was agony to hear it all again.

I think you've been lying to everyone, even yourself, sneered Cadyan.

A chorus of voices taunted her in overlapping cacophony, blending together until only one voice remained, louder and more strident than all the others. And finally, she realized who had been laughing.

You're Caerlon royalty, everything you touch, you ruin.

That was her own voice on the wind now, hissing the things she tried not to think.

A genuine cry rent the air, and for a second, she could see through the windstorm to the shoal beneath her. Drayk was thrashing on the ground, clutching at his head in pain, blood leaking from his ears.

"No, no, no!" cried Catanya. "Don't let him die too!" She gave an inarticulate shout as she spiralled through the air, frantically trying to move in one direction.

You should never have brought him with you, hissed the wind-Catanya. *Now he'll die just like the rest of them.*

More cruel laughter.

Catanya was panicking now. "I can't go through this again," she sobbed, watching Drayk writhe and scream on the ground. "I can't lose another person, please." She pleaded with the wind to release her.

The wind howled, and Catanya let out a bellow of frustration, tears swirling across her face as she continued to whip in every direction. "I won't let it happen again!" she yelled, finally getting angry. "I won't lose another person. Do you hear me?"

A sudden stillness settled around her and her body slowed. "Let me go!" she shouted, trying to muster all the authority she could find. She looked around, waiting for the next lurch, but it didn't come.

Help us, Catanya, came the voices of everyone she'd lost. *Don't leave us here.*

"Please," she said, begging them to stop. "Please! There's nothing I can do for you. I can't change what happened, but I swear I won't let it happen again. I won't let anyone else suffer the way you suffered. Just let me go."

She hung in the air for what felt like an eternity, then she felt herself begin to descend. With a great lurch, her body righted itself so her feet dangled below her once again. She held her breath as her toes touched down and the wind settled.

Drayk was still writhing in the sand and screaming. She rushed forward and hurled herself down beside him.

"Drayk!" She tried to pull his arms away from his head. "Drayk, can you hear me?"

He was shaking uncontrollably, with his eyes squeezed so tight that it looked painful.

"Make it stop," he moaned, and he sounded like a scared child whimpering in the dark.

"I'm here." Catanya grabbed him and pulled him close. "Just focus on my voice. Move towards it."

"Catya?" he asked, but his body spasmed and he kept his eyes closed.

"Yes, it's me. Come on, Drayk, listen to my voice." She didn't know what else to do. She couldn't let him die—she *wouldn't* let him die. "I'm real, just me. Nothing else. Listen to me. Ignore everything else. You can do it." She clutched his arms and squeezed.

His convulsions seemed to slow.

"You can do it," she repeated, brushing the sand off his face. "Follow my voice."

His eyes flickered and opened, and he stared up at her as though he couldn't see her. Slowly, the clarity returned. "I'm fine," he said after a while.

Catanya breathed a great sigh of relief and rested her head on his shoulder for a moment, taking slow, steadying breaths. Then she stood up and put her hands under his arms to help him to his feet.

"Is it over?" he asked, trembling as he looked at her. He spoke louder than usual, like he was having trouble hearing his own voice. His eyes were swollen, his hair was full of sand, and the blood from his ears had streaked down his face. Catanya supposed she must not look much better.

"I think so," she mumbled, trying to brush the grit out of her hair. She put her hands up to her ears, expecting to find blood just like Drayk, but there was nothing. Aside from a slight ringing sound, her ears seemed fine.

Catanya found this inexplicably unsettling. The old man in the cabin had lost his hearing out here, hadn't he? And it looked like Drayk had nearly suffered the same fate. But Catanya's ears were fine. No damage.

And the old man had still been able to hear *her*...

"That was..." Drayk's voice trailed off, and he looked at her helplessly.

Catanya didn't need him to explain.

Drayk let out a short hysterical laugh and shook his head like a dog, sending water and sand flying in every direction. Then he stumbled as though the effort had made him dizzy.

Concerned, Catanya watched him rub his face with his hands. She wanted to ask him what he'd heard, but she was nervous. So, she settled on something a little easier. "Are you all right?" she asked slowly. As exhausted as she felt, she thought Drayk looked worse.

"Me? I'm always fine." He was trying to sound confident, but his voice was unusually thin and he was still wobbling precariously. "Should we keep going?" he asked, gesturing forward half-heartedly.

Catanya took a deep breath and gazed along the shoal. There was still no end in sight, but she knew the voices wouldn't return—although she didn't know how she knew it.

She looked up at the darkening sky and sighed. "I can't change the past," she whispered. "But I can learn from it and use it to change the future."

"What?" asked Drayk. He was trying to rub the dried blood off his face as he stared at her.

"Nothing," said Catanya, shaking her head. "I think we should rest for the night."

Drayk nodded, and Catanya noted the obvious relief on his face.

They spotted an area where the shoal looked wider and more secure, so they continued until they reached that point. A small clump of shrubbery struggled to poke out of the deep sand, giving them limited shelter on one side.

"Do you think you'll be able to sleep?" asked Drayk as he slumped down beside the shrub. Dusk was giving way to night, but the moon had risen behind the clouds, draping a bluish-grey glow over them.

Catanya shrugged. "I doubt it... but I think we should try, don't you?" She was eyeing him closely. He still looked wan and agitated, but she thought he seemed a bit more like his normal self. "Who knows how much longer this will take."

"Or what's waiting for us at the end," added Drayk, giving her a significant look. "What does the next part of the map say?" He pulled off his bag and rummaged around for his canteen.

"The Burning Cove," said Catanya, reciting from memory. She'd memorized the locations on the map, but only now did she realize how utterly inadequate their names really were.

Catanya pulled out the parchment and read aloud the next lines of the poem, "*Delusions of yearning to burn and scold at innocence.*"

"Good, nothing cryptic about that." Drayk rolled his eyes and slumped backwards so he was resting against the shrubs.

Catanya laughed feebly and took a seat next to him. "You know, I think we should prepare ourselves. This journey is going to be difficult. More difficult than we expected," she said after a few minutes of silence. "What if each step is worse than the last?" She couldn't imagine what could be worse than hearing the voices of her dead friends taunting her. Or the sound of her own voice, so distorted and cruel.

"Well..." Drayk propped himself up on his elbows, grinning with the familiar twinkle in his eyes. "It wouldn't be much fun otherwise, now, would it?"

Catanya was flabbergasted. "How do you do that?" she asked. "How do you just take everything in stride like that, not a care or worry at all?"

Drayk put his hands behind his head and reclined. "I've never seen the point of worrying. I prefer to use my imagination for better things," he said, winking. Then he closed his eyes and drifted off to sleep.

Several hours passed before Catanya was able to fall asleep. Even then, her sleep was not restful. She was plagued by dreams once more.

She dreamed she was sitting with Diyah on the edge of the ocean in Faltir, chatting happily about the girls at the lodge and joking about the latest village boy who was smitten with Diyah.

But then the scene changed.

Catanya watched Diyah talking to Jémys.

"It's okay, Diyah. The only thing that matters is Catanya. As long as I know she's alive and fighting, I can endure anything," said Jémys. He smiled at Diyah, but there was something wrong with it. The smile distorted and cracked, and Jémys's face turned sour, like he was in pain. Then he fell to the floor, crying in agony.

"I loved her too," said Diyah, and she was bleeding as she crumpled to the ground beside him. Catanya suddenly realized they weren't the only bodies lying there. She spun around in circles, horrified by the sight of everyone she had ever loved, dead at her feet.

Then she felt someone touch her shoulder and turned around to see Drayk grinning at her. His face seemed taut and waxy and his smile contorted, just like Jémys's smile had done before it cracked.

"I've become sentimental and weak." Drayk's voice was distorted, and his entire body disintegrated into sand.

Catanya woke up with a start, panting and sweating. She twisted around, frantically looking for Drayk, and saw him sleeping peacefully a few feet away.

She took a deep breath and pressed her hands against her eyes until she saw bright spots inside her eyelids. Opening them again, she looked up at the stars. The clouds had dispersed. The evening was clear and calm, but Catanya wouldn't be able to fall back asleep.

She pulled out the map once more and began studying it in the moonlight.

The harkened pain and sorrow with resounding aches of defeat... She traced the words with her hands and thought about everything that had happened. It had been unbelievably painful hearing the voices of everyone tormenting her.

Was she destined to lose everyone she cared about? Had the

wind been trying to tell her that? Was that what she needed to learn?

When the sun returned to the sky and Drayk awoke, they sat together, eating a small part of their rations in silence.

Catanya was preoccupied, running over words in her head and trying to decide how best to say what she needed to say. Finally, clearing her throat, she spoke, "You don't need to come with me, you know?"

"What?" Drayk was lost in thought and seemed not to register what she said.

"I mean it. I think you should turn back... before you get hurt." She looked away from him, not wanting to see his reaction.

Drayk scoffed. "Turn back? Are you serious? I'm not turning back."

"Why not?" asked Catanya, giving him a hardened look. She needed to make him understand.

"What, you don't want me here, is that it?"

"No!" said Catanya. "I just mean it's not safe. I can do this alone, you know? You're not obligated... You don't owe me... You don't have to come," she finished lamely.

Drayk laughed. "I know I don't *have* to," he said, "but..." He swallowed his mouthful of bread and shrugged. "What else have I got? I don't have anywhere else to go... Besides, I love a good adventure, and this—the chance to find Túir-Avlea." He whistled and grinned. "No way I'm missing this. And I won't get hurt. I can take care of myself. I always have and I always will." He shook his head and stood up with his back to her.

"Drayk, you almost died yesterday," said Catanya, standing up beside him.

Drayk just shrugged. "Everyone dies eventually. At least it would have been an interesting end."

"Drayk, be reasonable," she said, annoyed by his dismissive attitude. "This is really dangerous. And eventually... everyone around me, everyone I care about gets hurt—or worse! It's not safe."

She put her hand on his arm. He turned to face her, wearing a wry smile.

"Well, I guess it's a good thing you don't care about me, then, isn't it?" he said, winking as he grabbed his bag and sauntered past her. "Come on, we're wasting daylight."

18

THE TOURNAMENT BEGINS

Diyah had only ever heard stories about the Maífírkon Tournament, but she'd always thought it sounded barbaric. She never would have believed that one day she'd not only witness it, but she'd actually be obliged to play a role in it. It all seemed surreal to her, and she couldn't accept that it was happening.

The castle was overflowing with people, between the Awnadh and all Caerlon's own soldiers, not to mention the hundreds of spectators pouring into the city for the tournament's entertainment.

In the two weeks since he'd been back in the city, Cadyan had expedited the preparations for the competition. He seemed determined to continue on schedule despite the recent upheaval of battle. Vendors and entertainers came from all over Mórceá. Extra makeshift barracks had been erected for the additional soldiers, and a large room near the armoury had been converted to an infirmary for the length of the tournament.

Diyah had been commanded to heal the fírkon and the Awnadh warriors in the aftermath of the battle. Injuries did not exempt anyone from the tournament, so Diyah worked day and night, under pressure to return everyone to fighting condition. Most of the superficial wounds healed quickly. But several soldiers had more severe damage, like broken bones and torn ligaments. Those men would be fighting at a significant disadvantage.

"It's madness out there," said Fehla as she came into the physician's quarters, closing the door behind her.

It had been an unusually busy day for Diyah. She'd just found time to sit down when Fehla arrived.

"It's been madness in here too," she grumbled, massaging her temple with one hand. She had an ear-splitting headache that wouldn't go away no matter what she tried, and her left wrist was still sore from when she'd sprained it in the dungeon.

"Really? Is there something going around?"

"Oh, yes," said Diyah, rolling her eyes. "A morbid sense of curiosity. Everyone wants to gawk at the poor girl being sold off to the winner." Strangers had been flooding the physician's quarters nonstop for days, but today was especially bad. It was the last day before the tournament began.

"Ah, I see." Fehla nodded as she sat down opposite her.

This was the first time Diyah had really seen Fehla for days. The queen looked thin and pallid, with dark circles around her eyes.

"Are you okay?" asked Diyah. "You don't look well."

Fehla shrugged, absentmindedly twirling the beaded bracelet on her wrist—the bracelet her daughter had made over ten years ago. "I have my good days and my bad days."

Diyah didn't need to ask what she meant. Everyone in the castle had heard.

The afternoon of his return, Cadyan had assembled his courtiers to watch as he triumphantly announced to Fehla that her daughter was dead. He'd made a spectacle of it, revelling in his mother's anguish. And now he never missed an opportunity to throw in a dig about it whenever he saw her.

"I don't understand my son," said Fehla abruptly. "Catanya is gone, so why is he still acting like this? You know, he never liked this tournament as a boy. It used to frighten him so badly he couldn't sleep. So why is he going through with it? He could cancel the whole thing if he wanted to."

"I suppose he doesn't want to," said Diyah. "I think we've established that he isn't the same boy he used to be." Diyah didn't mean to be so blunt, but she was tired and irritable.

Fehla rubbed her swollen eyes. "I just wish I knew how to fix him."

"Fix him? Fehla..." Diyah said it with a mixture of pity and reproach. "You can't help someone who doesn't want to be helped. And how do you expect to redeem a man who has killed so many people, including his own father and sister?" Diyah shook her head.

"But he didn't actually kill either of them, did he? *Slaedir* killed Catanya, and Casréyan... well..." Fehla was panic rationalizing now. "There has to be a way. This isn't who Cadyan really is."

"If you say so," said Diyah with a yawn, and they lapsed into silence.

Diyah welcomed the peace and quiet. She'd spent the better part of her day being ogled and interrogated by people from all over Caerlon. She was grateful not to have to talk, but she was also grateful for Fehla's quiet company. Whenever she was alone these days, Diyah struggled to keep the fear at bay. She was plagued by nightmares of what lay ahead, and she felt trapped and paralyzed. She had always sworn she'd never marry unless she found a true partner—someone she loved as much as her father had loved her mother. Now, it seemed, she wouldn't have a choice.

"Maybe Jémys will win," said Fehla. Diyah hadn't realized

she'd been watching her. "At least he's a good man, and he's your friend."

"Even if he does win, Cadyan will never let him be maífirkon," said Diyah. She had run through every scenario in her head a thousand times already. Cadyan would never trust a captain who had loved his sister. The only reason he wanted Jémys to fight was to watch him suffer, possibly even die.

"I suppose you're right," said Fehla. She reached out and took Diyah's uninjured hand. "I'm so sorry this is happening to you, Diyah."

Diyah gave her a thin smile. "None of this is your fault, Fehla."

"Isn't it?" She leaned back in her chair and closed her eyes in chagrin.

They spent the rest of the afternoon sitting together in silence and dreading the next day, when the tournament would begin.

***

The tournament was fought in two phases, and the first phase was the longest, comprising three rounds. Over a thousand firkon were slated to compete this year. Every soldier who'd ranked past the second phase in the previous tournament was required to fight. A random lottery selected the rest. Most low-ranking firkon saw it as their opportunity to advance and earn a more prestigious position. The high-ranking fighters used it to hone their craft and showcase their talent.

An enormous circular arena had been erected in the field off the west wing of the castle, north of the barracks. The arena had been partitioned into eight smaller segments to allow multiple fights at a time. As the rounds progressed and the number of fighters decreased, the partitions would be removed to give the fighters more space.

Wooden spectators' benches circled the arena, rising in levels to provide everyone a clear view. The enclosed royal box sat at the head of the stadium, where Cadyan, his courtiers, and select firkon could enjoy the tournament in privacy.

The first round would take over two weeks, and, to Diyah's dismay, she was obligated to sit in the royal box with Cadyan and Fehla throughout the entire tournament. No part of her relished the idea of watching countless gruesome duels, especially because she knew she'd be the one tending to their wounds afterwards.

Only the final round was meant to be a fight to the death, but, from what Fehla had told her, Diyah knew there were liable to be many more casualties. The fighters were not permitted to wear protective armour, and the impartial pairing system would set soldiers with decades of experience against young men with none. And according to Fehla, mercy was not a valued trait in this tournament.

Early in the morning on the first day of the tournament, Diyah was walking down the corridor towards the armoury, looking for Jémys, when she overheard some voices talking in low, hurried whispers.

"That's right. He has to survive," said a strict male voice.

"So, you want me to throw the match?" came a deeper baritone.

"I don't care what you do, as long as he survives."

"Okay, Lieutenant—"

The voices broke off quickly and a new voice said, "The maífirkon wants all competitors ready in two minutes."

Diyah heard the men exit the armoury into the training fields. She stepped into the now empty room, searching for any sign of who had been talking. Whoever they were, it sounded like they were interfering with the tournament's outcome.

Diyah didn't care about the cheating, but she was curious to know who "he" was.

Distracted, it took her a moment to recognize a new set of voices coming towards her. She heard Cadyan laugh and it made her skin crawl.

"What is it with this girl?" he exclaimed. "Why does every man in the kingdom seem to want her? Now even you?"

"Admittedly she is breathtaking, your majesty," said a voice Diyah recognized, "but in all honesty, it's her skill as a Heiltúir I'm most interested to acquire."

The king rounded the corner, accompanied by Lord Zadílar, who seemed startled to see her. They both looked especially garish, wearing finery with mixtures of fur, velvet, and brightly coloured silk.

"Ah, the woman in question herself," said Cadyan, a cruel grin spreading across his face. "Zad, here, was trying to convince me I should give you to him instead of the maífirkon. What do you think of that?"

Diyah was flustered. She looked at Zadílar for an explanation but he just shrugged and smiled as if he were perfectly nonplussed. "Well, I'd be remiss if I didn't at least suggest it," he said. "It's hard not to be jealous of the fírkon at a time like this."

"Is it?" Cadyan looked openly surprised. He surveyed Diyah, a strange expression on his face, like he was trying to see something hidden beneath the surface. "Well, regardless," he said finally, "I can't change the rules of the tournament now— well, that's not true... I suppose I *could*, but I won't."

"Why not?" asked Zad with a touch of urgency in his voice. He cast a furtive glance in Diyah's direction.

"Because the purpose isn't just to reward the fírkon, it is to punish her," he replied as he sneered at Diyah. "She needs to suffer. And a life with you, Zad, would be all parties and laughter."

Diyah glared at Cadyan, allowing her hatred to burn through her.

"Besides, she's still *my* Heiltúir, and I'm not letting her leave this city." He smirked as he walked away, leaving her and Zadílar alone.

Diyah waited until he was out of sight, and then she rounded on Zadílar. "What's happening?"

"My dear," he said, sounding unusually strained. "I am trying to get you out of this." He made a move as though to take her hands, but she backed away.

"By forcing me into marriage with you instead?" she asked, and her voice sounded a little shrill.

"Please calm down," said Zad, glancing around to make sure the guards couldn't hear them. "I merely hoped I could use it as a pretence to get you to Sidina and away from here... but, as you heard, our king is determined to move forward with this farce..." He trailed off, looking frustrated. "You could try to escape, but the likelihood of succeeding... and where would you go? I wouldn't be able to take you in. Sidina is always being watched."

Zadílar seemed flustered. It was uncharacteristic to hear him rambling.

"I can't escape," she said in a numb voice. "The firkon have people I care about, people I love. If I escape, Cadyan will kill them." She explained about Meya, Gréys, and Hahney and was surprised to see a slight glimmer appear in Zad's eye.

"Well, perhaps on that front, I can actually be of some use," he muttered. "I will make enquiries and see if I can locate them. Perhaps I can get them out of Caerlon City and somewhere safe. They won't be as difficult to extract as you are." He sighed and closed his eyes momentarily. "It's a start, anyway."

Diyah frowned at him. She was still having trouble deciding about this man, but he seemed genuinely interested in helping her. "Thank you," she said quietly. If he succeeded in finding the girls, Diyah would only have to worry about herself and Jémys.

A group of firkon came around the corner, and Zad straightened up, adopting an enthusiastic smile.

"Lads," he declared in a bright voice, "I'm trying to decide where to place my bets for the first round. Perhaps you would indulge me with your thoughts over breakfast? And it's never too early for a pint or two, is it?" His eyes darted over to Diyah briefly, but no one seemed to notice.

The firkon murmured sounds of agreement as they led the way down the corridor. Zadílar inclined his head towards Diyah before turning and following them.

Diyah watched him go, her stomach tight with a strange mixture of gratitude and nausea. Zadílar was trying to help her, but even he couldn't do anything about this. Nothing was going to stop the tournament from happening. Cadyan was determined to make her suffer and keep her trapped under his thumb forever. There was no way out.

Later that morning, as Diyah took her seat next to Fehla in the stands, she felt hundreds of pairs of eyes on her. A ripple of excited whispers moved through the crowd. She tried to ignore her queasiness.

"Here," said Fehla, handing her a leaflet.

The page detailed the order of the duels. It shocked Diyah to discover that nine sets were scheduled for today alone. Seventy-two fights.

"This is going to take ages," she groaned.

"Yes, but look." Fehla pointed at a spot partway down the list. Jémys was scheduled to fight in the fourth set that day. They'd paired him with one of the Awnadh fighters. Diyah didn't know if that was good or bad, but she hoped the Awnadh wouldn't be quite as driven to hurt Jémys, given that Awnell had been helping Catanya only a few weeks earlier.

Diyah hadn't seen Jémys much since that night in the dungeons. A few final visits to make sure he'd healed enough to fight, and then nothing. She missed his company, but she understood that he needed to focus if he planned to survive the tournament. After all, the fírkon and the Awnadh warriors were the most lethal fighters in Mórceá. And Jémys wasn't a soldier.

Cadyan strode into the arena, beaming at the sea of spectators.

"People of Caerlon, welcome!" he called out. "Welcome to this year's Maífírkon Tournament. As many of you may know, my great grandfather started this tradition to test the bravery, skill, and allegiance of his soldiers. The tournament runs every four years as a way to select the best among these honourable men to bear the maífírkon title and command the ranks of Caerlon's fírkon. Each fighter will be ranked based on brutality, efficiency, and skill. Winners progress to the next round and losers are disqualified. At the end of the tournament, all ranks will be tallied to determine individual soldiers' assignments and income for the next four years.

"Our current maífírkon, Slaedir, who returns this year to defend his title, has won the last three competitions." Cadyan gestured to Slaedir, who was sitting in the stands, watching the event. He stood up and waved at the crowd, clearly relishing the attention. "Join me in wishing our current maífírkon the best of luck in the coming weeks." Cadyan paused as the crowd clapped and cheered, then he raised his hands again to silence them.

"This year, our winner will not only claim the maífírkon title. He will also claim the hand of a *breathtaking* woman." He used Zadílar's word with deliberate emphasis. "Our own court physician, Diyah Aí-Murina, the last of the Heiltúir and a woman whose beauty is unparalleled throughout the kingdom." The cheering was even louder. Cadyan gestured at Diyah and smirked as he saw her glowering at him. "Without further ado, let the tournament begin!" Cadyan exited the arena and took his seat in the stands next to his mother.

Whatever Diyah had been expecting, this wasn't it. The duels were not only bloodier and more brutal than she'd imagined, they were also a lot quicker.

She rapidly realized that the first round of the tournament was a mere formality, a warm-up for the seasoned fighters as they wiped out the younger, inexperienced competition.

The only fight that even approached a fair match was the one between Jémys and his contestant. But even that fight had barely started before it was done. Jémys ended it cleanly, so neither he nor his opponent bore any serious injuries.

It surprised Diyah to discover that he was such an impressive and adept fighter. He moved with a powerful ease and agility that rivalled even the best fighters. And Diyah wasn't the only one who was impressed. She noticed a distinct sense of admiration coming from the audience as they cheered Jémys's victory. Even Cadyan had difficulty concealing his shock. For the first time since Jémys had told her his plan, Diyah thought he might stand a chance at winning. But then she reminded herself it was only the first round.

As the first day of the tournament came to an end, Diyah and Fehla were to be found in the infirmary.

"I can't believe it," grumbled Diyah, weaving in and out of patients' beds, carrying jugs of water and piles of fresh bandages. "I can't believe it! Look at them." She gestured around at the wounded fighters lying in cots throughout the room.

"Calm down, Diyah," said Fehla in a low voice.

"*Calm down*?" she repeated, a little hysterically. "How am I supposed to stay calm when I'm surrounded by this?"

"I know, but if you don't get a grip on yourself, you won't be any help to them, now, will you?"

Diyah closed her eyes in frustration and took a few deep breaths. "You're right," she said. "I know you're right, it's just so awful."

In all her years working as a healer, Diyah had never seen anything quite like it. She'd never had so many patients with life-threatening injuries that needed tending simultaneously. Even after the battle of Awnell, there hadn't been this many. She hadn't thought about it before, but she supposed Cadyan had deliberately left the dying men behind.

How many broken bodies had perished, alone and forgotten on the streets of Awnell? How many people could she have saved if she'd been there?

Diyah tried to shake away her morbid thoughts. She couldn't afford to think that way right now. She needed to compartmentalize, to prioritize wounds based on severity, and block out the rest.

"We're going to need help," she said finally. Her wrist was still tender and she was working slower than she normally would. "Can you get one or two servants?"

Fehla nodded and swept out of the room. When she returned, she brought two maidservants with her that Diyah vaguely recognized.

The four women worked for hours, Diyah dictating instructions to the others from across the room. It was well past midnight when the infirmary finally quieted. Diyah distributed a round of sleeping tonics to help the wounded men sleep, and then stopped at the foot of one of the cots. Despite all her hard work, this last patient wasn't improving.

He'd sustained a massive head injury and his stomach had been pierced with a sword. No matter what Diyah tried, she couldn't get the bleeding to stop.

"We could try cauterizing it," she said, looking at Fehla and seeing the exhausted bags under her eyes. "But I think that's just delaying the inevitable."

"Inevitable? You mean he's going to die?" whispered Fehla, evidently nervous to wake the sleeping patients. "There's nothing else you can do?"

Diyah sighed and wiped her bloodstained hands on her apron, eyeing the unconscious man. "I'm afraid not. At this point, all we can do is prolong his pain or else let him die, and hope he dies quickly." She heard the note of resentment in her voice.

"Diyah!" said Fehla reproachfully.

"I'm sorry. I didn't mean to sound so unfeeling, but in this case, a quick death is the best we can hope for. Death is better than living in agony."

"You can't mean that." Fehla was stooped with sadness as she watched the scene in front of her.

Diyah gave her a piercing gaze. "I *do* mean it, Fehla. I've been doing this long enough to know death is nothing to fear. Truly. Death is often a blessing instead of a curse, and that is certainly the case here." Diyah laid her hand on the man's forehead and felt his fevered temperature.

"But he's so young," said Fehla.

"I know." Diyah stared at him. He couldn't be more than seventeen or eighteen. This tournament was supposed to be the final step in his training to become a fírkon. He likely felt honoured to be chosen to fight.

Maybe it's better that he doesn't survive, she thought, but she didn't want to say that to Fehla.

Diyah sighed and brushed the sweaty hair off her neck. "I'm not saying it's fair, but it's the only thing he has left," she said.

At times like this, she wished she could do more to facilitate a quick passing. But the Heiltúir oath forbid it.

We do not mete out death.

Those words were a surprisingly heavy burden.

"I gave him another dose of sleeping tonic," she said more to herself than to Fehla. "And there's one more thing I can do." She grabbed a vial of numbing agent off the worktable and poured it liberally over his wounds. In large amounts, the numbing effects could become permanent, leading to paralysis and loss of sensation. But at this point, it didn't matter.

Diyah emptied the bottle and tossed it aside. "There. That should make him more comfortable... And it will be my honour to sit with him while he passes on." She gave Fehla a half-hearted smile and sat down on the edge of the bed, taking the boy's hand in hers. "Eva, Trayli, thank you for your help," she called to the maids who were standing in the corner, waiting for instructions. "I can take it from here. You should go get some rest."

The girls nodded and curtseyed before leaving the room.

There was a long pause before Fehla spoke again. "How is it that someone so young can be so wise?" she asked, sitting on an empty cot.

The compliment surprised Diyah. "I've never thought of myself as wise," she said with a faint chuckle. "I just try to remember what my father taught me."

"You've never told me much about your father," said Fehla. "I assumed you didn't remember him."

Diyah shrugged. "I was young when I went to live at the lodge. But I only went to live there after my parents died... there was a plague," she added, seeing the question in Fehla's eyes. "But I still remember my father treating the sick villagers. He told me not to be afraid. He said that death was just one part of our journey and it was something we would all experience eventually, so why fear it?" Diyah sighed heavily as she thought back on the lessons her father had taught her. "Then my mother died and my father fell ill, and before I knew it, I was an orphan living in Faltir."

Fehla watched Diyah with a hint of amazement in her expression.

Diyah sighed. "My entire village died because of that plague," she continued. "Murina was such a beautiful place. The limestone buildings sat along the south-western shores, with verandas overlooking the warm water. The white sand beaches stretched for miles, and the sun was always shining. In the summers, the whole village used to dine together under the stars..." She trailed off, lost in the memory.

A shadow clouded Fehla's face. "I remember that plague," she said in a dark voice. "I remember Casréyan meeting with delegates from your village. They pleaded with him to intervene, but he refused... He boasted to me about it later." Fehla was shaking with anger. "I'm so sorry, Diyah. You lost everything, all because my husband was an unfeeling and unjust ruler. I can never tell you how deeply sorry I am." Fehla stared resolutely at the ceiling, as though trying to collect herself.

"It's not your fault, Fehla."

"Please stop saying that," she said, refusing to look at Diyah. "So much of this is my fault. If I had never married Casréyan, none of this would have happened. If only I'd had the courage to follow my instincts."

"You can't blame yourself for Casréyan's decisions."

"No, maybe not, but I can certainly blame myself for Cadyan's."

"That's not fair, you know—"

"Life isn't fair, though, is it? And I deserve my share of the blame." Her voice was getting louder. "Oh, I wish I had never married Casréyan! I wish I had never been persuaded to go through with a political marriage. Oh, Diyah!" She stared at her with such intense pity that, for a moment, Diyah was truly scared. "I can't bear to see you suffer the same way I did. I'm so sorry you're going to share my fate, and I wish I could do something to help you."

Diyah's cheeks burned. "It's not the same thing at all," she said, trying to sound reassuring. "Please don't worry about me. I can take care of myself. Believe me, I have no intention of being forced into an abusive, loveless marriage…"

It was the truth. She had been thinking about it all day, and she knew she wouldn't allow this to happen to her. She just didn't know how to prevent it yet.

They spent the rest of the night sitting with their young patient until just before dawn, when he finally breathed his last breath. Fehla left to get a few hours of rest before the tournament recommenced, and although Diyah was exhausted, she was too wound up to sleep.

Despite everything she had told Fehla the night before, Diyah was full of anger and resentment. Tired of being calm and wise, she wanted to scream, to fight back. She wanted to punish someone for everything that was happening.

She stormed out of the infirmary and into the armoury, searching for someone to hate. Nobody was there, so she proceeded out the door towards the training yard where she found Julyán alone. He was standing several feet from a large wooden target board. A collection of daggers, blades, and axes were laid out on a table beside him.

When he caught sight of her, he looked surprised. "What are you doing here this early?" He glanced at the pale sky.

"Looking for someone to yell at!" stormed Diyah.

Julyán raised his eyebrows and Diyah thought she saw the corners of his mouth twitch, as though he were fighting off a grin. This just made Diyah even angrier.

"Okay," he said, lifting a blade off the table, and turning to face the target. "What would you like to yell at me about this time?"

Diyah found his easy tone irritating. "I just spent my entire evening cleaning up the mess you people made of each other yesterday."

"I didn't even fight yesterday," said Julyán.

"Well, I don't care! I just watched a teenage boy die a slow, painful death because of this stupid tournament. It's senseless and barbaric!"

Julyán ignored her and launched his blade at the target. It pierced the centre mark with a hard thud.

"Well?" spat Diyah, marching forward to stand beside him. "You have nothing to say?"

"What would you like me to say?" he asked, dropping his arm and turning to look at her. "People die during the tournament, that's just the way it is."

Diyah laughed derisively and put her hands on her hips. "*That's just the way it is*? Do you know how ridiculous that sounds?"

This time, Julyán didn't try to hide his smirk as he shook his head. "Are you done?" he asked. "I have work to do." He indicated the table full of weapons.

Diyah threw her hands up in the air "Oh, yes, by all means, don't let me distract you from improving your skills as a murderer!" She was about to walk away when she noticed Julyán flinch. "What was that?" she asked.

"What was *what*?" He tried to avoid her gaze, but his entire demeanour had stiffened.

"You don't like being called a murderer?" she asked hotly.

Julyán sighed. "Does anybody?"

"You never cared what I called you before, so what's changed?" Diyah stepped forward to scrutinize his face. "It's Jémys, isn't it?"

Julyán rolled his eyes.

"You should talk to him," she pressed, undaunted by his reaction.

"Why would I do that?"

Diyah's anger ebbed slightly. "Emotional pain can be just as deadly as the physical, you know?"

Julyán scoffed. "Emotional pain?"

"Yes!" shouted Diyah.

At this, Julyán rounded on her. "Well, *healer*, sometimes emotional pain is the only thing keeping us alive," he snapped, looming over her.

Diyah took a deep breath to steady herself before responding. "That is the stupidest thing I've heard all day."

Julyán's eyes flashed, and he took a sharp step towards her. Diyah resisted the urge to back away.

"Why do you think we fight?" he asked in a low voice. Then, without warning, he grabbed her hand and wrapped her fingers around the handle of a knife. He grasped her by the shoulders and spun her around so she was closer to the target. "Here. Channel all of your energy, all your hatred and your anger into the blade. Calm your mind and *will* it to hit the target board," he commanded, moving away from her.

"I don't have any anger," blurted Diyah, trying to cover up her surprise.

Julyán shook his head. "We all have anger. Some of us are just better at channelling it than others. Now throw the knife."

Diyah frowned at him, and then stared at the blade in her hand. Diyah used knives every day in her work. Scalpels, peeling knives, drop points, straight backs... She knew her way around a blade, but this one was different. It was a single, weighted piece of steel with no hilt—just the cold metal grip against her skin. For one brief moment, she imagined channelling her anger by using the knife on Julyán. She imagined what it would feel like to purposefully take someone's life. But shame and guilt quickly overtook that thought. Then came the anger again.

She hated to admit it, but Julyán was right. She needed to channel her emotions or they'd eat her up.

The target was a narrow circle on the board, but as she looked at it, she thought about everything that had made her angry or sad since she'd left Faltir—all the despair and rage she felt. She closed her eyes and took a deep breath. Then she opened them again, stepped forward, and threw the knife with every bit of force she had. The blade cut through the air until it pierced the target board on the far edge. It was well outside the circle, but it stayed there—wobbling, but not falling.

"Good," said Julyán, walking forward and yanking the knife out of the wood. "Now you understand."

Diyah was dazed and confused as she walked back through the armoury towards her quarters. She closed the door to her room and collapsed onto her bed, smiling to herself. She had no rational explanation for it, but she felt better than she had in a long time.

19

THE LIEUTENANT

As the first phase of the tournament ended, the infirmary was overcrowded with casualties of the game. Since the tournament had begun, Diyah had watched twenty men die from their wounds. Another ten had sustained such debilitating injuries that their lives as they knew them were over.

Diyah noticed a trend in the severity of the injuries too. The fights were always the bloodiest whenever they were fought between a fírkon and an Awnadh warrior. It was obvious that neither group was comfortable with their precarious alliance. Diyah didn't know which fighters were worse. The fírkon were definitely more brutal, but the Awnadh warriors had a precision and detachment in their fighting, which disturbed Diyah even more.

What made the entire situation worse was how most fighters had taken to leering at Diyah as though she ought to admire their skill and enjoy their shows of violence. It was clear to her that the soldiers (and spectators) viewed it all as some perverted mating display.

With each passing day, Diyah's options were becoming

fewer and fewer. She longed to run, to escape Caerlon and never return, but the more she thought about escaping, the more she realized she'd never succeed. She hadn't heard from Zadílar about the girls, so she couldn't risk doing something that might endanger them. Besides, she'd been trying for months to find a way out of the castle and out of the city, but everywhere she turned, guards were watching her. And now the castle was overrun with tournament spectators eagerly tracking her every move. Even if she wanted to risk it, she had no chance of escaping now. Her best bet was to wait until after the tournament. But the idea of spending even one hour as the unwilling wife to the maífírkon was enough to make her scream.

The rest of the city and the spectators seemed especially invested in this year's tournament. A large wooden scoreboard had been erected at one end of the arena to track the tournament progress. It also tracked the odds on each contestant. Dozens of bet takers flocked from across Caerlon to gamble on the outcome of the tournament. Everyone in the city was placing bets, not just the wealthy courtiers. The peasants, tradesmen, and farmers seemed to view it as an excellent opportunity to make some quick gold.

"All righ', I'll put up ten gold pieces that Slaedir wins again this year."

"Are you mad? Don't bet on the winner now, there's weeks left of the tournament. Anything could happen."

"Aye, tha's why there's good odds on it now. Get in on the game early an' all that. Besides, I'm sure it'll be him. He always wins."

Diyah was walking past the arena where a small group of women had gathered around one of the more dishevelled and dishonest-looking bet takers, counting the coins in their change purses and giggling. Diyah paused, not wanting to be seen (she'd had enough attention for one day), so she ducked behind the arena seats, waiting for the group to leave.

"Really though, how can you be sure he'll win again this year?" asked one woman.

"Yeah! Didn't you see that man Rey, that man from Awnell? He'll give Slaedir a run for his money. The way he moved... so fast and so calculated. If you ask me, we might be having our first Awnadh as maífírkon."

"Yeah, and I'd rather him than Slaedir. I mean... think about the poor girl."

There were murmurs of agreement and commiseration from the group. Diyah tried not to listen, but their voices carried through the empty arena, making them impossible to ignore.

"I like her, you know. She's a nice girl. She doesn't deserve to wake up next to that face every morning."

Even more laughter from the group. Diyah clenched her fists, holding back her anger. *So, they thought it was amusing, did they?*

"I tell you what though, ladies," came the bet taker's oily voice. "You don' want to go bettin' on gruesome things like battles and tournaments, now, do you? 'Ow about we do somethin' a little more your speed, huh? What do you ladies think 'bout our lovely lady healer? How long till she's anticipatin', do you think? One month? Two?"

The ladies all gasped and giggled and started chattering amongst themselves.

Diyah felt dizzy. Queasiness climbed up her throat. She sat there, listening as they made their bets and tittered cheerily. She waited for them to finish, all the while trying to push what she'd heard from her mind, but she couldn't.

Diyah wasn't naïve. She knew being married would involve all kinds of unpleasantness, but she had somehow never considered the possibility of that leading to a child. Anytime she'd ever imagined herself as a mother, the image had been bright—full of love. She'd certainly never pictured it happening like this.

"No," said Diyah out loud. "I won't bring a child into this." She stood up and strode from the arena without looking back.

Walking back to the infirmary, Diyah realized she really only had one option. She knew what she needed to do, though it wouldn't be easy. She needed some time to prepare.

But even as she thought about it, she remembered the girls. Would Zadílar be able to get them out? Would he be able to do it before she needed to act?

And then there was Jémys. She couldn't abandon him now, not if there was a chance that she could help him survive... help him exact revenge.

She still had some time before the final round sealed her fate. So, for now, her plan could wait.

The second phase of the tournament opened the next morning. It was obvious from the first minute that this phase would be even bloodier than the previous ones. A random lottery determined the pairings for the fights at the beginning of each round. Now that they'd weeded out most novices, the fights were growing steadily more violent.

Diyah hadn't had much opportunity to talk with Jémys since the tournament began. But late one evening, as she was leaving the infirmary, he caught up with her in the hallway.

"Diyah," he half called, half whispered. "Diyah, wait."

"Jémys," she spluttered, looking around to see if anyone was watching before pulling him into the empty armoury with her. She threw her arms around him for a tight hug. As she stepped back, she noticed how unsettling it was to see him in the firkon uniform. He looked so much like his brother.

"Sorry it's been so long," he said, brushing the hair out of his face. "It's nearly impossible to get away. I don't know how you can stand it, having every move you make observed."

"I *can't* stand it," said Diyah. "I don't know how much longer I can stand any of this. Have you seen the number of men lying in cots in the infirmary? It's unbelievable."

Jémys put his hand on her shoulder. "I know. But we have to stay focused. We owe it to Catanya to try." His voice faltered, and he looked away.

"Jémys... I know you want to do this. I know you want to avenge her, but... It won't bring her back, you know? And if you die in the process—"

"Then I die," said Jémys, shrugging. "I don't care as long as I take Slaedir with me, and as many of his soldiers as possible. And if I can, I'll take Cadyan too."

"I understand," said Diyah, and she truly did. She wanted nothing more than to take down the people who killed her friend.

They stood together in silence, each lost in their own thoughts until Jémys said suddenly, "I miss her so much." The pain in his voice was clear, and he gazed at the sword rack beside him. "And I'll never get a chance... I'll never get to..." He stared down at his feet ashamedly. "I'll never forgive myself."

"Forgive yourself for what?"

"I was scared, I was hurt, but I never—" He broke off, tears in his eyes. "Now she'll never know how much I loved her."

Diyah nodded, putting her hand on his arm. "I'm sure she knew."

But Jémys was shaking his head. "No, I don't think she did," he said. "I was so angry... I said so many hurtful things. And I never got the chance to tell her I forgive her and I... I need her. I realize now how much I need her, Diyah. I feel so empty, so broken." He turned to look at her, his eyes glistening. "Revenge is all I have left."

"All right." Diyah rubbed her tired eyes with her hands. She didn't really understand what Jémys was saying, but she could understand his grief and the sensation of emptiness. "What can I do to help?"

Over the next two weeks, Diyah watched the tournament with a newfound focus and attention. She noticed patterns in the fights, key weaknesses and vulnerabilities in the other contestants, which she used to help Jémys prepare.

They met under cover in the infirmary. As Diyah tended his wounds between fights, she slipped him notes about her observations.

Jémys spent every other waking minute in the armoury or the training yard. His desire for revenge had become an obsession, and he needed to train hard if he was going to stand any chance of making it to the final round.

His last two fights hadn't exactly been easy, but Jémys had managed to end them quickly and cleanly so his reputation in the tournament was growing. Diyah had even overheard Cadyan praising Jémys to one of his guards.

"I do hate the man, but it's nice to see someone fight as well as he does. It makes for a good show, doesn't it?"

That's what it all comes down to, thought Diyah. *A good show.* And for the first time since the tournament began, she allowed herself to feel hopeful. She imagined watching Jémys, the victorious maífirkon, turn against his king. She imagined watching Cadyan die, ending the years of tyranny in Caerlon. At times, she even imagined herself living a happy life, spared from the torment of an abusive marriage.

But when the pairings were announced for the eighth round and she saw Jémys had been paired with Rey, Diyah's hope evaporated. Rey's reputation as a superior fighter was well known, and all his fights had been favourites among the spectators. While Jémys was rising in public opinion, it was nothing compared to Rey, who was already considered a serious contender for the title.

The eighth round was scheduled over two days, with two fights slated each day. As the tournament progressed, each fight grew longer. At this point, there was no telling how long they'd take.

The excitement in the crowd was palpable as they filled the arena seats that morning. Slaedir and his opponent Bir—a burly man from Awnell with a long, braided beard—were scheduled for the first fight, followed by Jémys and Rey.

The first match lasted three times longer than the earlier fights. Bir was not very fast, but his size and strength made him a formidable opponent. More than once, Diyah thought Bir had bested Slaedir, but Slaedir was vicious, and he was crafty.

The crowd cheered and catcalled back and forth like enormous, grotesque vultures. Diyah wasn't sure what they wanted more: to see their current maífirkon prevail, or to see him suffer an epic, bloody death.

The fight grew more and more heated until finally Bir disarmed Slaedir and hurled him onto the ground. The crowd leaned forward, holding their breath. But just as everyone thought it was over, Slaedir rolled aside, pulling a dagger from his inside pocket. He slashed out at Bir's leg, slicing his calf and spraying the ground with blood.

Bir cried out in pain and fell on his knee just as Slaedir retrieved his sword from the ground and spun it through the air, cutting clean through Bir's arm and sending his severed hand and blade soaring into the sky.

The crowd erupted in cheers as Bir crumpled over, clutching his bloody stump and moaning. Slaedir turned to face the crowd, wearing a triumphant smile. Before he left the arena, he bowed and shot Diyah a lecherous glance.

There was a short break before the second fight. Although she wanted desperately to find Jémys and wish him luck, Diyah was obliged to tend to Bir in the infirmary.

Bir was in a lot of pain, and it surprised Diyah to discover he wasn't as tough as everyone thought. He was crying and writhing around on the cot, making it nearly impossible for her to help him.

"Hold still," she said, trying to wrestle his injured arm out where she could see it. Every time she tried to touch it, he cried out in pain and tried to push her away.

"Bir, you heard her. Do as the healer says!"

Diyah turned around to see Rey striding into the infirmary dressed in his tournament gear and wearing a bitter expression.

"Lieutenant!" gasped Bir, trying to sit up. "I'm so sorry. I failed, I failed!"

"Shh." Rey grabbed Bir's arm and pushed him back down onto the bed. "Nonsense. You fought bravely."

"But... but he lives!" cried Bir, his eyes bulging out of his head. "And you can't... because of the other one. What now?"

"We'll find another way," said Rey in a reassuring voice.

"I need to salve and cauterize this before he bleeds to death," muttered Diyah under her breath to Rey. "But he's too strong."

"I'll hold him," said Rey, nodding. Then he turned back to Bir. "All that matters now is we get you fixed up, huh? Think about what Niq would say." His voice was surprisingly gentle. "Now stay still and bite down on this." He handed Bir the wooden stick off the table and pushed down hard on his arms.

Ten minutes of screaming and writhing later, and it was done. Rey stared down at his now unconscious soldier and sighed.

"Thank you," he said in a tired voice, inclining his head towards Diyah.

Diyah nodded as she wiped her hands on her apron. "You seem to really care about him."

"I care about all of my people," he said. "Bir was a carpenter in Awnell. He carved the most beautiful pieces..." Rey touched one of the ornamental wooden beads threaded through the man's beard. There was a deep sadness in the Awnadh lieutenant's eyes that Diyah hadn't expected of him. In his fights he always seemed so brutal and unsympathetic.

"I'm sorry," she said, looking at the unconscious man between them and realizing what the loss of a hand would mean for him.

"As am I," said Rey. "For him, and for you. I had hoped..." He trailed off, staring blankly at his sword. "But it's out of my control now. I'm sorry." And he turned and strode out of the room, leaving Diyah utterly perplexed.

As Diyah joined the crowd that afternoon, she was distracted, thinking about her interaction with Rey. He had seemed genuinely upset. And Bir had seemed especially devastated, as though he'd disappointed Rey somehow. Something else was at play here, and she needed to learn more.

But Diyah couldn't afford to think like that, to have ambivalent feelings about Rey. If it came down to Rey or Jémys, she knew exactly whom she wanted to win, even if it meant Rey had to die.

The arena was packed, and the fight was about to start. Diyah suffered a slight twinge of guilt when she realized she hadn't had time to find Jémys and wish him good luck.

He doesn't need luck, she tried to reassure herself.

Diyah heard movement behind her and received her second shock for the day: Julyán was stepping over the rows of seats to sit in the space beside her. As far as she knew, Julyán hadn't watched any of the matches. In fact, the only times she'd seen him since the morning with the knives had been during his own fights.

"What are you doing here?" she asked before she could stop herself.

"Same as you. I've come to watch," he say, brushing his hair out of his eyes and staring down at the arena.

Diyah exhaled stiffly and rolled her eyes.

"What?" asked Julyán.

"Oh, nothing. I just think it's interesting you've come to watch your brother's fight even though you claim you don't care for him."

Julyán frowned slightly and looked back down at the arena.

The crowd cheered as Jémys and Rey walked into the centre of the field.

"Come on, Jémys," whispered Diyah, pounding her hands on her legs.

Now it was Julyán's turn to scoff.

"What?" spat Diyah.

"You might try to conceal your favouritism," he said. "When the tournament is over, you don't want your husband to know he wasn't your first choice."

"Are you mocking me?" asked Diyah hotly.

Julyán shrugged and smiled.

"Well, smirk all you want. But what if Jémys wins?"

"He won't," said Julyán with a sudden return to his usual brooding self.

"How can you be so sure?"

"Because if it's not Rey, then it'll be Slaedir, and if it's not Slaedir, it'll be me." His matter-of-fact tone surprised Diyah.

"You haven't even won your eighth round yet," she said, alarmed at how high-pitched her voice sounded.

"I will."

Any further conversation between them was prevented by the start of the fight.

Jémys was doing well. He was dodging Rey's strikes with a speed Diyah had never seen before. He seemed determined to win, and he was fighting just as aggressively as his opponent. But just as the crowd was inclining in Jémys's favour, Rey disarmed him. Jémys retreated against the walls of the arena. Rey raised his sword high in the air and Diyah closed her eyes, too terrified to watch.

The crowd cheered, and she opened her eyes again to see Rey, sword-less, locked in a fistfight with Jémys.

"What happened?" she asked, leaning forward, a wave of relief pouring over her. She looked at Julyán and saw a dubious expression on his face.

"Rey should have seen that coming. He left himself wide open," muttered Julyán.

But Diyah didn't care. She turned her attention back to the fight. The two men blocked each other's fists with speed and precision. Every once in a while, one of them landed a blow, forcing the other back a step. Diyah struggled to keep track of who was landing more blows.

Finally, Jémys's fist collided with Rey's face, and the two men broke apart. In Rey's moment of distraction, Jémys spun onto the ground. When he straightened up, he was grasping both swords in his hand. He kicked the side of Rey's leg, sending him crashing to the ground.

"Yield," he commanded, pointing the swords at Rey's neck.

Rey was panting heavily, but even at a distance Diyah saw him nod.

"I yield!" he called out, and the crowd erupted around them.

Diyah couldn't believe it. The fight had barely begun and now it was over. Jémys had won. She was so relieved she could have cried. Delighted, she turned around to look at Julyán, but he was still frowning.

"What's the matter with you?" she asked, her good mood evaporating in an instant.

Julyán just shook his head and stood up.

"Ugh." Diyah turned away from him, but Julyán grabbed her arm and stopped her.

Leaning in, he said in a low voice, "There's no way my little brother defeats Awnell's best fighter that easily. No. Rey let him win."

"What?" Diyah yanked her arm out of his grasp and looked back at the arena where Jémys stood, grinning at her. "No, I don't believe it. I don't—" But then she remembered the strange conversation between Rey and Bir. "Why would he do that?" she asked.

"I don't know. But he has done my brother no favours," said Julyán, turning to leave.

"Wait!" called Diyah, running after him. "Wait, what do you mean? Surely not—"

"Rey is a cunning warrior—a strategist. If he let Jémys win, it is for one reason and one reason alone. Because he wants him to die, but not at his own hand."

"No!" shouted Diyah, and several nearby people turned to stare at them. "No," she repeated in a quieter voice. "That doesn't make any sense. Please." She grabbed Julyán's arm to stop him from leaving. "You can't let that happen. Please!"

Julyán looked down at her, almost in pity. Then he strode off, down the steps and out of the arena.

Diyah felt numb. She heard feet thumping and the clamour of conversations and laughter, as though the sounds came to her through a thick wall. It couldn't be true. Why would Rey want Jémys dead? And why not kill him himself? It made no sense.

"Diyah? Are you all right?" It was Fehla's voice that finally broke through her daze.

"I—I don't know... Something Julyán said..."

"What did that awful brute say?" asked Fehla in an irritable voice, glaring after Julyán.

Fehla listened as Diyah explained their conversation.

"You're right, that doesn't make any sense. Unless..." Fehla broke off, glancing behind her. "Maybe Rey *did* let him win, but not for the reason Julyán suspects," she whispered.

"Then why?" asked Diyah, somehow hopeful and apprehensive at the same time.

"Perhaps because of Catanya?"

"What, you think Rey is still loyal to her? Even though he betrayed his own queen?" Diyah found it hard to believe.

"It doesn't seem very likely, does it?" said Fehla, looking back at Rey, who was exiting the arena in the opposite direction. "But I can hardly believe he let Jémys win just so he could die during the next round. That's idiotic."

"But only the final round is supposed to be a fight to the death," said Diyah. "Maybe he won't win, but he won't die either."

Fehla raised her eyebrows and nodded. "It depends on who he fights."

20

THE BURNING COVE

Catanya had completely lost track of time. The hours seemed to pass in unmeasurable patterns. At times the days felt unnaturally long, and the nights never fully settled over the world. At other times, the overwhelming gloom of the sky was so oppressive, it gave the impression of everlasting darkness.

Catanya had no idea how long she and Drayk had been traipsing along the shoal. The isolation of the sandbar and the uncertainty of it ever ending were sapping her energy.

So, when she looked up after an eternity of endless sand, wind, and mist and saw the hazy shape of a landmass hovering in the distance, she hardly believed her eyes. She blinked several times to make sure it was real.

"Drayk," she croaked, grabbing his arm. "Do you see that?" She pointed at the island in front of them.

Drayk had been stumbling along beside her, looking just as miserable as she felt. He turned his gaze towards the island and sighed.

"Finally," he said.

They quickened their pace, both desperate to reach solid land again and feel the strength of the earth beneath their feet.

But as they drew closer to the island, Catanya noticed something strange happening. Thick veins of darker sand were mixing in with the white. The farther they walked, the more marbled the texture became, until the white gave way to a deep, dark burgundy. She knelt down and ran her hand through it, rolling the grains between her fingers. It was unusually dry, and it left a rusty stain on her fingers as she brushed it away.

"Have you ever seen sand this colour?" she asked, looking up at Drayk.

He shook his head and frowned. "It looks... burnt. But that's impossible."

"The Burning Cove," said Catanya flatly. "This must be it."

They exchanged apprehensive looks and continued walking with caution.

As they approached the island and it came into sharper focus, they realized just how enormous the landmass really was. It seemed to stretch on for miles. The only part facing them was a sheer wall of solid grey rock, reaching at least fifty feet above their heads, with a precipitous drop into the depths of the ocean beyond the shoal.

Catanya wasn't sure how they were supposed to reach the top. There was no path or slope, and she didn't relish the idea of climbing the treacherous cliff face. It wasn't until they were standing directly in its shadow that she noticed the sliver of a gap at the cliff's base where the shoal ended.

"That must be the entrance to the cove." Catanya pointed towards the opening, her arm shaking with what could have been either exhaustion or nerves. She couldn't separate her emotions anymore.

As they approached the entrance, the water level rose, lapping at their feet. The sandbar was disappearing beneath them, slowly becoming submerged. Water soaked through their boots, rising up their ankles and drenching their breeches. The strong current tugged their legs as they walked, and the water level climbed steadily higher and higher until they were standing waist-deep at the foot of the cliff.

The entry was long and narrow, like a crack in the island's foundation. It was barely wide enough for them to pass through, and the shadows of the looming rock walls cast a dark, foreboding gloom.

Catanya took a deep breath and led the way forward.

The water was surprisingly warm, and it grew warmer as they went, though the air was still biting. Gradually, the water level crept up their waists and towards their necks. They were forced to start swimming, the tips of their fingers brushing against the rock walls beside them.

Somewhere above, they heard a faint crack, followed by the sound of rock hitting rock. A chunk dislodged from the cliff and ricocheted off the walls before splashing into the water behind them.

Catanya let out an involuntary yelp and urged herself to swim faster, eager to leave the cramped passageway.

They swam until the passage widened, and they emerged into a sheltered bay. It was carved inside the island, as if a seamless bubble had expanded over time, forcing the earth to mould around it.

And in the fading light of the late-afternoon sun, Catanya was struck by the unusual colour of the water. It was almost purple. The brilliant blue of the sky reflected above the burgundy seabed, bleeding their colours together.

Catanya started treading water as she looked around the bay, bracing for something unnatural to occur. But nothing happened. She spun around in a circle, examining her surroundings. Other than its unusual location and fascinating colour, this cove seemed unremarkable.

Catanya and Drayk made their way towards the narrow,

red-sand beach at the head of the bay. When Catanya's feet brushed the sand bottom, she stood up to walk the remaining distance.

They waded to the shore and emerged onto the beach, shaking water out of their heavy, drenched clothes. Catanya stared back out at the water, feeling a slight uneasiness. Something about this place made her nervous. Her skin was tingling and not just from the cold breeze blowing through her clothes. She could sense the energy coursing through the air as if it were circling them, coming ever closer until eventually it would strike.

"Okay, now what?" asked Drayk, shivering. His clothes dripped onto the ground and the sand clung to his boots. He dropped his sopping travel bag at his feet.

"I'm not sure," said Catanya. She pulled off her own bag and rummaged around for the wet bit of parchment that was their map. She carefully unfolded it and laid it out on the sand to dry, pleased to see that the water hadn't damaged the images too much. The words, though slightly smudged, were still legible.

"Soggy bread?" Drayk grimaced, holding out the now waterlogged loaf that was once their rations. He tossed the bread aside as he continued pulling the rest of the contents out of his bag. "The rest of the food is fine, though," he said.

Catanya sighed and rummaged through her own bag to check the contents of their water skins. "We're running low on fresh water. This one filled with ocean water," she groaned, emptying the saltwater onto the beach. "We need to find fresh water somewhere." She was trying to sound calmer than she was. They only had half a canteen left, and this bay made her feel trapped and confined.

"Right, okay." Drayk climbed to his feet. "There's no sense waiting around, then. Where do we go next?"

Catanya glanced at the damp map and read aloud, "The

Reflecting Channel." Then she scanned the images on the map. "It looks like there's an entrance to a waterway somewhere on the beach!" she called out with a jolt.

They walked the length of the beach all afternoon, scouring it for any sign of the channel. Not only was there no channel to be found, there didn't appear to be any way off the beach. A continuous wall of rock surrounded the entire cove with no path through, over, or around it.

"Now what?" asked Catanya after her fourth survey of the area. The sun was setting, and she was tired and damp.

"I don't know," grumbled Drayk, sounding frustrated and irritable. "Let's make camp, I guess. We can search again in the morning with fresh eyes."

Catanya sighed. "Okay. But let's make a fire, I'm freezing."

Drayk nodded. But as they scanned around, they suddenly realized there were no trees or plants on the beach. There was no wood, nothing they could use to build a fire.

"Great," said Drayk through clenched teeth. "No fire, no water. Nothing but sand, sand, and more sand!" He kicked the beach in frustration.

"It's okay," said Catanya. "We just need to make it through the night. I'm sure tomorrow we'll find the way off this beach."

"You really believe that?" asked Drayk sceptically, as he slumped onto the ground.

Catanya wasn't sure what she believed anymore, but she needed to stay calm. "We've made it this far," she said with a shrug, as she sank down next to him.

As they sat together on the beach with nothing to do but wait for the night to pass and their clothes to dry, Catanya lay back, watching the stars and listening to gentle waves lap against the shore. It sounded like home. For a while, she managed to block out the prickling sensation on her skin and the tightness in her chest by pretending she was back in Faltir, surrounded by everyone she loved.

She tried not to wallow in regret, remembering how many of those people had been taken from her. Instead, she urged herself to be grateful for all the love she'd experienced in her life. She reminded herself that not everyone was lucky enough to experience love like that.

"Drayk?" she said after a while, propping herself up on her elbows to see him. "I've been thinking about what happened on the shoal. About what I heard." She paused, waiting for him to say something, but he didn't. "I was wondering... What did you hear?" she asked.

Drayk turned his head to look at her, and even in the dark she saw his uncomfortable expression.

"In the wind. What did you hear?" she pressed.

"Memories," he said stiffly, turning his gaze up to the stars. "Bad memories."

It was clear from his tone that he wouldn't elaborate, so Catanya decided it was best not to push for more detail. Besides, she thought she knew what his answer would be, anyway. If the voices were meant to cause them pain, she suspected she knew exactly whose voice he'd heard and what it had said.

Catanya felt even worse as she lay back in the sand and closed her eyes. Lately, it seemed she was surrounded by nothing but pain. Every time she found even a glimmer of happiness it was taken from her. But she couldn't rewrite her past or erase her pain, so she had to move on. It just didn't seem fair.

She let out a soft sigh and rolled onto her side. *Fair,* she thought bitterly. *Of course, it isn't fair. None of this is fair... But maybe that's the point. Maybe we're not supposed to get what we want.*

And with that thought, she drifted into an uneasy sleep.

Catanya opened her eyes and cried out in surprise. The world was alight with a blinding red blaze. A wall of fire stretched the length of the beach, licking at the cliff rocks and burning the darkness out of the sky.

Catanya scrambled to her feet in terror, snatching the map and her bag off the sand. Drayk jumped up next to her.

They cast around for an escape, but there was no way out. The fire surrounded them in a seamless sheet of flames that stretched at least forty feet high.

But the blaze was unnatural. It didn't seem to spread. Rather, it enveloped the beach like a shield, dancing above the sand but never actually touching it. The flames were self-contained. They flickered and flapped calmly, as though waiting for something.

Catanya froze, momentarily mesmerized by the unnatural display.

Then slowly, the flames contracted. The wall drifted forward, creeping its way along the beach towards them. Catanya stumbled backwards into Drayk and they exchanged looks of horror.

The flames crawled ever closer, driving them back towards the water.

"Come on," said Catanya, sliding the map in her pocket. She hurled her pack over her shoulder and grabbed Drayk's arm to pulled him into the bay with her.

They splashed out into the depths, trying to put as much distance as possible between themselves and the fire. Catanya threw herself forward, paddling into the deeper water, hoping against all hope that she'd have enough energy to keep afloat as long as she needed.

She heard Drayk swimming along behind her. When she thought she'd gone far enough, she stopped and stared back at the beach.

The wall of flames had stopped moving. It flickered and

danced playfully on the edge of the shore. Catanya had the strange impression that it was watching her.

Then, suddenly, the flames accelerated, careening towards the water.

"What?"

Catanya heard Drayk gasp and gargle on the water, but she didn't have time to react. She watched in shock as the flames connected with the water and it ignited. The waves mutated and transformed into a firestorm, engulfing the bay.

A sudden lurch behind her navel, and she was pulled beneath the surface.

She and Drayk dropped through an ocean of flames that licked and snapped at them like fiery serpents.

It was hot and suffocating. The temperature mounted to unbearable heights, but, curiously, the fire didn't burn. The flames blanketed Catanya, tracing her skin, but never fully connecting.

Catanya flipped around, searching for Drayk and saw him flailing a few feet from her. She tried to propel herself towards him, but nothing happened. She tried to call out to him. Her mouth filled with hot air and ash and she choked, spluttering and spinning in a whirl of fire.

The flames hissed and sparked, exploding in flashes of blinding light. They twisted and contorted, forming a series of unusual shapes that writhed in hypnotic patterns.

Catanya swam through the blaze, entranced, as images flashed amidst the fire. At first, they moved too fast for her eyes to register. But gradually, the images solidified. She could see people and places she recognized. They fluttered past her at blinding speed, taunting her and drawing her closer.

Her eyes burned in the heat, but she couldn't look away. Something magnetic was pulling her towards the images.

Another wrench behind her navel and she was hurled forward.

Catanya gasped as her knees crashed into something hard and she doubled over, panting. She heard Drayk thump down next to her. The smoke cleared and the heat abated. They were sprawled beside each other in a dark, wooden room. The fire had retracted up the walls, licking at the space like a frame on a painting.

"What is this?" asked Drayk, scrambling to his feet and surveying his new surroundings.

It was a small, inviting space, set up like a nursery, with two cozy cribs in one corner and various toys strewn across the floor. In the room's corner, a woman sat in a rocking chair.

Catanya climbed to her feet. "Hello?" she called, trying to get the woman's attention.

The woman didn't react. She didn't seem to notice the two strangers who had fallen onto the floor behind her. Nor the fire that snaked up the walls.

Catanya stepped forward to see her properly. The woman had long dark hair and sympathetic eyes. She laughed as the twin infants on her lap giggled and hugged her.

Catanya's chest tightened. She gaped at Drayk and realized he'd arrived at the same conclusion as her. Before either of them could speak, an almighty lurch plunged them into flames once again.

Tumbling, spinning, whirling. The flames flashed brighter around them.

Crash.

They landed again, and the flames retreated. Winded and out of breath, they stood up to take in their new surroundings.

This time, the room looked familiar somehow. Catanya turned around, trying to get her bearings, and saw a different, slightly older woman. The woman beamed as she lifted a young boy into her arms and hugged him, spinning around in circles. The boy squealed in joy as she deposited him back on the ground, his bright blue eyes shining with joy.

Catanya clapped one hand over her mouth and grabbed Drayk's arm. As soon as her fingers made contact, she fell through flames again.

Crash.

The lurching sensation was nauseating. The wall of heat evaporated, and the flames withdrew like curtains.

They were standing on the beach now. But it wasn't the Burning Cove. No, this was the beach at Faltir. An elderly couple was strolling leisurely along, hand-in-hand as they watched the sunset. Under the grey hair and lined skin, Catanya recognized her own face... and Jémys.

She stared at the image, transfixed, as the flames crept back from the corners of her vision, mixing into the glow of the sunset and giving it a strange, inviting warmth.

Catanya let out a single sob as the flames flickered and snapped, tossing them back into the unknown.

The next setting was dark and jarring after the peace of the beach before.

She and Drayk stood on the deck of an enormous ship. A group of unknown figures dragged a man, kicking and screaming, off the deck. They hurled him onto the ground, where they took turns flogging him with canes and whips until he lay still, bloodied and unconscious.

The scene made Catanya queasy. She couldn't reconcile it with the other, more peaceful scenes they'd watched. The man's screams echoed in her ears as the setting shifted again, churning her already upset stomach.

The new scene was dim and quiet. A string of hanging lanterns emitted a warm, inviting glow. Catanya was standing in a room, watching as a second Catanya and a second Drayk slowly intertwined in a steamy, amorous embrace.

Her jaw dropped, but she had no time to react.

Snap.

She watched a version of Drayk, sitting atop a massive black horse, ride through a raging battlefield and strike down every enemy that stood before him.

Snap.

She saw herself sitting with Diyah in the beautiful meadow outside Finnua. They were carefree, laughing and talking as they watched Jémys play with Olly nearby.

Snap.

Catanya and Drayk tumbled out of the flames, and this time, the image took longer to solidify.

Catanya saw herself standing with a man she didn't recognize. But then the smoky edges settled together, and his face became clear. He was tall with jet-black hair and steely eyes, but they were full of warmth. He smiled widely as he walked over to his sister, put his arm over her shoulders protectively, and hugged her. They walked away, arm in arm, as the flames slowly eclipsed the image.

Catanya fell again, flailing through flames in rapid, sickening circles. She cried out. The tears on her face sizzled in the heat and evaporated almost instantly.

She wanted it to stop. She couldn't take it anymore. "I've seen enough!" she shouted into the scorching waves around her. "Do you hear me?"

The flames hissed. The heat intensified, choking her and swamping her mind. She was lightheaded.

Catanya gasped and clutched at her throat. She couldn't breathe. Her lungs were filling with fluid. She blinked rapidly, watching the red flames fade into blue. A dense wave of water enveloped her as she found herself submerged in the bay. The warm, salty seawater cloaked her skin where flames had been a moment before.

Turning to face the surface, she kicked as hard as she could, ignoring the blinding pain in her chest and the bright spots on her vision.

She burst forth into the open air, spluttering and gasping as she coughed saltwater from her lungs. A second splash nearby told her Drayk had made it back too.

The sky was burnt orange, but it relieved Catanya to see the colour coming from the sun, which sat low on the horizon, heralding the new dawn.

The fire was gone.

Catanya pushed herself to swim back to the beach, where she collapsed on the sand, heaving great gasps of air as tears streamed down her face.

It was a long time before she managed to settle herself down. She lay huddled in a ball, half in and half out of the water, sobbing and shaking uncontrollably until the sun had fully risen.

"It's impossible," she mumbled, face buried in the crook of her arm. "Those things... impossible."

Something tugged on her sleeve and she tried to swat it away, but her muscles felt like lead.

"Never going to have them," she mumbled. "I understand now."

"Catya, you're babbling," came Drayk's voice, as he grabbed her and hauled her to her feet.

She opened her eyes to peer at him. He looked just as exhausted as she felt.

"I'm never going to have what I want," she said in a pitiful voice. "Am I?"

Drayk backed away slowly, as if nervous she might fall if he let go. Then he dropped his hands. "No, probably not," he said bluntly. "It's already too late for most of it. We can't go back." He shook his head. "You saw it. Your mother, my mother, Jémys... they're all gone, it's—" He broke off and walked away from her.

The sting of disappointment pierced Catanya like a knife. He was right. She stared at the water and wanted to scream. She was so angry—so exhausted and frustrated—and she was tired of pretending to be okay.

"So why show us? Was it just more of what happened on the shoal?" she cried to the air. "More pain and suffering, torturing us with images of things we'll never have?" She kicked a stone off the beach so it soared across the bay and rebounded off a protruding rock in its centre before plunging below the surface. She let out an inarticulate shout and slumped down onto her knees. Her anger seeped out of her as quickly as it had come. Now all she felt was bitter sorrow.

Drayk was watching her with mingled pity and exhaustion on his face.

"What?" she asked defensively.

"You told me when you first read that poem, you thought it was a series of lessons, didn't you? Well, *fine*. I've learned my lesson. Those fire images—whatever they were—it's time to let go of them. Wanting those things has only brought us pain. They've been holding us back, and it's time to move on."

Catanya gaped at him. This was the last thing she imagined he'd say. "What if I can't let go?" she asked. "What if I don't want to? I know I can't have *everything* I want... But I can't just give up. I can't because—" She broke off, anger bubbling inside her again.

"Because what?" asked Drayk, rubbing his forehead tiredly.

"Because then *what's the point*?" she snapped. "If we're not fighting for what we want, we might as well lie down and die right here on this stupid beach."

Drayk looked surprised, but then his face soured and he shrugged. "Why waste our time striving for something we'll never have?" he asked. "Caring isn't worth the pain."

A bitter silence settled around them.

Catanya heaved a great sigh and wrestled her emotions into check. "That's not true," she said. "I don't want to live my life without hope. So... maybe it doesn't matter if we can't have what we want, or if it hurts. We should never stop trying. The moment we give up on what we want, we give up on ourselves. That's the moment we die."

A low rumble sounded in the distance, and the earth trembled beneath them.

"What's happening?" she asked, looking around in panic, thinking the flames had returned. But all around her, the beach was tranquil and harmless.

"Um, Catya," called Drayk, and there was an oddly bright note in his voice. "You should probably come look at this."

Catanya turned around, surprised to see him standing several feet down the beach, facing the opposite direction.

"What is it?" she said, standing up and walking over to join him. But as she stopped beside him and followed his gaze, she saw it. There was a slight opening in the cliff where a gentle stream poured out into the bay.

"I didn't see that yesterday, did you?" asked Drayk.

"No. But I checked this entire area. There was nothing here."

They exchanged bewildered looks. Drayk let out a short, nervous laugh. His tension seemed to melt away, and he grinned, looking more like his usual animated self. He ran forward to peer through the crack.

It was just large enough for them to walk through.

"All right," he said, stepping back and taking a deep breath. "Onwards?" He raised his eyebrows and smiled at her.

Catanya sighed. Whether it was genuine or contrived, she couldn't tell. But Drayk's improved mood revitalized her. And she'd said it herself, hadn't she? She couldn't give up.

"Onwards," she said, nodding and following him through the gap in the cliff.

21

A NEW WEAKNESS

The eighth round of the Maífírkon Tournament carried on with two more fights. The first was between two fírkon, both close in age to Slaedir. Their fight was nothing short of vicious. Diyah couldn't help thinking that after years of losing the tournament to Slaedir, they were both equally determined to progress to the final round. Their fight lasted longer than all the others. It was well past midday when it finally ended with one man lying in a bloody heap at the other man's feet.

Although only the final round was meant to end in death, Diyah had already witnessed the deaths of nearly thirty men. The knot in her stomach that had started after Jémys's fight with Rey tightened uncomfortably as she watched the latest broken body being dragged from the field.

The last fight of the eighth round would be between Julyán and a fírkon named Holun. Diyah had never met Holun, but she'd heard stories about him from the other fighters. Apparently, Holun had been born and raised at the castle. His father, Hamir, had been the maífírkon before Slaedir killed him in the tournament twelve years ago. Holun had trained from infancy to take his father's place, but he had yet to progress past the eighth round of a tournament.

The atmosphere in the arena was tense and excited. It seemed Holun had been a source of interest for some time. Everyone yearned to know if this year he'd make it to the ninth and second-last round. The bets were high on this fight. Diyah was nervous, even more nervous than she'd been for Jémys's fight with Rey.

"What's the matter?" asked Fehla as she took her seat next to Diyah.

"I'm scared," said Diyah, wringing her hands in her lap.

Fehla nodded. "I understand. Whoever wins today might well be facing Jémys next. But don't worry. Jémys can handle himself. He'll be fine."

"Right," said Diyah mechanically, but there was something more. She was starting to think Jémys wasn't the only one she was worried about.

They watched as Julyán and Holun strode out onto the field. Holun seemed agitated and eager, but, as usual, Julyán only seemed calm and detached. This served the dual purpose of intimidating his opponent and stirring up admiration from the spectators. But Diyah was beginning to suspect it was all a façade, that Julyán was just adept at hiding his emotions—or *channelling* them, as he called it.

He couldn't be as calm as he looked.

Of all the fights so far, this was by far the most impressive. Both men spun across the arena with an unexpected fluidity and lightness of foot. It was ages before either of them managed to land a blow without it being blocked, and by that point, the entire energy of the duel had changed.

Holun was growing impatient. The more he lost control of his temper, the more rashly he acted. Julyán, however, remained as cool as when he'd first stepped onto the field.

"How does he do that?" said Diyah, awed in spite of herself. "How does he stay so calm?"

"I don't think there's any great secret there. The man has no feelings. He doesn't care," muttered Fehla, shaking her head.

Diyah frowned at Fehla, but decided it was best not to argue. Instead, she turned back to the fight.

Their swords were moving faster now, so they looked like nothing more than blurry waves of steel. The clanging of metal reverberated across the arena, and the audience barely had time to react between moves.

Julyán cried out and stumbled backwards, clutching at his arm. Diyah could see a long gash from the inside of his elbow up to his shoulder, and she gasped, raising her hand to her mouth. Julyán's sleeve was turning red with his own blood as it poured from the long wound on his arm.

"Oh no," said Diyah, sitting up straighter.

Holun seemed pleased with the damage he'd caused. He smirked as he launched his next assault. Julyán blocked the attack with his injured sword arm, wincing as he did it. Then he lifted his leg and kicked Holun in the chest, sending him stumbling backwards.

For a brief moment, as Julyán stared at his wounded arm, doubt seemed to cross his face. But it was gone as quickly as it came. He tossed his sword into his uninjured hand, meeting Holun with the same precision he'd shown throughout the entire fight.

But Diyah could tell he was losing steam. The wound on his right arm was obviously painful. It was distracting him as it trickled blood onto the ground beneath him. Diyah knew if he didn't get help soon, the blood loss would kill him. All Holun needed to do was keep him fighting.

But the ground was muddy and wet with Julyán's blood, making it dangerously slippery as the two men continued their dance. Julyán dodged another blow and slipped backwards, throwing out his injured arm to break his fall. The crowd flinched in unison and cringed as he brushed the dirt out of it, rolling away just in time to avoid Holun's next advance.

Julyán was on his feet again, but his face was ashen. He wasn't going to last much longer. Diyah wanted to do something to help him.

Holun was advancing again. Julyán blocked his sword with his own, but Holun brought his free fist around where it collided with Julyán's injured shoulder and sent him crashing to the ground again. Holun stood looming over Julyán in the mud.

Diyah was panicking now. Before she knew it, she was on her feet. "Oh, get up!" she shouted. "Get up and fight!"

A chuckle ran through the audience and several people looked around at her. Diyah thought she saw Julyán smile as he rolled out of the way of Holun's incoming kick. He pulled himself up and spun his sword out in front of him, leaving two deep slices on Holun's thighs.

Holun cried out in pain and slipped on the wet ground, crashing down. Julyán stood upright and kicked out hard so his boot met the underside of Holun's chin, knocking him out cold.

There was a long pause while the audience absorbed what happened, and then the entire stadium erupted in noise. Whether the noises were happy or angry, Diyah couldn't tell. She raced down the steps towards the arena where Julyán stood, looking like he might faint.

"Come with me." She tried to pull him off the field, but he wouldn't budge.

"I'm fine," he said, trying to shrug her off.

"You're not fine!" she shouted, surprised at her own anger. "You need help now."

When Julyán just ignored her again, she lost her temper completely and smacked him hard on the side of the head.

"Ow!"

"Get to the infirmary now or I swear I'll kill you myself," she hissed.

Julyán's eyes widened, but he nodded and followed her out of the arena.

"You there!" called Diyah, as she passed a castle guard. "Get some of the others to help you bring Holun to the infirmary."

"I don't take orders from you, woman."

"Oh, yes, you do!" she snapped. "Now, go get him this instant before I take this sword and use it to run you through! How long do you think you'll last before I have you crying for your mother?"

The guard looked flabbergasted. He gaped at Julyán, but Julyán just burst out laughing. Diyah looked at him, shocked. It was the first time she'd ever seen him really laugh, and she found it both beautiful and unnerving.

"Well, you heard her," he said with a chuckle. He was slurring his words and stumbling slightly as he followed Diyah past the guard.

Diyah reached out and grabbed his uninjured arm.

"Here." She gripped him by the waist and started steering him towards the castle. "I've never seen you laugh," she said as they approached the infirmary door.

"Mmm." Julyán's eyes slid in and out of focus.

"You're delirious. Here, lie down." She pushed him onto a bed near the fire. Then she ran and grabbed a set of wool blankets and threw them over him. "Take off your shirt," she called, rummaging around for her suture needle, sealants, and blood replenishing tonics. She turned around to see him fumbling with his vest. "Oh, for crying out loud," she exclaimed, exasperated. She hurried over to him, pulled a knife from her bag, and used it to slice through the laces.

"Hey!"

"Shut up!" she snapped, ripping his vest off and throwing it to the ground. Half of his tunic was stained red, and it was sticking to his arm, but she pulled it up and yanked it unceremoniously over his head. Julyán clenched his jaw in pain as it tugged at his wound.

"I need to clean this," said Diyah. "Here, drink." She thrust the tonic into his hand.

"How much?" he asked.

"All of it." She poured cleansing oils into a basin of hot water and brought it over to the bed with a pile of clean rags. "Now lie down." She gently pushed him back and began wiping the mud out of his wound, ignoring his winces. The cut was deep. Thankfully, Holun hadn't severed the artery, but blood was still gushing down Julyán's arm.

Diyah swore under her breath. Without hesitating, she yanked Julyán's belt off his waist.

"What—"

She ignored him, buckling the leather strap around his upper arm.

"Hold on to the cot," she said. He did as he was told. Then she braced his forearm with her knee and heaved with all her might, tightening the belt to cut off his circulation and stem the blood loss. Julyán grunted and shut his eyes, but he didn't budge.

Then she snatched the sealant off the table and poured it over the wound.

"Ah, that's cold," he mumbled.

Diyah held up her needle, threading it by the firelight. "This will hurt," she said, glancing down at him. She didn't want to risk the numbing tonic so close to the artery. "Try not to move."

The door burst open and the guard from earlier backed into the infirmary, carrying an unconscious Holun.

"Put him over there," she said, indicating an empty bed by the wall.

"Can I help?" came Fehla's voice by the entrance. She had arrived just after the guards, looking harried and concerned.

"Yes, please. Can you examine Holun and let me know how bad his wounds are. Does he need the blood tonic?" she asked, knowing full well she'd just given the last vial to Julyán.

"I-I don't think so," said Fehla, bending over him and examining his wounds.

She was murmuring something to him, but Diyah wasn't listening.

"He'll be fine," muttered Julyán. "Wound, don't kill... good man..."

"A good man?" scoffed Diyah in a shrill voice. "He nearly killed you!"

Julyán shrugged. "He wanted to win."

"Don't you all?"

Julyán frowned and closed his eyes. "No. I needed... *need* to win," he stammered as he slid out of consciousness.

Diyah spent the rest of the evening tending to Julyán and Holun's injuries. But Julyán was right. Holun's wounds were only superficial. They were only enough to incapacitate him, not to kill him. After a few days' bed rest, Holun would be back on his feet.

This got Diyah thinking. She thought back over Julyán's duels throughout the tournament and realized that none of his opponents had been injured badly enough to stay in the infirmary longer than a couple of days. Julyán had been careful and precise. He hadn't caused any unnecessary damage.

"It doesn't make sense, though," whispered Fehla later that night as they were watching over the sleeping patients. "He has killed countless times before. Why should this be any different?"

"I don't know," said Diyah, frowning. "Maybe... it's about honour?"

Fehla raised an eyebrow. "Honour? Really?"

"Well, I don't know," said Diyah, exasperated. "But it almost seems like he doesn't want to kill unless he has to, doesn't it?"

"Hmm, I'm not sure…"

"Well, whatever the reason, I'm grateful. For once, he hasn't been the source of my problems." Diyah smiled weakly, then stood up to go check on Julyán. She laid her hand on his forehead and realized he was shivering. She pulled a few blankets off the stool by the fire and threw them over him. As she was straightening out his pillow, she realized Fehla was watching her.

"He was cold," said Diyah defensively.

Fehla nodded and said nothing. But as Diyah walked back over to sit with her, she noticed Fehla still eyeing her.

"What now?"

"It's okay to admit you care about him," said Fehla.

"What?" Diyah was surprised. "I-I don't care about him… I don't!" The sympathetic gleam in Fehla's eyes irritated her. "Really, Fehla, I don't… At least, not as anything other than a patient. I care about all my patients. That's it."

"I see. So, let me ask you, if it were Slaedir lying on that bed, would you be worried about him too?"

Diyah let out a derisive laugh.

"That's what I thought," said Fehla with a smile. Then she stood up and stretched. "Well, if you don't mind, I'm going to sleep. Don't stay up all night, Diyah."

Diyah nodded and watched Fehla leave the room. She stared blankly at the door, lost in thought, until—

"So, I take it, if Slaedir were lying here instead of me, you would just let him die?" asked Julyán, propping himself up on his uninjured elbow and staring at her.

"You're awake," said Diyah, jumping up and walking over to his bed. "How do you feel?" She tried to cover her own embarrassment.

"Better," he replied. "Thank you."

"Are you warm enough?"

Julyán nodded and laid his head back on the pillow, not taking his eyes off her.

"Good... that's good..." Diyah trailed off into an awkward silence and rubbed her neck. "Well, if you're feeling better, I suppose I don't need to wait here overnight... I think I'll go get a couple hours of sleep."

She patted him on his uninjured arm before turning to walk away. But before she had taken two steps, Julyán's hand grabbed hers. She looked down, startled. His skin was warm as his thumb traced the tops of her fingers. She stood stunned for a few seconds before pulling her hand free.

"Um... Goodnight, then," she mumbled, turning and leaving the room without a second glance.

The next day, when Diyah awoke, she dressed in a rush and headed to the infirmary to check on Julyán. The ninth round wasn't meant to start for several hours, but Julyán would have to fight, and he'd be doing it at a serious disadvantage.

As she hurried down the hallway, she heard someone call her name. Turning around, she saw Jémys.

"Oh, Jémys, you must be so worried, but everything's okay, he's fine—what's wrong?" Diyah had just noticed the expression on Jémys's face. "What is it?"

"They announced the pairings for the next round," said Jémys, and something about his tone made Diyah uneasy.

"And?"

"And I've been paired against Julyán."

Diyah's stomach dropped, and she stared at Jémys in horror. "What? No, you can't fight him, he's your brother."

"I don't really have a choice... Besides, I wouldn't mind the opportunity for payback."

"Jémys!" Diyah gave him a reproachful look.

"What, Diyah? He's not my brother, and he's certainly not our friend. He's one of *them*. One of the people who killed my family... who killed her..." He trailed off, a dark shadow obscuring his features.

Something unpleasant twisted inside Diyah, and for a brief moment, she welcomed the idea of watching Julyán die. But that sensation vanished as quickly as it arrived, leaving a deep shame in its place.

"When is the fight?" she asked in a hollow voice.

"This afternoon. First it's Slaedir and Niral."

Diyah nodded. Her mind was completely blank, and she didn't know what to say.

"So, how is he?" asked Jémys. He was trying to sound nonchalant, but Diyah heard the concern in his tone.

"He was doing much better last night when I left, but I should check on him, actually... Do you want to come with me?" she asked, hoping he would say yes.

"No," said Jémys, his jaw set with tension. "No, I'll see him on the field this afternoon."

"Right," mumbled Diyah. Her breathing was shallow, and she felt lightheaded. As she watched Jémys walk away, she stood rooted to the spot, unable to move.

When she entered the infirmary several minutes later, she found Julyán sitting propped up in his bed. He looked much more alert and his face had regained its colour.

"So, I take it you've heard." He was watching her as she crossed the room to stand beside his bed.

Diyah didn't need to ask what he meant. "Yes, I heard," she replied, taking his arm and checking his bandages. "But how can you even consider fighting with a wound this severe? It's a wonder you survived at all."

"I've fought with worse wounds before, and I still killed my opponent," he said.

"But you can't kill your brother!"

Julyán's face fell slightly, and he looked away from her. "I will do what I must."

"You don't mean that," grumbled Diyah, unwinding his bandage to replace it with a fresh one. "He's your brother, I know you care about him."

"You're wrong," said Julyán in a dull voice. "There's no one I care about. I learned a long time ago that attachments are just weaknesses, leaving you open and vulnerable to manipulation. You should understand that too by now. You've allowed yourself to be used by others because of your sympathies, your weaknesses."

He winced as she pulled off the bandage and cast it aside.

"What are you talking about?" she asked.

Julyán gave her a sidelong glance. "The girls... Those orphan girls. You left yourself wide open to us because you cared more about them than your own safety. Your affection made you weak."

Diyah was working hard to hold back her anger. "You're equating strength with selfishness," she said, shaking her head. "But they aren't the same. Not at all."

Julyán snorted under his breath. "Please. There's no strength in being selfless."

Diyah stared at him in disbelief. "I don't believe that, and I don't think you really do either." She met his eyes with hers. They were the same brilliant green they'd been all those years ago, and her stomach flipped uncomfortably as she remembered that day. "The young man who stood up for me in the woods... you remember him?"

Julyán just smirked and said nothing.

"He had a vast deal more strength than this man sitting in front of me."

"How do you reckon?"

"Well, that boy was brave enough to stand up to the petulant brat this coward in front of me now serves," said Diyah, as she began wrapping his arm in fresh bandages, a little more callously than she might have done otherwise.

"I'm not a coward." Julyán's voice was deadly quiet. "You know nothing about me. Not then, not now, not ever."

"Right," said Diyah, rolling her eyes.

"So, tell me," snapped Julyán, finally losing his cool, "where will all of your so-called strength be when you're forced into marriage with whichever one of us wins this tournament?"

He glared at her with a hardness in his gaze that hadn't been there moments before.

Diyah finished wrapping his bandage and tied it off in an unceremonious knot, taking pleasure in making him wince.

Then she stood up and glared down at him. "Well, lucky for me, this wound makes it a lot more likely to be Jémys, doesn't it?"

Then she turned on her heel and stormed out of the room.

22

A BROTHER'S PAIN

Diyah was still fuming as she sat in the stands that afternoon. The first match that morning had been long, and she felt no sympathy for either Slaedir or Niral, so she found it especially difficult to sit through it. When it had finally ended with Slaedir standing over Niral's unconscious body, Diyah wasn't surprised. She always knew it would come down to Slaedir at the end. All that remained to determine was whether Jémys or Julyán would fight him in the final round.

As with the earlier rounds, there was a short break between fights, but for the first time, Diyah didn't leave the arena. She couldn't decide if she should check on Julyán, or go find Jémys. She worried Julyán's wound would leave him weak, and part of her wanted to find Jémys and talk some sense into him. But she was too angry, too confused, and too terrified.

So, Diyah just sat there, wracked with guilt and anxiety, waiting for the fight to start.

She wondered how many people in the crowd knew Jémys and Julyán were brothers. It wasn't a widely known fact, and

Diyah suspected the fight would draw a bigger crowd if more people knew.

The stands creaked, and she turned to see Fehla coming to join her.

Diyah waved feebly and watched Fehla take her seat. For a while, neither of them spoke. Somewhere far off, a thrush chirped in the trees, and it reminded Diyah vaguely of spring-time and all the joys that time usually brought.

But there would be none of that joy this year.

"It's a nice day," said Fehla, looking up at the clear blue sky. There were no clouds in sight, and the breeze smelled faintly like sweet grass. It was warmer than it had been all month.

Diyah just nodded and continued to stare at the arena.

"It's going to be okay, Diyah." Fehla's voice was soft and reassuring. "You said it yourself, Julyán hasn't been killing anyone all tournament. Why would he start now? And his own brother?" Fehla sounded sceptical.

"Of course, the idea of a brother killing his sibling is so foreign to us," said Diyah. She regretted it immediately and turned to see Fehla's stunned and sad face. "I'm sorry." Diyah reached out to take Fehla's hand. "I'm sorry, I shouldn't have said that. I'm just—" But she couldn't articulate it.

"It's okay, I understand," said Fehla, patting Diyah's arm. "And besides, maybe Jémys will win, right?"

"Yeah... But I'm not sure that's any better. He's so angry, Fehla. Julyán might have the restraint to stop himself from killing, but I'm not sure Jémys does."

"And would that be so terrible?"

Diyah rubbed her face hard with her hands. "No... er... yes. I don't know!" she blurted, throwing her hands up in the air. "I honestly don't know."

Fehla looked mildly stunned, but she nodded. "I suppose we shouldn't hope for Jémys to kill his own brother. I'd hate to think what it would do to him."

"Exactly," said Diyah. "Yeah, I just don't want Jémys to have to live with his guilt. It would wreck him." It relieved her to have an explanation. "That's all it is."

"Are you sure?" asked Fehla, giving her a shrewd and piercing stare.

"Yes, I'm sure." But Diyah was careful to avoid Fehla's gaze.

People were filtering back into the arena, and Diyah was grateful for the distraction. The bet takers gathered near the scoreboards, calling out odds as people passed by, occasionally stopping to place their bets.

"I hate this," said Fehla suddenly. "I've always hated this stupid tournament. It makes no sense! We should train our soldiers as a unit, instilling loyalty and trust as values, not this." She gestured helplessly towards the arena. "This teaches them to be selfish, to be ruthless. I don't know how any of them can trust their leader knowing how he claims his title."

"It's not about them, Mother," came Cadyan's drawling voice from behind them. They turned to see him standing in the highest row. "It's not about trust. It's about proving their loyalty to the king. Tell me, with powers like these"—he pulled a gold piece out of his pocket and began spinning it through the air a few inches above his palm—"why does Caerlon even have soldiers? Why bother with the tournament or the firkon at all? It's not as if I need them."

"Because you're bored?"

Cadyan smirked and closed his fist around the coin. "No," he said coolly. "It's to remind them—to remind everyone—how much they need me. Because even their strongest fighters can't win against *me*." He took his seat at the top of the risers and smiled. "That's comforting to know, isn't it?" He laughed and turned to welcome the courtiers now filing into the seats beside him.

"I suppose he's right, isn't he?" mumbled Diyah, looking back down at the arena. "This just proves that everyone is his puppet. Even our best fighters can't escape. We're all trapped, aren't we?"

Fehla gave a heavy sigh. "I'm afraid so. Catanya was our only hope and now even she's gone..." She trailed off, staring at the sky. "I should never have sent her away. Or I should have found a way to protect Cadyan too. Perhaps if—"

"Stop it, Fehla," said Diyah. "There's nothing you could have done. This is the way it is now. We can't look back."

Fehla nodded and cleared her throat, wiping her eyes on her sleeve. "You're right. I know you're right, but a mother's love never dies. And a mother's guilt never fades. You'll understand one day."

Diyah's insides twisted, and she resisted the urge to run screaming from the arena. She would rather die than experience what Fehla went through. She'd rather die than conceive a child with a man she loathed as much as Fehla had loathed Casréyan.

With a half-glance back at Cadyan, she thought what a shame it was that neither he nor his sister had ever had a real family. *Just look at what happened to them*, thought Diyah. *One dead, and one twisted and mutated beyond recognition.* She felt a sudden and profound sadness as she imagined Cadyan as a child, an innocent little boy suffering at his father's hands. *No child should have to endure such pain and misery.*

She suddenly realized she was sympathizing with the man she hated most, and she had to fight the urge to laugh out loud at the absurdity. Shaking her head, she turned her attention back to the arena.

Jémys and Julyán were walking onto the field and Diyah felt the familiar mixture of fatigue and apprehension she'd come to associate with this tournament. As she watched the two men approach and shake hands, her chest tightened, making it diffi-cult to breathe. She didn't know what to expect, and she certainly didn't know what outcome she wanted.

Julyán held his sword in his left hand, which told Diyah his right was far too damaged for him to be fighting so soon. One wrong move and he'd aggravate the wound all over again.

Jémys looked uneasy standing there, facing his brother. In all his other fights, he had remained focused and determined, but now he seemed unsure. His eyes kept darting to Julyán's injured arm as though he were just as concerned as Diyah.

The bell sounded for the match to begin, and everyone held their breath, waiting to see who would strike first. But neither of them seemed inclined to make the first move.

Diyah squinted down at them.

"Are they... talking?" asked Fehla, leaning forward to get a better view.

"Yeah, they are," said Diyah, confused. "But I can't make out what they're saying, can you?"

"No."

The crowd grew impatient, waiting for the fighting to start. People started heckling from their seats and calling down at them.

Suddenly, Julyán's face cracked into a wide grin. He tapped his sword on the ground and held it out in front of him, as though inviting Jémys to attack.

The crowd grew unusually quiet, so Diyah heard a small snippet of what Julyán said next.

"You're a grown man now, *Jémie.* Time you act like one."

"You don't even care. Nelle's dead, you know?"

Whatever Julyán said next was lost to the sound of the crowd cheering, as Jémys suddenly lost all composure and lunged. Julyán blocked his attack with ease, and the fight began.

Jémys launched assault after assault with a ferocity that betrayed the anger he must have been feeling. But Julyán seemed moderately amused, almost bored, as he blocked each hit one after another.

"You can do better than that!" he taunted as he blocked another hit and sent Jémys's sword flying out of his hand.

Jémys scrambled to pick it up, and though Julyán could have attacked, he just waited for Jémys to retrieve his sword before resuming the fight.

For all Diyah had been worried about Julyán's arm, it surprised her to see how well he fought without it. He seemed to fight as well or better with his left hand. Diyah was sure if he'd wanted to, Julyán could have ended the fight in a few quick moves, but for whatever reason, he continued blocking Jémys's hits, instead of launching his own.

"He's not even trying," said Diyah, looking at Fehla with her eyebrows raised.

The fight carried on like this for some time.

Jémys lunged. As Julyán side-stepped the attack, he brought his sword down, leaving a deep slice across Jémys's cheek. Jémys straightened up, touching his face to feel the blood on his fingers.

"Just tell me why!" he shouted, his voice carrying over the hushed voices of the crowd.

"When are you going to get it through your thick skull?" said Julyán. "I just don't care!" He punctuated every word with venom as he glared tauntingly at his brother across the arena.

Diyah saw something snap in Jémys. He lost all sense of remorse. As he raised his sword, Diyah could see it unfolding before it began.

Jémys struck out. Julyán blocked him with his own weapon just as Jémys lifted his leg and kicked Julyán hard in the knees, causing him to buckle. Jémys lowered his sword and threw his fist out, where it collided with Julyán's injured arm, sending blood spraying onto the ground. Then Jémys kicked Julyán's blade out of his grasp and stood looming over him.

The entire arena went quiet, waiting.

"Well, go on," said Julyán, kneeling before him. "Go on, do it!"

But Jémys stood perfectly still.

"Go on, kill me, little brother! Prove just how easy it is!"

Diyah sat there, frozen in terror, as she watched. But Jémys still didn't move. He let his sword fall a few inches, and the weight on Diyah's chest lightened. She knew in that moment that Jémys never would have killed his brother.

But her relief was short-lived.

In the span of a heartbeat, Julyán smacked the sword out of his face and spun his leg around, kicking Jémys's legs out from underneath him. As Jémys toppled to the ground, Julyán reclaimed his sword and stood up with surprising grace. He smashed the hilt across Jémys's head, knocking him unconscious.

And just like that, it was over. Julyán had won.

The crowd was cheering all around her, but Diyah sat motionless in her seat, her head still spinning.

Jémys had lost.

"Excellent," said a voice behind her. She turned to see Cadyan rubbing his hands together and smiling. "I was hoping he'd make it to the last round." He was talking to the man seated beside him. "Oh, I think Julyán will make a fine maífírkon. And it's time for fresh blood. New king, new maífírkon, don't you think? And Julyán has already proven himself to be a most worthy and loyal subject. This proves it even more."

The man beside him nodded.

"Oh, I'm excited to see how this ends now." Cadyan grinned from ear to ear as he stood up and left the stands.

It was well after dark before Jémys regained consciousness in the infirmary. All the other injured fighters had been healed and released, so the room was unusually quiet.

"How long have I been out," he asked, pushing himself into a half-seated position.

"A few hours," said Diyah. "Here, drink this. It should help with the pain." She handed him an opaque vial of pain reliever.

"I'm not in pain," said Jémys, but Diyah just stared at him sceptically. "Oh, all right," he grumbled, drinking the tonic in one gulp. Then he touched the spot on his face where Diyah had bandaged his cut.

"It's only superficial," she said. "It should heal just fine."

Jémys nodded and closed his eyes tightly. "I'd hate to lose my good looks," he grumbled.

"Are you okay?" asked Diyah after a pause.

Jémys opened his eyes, and she saw the torment in them. "No, not really," he said in a thin voice.

"What happened out there? You had him. You were about to win—"

"I don't know." Jémys raked his hand through his hair and clenched. "I just hesitated. I'm such an idiot."

"You're not an idiot!"

Jémys shook his head in frustration. "When I was a child, I idolized him, you know? He was my hero, my big brother. But now..." He trailed off, staring into the fire. "I don't even know who he is."

"He's still your brother," said Diyah.

"No, he's not." Jémys took a shaky breath, trying to steady himself before continuing. "When I was a boy and my father died, everyone told me Julyán was the reason—that he sold our father out to the king. But I never really believed it, you know? There was no way my brother would ever do that. He loved our father even more than I did. He'd never betray him... But my aunt never talked about it and I refused to believe what people said, so eventually they stopped trying to tell me. We stopped talking about him altogether, pretending he'd never existed. But a part of me always thought... or hoped... but now—" He broke off, tears pooling in his eyes. "I've lost everyone I've ever loved, Diyah. *Everyone.*"

Diyah watched Jémys for a while, feeling so overcome with sadness she could have drowned in it. She couldn't believe Julyán would betray his own family like that. She'd been hoping for any reason to think well of him, any reason at all—but now this?

The infirmary door opened and in walked the man himself. Diyah's entire body tensed as he strode over to join them, looking as cold and unfeeling as ever.

"What do you want?" she asked bitterly.

Julyán ignored her tone. "How is he?"

"I'm fine," said Jémys through gritted teeth.

Julyán just stood there, staring down at his brother impassively as though he hadn't heard what Jémys had said. Then, without speaking, he nodded and turned to leave.

"I used to pretend you were dead, you know?" called Jémys. "As a boy, I used to pretend you were dead. It was easier than accepting the truth. People tried to tell me, but I wouldn't listen. And Nelle was too broken to talk about it. Too hurt."

Julyán just stood stock-still and listened.

"How could you?" continued Jémys in a strained voice. "How could you just stand there and let them kill her— slaughter the entire village? Don't you remember how much you loved it in Finnua? How happy we were?"

"I told you on the field, Jémys. I didn't care." Julyán turned to face him. "Nelle's death meant nothing to me. I don't care. I watched them burn Finnua, and I felt nothing."

Diyah's mind was racing, trying to keep up. "Wait a second," she said, frowning at Julyán.

"I should go." He cast her a furtive glance before turning to leave.

"I used to think there was still hope for you," called Jémys. "But now I understand. It would have been better if you actually had died. That's what hurts the most. I would rather you'd died than become this." He gestured up and down, wearing an expression of utmost contempt.

Julyán stood rigid, with his back to his brother. "Well, Jémys, tomorrow you may get your wish," he said, sweeping out of the infirmary before anyone could say anything else.

As the door closed behind him, Diyah frowned at Jémys.

"What is it?" he asked, sounding miserable.

Diyah faltered. She wasn't sure what to tell him. "Julyán wasn't there," she said, finally settling on the truth. "Julyán didn't go with them to Finnua. He wasn't there when your aunt died."

"Wait, what?"

They stared at each other in confusion for a moment. Then Diyah jumped to her feet. "I'll be back," she said, racing towards the door and wrenching it open. She heard Jémys call after her, but she didn't stop.

The corridor outside was empty and there was no sign of Julyán. Somewhere deep inside the castle she heard a bell tolling for dinner, and she set off towards the soldiers' mess hall. As she turned the corner, she ran headlong into someone.

"There you are," she blurted, assuming it was Julyán.

"Here I am," responded an oily voice she recognized all too well. The smell of sourwood rum and sweat reached her nostrils, making her gag. "You've been looking for me?" Slaedir reached out to grab her arm.

"No." Diyah tried to tug her arm out of his grasp. "I just thought you were someone else."

"You don't have to pretend. We'll be married soon, you and I, and there will be no more secrets between us. There will be nothing between us at all." He grinned as he tightened his grip and pushed her into the wall, knocking the wind out of her.

His hot breath clung to her neck as he ran his hands over her body.

"Stop it, let go of me!" she shouted, trying to wrestle free. She elbowed him in the stomach and kicked him hard in the shins, so he backed off, scowling.

"Just you wait, girlie. Tomorrow night, you'll be all mine."

"I would rather die," said Diyah in a cool, carrying voice. "I *will* die rather than marry you, or anyone else whom I do not choose."

Slaedir cackled tauntingly. Just as he was about to grab her again, Julyán appeared around the corner.

"What's going on?" He glanced from Slaedir to Diyah, wearing something close to concern on his face.

"None of your business," snapped Slaedir, reaching forward again.

But Julyán grabbed him by the wrist. "Keep your hands to yourself, Slaedir."

"She doesn't belong to you, boy."

"Nor does she belong to you."

"Not yet. But you should have heard her, Julyán." Slaedir leered at Diyah. Then, in a mockingly high-pitched voice, he continued, "*I will die rather than marry you, or anyone else I did not choose. I'd rather die!*" He threw his head back, cackling. "Well go on, then. Hop to it. If you'd rather die, you're running out of time, aren't you? Why not off yourself now and be done with it? Want help?"

He pulled a dagger out of his vest and waved it in front of her, snickering.

Diyah stood perfectly still, not wanting to take the bait, but she couldn't help chancing a quick glance at Julyán who, she was surprised to discover, was staring at her with pity.

"Oho!" Slaedir clapped his hands together and stared from

Diyah to Julyán. "This is rich. You think Julyán might win tomorrow? Ha! Is that what you want?"

Diyah's face burned with embarrassment and anger. She took a step forward, so she was staring right at Slaedir. "All I want is to live just long enough to watch you die tomorrow. To watch you die the slow, painful death you deserve."

Then she pushed past them both and marched back down the corridor towards the infirmary without a second glance.

23

THE REFLECTING CHANNEL

Catanya and Drayk sat face to face in a small rowboat. They made their way upstream along the winding channel that had carved its path through the dense rock. On either side, the steep cliffs stretched up towards the stars. It gave the illusion that they were holding the sky in its place.

The water beneath them was the most brilliant shade of blue that Catanya had ever seen—bright and luminous as it reflected the light of the moon. It was also eerily calm and quiet, despite the boat now cutting gently through it, sending small waves rippling into the distance. The ripples faded faster than normal, returning the water to its glass-like quality.

The air was perfectly silent except for the sound of water lapping against the boat and the creaks and clunks of the wooden oars rolling in circles overhead and plunging back into the water.

They had been rowing all day, taking turns to row and rest. Catanya wondered how far they'd have to go before they reached the end of the channel. And what—or who—awaited them when they arrived.

When they'd walked through that gap leading away from the cove that morning, the last thing they'd expected to find was a rowboat, pulled onto the rocky shore, waiting for them.

"What do you reckon?" asked Drayk, circling the boat and knocking on the wood.

"Is it safe?" asked Catanya.

"Seems to be." Drayk shrugged and ran his hand along the side like he was searching for imperfections.

Catanya glanced out at the channel in front of them. It was long and narrow, and it snaked through the mountainous rock until it curved out of sight. There was no telling how far it stretched.

"Well, it's not as if we have many options," she said.

The water was deep and the shoreline quickly dropped off as the sheer rock walls closed in around them. There was no way to walk along the side. She knelt at the edge of the water and dipped her fingers in it. It was ice cold, and it sent a shiver up her spine. "It's too cold to swim," she said, standing up and turning around to face Drayk. "And I can't see any other way along."

"But it's peculiar, isn't it?" Drayk was still staring at the boat. He straightened up and looked around, frowning. "How did it get here?"

Catanya shook her head. "And who put it here?" Another shiver ran up her spine that had nothing to do with the cold water. "Do you think they're waiting for us?" she asked in a whisper.

Drayk narrowed his eyes and squinted out towards the water. He looked stiff and wary, as though his instincts were preparing to fight. "Well," he said finally, "I suppose there's only one way to find out." He lifted the oars and slid them into the boat.

Catanya sighed and nodded, casting one last uncertain glance around.

Together, they had manoeuvred the boat into the water, fastened the oars into the oarlocks, and set off along the channel towards the heart of the island.

It was just past nightfall now, and Catanya had taken the oars so Drayk could rest. She watched him rubbing his sore arms and stretching them out to the sides. He stared into the water and frowned.

"Should we fill the canteens?" he suggested. He reached out and touched the surface, watching the small slipstream form behind his hand. "We're almost empty, and this may be the only fresh water we'll find for a while."

The water seemed to turn a brighter and more radiant blue the farther inland they travelled. Even the night's darkness did nothing to dampen its effect. On the contrary, the water illuminated the world around them as though it had been storing sunlight for that very purpose.

"Yes, we probably should," she said despite the tightness in her stomach. She couldn't explain it, but she sensed that something was off about this place. "The Reflecting Channel," she mumbled under her breath as Drayk leaned over and submerged the canteen in the water, allowing it to fill to the brim.

He shook the excess droplets off it and stared at it momentarily. Then, holding it out to her in salute, he raised the canteen to his mouth and took a sip.

He shrugged, smacking his lips. "Seems fine," he said, taking another drink. "Here." He handed it to her and turned to fill the second one.

Catanya hesitated, but ultimately her thirst got the better of her. The water tasted fresh and it was cool as it passed over her parched lips and soothed her throat.

She felt better.

After a while, Drayk settled at the base of the boat and fell asleep, leaving Catanya alone with her thoughts as she continued rowing through the night.

It felt like days had passed since their experience on the cove, but she was still consumed with thoughts about the images they'd seen in the fire. It was bothering her, and she didn't know how to talk about it with Drayk. She didn't know how to explain her feelings because the more she thought about it, the more certain she became of what those images represented.

The image of her and Diyah, her and Jémys—all of it. They were her hopes and dreams. The flames had shown her and Drayk the things they desired, everything they longed to have. And that was what frightened her the most.

Some desires had been fairly self-evident. Of course, she longed to laugh with Diyah, and grow old with Jémys. Of course, she longed to see her mother... But who was the man on the ship? And then there was Drayk... Had that been her desire or his?

But it was the last image that unsettled Catanya most. The man with black hair and eyes full of brotherly affection. She knew what it meant, but she couldn't acknowledge it. She felt like she was betraying everyone, dishonouring their memories and disgracing herself.

All of a sudden Drayk sat bolt upright, sweating and looking panicked.

"What is it?" blurted Catanya, nearly dropping the oars in her surprise.

Drayk swivelled around, frantically searching the area, and then relaxed. "Nothing," he breathed, brushing the hair out of his face with shaky hands and laughing in relief. "Just a dream."

He rubbed his eyes and took a few deep breaths to calm himself. Then he reached into his bag and pulled out the canteen again, taking a deep sip. He shook his head as though trying to cast the memory away.

"What happened in the dream?" asked Catanya, eyeing him. He seemed strangely vulnerable in this moment, and she wanted to comfort him.

Drayk looked at her quizzically before his face split into a disarming grin. "I should blush to tell you," he said with a wink, reverting to his usual self.

"Right." Catanya rolled her eyes and picked up the oars again. "I almost forgot who I was talking to." After travelling alone with Drayk for so long, she had grown both accustomed to and increasingly frustrated with his facetiousness. Usually his levity helped her, but sometimes she wished he would just drop the pretence.

"It was nothing of consequence," said Drayk, shrugging as he took another swig from the canteen before passing it to Catanya.

They sat in silence for a few minutes as she drank. She watched Drayk absentmindedly rub the side of his ribs where she knew he bore several scars and burns. In all the time she'd known him, she still hadn't found the courage to ask him about them. After all, why bring it up? Why make him say it?

Catanya sighed and shook her head. Then she returned the canteen to her bag and lifted the oars to row again.

After another few hours, Drayk and Catanya switched places. She wrapped her cloak tightly around her arms and squished down into the base of the boat, resting her back against the seat. Then she closed her eyes, hoping she could fall asleep despite how uncomfortable she was.

She dozed unevenly as strained dreams and images passed through her head, twisting and warping through the haze of her fatigue. Her muscles seized from the contorted position, so she finally abandoned the idea and returned to her seat.

"Can't sleep?" asked Drayk casually. He hoisted the oars

over and around in circles, propelling the boat silently through the glassy water.

Catanya shook her head and wiped her eyes.

"Anything on your mind?" he asked with a slightly mocking smirk.

Catanya snorted and gave him a sour look as if to say, "why would I tell you?"

They continued in silence, with only the sound of the oars splashing into the water.

After a while, Catanya thought she caught a new sound encroaching on the silence. A faint crackling came from somewhere nearby. She turned her head to check behind them, but there was nothing. The sound seemed to stop, so she shrugged and turned back in her seat.

The crackling started again, slowly vibrating through the unnatural stillness.

"Do you hear that?" she asked, glancing around. The sound continued, growing louder and rising in pitch.

"Yeah, I—" Drayk broke off, squinting at an area a few feet away, where the water connected with the sheer rock wall.

Catanya followed his gaze. Crystals of sapphire ice bloomed in the water along the edges, branching out into veins of frost that crept towards the centre of the channel. Slowly, the icy claws extended farther. They twisted and broke off in different directions, tangling together to form a web.

Vein after vein, the frozen lines converged, filling in the remaining pockets of water until a solid sheet of ice emerged.

There was a sharp crack, and the boat lurched. Catanya glanced over her shoulder. The ice had already reached the other side of the boat and begun to seep between the slats of wood, bursting forth like icy spores.

The boat shook again and again. Icy tendrils wove their way along the surface of the wood, inching closer and closer to where Catanya and Drayk sat, watching in awe.

A sudden instinct told Catanya she couldn't let those tendrils touch her. She jumped to her feet and yanked Drayk up beside her.

"What do we do?" he asked with an uncharacteristic level of panic in his voice. "It's everywhere, we're trapped."

He was right. All around them, the world was turning to ice, and there was nothing they could do but watch the tendrils inch their way closer and closer.

Catanya tried to summon her magic, she tried to force the ice to retreat or melt it back into water, but nothing happened. She shook her hands out impatiently, trying to focus. But there was nothing to hold on to. She had nothing but her own fear and doubt.

"It's not working!" she exclaimed. "I don't understand." As much as she hated her powers, she would have given anything to be able to use them now.

Mere inches away, the icy fingers extended their grip towards her.

Catanya closed her eyes and braced herself, waiting for a deathly chill to connect with her feet and make its way up her legs.

She felt the pressure of it first, the weight of the ice on her body. She looked down and watched the ice coil around her shins like vines, leaching the warmth from her and replacing it with a biting chill.

Her skin smarted, and she gasped. She tried to take a step, but nearly buckled over at the knees. She was frozen where she stood.

Drayk swore as he twisted at the waist, looking down at the tendrils that encircled him. He frantically tried to pull himself free.

Catanya was shivering uncontrollably now. "If it covers us completely..." she said, exchanging nervous glances with Drayk. The cold was excruciating, but the pressure was worse.

The weight of the ice was agonizing as their muscles seized and locked.

"All right, I'll ask again. What do we do?" said Drayk. The ice had crept up past their knees and it showed no sign of slowing or stopping.

"I don't know," said Catanya. The weight was dragging her down. She tried to move her legs, but she was afraid to push too hard. Her body felt brittle, like it might snap and shatter at the joints. She tried to keep her arms above her waist and wiggle herself free, but she slipped and her hand slapped against her knees, leaving a stain of frost along her palm.

She let out a sharp gasp as the area began to crystallize and spread. "We're going to die here," she said a little hysterically. She winced as the pain in her hand scorched and seeped through her skin, into her bones.

"Oh well," said Drayk through clenched teeth as he teetered at the waist. "I've always wanted a statue of myself somewhere in the world. Guess an ice sculpture will have to do... shame nobody will ever see it." His grim attempt at humour barely penetrated the sheer panic taking hold of them both. "So much for you mastering your powers and becoming queen," he spluttered. He was shivering and panting from the fear and exertion as he tried to fight the ice.

Catanya let out a sharp, hysterical laugh. After everything she'd been through, she couldn't believe this was how it was going to end, but...

"I guess something good will come from this after all," she said, her voice shrill. The ice on her arm had crept up past her elbow now, locking her arm inside like a cast. Her heart was thumping faster and faster like it knew it was about to beat its last beat.

"You don't mean that," said Drayk in a surprisingly stern voice. He shook his head and convulsed as the ice finally spread to his arms.

Catanya was taken aback. "Yes, I do," she said, looking him dead in the eye. She lurched as the ice connected with her ribs and the blinding pain shot through her spine. She was having trouble breathing now, but if she was going to die, she might as well be honest. "Drayk, I don't want to be queen of anything... I never did."

She watched in horror as the ice crystals reached his neck and began creeping towards his face. The colour leached from his skin, as the life drained out of him. He clenched his jaw, fighting the pain, and stared at her with bitter scepticism.

He still didn't believe her.

"I'm telling you the truth," she said, fighting the urge to close her eyes. The weight on her chest was excruciating. She needed to get the words out before she ran out of time. They'd spent so much time lying to each other and holding things back. Now, at the end, she needed him to believe her. "I never wanted these powers, Drayk. I never wanted any of this. All I've ever wanted is to be free. I wanted to see the world and find my place—somewhere I could... *belong*."

The air stilled. The cracking sounds ceased abruptly and the ice ground to a halt.

Catanya and Drayk stared at each other, waiting with bated breath. But nothing happened.

The seconds dragged on and nothing changed. They were still alive and frozen in place, trapped in excruciating pain.

"Oh, this is perfect," said Drayk. He could barely move his lips, and his entire face had a ghostly blue tinge. "So, now we get to starve to death, is that it?"

Like bitter truth that bites the years of tart neglect.

"Wait a moment," said Catanya, an idea forming in her mind. "I told the truth."

"Good for you," retorted Drayk, grimacing underneath his mask of ice.

"No, I mean... maybe that's what this is all about. *Bitter truth...* I have an idea. Tell me something! A truth," she said frantically. "Something you haven't said before."

This had to work, it had to. She was sure she was right.

"Uh..." Drayk seemed hesitant.

"Tell me what your nightmare was about." In her excitement, Catanya's pulse quickened again. Her breathing accelerated, but her chest ached as it expanded into its frozen cincture. "Please!" she gasped.

"Fine. I dreamed about my childhood, all right?"

A sharp crack, and the ice on his face and head broke free, disintegrating as it fell like snow in the air. They watched it descend, momentarily mesmerized.

"I knew it," hissed Catanya in triumph. "Quick, tell me more! What else happened in your dream?"

Drayk's expression was stunned. "It was nothing," he said. "I have the same nightmare every couple of months. Just memories."

"Memories of your mother?" she asked.

Drayk gave her a dark look and nodded.

There was a light crack, but nothing moved this time.

"It's not enough," she said, looking around at the frozen water. "Okay, so... the vision in the flames." She remembered the woman laughing and playing with the young boy. "That was you and your mother we saw, right?"

Drayk looked uncomfortable, but he nodded again, averting his eyes. Then he exhaled and squinted out at the frozen channel. "You saw my father briefly too," he said, and his voice grew bitter.

Catanya frowned, wracking her brain for the memory. "You mean the man on the ship?" she asked, surprised. The image of the man being dragged off the ship and flogged had seemed so jarring amongst the other visions. Catanya hadn't understood what it was, but now she thought it was becoming clearer.

"Yeah, that's him," grumbled Drayk, his face marred with revulsion.

There was a shudder and a crack, and the boat teetered. The ice on Drayk's neck broke free. But it still wasn't enough.

"But I thought..." She needed to ask the question but she couldn't find the words. "I thought your mother was... I thought that's why she..." Catanya broke off, embarrassed and unsure how to continue.

"Yeah," said Drayk, grimacing. "But I *have* met him. I know his name and I know where to find him."

Catanya didn't like the morbid curiosity she felt.

"All right, your turn," said Drayk brusquely, cutting her off before she could ask another question.

"Me?" Her voice sounded high-pitched. "I... um..." She would have fidgeted if she could have moved at all. "Well, all right... sometimes, I think—" She stopped herself, casting around for a more banal secret to reveal, anything but the one on the tip of her tongue. She opened her mouth to say something else, but the words came tumbling out. "Sometimes, I think Mórceá would be better off if I'd never been born. Sometimes I think I should just let Cadyan kill me."

Crack. The ice surrounding their chests and arms shattered.

Drayk stared at her for a long pause, an intense sorrow in his eyes.

Now it was Catanya's turn to avert her gaze. "What? It's true," she muttered, shrugging. Then she shook her head. "I can feel it, Drayk." She took a deep breath, reluctant to continue. But after everything they'd been through together, he deserved to know. She needed to prepare him. "I can feel the power inside of me. The more I use it, the more it takes hold, and... I-I don't want to become like him." She turned her gaze back to Drayk. "I *can't* become like him."

An enormous crack rent the air and the ice around them burst apart. The force of it nearly knocked them over as the boat teetered and they slammed into each other, trying to steady themselves.

They slumped down into their seats, groaning as they massaged their sore muscles and tried to rub the warmth back into their limbs.

Catanya rolled onto her side to glance over the edge of the boat. The surrounding ice was wet, like it had started to melt, but the channel was still frozen solid.

"I say we get out and walk the rest of the way," she said.

Drayk groaned and grabbed the frozen oar beside him, hoisting himself up into a better position.

"That won't work, Catya, you know it won't."

"Why not?" she asked, a bit more defensively than she needed to. "I'm sure the ice is sturdy enough to support our weight, and it would be nice to stretch our legs."

Drayk watched her closely, not saying a word.

"Honestly, I'm sure it's fine," she continued babbling, trying to ignore his knowing look.

"Catya."

She was thrown off guard by the sudden tenderness she heard.

"Say it." He spoke calmly and his eyes were full of understanding.

"I don't want to."

He knelt down in front of her, eyes boring into her. "You have to."

Catanya groaned dejectedly. "I don't want... I don't want to do it," she blurted before she could stop herself. "Cadyan, I don't want to fight him. I don't want any of this. I never realized it before, but... he's my brother! Why can't he just be my brother?"

With a final deafening crack and splash, the ice shattered into dust, disintegrating slowly into the water.

Tears pooled behind Catanya's eyes, and the heat of embarrassment burned on her cheeks. She turned her face away from Drayk. "Maybe... if I could just talk to him..." But she broke off. "Ugh," she grumbled, burying her face in her hands, "I'm pathetic."

It mortified her how juvenile she sounded. It was absurd to believe she and Cadyan could ever actually care for one another. But she couldn't help it. Ever since she'd discovered she had a family, she'd been struggling to come to grips with the overwhelming regret underneath her other scattered emotions. She had a brother. She couldn't help her childish longing to connect with him, to be loved by him.

The boat shook slightly, and she knew Drayk had taken his seat at the front, preparing to row.

"You're not pathetic, Catya," he spoke in a slow, firm tone. "But take it from me, just because he's your blood, doesn't mean he's your brother. In my experience, blood has very little to do with family."

Catanya sighed and looked up at him. "You're right. I know you're right. But I can't help but wonder... I wonder how different our lives would be if we'd grown up together. If we'd been there for each other all along... I have to believe there's some good in him somewhere. And I have to know he can be redeemed because..." She trailed off, nervous to say it aloud.

"Because why?" said Drayk.

Catanya looked out at the glittering water, watching the last bits of ice melt away. Then she took a deep breath. "Because then maybe I can be too," she said.

24

———

TO THE DEATH

On the morning of the final round of the Maífírkon Tournament, the entire castle was already buzzing with excitement. The fight was scheduled that afternoon, followed by a celebratory feast and party in the Great Hall to honour the new maífírkon.

Diyah sat in the infirmary, waiting for Jémys to wake up as she watched the sun rise slowly through the window. The sky was a pinkish hue with orange hints where the light peeked through the trees. It was truly beautiful, and it filled her with a sense of peace that she desperately needed.

"Miss," said a voice behind her, causing Diyah to nearly jump off her chair. A maidservant stood a few feet away. "A letter for you, miss." She spoke in a whisper, clearly nervous to wake Jémys.

"A letter?" Diyah was surprised, but she took it, turning it over to examine the seal. The wax was already broken, and she realized with a stab of irritation that the guards had read it. "Thank you," she said sourly, dismissing the maid. Then she unfolded the parchment to read the writing inside. She didn't recognize the strangely neat, loopy script, and there was no name on the bottom.

My dear,

She received a jolt when she read that, wondering if the letter was from Lord Zadílar.

I'm sorry it has taken me so long to write, but the task proved even more difficult than expected. However, I have finally located the three ingredients you requested, and they have been dispatched. I feel certain this remedy will prevent a great deal of pain.

Sincerely yours...

Diyah read the cryptic words multiple times, trying to make sure she understood.

Zadílar had done it. He'd found Meya, Gréys, and Hahney and he'd gotten them out of Caerlon. She didn't know how he'd done it, and right now she didn't care. She felt a great weight lift off her shoulders. The girls were safe. Zadílar had been true to his word, and now she was free to make her decision without regrets.

She folded the letter and tucked it into her pocket, closing her eyes in silent thanks.

When she opened them again, she began rifling through her bag of medicines. She was searching for two particular vials that, when mixed, would create a powerful, fast-acting toxin.

"Diyah?" said Jémys, sitting up in bed.

"I'm here," she called, hastily shoving the vials in her pocket and pushing her bag aside. "I'm here. How are you this morning?" She walked over to his cot and surveyed him.

"Oh, my head feels like a bruised apple, but otherwise I'm

okay." He smiled wryly as he rubbed his temples. Then he tilted his head. "How are you doing?"

Diyah gave a nervous laugh. "I'm fine. It'll all be over soon."

Jémys reached out and took Diyah's hand. "I'm so sorry, Diyah. I wanted to win, and I tried so hard. Not just to avenge her, but also—" He broke off, as if he couldn't bring himself to say it. "But whatever happens next, I promise you I'll be here for you. We'll find a way out of this together. I think Catanya would be happy to know we have each other. She loved you so much, you know?"

Diyah nodded. Her hand trembled slightly as she pulled it back. She felt guilty lying to Jémys, but she'd made her decision, and he would only try to talk her out of it.

"Are you going to the fight?" she asked, wanting to change the subject.

"No."

"But..." She looked at him, filled with sorrow, "What if Julyán dies? This could be your last opportunity to say goodbye, don't you want to take it? You didn't get a chance with your father."

Jémys screwed his face up into a painful expression, as though he were trying to hide his emotions. "No, Diyah. My brother died the same day as my father. I've already mourned him."

"Jémys—"

"I'm not going, Diyah." His voice was stern and Diyah knew the conversation was closed.

"Fine," she muttered, standing up. "I need some air. I'll be back later."

She walked past the rows of cots and left the infirmary, closing the door behind her. She stood there, with her head pressed against the wooden door, trying to fight the dizzy sensation coming over her in waves.

A Heiltúir does not mete out death, said a voice in her head.

But this was different.

She clutched the vials in her pocket and tried to cast the guilt aside. *Am I being selfish?* she wondered, as she walked down the corridor with no sense of direction or destination.

"Jémys will be fine," she tried to reassure herself. "He'll be fine. He doesn't need me. And I can't, I *won't!*" She halted and stared out the window at the arena. "And Catanya wouldn't want me to, either. *She'd* understand. She'd never accept it either."

"Are you talking to yourself?" came a voice from behind her.

"What?" She spun around to see Julyán standing with his hands behind his back, watching her curiously.

"No—well, yes. I'm just working through some things." She turned back to the window, embarrassed. "Shouldn't you be getting ready? Why are you here?"

"I was looking for you, actually." He took a few steps towards her. "I came to ask about... about Jémys. How is he doing?"

Diyah frowned. "Physically, he's fine, but emotionally, well..." She shrugged as if to say, "what do you think?"

Julyán nodded and turned his gaze out the window.

"Why did you lie to him?" she asked.

He looked surprised and turned to meet her gaze. "About what?"

"About your aunt," she said. "You weren't even there when she died. I remember. You were here when Slaedir and the others destroyed Finnua. So why did you tell Jémys you were there? Was it just to upset him?"

Julyán's face fell, and he sighed. "It is easier for Jémys to hate me than to accept the truth."

"Well, you're not even giving him a choice. How is he supposed to accept the truth if you don't give it to him?"

Julyán smiled dryly. "I've never been a very good brother... or person, for that matter," he said, shrugging.

"What?" His sincerity caught Diyah off guard.

"It's true. I've only ever caused our family pain. Whatever happens today—whether I live or die—it's better for Jémys to know as little as possible. Hate is easier than pain." His voice sounded distant, and his eyes gazed, unblinking, at the window.

"Hate may be easier, but that doesn't mean it's better," said Diyah calmly. "And besides, I don't think it's fair to say you've never been a good brother. Jémys certainly thought you were wonderful as children. And I know for a fact you weren't always a bad person. I remember the boy you used to be."

"That boy is gone." He shook his head and turned to walk away, but Diyah grabbed his arm. He reluctantly turned around to face her.

"I don't believe that." She spoke in a voice so low it was barely a whisper. "I think he's still in there somewhere, buried deep, maybe, but he's in there. You just have to look for him. I'm sure you can find him again before... before the end."

The corners of Julyán's mouth twitched as he lifted her hand off his arm. "Even if I do, how will you know?"

"What do you mean?"

"I heard what you said last night. You would rather die, and..." He reached down and pulled the two vials out of her pocket, smiling. "It seems you meant what you said." He turned the vials over and read their labels. "That's one way to do it, I suppose."

"I—" An icy chill ran through Diyah's body. *He knew.* Now what was she going to do?

"So, you would rather die?" repeated Julyán.

"I... I would," she responded, finding her voice. "Yes." She said it unapologetically. She didn't owe him anything and she wouldn't let him make her feel bad about her decision.

Julyán nodded and handed her back the vials. "Understood."

"Wait, what?" blurted Diyah, as she watched him turn to walk away. "That's it? You're not going to stop me?"

"No," he said with a shrug.

She couldn't believe it. "Really? Not even if you win?"

Julyán frowned as though he were considering his answer. Then his face contorted, and he looked almost deranged. "No, my victory will be its own reward." His eyes flashed. He stared at her like he was seeing through her. "I've been waiting for this for over ten years. All I've ever wanted is to see that bastard dead at my feet, to finally make him suffer—make him pay. I've waited long enough." He seemed to pull himself out of his trance. He inclined his head slightly and said, "This is goodbye, then." Without waiting for a response, he turned and strode away.

Diyah was speechless. "Goodbye," she murmured, watching him go. She was too stunned to stay anything else.

She spent the rest of the morning wandering around the castle in a kind of daze. The vials in her pocket grew heavier with every passing minute. Their weight bounced around, taunting her as she took each step.

Her mind kept returning to the same question—what truth was Julyán hiding from his brother? What could be so bad that telling Jémys he'd destroyed their village would be better? Why did he want his brother to hate him?

She ran through every interaction she'd ever had with Julyán. None of it added up. How could he change from a man of honour, a man his brother admired, to someone willing to kill indiscriminately?

But maybe he wasn't willing to kill for no reason. After all, he hadn't killed anyone in the tournament, unlike many of his fellow soldiers. He'd shown mercy on numerous occasions. He always kept his emotions buried so deep, and his face so neutral, he was hard to read. But maybe Julyán had been playing a different game.

Could this all have been about revenge? Diyah paced up and down the hallway outside the infirmary. Hadn't Slaedir killed Julyán's father? Maybe Julyán had been biding his time before he could get his revenge.

Yes, that's it, thought Diyah, breathing deeply as a burden lifted. But no sooner had this thought occurred to her than a nagging voice said, *didn't Jémys tell you Julyán betrayed their father? Julyán is the reason their father died, so why would he care?*

"I don't know!" exclaimed Diyah aloud. She threw her hands up in frustration, startling two maids who were walking past her.

An intense curiosity was overcoming her. It was almost enough to overpower the fear and anxiety that had been growing stronger with each passing day. She needed to know the truth. She needed to talk to Julyán again. Before it was too late.

She turned around and marched straight down the hallway towards the arena. As she rounded the corner, she found her way barred by two burly guards.

"The king says you're to head to the arena," grunted one of them.

"Well, that's where I'm—"

"The fight is about to start."

"What?" Diyah looked out the window, and to her horror, she realized they were right. The arena was rapidly filling with spectators.

She had run out of time.

"No, it's too soon," she muttered to herself.

"Come on." One of the guards grabbed her by the elbow and started steering her down the hall.

"Let go of me. I can walk by myself," she snapped, yanking her arm away.

As she took her seat in the stands next to Fehla a few minutes later, she felt dizzy and nauseated. How had this all happened so fast? She wasn't ready. She needed more time, and she needed more answers.

"All right, dear?" Fehla took her hand and squeezed it.

"Hmm," was all Diyah could say, as she looked at Fehla without seeing her.

"Everything will be okay," said Fehla, but Diyah felt the emptiness of those words.

"Right, of course," she replied.

"I suppose if we're going to hope for the lesser of two evils, that's Julyán, isn't it?"

"What?" Diyah was shocked out of her stupor by the sound of Julyán's name. "Oh, yes. Yes, he is definitely the better choice."

"Still not great though." Fehla looked at Diyah with sadness. "But you'll be fine, and I'll help you. I have experience in these... these *things*," she added bitterly. "And if it's any consolation, I don't think my son wants Slaedir to win any more than we do."

Diyah just nodded. She was afraid if she opened her mouth, she'd be sick.

Time raced ahead at an unnatural rate. Julyán and Slaedir were already on the field, and before she knew it, Cadyan was on his feet.

"Welcome, everyone," he called out to the arena. "Thank you for coming to show your support for our brave fighters throughout this tournament. It truly has been a tournament unlike any other! As you know, today's match is a fight to the death to determine who will be Caerlon's next maífírkon, and of course, who will claim this beautiful woman's hand." He pulled Diyah up to stand beside him. "Our very own court physician and one of the last remaining Heiltúir!"

Whistles and cheers came from the spectators. Diyah had to

work hard to avoid passing out, as the sea of faces pointed in her direction. She glanced down at Slaedir and Julyán, who were both staring up at her. Slaedir was wearing a self-satisfied smile on his face, but Julyán just looked determined and focused.

"Defending his title for the fourth time, we have Master Slaedir Aí-Camwin, and challenging him we have Master Julyán Aí-Finnua," said Cadyan, gesturing to each of them in turn. "Well, gentlemen, I thank you for your loyalty, and may the best man win." Cadyan took his seat and gestured for a servant to sound the bell and start the match.

Before the bell finished sounding, Slaedir made his first attack. The crowd booed and hissed as his blade nicked Julyán's shoulder. But Julyán reacted quickly. He barely flinched, using the momentum of the hit to spin around and kick Slaedir's legs out from under him.

It was the most brutal fight Diyah had ever seen. Both men seemed driven by some personal vendetta to cause the other the most pain possible. Before long, they were both sporting cuts along their arms and chests, and purplish bruises formed on their faces.

Julyán, especially, seemed motivated by a carefully controlled rage that Diyah had never seen in him before. He told her he'd waited over ten years for this and now, watching him fight, Diyah knew it was true. She saw the years of anticipation coming to fruition as he parried and stabbed with everything he had in him.

Slaedir lunged and Julyán blocked his sword with a crash of metal. Julyán's fist connected with Slaedir's jaw with a near audible force, and they broke apart.

They were circling each other now, and Slaedir's voice carried into the stands.

"I should have killed you when you were a boy!" he shouted, spitting blood out on the ground. "Ungrateful little shit!" He lunged with his sword outstretched, but Julyán was too quick. He spiralled out of the way and brought the hilt of his own sword down on Slaedir's back, propelling him into the mud where Julyán kicked him several times in the chest. But as Julyán prepared to plunge his sword down, Slaedir rolled over and kicked his shin. Julyán teetered and Slaedir sprang forward to tackle him. Both swords flew out of their grasps and they became locked in a fistfight on the ground. They were a mass of whirling limbs and Diyah couldn't tell whose were whose.

Finally, they broke apart. Julyán was sporting a split lip, while Slaedir's left eye looked bloody and bruised. He was wincing as though he'd broken a rib.

Backing away, Slaedir pulled a six-inch dagger from inside his jacket. He exposed his bloodstained teeth in a vicious smile and advanced on Julyán. But Julyán was prepared. He pulled his own dagger from his belt, holding it with a reverse grip.

Slaedir scowled and launched at him. Julyán deflected with his left arm and hooked with his right, slicing Slaedir's cheek from his ear to his nose. Slaedir cried out in rage and clutched at his bloody face.

The crowd winced together. Some cheered, while others hissed. The bets were high on this fight, but Diyah hadn't checked the odds. She couldn't bear to know.

Slaedir lunged again. Their forearms collided in a deadlock, and Slaedir stomped on Julyán's knee. Julyán cried out and crashed onto his back. Slaedir bore down on him, but Julyán twisted out of the way and kicked up onto his feet.

They carried on like this, lunging and blocking each other's daggers, until Julyán hit Slaedir's arm so hard, it sent his weapon flying out of his hand. Unarmed, Slaedir retreated to the edge of the arena. Julyán seemed to contemplate his options for a moment. He tossed his blade between his hands a few times, watching Slaedir. Then, without warning, he hurled his dagger through the air.

Slaedir dodged just in time. But the blade still grazed his arm before lodging into the wooden wall behind him. The force of the hit was so strong it splintered the board, scattering shards into the air.

The two men stared at each other across the arena. Slowly, as if moving with one mind, they turned their eyes to the swords lying discarded at the centre of the ring.

The noise level mounted, as the audience seemed to guess their thoughts.

Both fighters launched forward. Julyán arrived first, but before he could retrieve the weapons, Slaedir descended on him and started pummelling every inch of Julyán that he could reach. Julyán cried out in pain and tried to wrestle Slaedir off of him. He finally landed one good blow on the side of Slaedir's head, knocking him down.

In the split second it took for Slaedir to climb back to his feet, Julyán managed to retrieve the swords. With one in each hand, he stood staring at Slaedir, whose eyes were wide with alarm.

With a speed and ferocity unlike anything Diyah had ever seen, Julyán whipped the blades through the air like the sails of a windmill and advanced on Slaedir. But as Julyán brought one blade down, Slaedir grabbed his arm and elbowed him squarely in the chest, causing Julyán to drop the weapon and stumble backwards a few paces.

By the time Julyán had straightened up, Slaedir had already retrieved his sword and was lunging at him. This time, Julyán had to grab Slaedir's hand to block his attack. Holding Slaedir's arm with his left hand, Julyán brought his sword hilt down hard on his wrist. Slaedir shouted inarticulately and stumbled, dropping his sword. Julyán wasted no time. He launched onto the ground, collecting both blades.

But Slaedir hadn't noticed, and as he took another step, Julyán thrust both swords upwards with all his might, piercing straight through Slaedir's chest. With one final effort, Julyán drove the blades through with a sickening crack and Slaedir fell to his knees, spluttering and choking on his own blood.

The entire arena erupted into an explosion of cheers and howling.

Julyán moved to straighten up, but Slaedir grabbed him by the leg and yanked him down next to him. Everyone held their breath, not daring to move, but what happened next was completely unexpected.

Slaedir laughed hysterically. He spluttered, blood pouring out his mouth, as he grabbed Julyán's vest and pulled him close to whisper something in his ear.

"What was that? What did he say to him?" asked Diyah, looking at Fehla.

"I don't know."

Julyán jerked himself free of Slaedir's grasp and stood up, wearing a grimace. Slaedir cackled even louder, twitching as blood streamed down his chest, pooling around his knees. Julyán watched him for a moment. Then he slowly pulled the swords out of Slaedir's chest and tossed one aside. He paused briefly, examining the second blade—an ornate, gilded broadsword that gleamed in the sunlight. Julyán turned the tip towards Slaedir, so blood dripped from the blade onto his face.

Even at a distance, Slaedir's fear was visible. But he continued to cackle hysterically, almost as if he couldn't stop.

Slowly, as though relishing every moment, Julyán positioned the maífírkon's own sword against his neck. Slaedir made one final, strangled noise before Julyán wound his arm back and brought it down in a whirl of metal. Slaedir's body slumped to the ground, and his head rolled away into the mud.

Julyán stared down at Slaedir's lifeless body as the crowd's cheers filled the arena. When he finally turned to face the audience, Diyah thought she noticed some uneasiness in his expression. He looked back at Slaedir, frowning before turning to walk towards Cadyan, who was striding into the arena with a wide smile on his face, his arms outstretched in a brotherly manner.

Diyah couldn't hear anything that was happening anymore. Realization had suddenly dawned on her. Slaedir was dead. He was gone and Julyán had won—he had won the maífirkon title and he had won *her*. Relief flooded through her, washing away most of the anxiety she'd been battling all day. She didn't know whether to laugh or to cry.

She put her hand in her pocket and thumbed the tops of the vials. Until now, she hadn't realized how much she'd been counting on Julyán to win the tournament. She smiled to herself and pulled her hand back out of her pocket so she could clap along with everyone else.

25

THE SHROUDED CAVES

atanya was losing track of time. Hours seemed to pass differently in this strange, mystical place. She couldn't remember how long it had been since she and Drayk first stepped onto the shoal, starting this journey. Time was bleeding together unnaturally, making her increasingly impatient and despondent.

After what felt like a week sitting cramped in a small boat, they finally reached the end of the valley. They disembarked onto the rocky, desolate shore.

"That wasn't so bad," said Drayk, staring at the water. "At least we didn't freeze to death." He laughed as he hauled the boat up onto the rocks. Then he shook his head as though he were trying to clear it.

"Right." Catanya was barely listening. She had taken the map out again and was studying it, trying to make sense of the images. It showed an entrance to a set of caves somewhere nearby, but as she glanced around, she couldn't see it. She looked back at the map, tracing her finger over the words scrawled at the top.

"Shrouded Caves," she read out loud. "*Jagged fear cracks and grinds, paring down to soothe the dread.*"

"Great. *Caves*," mumbled Drayk. "I can hardly wait." He tossed the oars into the boat and threw himself down on the ground, looking exhausted.

Catanya looked at Drayk sprawled on the damp stones with his eyes closed and his arm draped over his face. He didn't seem eager to start the next leg of the journey. Catanya didn't like the idea either. She had never enjoyed any activity that took place in a cramped, dark space. It made her anxious just thinking about it. Being trapped in the dark, struggling to breathe as the air grew thinner and thinner...

Catanya suppressed a shudder. "Maybe we should rest for a while," she said, sitting beside him on the ground and pulling out their dwindling rations. "We need to regain our strength, and who knows what these caves might hold."

"Agreed." Drayk nodded without opening his eyes.

They shared a small portion of their remaining cheese and dried boar in silence. When they'd finished, Drayk reclined on the rocks again.

Catanya knew she should use this time to rest, but she wasn't tired. She couldn't stop thinking about everything that had happened on their journey so far and running over the map's instructions in her head.

The harkened pain and sorrow,

With resounding aches of defeat

She recalled the beginning of their journey and everything she'd heard while making her way across the shoal. Snippets of so many painful memories, and the voices of everyone she'd loved and lost. She'd been helpless as the voices taunted her, reminding her of everything her powers cost. Reminding her there was nothing she could do to change that.

Shows delusions of yearning

To burn and scold at innocence

The firestorm images had been a torment. Seeing all the things she yearned to have, the fantasies she clung to… Fantasies that belonged to a younger version of herself, a version that no longer existed. Most of what she longed to have was already beyond her reach forever. But there were some things… certain things might still be possible. Those were the things she needed to focus on. She couldn't let them slip away. Not now they were all she had left.

Like bitter truth that bites

The years of tart neglect,

Now she understood what her greatest hopes and darkest fears were. She had finally admitted them. A strange sense of relief came with that. She didn't have to pretend anymore, or shut a part of herself off, restraining her emotions. She could finally move forward and take the path that lay before her. There was no escaping what needed to be done. She was the only person who could do it, and there was only one place she could go to learn how.

"All right, I think we should keep going," said Catanya after a while. She stood up and returned the map to her pocket, taking a deep breath to prepare herself. "The cave entrance shouldn't be far from here."

Drayk sighed heavily. He stood up and walked over to join her.

"All right," he said. "But if we get to these caves, and there's something living inside, I'm turning back." He grinned and nudged her shoulder with his own before striding confidently inland.

They moved slowly, hiking along the uneven and rocky shoreline until the steep cliff face blocked their path. They turned and followed the rock wall deeper inland until finally they found an opening. It was a narrow cavity, just big enough for someone to walk through, and it stretched out of sight into the earth.

"This must be it." Catanya peered apprehensively into the opening. "It's pitch black in there. We won't be able to see a thing." She glanced at Drayk, but he just smiled and clapped his hands together.

"Come now, don't tell me you're afraid of the dark." He stepped forward and glanced into the entrance. "What's the worst that could happen?" he asked with artificial cheer, like he was pretending to be more carefree than he was.

Catanya bit her lip, trying not to think about the possible answers to his question. Her skin prickled ominously and every fibre of her being told her not to go inside—to turn back. But she knew she couldn't.

She looked at him and nodded. Then she took a deep breath and crossed the entrance into the cave. Drayk stepped in after her.

They walked cautiously, allowing the light from the entrance to show them the way. As they delved deeper into the caves and the light grew dimmer, Catanya's heart beat faster and faster. She reached out and gripped the cave wall, touching the rough stone under her fingertips. By the last ray of light, they saw the tunnel turn sharply out of view.

They paused briefly, exchanging anxious looks in the dimness.

"Well, here we go," said Drayk, rounding the corner and stepping into the dark.

The air was stale and moist. It grew dense as they walked deeper into the caves, making it harder and harder to breathe. They continued at a much slower pace, using their hands to feel their way along the walls.

Catanya's tension mounted with each step she took. She was overwrought, twitching and jumping at every new sound she heard. Her fingers chafed from being dragged along the rocky walls.

The tunnel twisted and turned countless times, so they lost

all sense of direction. For all Catanya knew, they were just moving in circles. Several times, they found themselves trapped in a dead-end cavern and had to stumble their way back out in the same direction they'd come, hoping to find a different route.

It was exhausting and strenuous, and they made very slow progress, tripping on the uneven ground and colliding with low-jutting ceilings and protuberances.

Before long, Catanya was covered in all manner of cuts and bruises. Her body ached, and her head was dizzy from struggling to breathe the narrow air.

She couldn't tell how long they'd been underground, but she longed to be outside again. In the absolute darkness, they had no sense of time. Only the burning in her legs told her how far they'd gone and whether they were climbing or descending.

However, after a while, she noticed the temperature in the caves fluctuating at a disturbingly unnatural rate. At times, the air was swelteringly hot and moist as it clung to their skin and pressed upon them, suffocating them. But at other times, it was frigid and dry, and their throats chafed and rasped on the barren draught.

The rapid changes made it difficult for Catanya to regulate herself or her breathing. She felt strained—out of control and vulnerable.

I have to make it through this, she thought over and over again. *People are counting on me. I have responsibilities. I have to be strong enough.*

Her legs shook and her body twitched. Every tiny creak and crack sounded enormous to her. She felt like a frightened child again, stuck in a cabinet, crying and suffocating—afraid of the dark. And there was no Lady Genna to save her this time.

She closed her eyes and squeezed, willing the fear to go away. Then her legs shuddered violently underneath her and she nearly collapsed.

But that tremor wasn't just in her legs.

"Drayk," she croaked, "do you feel that?" She hoped she was imagining it, but it felt like the ground was quivering beneath her feet.

"I feel it," he replied. And even in the dark, she thought she could sense him looking around nervously.

They stopped moving, and Catanya stared at her feet blindly. The vibrations reverberated through her legs and into her spine, rattling her bones and shaking her body.

"What is it?" she whispered, her heart racing as the dread mounted inside her.

The tremor intensified, making it harder for them to stand upright, let alone move. It sounded like thousands of stampeding feet thumping in time with a great host of drums. The sound echoed through the cavernous passageways. The walls shook with an intensity that threatened to trigger a cave-in.

A loud grinding, groaning sound rent the air, as the ground trembled even harder. The walls writhed and came to life, rolling in on themselves. The ground sagged and swelled beneath their feet like a great serpent trying to hurl them from its back.

Catanya spun around, sightlessly trying to grab hold of anything that could stabilize her. With a mighty jerk, the ground lurched, and she fell forward, breaking her fall with her forearms and cutting them open on the jagged floor.

"Drayk!" she called, panicking completely. She grasped around and tried to push herself onto her knees, without success. The ground was undulating too violently, jerking her body every which way, so she crashed against the stone walls and ceiling. She could no longer tell which direction was up or down as the cave hurled her body around.

"Drayk!" she called louder. She could hear him gasping and shouting as he slammed into the rocks. She needed to get to him. "Drayk, where are you?"

"I'm here!" he choked, and his voice came from a few feet away.

The ground gave another mighty heave, propelling her sideways, away from the sound of his voice.

"No," she groaned, grasping blindly.

Something struck her chest, knocking the wind out of her entirely. She collapsed on the ground, coughing and spluttering as what felt like rain began to pelt against her.

But it wasn't rain, it was dirt. And it poured over her like a terrible waterfall, crushing her into the ground and burying her alive.

"No, no!" she cried out in a panic, getting a mouthful of dirt. "Drayk!" she tried to call for help, but her voice was muffled. The ceiling had caved in around her, cutting her off from him completely.

Gradually, the surges and swells lessened. The ear-splitting crunch of rolling boulders dimmed, and the world righted itself.

With one last grinding shudder, everything stopped, and an unnatural stillness settled in its place. Catanya was trapped under a pile of rubble, slowly suffocating in the dark, unable to move.

"No, no, no," she spluttered, as tears flooded her eyes. She started crying just like she had as a child. Great, desperate sobs of isolation and inevitability. She needed to stop. She shouldn't waste her air, but she couldn't control it. Each breath was excruciating. Jagged stones pressed into her body, and her eyes and mouth filled with dry, abrasive earth.

Panting and heaving as the tears came in droves and her lungs burned, she tried to focus her mind. She tried frantically to move the rocks, but they wouldn't budge. Her arms and legs were stuck, growing numb as the weight pressed down on them.

Frantic, she tried to summon her magic, anything that might help her out of this. But nothing came.

Again and again, she tried, but her body was trapped. Her powers had abandoned her just like they had on the channel. There was nothing she could do.

"Catya!" Drayk's voice came through the barrier, muffled but clear.

"Help," she tried to croak, but it was barely a whisper, and she choked on the new influx of dirt. She tried to wiggle her legs enough to jostle the stones and give him a sign of where to look, but nothing happened.

He's not going to find you, said the voice in her head. *He'll give up eventually. And then he won't even mourn you.*

"No," she spluttered. "Drayk will find me. He won't leave me here."

The voice in her head laughed, but she closed her eyes tight, urging herself to ignore it. She had to trust Drayk. After everything they'd been through, he wouldn't let this place become her tomb. He'd help her. She could count on him.

A discouraging silence slowly settled around her, and dread filled her heart.

But then the sound of grinding and clattering rocks reached her ears, and she knew she was right. Drayk was searching for her.

She closed her eyes tighter, trying to calm herself as she waited to be found. It was agony. She felt feeble and impotent, leaving her fate in Drayk's hands. But she knew he would never abandon her.

A slight breeze on her face signalled for her to open her eyes. They burned as she blinked away the dirt. It was still pitch black, but this blackness was somehow brighter.

"Drayk," she choked, coughing on the dusty air.

He swore in relief, and then she felt his frantic movements

as he tore the remaining rubble away and dug through the dirt to reach her.

She could move her arms again. She grasped around until her hands brushed his vest and she reached forward and pulled him closer to her.

"Catya," he spluttered as he yanked her free of the remaining rubble and slumped back against the cave wall.

She sobbed tears of relief, trembling as she gripped him tightly in the dark. They remained huddled together, frozen in shock as they tried to calm their racing heartbeats and regulate their breathing.

"That was—" But Drayk didn't finish his sentence and Catanya noted the anxious edge in his voice. She nodded into the dark. Her stomach was tangled in knots, so she closed her eyes, waiting for the nausea to pass.

"For a second there, I thought I'd lost you," mumbled Drayk.

Catanya half sobbed, half laughed into his shoulder.

They sat perfectly still for several minutes, too terrified to move for fear that the entire ordeal might begin again.

If Catanya's body had been aching before, it was nothing compared to how she felt now. She wanted nothing more than to melt into the wall and sleep forever. She didn't think she'd ever been this exhausted or battered in her life. The physical assault alone had been devastating, but the fear and tension were torturing her from the inside out.

"Should we... should we try to continue?" she asked reluctantly after a while. She was afraid to move, but she didn't think she could stand much more of these caves. And the only way out was through.

Drayk moved to stand up.

"Wait," said Catanya. She stood up beside him and took his hand firmly in hers. "Don't let go."

There was a slight pause before Drayk squeezed her hand and said, "I wouldn't dream of it."

As they turned to walk on through the dark, he spoke again. "You know, normally I prefer to do more pleasurable activities for hours in the dark, but under the circumstances..."

Catanya could hear the smirk in his voice, and she laughed a little hysterically. "We need to stick together," she said, recollecting herself.

"Any excuse to hold my hand, right, love?"

"Shut up," she muttered, but she smiled despite herself. She had to admit that his levity was helping her stay calm.

They stumbled along, hand-in-hand for hours, stopping once in a while to drink water or regroup when they hit a dead-end. The cave walls grew increasingly grimy. At times, the ceiling hung so low, they had to crouch to pass through. But they pushed onwards, all the while staying alert for any sign of movement.

But the caves remained perfectly still, showing no sign that anything strange or abnormal had ever occurred. Whatever had happened, it was over now, and Catanya was immensely grateful for that.

After a while, the cave brightened slightly and they could finally see where they were going.

"Over there," said Drayk, pointing ahead.

There was a narrow opening in the rocky ceiling, which allowed some moonlight to flood inside, illuminating the cave.

"M-maybe we should rest here," said Catanya. Her entire body was in knots and she was jittery from the strain on her nerves.

As they walked into the light, Catanya noticed Drayk's face was covered in cuts, bruises, and filth, and she realized she must not look much better. She raised her shaky hands up to her face and brushed the sweaty hair off it. She wobbled, momentarily lightheaded as she breathed the fresh air wafting through the ceiling.

Drayk stood with his back to her, staring up through the gap at the stars above.

"What is it?" asked Catanya, walking over to join him.

Drayk made an odd movement, like he was suppressing a shudder. "It's just nice to see the sky," he said, taking a deep breath and turning around to face her. "I've spent the better part of my life living free under those stars."

Catanya nodded and looked around the cave. She knew that he, like her, was longing to be outside again.

"I wonder how far these caves continue," she said, hoping they were nearing the end. The confinement and darkness were making her skittish.

"With any luck, not much farther," he said. "Why don't you rest. I'll take the first watch."

He moved to walk away from her, but she grabbed his hand to stop him. He looked at her quizzically, but she just shook her head. These caves were dangerous and unpredictable, and she didn't want to be separated from him.

She pulled him towards one side of the cave and they slid down, side-by-side, with their backs against the wall. They sat, holding each other and staring at the stars.

"I'm grateful you're here with me," she said, resting her head on his shoulder and closing her eyes. "Thank you."

When she'd started this journey, she knew there would be risks. But she never could have predicted any of this. She had seen and experienced things she never would have believed possible, and throughout it all, Drayk had stayed by her side.

She felt braver knowing he was with her. Drayk had seen the worst sides of her, but he was still there, braving all manner of peril alongside her, helping her. She trusted him to watch out for her just as she would watch out for him. After all this time, he had become her friend and for that, she was grateful.

He cared about her—she knew that. But this was different. It was so much more than that.

Since the moment she'd met him months ago in the forest, Drayk had seen something in her she didn't know was there. He believed in her. He believed in her so much he was willing to risk his life to make her believe too.

She smiled to herself as she realized why that made her feel so safe. She realized who else had believed in her like that.

And before long, she drifted off to sleep.

When Catanya awoke, she was lying on the cave floor with her head on Drayk's leg. He had fallen asleep, sitting with his back against the wall and his arm resting on her shoulders.

She nudged him gently, and he woke with a start.

"What's happening?" he blurted, reaching for his sword.

"No, everything's fine," she said, sitting up straight. "We just fell asleep. It's early."

The pale sky was visible through the hole in the ceiling. In the soft light of early morning, the caves looked almost cozy compared to the gloom of the night before.

"Oh." Drayk relaxed slightly and looked up at the sky.

They sat there in silence for a few minutes, neither one wanting to suggest that they keep moving and return to the suffocating darkness.

"We're nearly there," said Catanya, more to herself than to Drayk.

"Remind me, what happens after the caves?" he asked, not taking his eyes off the ceiling gap.

Catanya hesitated, reluctant to answer.

"Catya?" He gave her a piercing look.

She sighed and pulled the map out of her pocket to read the final location. "The Dead Wood," she said, glancing at Drayk before reading the last words of the poem. "*Where balms of closing breaths respire their final essence.*" She suppressed a shudder as she folded the map.

"The Dead Wood," repeated Drayk in a hollow voice. "Sounds cheery, doesn't it?"

Catanya laughed out loud and stood up, holding her hand out for him. "Onwards?" she said with a stab at light-heartedness.

Drayk's face cracked into a wide grin. "Onwards," he replied, taking her hand.

26

THE DEAD WOOD

It was just past dawn the next day when Catanya and Drayk emerged from the Shrouded Caves and stepped into the open air. They stood hand-in-hand and gazed in wonder at the immense forest ahead, struggling to contain their awe.

When Catanya had pictured the Dead Wood in her mind, it had always been dry and desiccated—dead. But this forest was anything but dead. It was an endless assortment of massive trees, packed densely together with their gnarled roots painted green with thick layers of springy moss. The morning dew still gleamed on the leaves, and a hazy layer of mist hung in the air. Pale rays of sunlight seeped through the dense canopy, reflecting off the water droplets like glitter in the air.

The leaves fluttered gently, and a stream trickled in the distance. The air teemed with birdsong and, somewhere nearby, a dove cooed its affectionate greeting.

A soft breeze rustled through Catanya's unkempt hair, bringing with it a sweet assortment of smells. She inhaled and allowed the bouquet of aromas to transport her mind to different places and times.

There was the smell of wildflowers that reminded her of the meadows in Finnua, mixed with the smell of ocean air she associated with Faltir. And there was something else she couldn't quite distinguish. It was something smoky and earthy, somehow warm and sweet at the same time. She couldn't place it, but whatever it was, it warmed her from the inside out.

This place was a welcome change after the stale air of the caves. The gentle mist felt refreshing on her face as Catanya stepped onto the leaf-strewn ground, gazing up at the thick canopy above her.

There was something otherworldly about this place. The forest was ancient, but an energy reverberated from the trees. It was hypnotic, and it flowed through the leaves and the plants, beckoning for Catanya and Drayk to follow it deeper into the wood.

They exchanged curious glances as they walked. There was no clear route to follow, but with each step they took, the area ahead brightened as if it were highlighting their path.

They walked in silence, listening to the forest sounds and observing how the trees tangled and bent into distinctive shapes. The thick tree bark was crinkled and corrugated with knobs and hollows dotted along the trunks and branches. The ancient roots wove in and out of the ground and stretched far and wide, interlacing with others to form an irregular knitted tapestry.

And, peppered between the tangled roots, smaller saplings poked up through the densely packed earth, reaching towards the sky with youthful hope.

The earth was uneven, littered with a fine dust of twigs, fallen leaves, and an assortment of pinecones, acorns, and other nuts. Gentle crunches from their footsteps echoed through the air, and the wind whistled through the branches, carrying new waves of familiar scents with every gust.

The forest floor sloped downward, leading them underneath a mass of fallen trees that had tangled to create a roof of branches. Drapes of vines and tendrils of wisteria flowers brushed their faces as they passed.

When they emerged from the hollow, Catanya thought she saw something move just outside her vision. But when she scanned the trees, nothing was there. She shook her head and continued walking, assuming it was a trick of the light.

They continued on for a while, enjoying the fresh air and the tranquillity. Catanya was beginning to think the Dead Wood would be just this—a pleasant repose after the perils of the caves, but then she saw it again.

Out of the corner of her eye, she glimpsed a dark shape passing out of sight behind the trees.

"Did you see that?" she asked. Her voice sounded unfamiliar and airy, like it was coming to her from inside a dream.

"Hmm?" Drayk didn't seem to register what she said.

"Something's out there," she whispered. "Something moving in the trees."

But Drayk wasn't listening anymore. His attention was being drawn in the opposite direction and he staggered forward with his hand outstretched, oblivious to everything else.

His fingers slipped out of hers. Catanya wanted to follow him, but then she saw it again. It darted on the outskirts of her vision, so she couldn't tell what it was.

"Hello?" she called, her voice echoing through the trees.

She felt Drayk moving farther away from her, but she didn't have time to follow him. She needed to follow whatever was behind that tree. It was important, she was sure of it.

She heard leaves rustling and turned to see the dark shape take off into the forest.

"Wait!" she called, hurrying after it. "Wait, please!"

But whatever it was, it showed no sign of slowing down. Instead, it moved faster and faster until Catanya had to run to keep up. Deeper and deeper into the forest, weaving through trees and stumbling over roots, she ran without a second thought.

Until suddenly, it wasn't just one shape she was following. The air was thick with shadowy outlines scattering in different directions. Catanya didn't know which way to turn. Ghostly figures crowded the trees around her. They were indistinct and faceless, but somehow she knew they were looking at her.

She stopped dead in her tracks, realizing how deep in the forest she was. Drayk was nowhere to be seen. She was lost and all alone, with these creatures bearing down on her.

Catanya stumbled backwards and tripped. She crashed to the floor with a heavy thud and grazed her hand on a jagged rock. She gasped and pulled her hand into her body, taking her eyes off the spirits for only a second.

When she looked up, the ghosts had formed a barricade as one stepped forward, gliding towards her.

Catanya sat there, frozen in fear, waiting for it to approach.

The ghost's shape was blurry around the edges, but as it moved closer, it came into focus. Its features grew more human until Catanya realized it was the ghost of a young woman. Her long, chestnut brown hair was undercut and pulled back in a series of tight braids, each coiled around a sequence of small iron rings. She wore a black outfit that seemed strangely familiar.

As the spirit's face became clearer, Catanya suddenly recognized who it was.

"I know you," she said, barely believing her eyes. "I've seen you before—or a statue of you, anyway. In Awnell... You're *her*! You're the Warrior Queen."

The woman nodded as her outline solidified. Her expression solemn, she stopped in front of Catanya and held out her hand.

Catanya hesitated before taking it. The queen's hand was

cold and somehow neither solid nor smoke, but she helped Catanya to her feet with ease.

"In life, my name was Ana." She spoke in a cool, resonant voice that echoed through the air, and she had a strange accent Catanya didn't recognize.

Catanya gawked at her. "I don't understand," she said. "How can you be here? You lived thousands of years ago."

"I am not here," replied the queen, staring vaguely off into the distance. "Not really."

Catanya frowned and shook her head, even more perplexed. "What does that mean?" she asked.

Ana smiled complacently. "Walk with me." She motioned for Catanya to follow as she moved away from the other spirits, deeper into the forest.

Catanya lingered. "What about Drayk?" she said, biting her lip and looking back over her shoulder. "I shouldn't have left him. I don't know what came over me."

"Your companion is fine. He has nothing to fear from this place. He will be waiting, and when you are ready, you can join him again. Now come." Ana's voice was cool and patient, but Catanya's instincts told her it wasn't a suggestion.

"Where are we going?" she asked, eyeing the other ghosts as she passed. But they no longer seemed interested in her. They were drifting away in different directions with no sign that they'd ever seen her at all.

"Forward, I should think," said Ana blandly.

They walked silently through the woods for some time until they came upon a stream and stopped. Catanya stayed a few steps behind Ana. She felt nervous, like she should show respect and deference, but she wasn't entirely sure how.

Finally, Ana spoke again. "Why are you here, Catanya?" she asked.

"You-you know my name?" Despite her shocked and nervous state, Catanya was slightly flattered.

"Yes." Ana offered no further explanation. "Why are you here?" she repeated.

"I-I'm looking for Túir-Avlea," said Catanya.

Ana nodded. "I know that," she said, turning to face Catanya. "But I'm not interested in where you are going. I am interested in *why*. Why are you looking for Túir-Avlea?"

"Why?" repeated Catanya, frowning. "Because I need their help."

"Help with what?" Ana was still smiling, and her tone was pleasant, but it had an undertone of impatience.

"Well... I suppose... I need their help to understand my magic," said Catanya, shaking her head and shrugging. "I need to learn how to control it."

Ana nodded once again. "And is that all?" she asked like a parent waiting for their child to understand something important.

"I—" Catanya broke off, confused. She didn't know what else Ana wanted her to say. "Yes. Yes, that's all," she finished, a little less confidently.

"I see." Ana turned away from Catanya and starting walking again. She seemed disappointed with Catanya's answer.

"You disagree," said Catanya, hurrying to catch up with her. "You don't think that's why I'm here?"

"What I think doesn't matter," said Ana.

As they continued walking, they passed by other spirits, wandering aimlessly through the woods with no direction or purpose. The sight of it made Catanya sad.

"Are you trapped here?" she asked when they passed by another spirit just floating between two trees. "Are you all trapped in this forest?"

"We are neither trapped, nor are we free. We are here because it is where we must be for now."

"Why?" Catanya smiled wryly to herself. "*Why* are you here?" she asked, repeating Ana's words.

Ana turned to look at her, beaming. "Now you are begin-ning to understand," she said, nodding. "I cannot speak for the others, but I believe I am here for a very clear purpose."

Catanya waited for her to elaborate, but she didn't. "Can you tell me what that purpose is?" she asked.

"I could." Ana tilted her head to the side, thinking. "But I won't."

"Oh..." Catanya couldn't help feeling a little disappointed. "Why not?" she asked, hoping it wasn't an intrusive question.

"Because it is mine," replied Ana. "And you have your own purpose, which, if I am not mistaken, will change the outcome of mine quite dramatically." A hint of eagerness tinged Ana's voice as she squinted out into the trees.

"I don't understand," said Catanya, shaking her head. She felt dense as she struggled to keep up with the conversation.

"No, I wouldn't expect you to... at least, not yet. But all souls are connected, Catanya—all spirits. We are united in our shared human experience. It is a heavy burden to perceive that connection and an even heavier one to wield it."

Catanya's breath caught in her throat. "Wield it?" she said, suddenly intrigued. "How?"

Ana looked thoughtful. "I never did learn how," she said with a sad smile. "Which, at the time, I considered a great injus-tice. But now I understand..."

There was a long pause as Catanya tried to decipher Ana's words, but she couldn't. "Understand what?" she asked.

Ana sighed and closed her eyes briefly. "That it was never meant to be wielded," she said, turning to face Catanya with a serious expression.

Catanya frowned, unsure how to respond, but she was spared the trouble when Ana spoke again.

"You've learned much on your journey to get here. But there is one more lesson you must learn. Do you know what it is?"

Catanya thought about her answer as she gazed at the

wandering spirits around her. "I think so," she said slowly, an odd mixture of relief and dread settling in her heart. "Yes, I know."

Ana nodded, wearing a sympathetic expression. "You have made many sacrifices already, but there will be more. Are you ready?"

Catanya swallowed heavily. "Yes, I'm ready."

Ana tilted her head, scrutinizing Catanya's face intently. "No," she said after a pause. "Not yet. But I believe you will be."

The queen's outline was blurring again. Her features were blending together in shadow.

"Wait," said Catanya, reaching out towards her. She wasn't ready for Ana to go. She still had so many questions.

"Trust your instincts, Catanya," called Ana, and her voice sounded distant and faint as she faded back into the mist, leaving Catanya standing alone in the forest.

A powerful gust of wind blew through the trees, carrying a warm, smoky smell that reminded her of something.

Drayk.

She shook her head and turned away from the spot where Ana had disappeared. As confused and disappointed as she felt, right now it didn't matter. She needed to find Drayk, and they needed to keep moving.

Catanya started walking again, and, as it had done before, the path ahead brightened to show her the way. She followed the winding trees deeper into the forest until, at last, she spotted him. He was standing in a clearing, gazing forward as if entranced by something.

"There you are," she said, relieved as she stopped beside him. "I'm sorry I—" She broke off when she caught sight of his face.

Drayk didn't look like himself at all. His eyes had glazed over with a milky white sheen and his features were rigid and mask-like.

"Drayk?" She reached out to touch his arm but stopped herself, feeling strangely nervous. "Can you hear me?" she asked, dropping her hand.

"I hear you," he replied in a voice almost as distant and echoing as Ana's had been. "It's beautiful here, isn't it? Let's stay forever."

This unsettled Catanya more than anything. Something was wrong... But Ana had told her Drayk would be fine. She'd said he had nothing to fear. Had she been lying?

"No... we can't stay here," said Catanya, crossing in front so she could face him. It terrified her to see him looking so lifeless and numb.

"Why ever not?" he asked, frowning. "It's so peaceful." He wore a small smile now and stared blankly without seeing her.

"Drayk, you're scaring me," said Catanya in a slow, cautious voice. "Let's go."

"Go?" he repeated, frowning as he finally turned his glassy eyes towards her. "But I just got here. I can't go now. They've been waiting for me—calling me. I need to stay."

"No," said Catanya, her distress rising with every word he spoke. "No, you need to come with me now. Come on, Drayk, snap out of it."

She reached out and took his hand, alarmed by how cold it was.

But as soon as she laced her fingers through his, the trance seemed to break. The milky film on his eyes dissolved, returning them to their brilliant blue. He blinked and focused on her, bewildered.

"There you are," he said, sounding relieved. "I turned around, and you were gone. What happened?"

Catanya gaped at him, baffled by his sudden change. "What just happened?" she asked. "Are you all right?" She stepped closer to examine his face.

"Me?" Drayk looked at her, completely nonplussed. "Of course I am. Why wouldn't I be?"

Catanya surveyed him up and down, but he seemed fine. She turned instead to examine the clearing.

Drayk's eyes followed her with concern. "What's the matter?" he asked.

Catanya didn't know how to respond or how to describe what had just happened. She fumbled her way through an explanation, seeing the slight incredulity on his face as he listened.

"I'm telling you, something very strange is going on," she finished. "You just have to believe me."

"I do," he said, taking her other hand in his. "But whatever it was, it's over. I'm all right now, we're both all right."

"But... did you see them?" she asked in a hushed voice. "The figures in the trees." She glanced around nervously. "They... they're..."

"They are spirits," said a soft voice behind them.

Drayk and Catanya spun around to find themselves face to face with a short elderly woman. Unlike Ana, this woman was flesh and blood. She wore a thick shawl over a set of flowing white robes that bunched up at her feet and dragged across the floor. Perched atop her willowy hair was a thin circlet of woven silver and partially wilted yew branches. She was smiling at them, her eyes twinkling from beneath her bushy white eyebrows.

"The Dead Wood holds the spirits of many of those who have lived and died. All spirits are connected. If you enter the wood with a clear intention, the spirits will show you your path."

"Who are you?" asked Drayk, his hand resting poised on the hilt of his sword.

"Oh, yes, of course." The old woman tapped herself on the forehead and chuckled. "Where are my manners? I am Laylian,

Maílehr of this community. Welcome to Túir-Avlea," she said, turning and gesturing behind her.

A shadow slowly stretched across the forest, dampening the vibrancy of the trees with an almost ominous shade. Catanya craned her neck up, and blinked in astonishment. The clear blue sky was no longer visible, eclipsed by the outline of an enormous mountain. Silhouetted in sunlight, rays glimmered and danced off its peak like diamonds.

It was the most glorious mountain Catanya had ever seen.

EPILOGUE

AYR

THE DISTRACTION

Ayr sat cross-legged on the dungeon floor. She kept her back straight and her eyes closed, counting her breaths and listening to the steady drip of water in the dark. It was meditative. It helped pass the time while she waited, alone in the dark.

A slight fluctuation in the air quality told her someone was coming long before she heard the footsteps in the corridor. She kept her back to the door and waited for the torchlight to flood her cell before opening her eyes.

"Well?" she asked, still facing the wall.

"It's done. Slaedir is dead," said a familiar voice.

Ayr held her breath. "Any casualties among our men?" she asked.

"A few injuries but nothing fatal."

She released the air from her lungs and felt weeks of tension melt along with it. "Good," she said, climbing to her feet and turning to face her first lieutenant. "That is good. Well done, Rey. I knew I could trust you." She held her arm through the bars.

Rey grasped it with enthusiasm and smiled. "Tenacious and loyal," he said, inclining his head.

Ayr beamed at him.

Rey. One of her most faithful and capable soldiers. Months ago, she'd sat this man down and explained what needed to happen. That he needed to betray his kingdom and his people, he needed to desert his home, his friends, his wife, and join forces with the enemy. There was no one else she trusted to do it. Infiltrate Caerlon and protect her people. Distract Cadyan long enough for Lia to regroup and Catya to return.

Rey hadn't balked, he hadn't complained. He'd done his duty to Awnell. His duty to Mórceá.

"Thank you, Rey," she said, withdrawing her arm. "I promise this will all be worthwhile. When Catya returns, we'll be ready."

Rey nodded. "Lia sent word this week. The women's army is recuperating. The last shipments from Sidina are being carried through the port. You were right about the smugglers."

Ayr scratched her chin, thinking about every dubious deal she'd made to ensure her plan's success. "Yes, Osrin may be a greedy, despicable snake, but he is effective..." She hated working with him and his smugglers, but her options were limited.

Rey pursed his lips. "Drayk won't be happy when he learns about it."

Ayr snorted. "Drayk's happiness is not my concern. We're fighting a war. We'd be foolish not to exploit every resource."

"True. And Osrin has access to our men in Bratia. We need to free them as soon as possible. I've heard stories about Bratia..." Rey's face fell into a deep scowl. "The place is torture. The firkon there are so miserable, they spend most of their time abusing the workers for sport."

"I know," she said, trying to reassure him. "I don't like the idea of our men enslaved there any more than you do. But the

Awnadh are trained to withstand anything. They only need to wait a little longer. And we still have work to do here."

Rey sighed and nodded. "On that note, I'm concerned about the new maífírkon, Julyán. He is difficult to read, but he's intelligent—far more so than Slaedir. He has tremendous self-control and patience. I think he could be a problem for us."

"Should we eliminate him, then?"

Rey frowned slightly. "No... not yet. I think, perhaps we can distract him. I suspect the healer, Diyah, may have some influence over him... I have an idea for a distraction that involves them both."

"Do I want to know what this distraction entails?" asked Ayr.

Rey's mouth twitched like he was fighting off a grin. "Let's just say Caerlon's illegal delirium trade is... *unpredictable.*"

Ayr stifled a laugh. She privately wished she could be free to watch the chaos. But she couldn't escape yet. Cadyan needed to think he was in control. "And what about the other matter?" she asked. "What about Cadyan's ring? Is it really losing its power?"

Ayr remembered the strange sensation she'd felt when she'd grasped hands with Cadyan in Awnell. Her spies had informed her about the ring months ago, so when Cadyan arrived in Awnell, she was prepared. She'd expected the ring's power to be harder to resist, but the compulsive effect had faded so quickly, it surprised her.

Rey folded his arms and nodded. "Yes. It seems, the ring hasn't worked reliably since Cadyan fought Catya on that beach. The fírkon who witnessed the altercation have been whispering about what happened that night. I believe the ring was damaged."

"Interesting..." Ayr's mind raced with ideas and questions. "What about the other relics? Any sign of them in Bratia?"

"No. Most of the fírkon have given up expecting to find

them... But Cadyan hasn't. As you predicted, the son has embraced the father's obsession. He's desperate to find that crown."

Ayr shook her head in exasperation. "Fools," she said. "So preoccupied with immortality that they can't see the threats right in front of them."

"It works out well for us," said Rey with a smirk. "Casréyan's blindness made him an easy target. Cadyan's will too. He will never see the attack coming."

Ayr nodded. She bent her knees and lowered herself onto the cold, hard floor to resume her meditation. With her eyes closed, she inhaled deeply and filled her mind with visions of things to come. "Yes," she said, "with Catya's help, we will tear this kingdom apart from the inside out, and reforge its remains into something greater. And Mórceá will finally be free."

THE END of
Book Two of
THE QUIESCENCE TRILOGY

ALSO BY KATHRYN KNOWLES

THE QUIESCENCE TRILOGY

The Relics of Illayan

The Warrior Queen

Book Three, Coming Fall 2022

OTHER STORIES OF MÓRCEÁ

The Last Verratrí, a Short Story Prelude

Subscribe to the Mad Endeavour Newsletter to get a free copy of The Last Verratrí.

www.madendeavour.com

ACKNOWLEDGMENTS

Thank you, as always, to my friends and family. Your support and encouragement give me the confidence to keep writing and to keep trying new things! Thanks, especially, to Mom and Colin for reading the drafts and giving me such wonderful feedback. So many improvements were made because of our speaker phone chats!

Thank you to Rebecca—my beta reader, my editor, my friend! 1228 comments to take this book across the finish line (and that's just the number tracked by the computer). Thank you for all your amazing—and sometimes ruthless—insights, and for being my champion through the entire writing, editing, and publishing process. I love floating ideas past you and hearing your thoughts. Thank you for our chats at the park and our mental health check-ins. I'm so lucky to have you in my corner.

Thank you to Massimo for reading and re-reading the drafts. For being my "coworker" through the editing process and letting me talk at you for hours about the book. This has been the best nine months ever. So much happiness and so much support!

To Karin, thank you for the hilarity and joy of your chapter reactions, and for the amazingly wonderful friendship. For encouraging me to rest and relax, and for being my vent friend on days when the balance just isn't working. Here's to more wine and pools with squirrels and raccoons! Oh, and hopefully some music too!

Thank you to everyone who read it when it was still one book: Heather, Jeff, Jesse, MacKenzie, Martha, Vicki. Your comments and encouragement inspired a trilogy!

And finally, thank you to everyone who read *The Relics of Illayan* and enjoyed it enough to want book two! I am honoured and thrilled to be able to share this story with you. I promise you there are many more stories to come. Writing (words and music) is a true passion for me, and it makes me unbelievably happy knowing you are out there reading my stories. I hope you enjoy them as much as I do!

ABOUT THE AUTHOR

Kathryn Knowles is a composer, cellist, conductor, and writer currently based in Toronto, Ontario. She splits her time between writing, teaching, conducting, composing, and running Mad Endeavour.

Photo Credit: Claire Bouvier Photography

Kathryn received honourable mention in the Writer's Digest 89th Annual Writing Competition for her poem, Beyond the Black Horizon's Crease, and her short story, Lester's Bird Feeder. Her musical works have been played in workshops by the Toronto Symphony Orchestra, the New Orford String Quartet, and the Penderecki String Quartet. She holds a Bachelor of Music and a Master of International Business from Queen's University, as well as a Master in Music Composition from the University of Toronto.

In her spare time, Kathryn enjoys taking on new creative projects (i.e. filling up that "spare" time), spending time with friends and family, tending her ever-growing plant collection (obsession), and looking at pictures of puppies and dreaming of the day she can have one of her own.

Learn more at www.kathryn-knowles.com

instagram.com/kathryn.knowles_

www.ingramcontent.com/pod-product-compliance
Lightning Source LLC
Chambersburg PA
CBHW061346190726
48288CB00005B/1613